A Sportsman's Notebook

Ecco Art of the Story

A Sportsman's Notebook

STORIES

IVAN TURGENEV

HarperCollins books may be purchased for educational, business, or sales promotional use. For information, please email the Special Markets Department at SPsales@harpercollins.com.

Translated from the Russian by Charles and Natasha Hepburn.

Originally published in 1992 by Everyman's Library, an imprint of Penguin Random House.

FIRST ECCO PAPERBACK EDITION PUBLISHED 2020.

Designed by Suet Chong

Library of Congress Cataloging-in-Publication Data has been applied for.

ISBN 978-0-06-296847-0

HB 07.09.2024

CONTENTS

INTRODUCTION

A Sportsman's Notebook, the first of Turgenev's masterpieces, was written in several stages, mostly between 1846 and 1851, with two of the stories in this volume ("The End of Chertopkanov" and "The Live Relic") added later for an edition of 1874. Most of the stories appeared first in the Russian literary magazine *The Contemporary* between 1847 and 1851 and were published together in 1852 to the anger of the authorities. These coincided with a happy time in Turgenev's relationship with the Spanish opera singer Pauline Viardot, especially those written in France in 1847 and 1848. Some of the inspiration for the book may have come from the infinitely more dreary *Souvenirs de Chasse* published by Pauline's French husband Louis in 1846. Louis Viardot, a theatrical producer and impresario, was also a keen sportsman. This perhaps contributed to the curious fact that Turgenev and he seemed to have remained friends in spite of the novelist's love for his wife.

Ivan Turgenev came from a landowning family in the Russian province of Oryol. Born in 1818, he grew up on the family estate at Spasskoye in the care of his irascible and tyrannical mother whose behavior led to his early disgust with serfdom. She appears in several of his stories, most notably "Mumu," "Punin and Baburin," and "The Inn," a forbidding and philistine figure who terrorized her serfs, quite different to her remote philandering husband who died in 1834 without apparently playing a great part in his son's life except to suggest the romantic apartness of the distant parent in "First Love." Turgenev attended schools in Moscow and universities in Moscow and St. Petersburg before leaving for Berlin. While he was away his mother missed him dreadfully. Later he worked briefly as a civil servant before resigning much against his mother's will to devote himself entirely to writing. He met and fell in love with Pauline Viardot during her visit to St. Petersburg in 1843. Turgenev followed her and her husband to Paris and then to wherever she might be in Europe. In 1850, after his mother's death, he inherited Spasskoye. However, his infatuation with Pauline and the hostile reception given to *Fathers and Children* in Russia after its publication in 1862 (particularly by radicals who thought it caricatured their beliefs) made him reluctant to visit his homeland for long.

Like many novelists, Turgenev began as a poet. He was introduced to Pauline Viardot as "a young Russian landowner, a good shot, an agreeable companion and a writer of bad verses." These words imply a dilettantism of which Turgenev would be sometimes accused. Dostoyevsky caricatured him as the precious and foolish Karamazinov in *The Devils*; Tolstoy condemned his frivolity. Turgenev was not a novelist of belief. In time he follows Pushkin and Lermontov, and early stories such as "The Duellist," "Three Portraits," and "The Jew" show the influence of their Byronic romanticism. He was also the heir to the more naturalistic Gogol, and his first true mentor was the liberal critic Belinsky, a westerner as opposed to a Slavophile. The nearest Turgenev gets to mysticism is in his descriptions of human or natural phenomena, not in some evocation of an unearthly divinity. He has no religion in the sense that Tolstoy or Dostoyevsky have.

A Sportsman's Notebook has no backbone of plot or schematic narrative. The episodes are not stories but glimpses of situations or characters, occasionally descriptions of scenery or landscape. For inspiration, Turgenev went back to his youth at Spasskoye, his mother's estate, where hunting expeditions had been a way of escaping briefly from her tyranny. His motive in writing about the countryside must have been at least partly political. The reactionary Tsar Nicholas I was still on the throne and there seemed no prospect of reform. A landowner like Turgenev's mother was the complete mistress of her domain and the serfs who were in bondage to her. Flaubert might remark on how the *Notebook* made him "want to be shaken alone in a

telega through snow-covered fields, to the sound of wolves howling";
for Turgenev, however, there was the added purpose of describing
these conditions to readers of influence and education, a very small
class in Russia at that time. It is said that a reading of *A Sportsman's
Notebook* contributed to Tsar Alexander II's decision to liberate the
serfs.

The book is both a work of imagination and of description; Belinsky had advised Turgenev to observe the facts and then filter
them through his imagination. *A Sportsman's Notebook* conveys the
vastness and beauty of rural Russia. It shows also the eccentricity,
cruelty and nobility of many of its inhabitants, a varied collection of
peasants, landlords, bailiffs, overseers, horse dealers, and merchants.
Turgenev observes them from a certain distance; he is a hunter travelling in search of game, often in the company of his faithful guide
Ermolai who is probably based on one of his mother's old house
serfs, Afanasy Ivanov. It was also from Ivanov that he took down
the touching words of the short reminiscence "About Nightingales."
Descendants of the serf were still living at Spasskoye in 1955.

Ermolai and the narrator wander across the huge landscape of
forest and steppe, usually with one or two hunting dogs, travelling sometimes for several days on end, walking or riding in carts,
staying in village inns or with hospitable neighbors. Turgenev was
fond of dogs. Later he was to write an elegiac memoir of his beloved Pegas, a half-bred retriever who would accompany him on
similar shooting expeditions near Baden-Baden. This was the sort
of sport which Turgenev enjoyed. No great numbers were killed;
the spirit of the countryside and its people were as important as
the bag itself, a different concept of pleasure to the great massa-
cres of driven birds which were popular in England and Scotland
at this time. Turgenev tried these and seems not to have enjoyed
the experience. "Such expeditions—without dogs—are somewhat
monotonous," he wrote to Tolstoy in 1878. "In such circumstances
one has to shoot very accurately, and I have always been only an
average shot." Louis Viardot, Pauline's husband, was also scornful
about shooting in England, disliking the game laws which he said
unduly hampered his sport.

Turgenev did not possess what one might call the killer's instinct. Birds and animals could arouse not only his affection but his sentimentality as well. In another reminiscence called "The Quail" he remembers a hunting trip with his father and an old dog Trezor during which a quail sacrifices itself for her chicks. Later he sees a black-cock do the same; "after that day," he writes, "I found it harder and harder to kill and shed blood." Indeed, he declares, "I never became a real sportsman." Yet Turgenev was a true countryman. During his time of imprisonment in 1852 after the publication of his eulogistic obituary of Gogol he thought longingly of those sporting expeditions of the past. Part of the reason he became so fond of Baden-Baden was because of the woods and forests that encircled the town.

It was the enthusiastic reception accorded to the first sketch of *A Sportsman's Notebook*, "Khor and Kalinich," that led Turgenev to decide not to abandon literature. Although his poems had been praised initially by Belinsky (whose habit it was to be indulgent towards a writer's first work), they began soon to be met by a certain indifference. In another of his reminiscences Turgenev declares that "I quite soon realised myself that there was no need for me to carry on with such-like exercises and—made up my mind to give up literature altogether." However I. I. Panayev, the editor of *The Contemporary*, was looking for articles and Turgenev gave him "Khor and Kalinich." Paneyev added the words "From the sketches of a sportsman"; the piece aroused such interest that Turgenev was encouraged to do another.

He was a careful writer, alive to each nuance of language and subtlety of style. Words fascinated him; he regarded Russian as an exquisite instrument. Constance Garnett, whose translations introduced Turgenev to the English-speaking world, wished later that she had come first to Tolstoy who wrote in a much less artful way. She found *A Sportsman's Notebook* particularly difficult because of the author's use of dialect. Some translators baulk at rendering the idiomatic speech of the peasants or the backwoods landlords into an English equivalent; others attempt what can seem like a version of *The Archers* transposed to the steppes.

Probably much is lost in translation. The Russian critic Zhdanov said he believed it to be impossible to translate Turgenev and retain the effect of the original. Constance Garnett herself declared that "Turgenev is much the most difficult of the Russians to translate because his style is the most beautiful." I do not read Russian. Yet to me an atmosphere and beauty of description come through in English. The book's extraordinary evocation of the countryside, its life and climate, the often pathetic condition and struggles of those who live there: these are there in this version as well.

Rural Russia could be a brutal place. There was poverty and cruelty, ignorance and disease. Even the narrator's faithful companion Ermolai is described in "Ermolai and the Miller's Wife" as a wife-beater who kills winged birds by biting into their necks. In "Raspberry Water" a manor house has burnt down and been abandoned by its family. Only a pathetic gardener remains in a hut nearby. It is his job to supply vegetables for the manorial table a hundred and fifty miles away; his wife tries vainly to milk a barren cow. Another peasant tells of the house's previous owner, the wastrel Count who died bankrupt in a St. Petersburg hotel. Once there were wild parties, decadent extravagance, hounds kept on silver leads, rapacious mistresses, unthinking severity towards the serfs. Yet "the master was everything a master should be," the old man says. "They were good old days, all the same!" Almost anything can be transformed by memory into human nostalgia and its longing for a golden age.

Coming as he does from a landowning family, the narrator cannot escape the occasionally brutal deeds of his forebears. In "Ovsyanikov the Freeholder" Ovsyanikov cheerfully relates how the narrator's grandfather seized some of his family's land, reacting to their protests by sending his huntsmen and a gang of ruffians to fetch the freeholder's father and beat him under the windows of the manor house. The narrator also shows a Russian vagueness about his ancestral possessions. In "The Live Relic" he and Ermolai are caught in the rain. The serf tells him they can shelter at "a little farm belonging to your mother; eight versts from here." Previously he did not know of the place's existence.

Throughout the book there is this dichotomy: an obvious distance between the narrator and the country people he meets, yet also a strong sense of them as individuals. The distance comes from class and education; the clear characterization from a country upbringing and solitary childhood during which Turgenev came to rely on the peasants for company. A youthful affair with a seamstress at Spasskoye resulted in an illegitimate daughter; there may have been other involvements with peasant girls, as was common then on Russian estates. Turgenev could write with sympathy of the landowner Chertopkhanov's love for the peasant girl Masha in "Chertopkhanov and Nedopyuskin" and "The End of Chertopkhanov," a precursor of Kirsanov's feelings for Fenitchka in *Fathers and Children*. His own affairs were probably not so intense as the one in the story. No woman in Turgenev's life ever matched Pauline Viardot.

A lack of intensity has always been one of the charges laid against Turgenev. It does not diminish his powers of sympathy or feeling. In "The Live Relic," first published in 1874, long after most of the other stories, the fresh beauty of the sunlit garden after the rain offsets the pathetic predicament of the diseased but once lovely peasant girl who had led the dancing in his mother's household to create one of his most affecting portraits. The blameless Lukerya was doomed before the age of thirty. Turgenev compares her to Joan of Arc and in the context of her suffering the comparison seems apt. Like Tolstoy's Ivan Illyich, she has contracted a mysterious illness after a fall. Her fiancé, the wine butler, grieves for her, then marries someone else. She has been lying in the hut for seven years, looked after by the locals, dreaming and watching the animals and birds, close to the natural beauties around her. There is a sad irony in the local constable's claim that she has been "smitten by God, for her sins no doubt."

The theme is that of submission to fate. It is a constant presence in Turgenev's work: in the shocking return of Lavretsky's wife in *The Nest of Gentlefolk*, in Sanin's ill-fated courtship in *The Torrents of Spring*, the death of Insarov in *On the Eve*, the crumbling of Bazarov's strength in *Fathers and Children*. The image of inaction, of the withered body lying on a sick bed, is characteristic as well. At this point all activity can seem to be ultimately futile, even doomed.

This, however, does not lessen the moral power or simple strength of the Lukeryas: those who suffer with resignation and even a certain strange joy.

Fate hovers over "Bezhin Meadow" with an almost supernatural sense of foreboding. On a summer night, peasant boys sit by fires, guarding the horses. They cook potatoes and as the narrator lies near them pretending to sleep he hears their talk of ghostly apparitions and the imaginative world of childhood. Ahead lie the uncertainties and probable hardship of their adult lives; for the moment they are excited innocents. Later the narrator hears of the tragedy that strikes down the most memorable of them. With that characteristic concision of sympathy, Turgenev writes "A pity, he was a splendid lad!" People and their fate: for Turgenev the elusive link was of ceaseless fascination. In "King Lear of the Steppes" he writes "Everything in the world, good and bad, comes to man, not through his deserts, but in consequence of some as yet unknown but logical laws which I will not take upon myself to indicate, though I sometimes fancy I have a dim perception of them."

Turgenev's characters live in a way that those of few other writers can. He told Henry James that his stories had their origins not in an idea but a human image; then he would seek a plot or situation in which to place this. The characters in *A Sportsman's Notebook* are precursors of his later often blighted and occasionally heroic inhabitants of rural Russia: the tormented Harlov in "King Lear of the Steppes," the broken down nobleman in "The Brigadier," the curious couple in "Punin and Baburin." Like these, the people of *A Sportsman's Notebook* convey the sense of their time and position: the way these can bring nobility to some, also lead to frustration or almost absurd stoicism and occasionally create monsters. In "My Neighbor Radilov" the courteous but preoccupied landowner with whom Turgenev dines is a victim of the Orthodox Church's refusal to allow a man to marry the sister of his dead wife. "The Bailiff," with its picture of the cruel dandy on his rarely visited property, shows the peasants at the mercy of the landowner's vicious but sycophantic agent; in "The Office" we see the workings of the capricious bureaucracy of a landed estate. The absurdly pompous Major-General Khvalinsky in "Two Landowners" is almost as detestable as his neighbor, the bachelor Stegunov who declares "As I see it, the master is the master and the peasant is the peasant . . . and that's all there is to it." Stegunov hums as he listens to the sound of his butler being beaten; what makes the incident even more pathetic is that the butler tells Turgenev later that he is sure he deserved his punishment. The serf declares admiringly that "you won't find another master like him in the whole province." Turgenev writes simply "there's old mother Russia for you, I thought on my way home."

It is partly through this suffering that Turgenev gives a unique spiritual dimension to the Russian peasant. The dying Lukerya in "The Live Relic" has it, as does the mysterious dwarf Kasyan in "Kasyan from Fair Springs" who is said to possess the power of healing. In "The Bear" it seems as if the giant solitary forester is almost at one with the woods he is protecting on behalf of his master. The death of a man crushed by a tree in "Death" shows such simple acceptance that Turgenev is moved to write "Strange how death takes the Russian peasant! His state of mind at his last hour cannot be called indifference or dull-wittedness; he dies as if he were going through a ceremony: coldly, and with simplicity." By contrast the landowners are usually portrayed in a less attractive light. There is not much spiritual awareness in the arrogant remount officer Prince N. and his toady Lieutenant Khlopakov in "Lebedyan."

It is generally the peasants who supply the moments of transcendent beauty. In "The Singers" the singing competition between Yasha the Turk and the huckster in the "Snug Nook" pot-house takes place amid squalid and pathetic surroundings but once the music begins each competitor "climbs out of his skin," the winner attracting "silent passionate attention" as "with every note there floated out something noble and immeasurably large, like familiar steppe-country unfolding before you, stretching away into the boundless distance." The narrator forgets the low pot-house; he thinks of "a great white gull" slowly stretching its long wings "towards the familiar sea, towards the low, blood-red sun." It is a triumph of simplicity, of a skill as natural as the vast countryside itself. At the end another human reality returns; as the narrator leaves he hears a child calling out to one of its siblings to come home to be beaten by their father.

In Turgenev's landscape of forest and steppe lurk those traits of character which he would develop later in his novels. "Khor and Kalinich" represent two sides of human nature: the one cautious, reserved and calculating; the other instinctive, talkative and idealistic, a more typical Turgenev hero. The provincial Hamlet of "Prince Hamlet of Shchigrovo" proves in his dispiriting soliloquy the disastrous effects of self-pity and irresolution, describing his perverse pleasure at having reached "the extreme limit of misfortune." It is a study similar to that of the *Diary of a Superfluous Man*, the weakness of will typical also of the main character in *Rudin* and the almost masochistic descent into failure and farce of Nezhdanov in *Virgin Soil*. Turgenev would write later of the contrast between the Hamlets and the Don Quixotes of this world: the men of indecision and introspection and those who are decisive and free from egoism. Objectively he favored Don Quixote's questing active spirit; he knew, however, that he himself had much more of Hamlet's temperament. This made him understand the failure of the nameless man from Shchigrovo, the thwarted hopeless love of Pyotr Petrovich Karataev for Matrona, of Radilov for Olga in "My Neighbour Radilov," of Chertopkhanov for Masha. Turgenev believed love to be doomed generally to end in a sense of disappointment or loss.

Turgenev seems at times almost to cherish weakness. Of his central figures, perhaps only Bazarov in *Fathers and Children* and Insarov in *On the Eve* are strong and even they at the end become victims, pathetic in death. One may perhaps look to Turgenev's own life for an echo of this in the follower of the Viardot family around Europe. Turgenev was accepted by Pauline's elderly husband Louis and their children; they were happy even that he should have his own illegitimate daughter by a serf at Spasskoye brought up in their family. But Pauline put her art above all other attachments, whereas Turgenev would have been prepared to give up everything for her. Whether they were ever lovers is doubtful; Turgenev's love for her is not in doubt. It was the strength of her ultimate indifference against the weakness of his devotion. His work seems often to proclaim that lasting mutually satisfying love is unattainable, especially when the passion of one of the lovers is particularly great. The liberal exile Alexander Herzen wrote of the middle-aged Turgenev at Baden-Baden: "he is in love with the Viardot like an eighteen year old."

Melancholy, doubt and occasional timidity molded Turgenev as a writer. He found it more than usually hard to bear the dislike of others; he distrusted the grand solution or the strident campaign. No wonder Tolstoy and Dostoyevsky despised him; he could not share their certainties or vigorous determination. In love he was not exactly thwarted but almost certainly unfulfilled. In politics he found himself often cursed by revolutionaries and conservatives alike; perhaps this is always the destiny of the liberal at a time of extremes. Yet the political message of *A Sportsman's Notebook* is simple, if necessarily not too obvious because of the Tsarist censor. The abolition of serfdom was a great radical cause in the 1840s and 1850s. With this, Turgenev was in full agreement. For a few years the book made him immensely admired among educated people in his homeland before the disapproval that followed the publication of *Fathers and Children* in 1862.

He was too subtle a writer to produce a mere political tract. It was partly the Hamlet in him which prevented this, the irresolution his more certain contemporaries castigated and that now seems often a relief from their didactic sermons. His artistry was a barrier to propaganda or preaching. The propagandist or the preacher must put a detailed case; Turgenev wrote once that "the secret of being tedious was to say everything." In this book, the first of his masterpieces, he proved the truth of this, impressing others with it as well. Herzen had previously believed Turgenev to be "educated and clever" but "superficial and fatuous." He changed his mind after reading *A Sportsman's Notebook*.

Turgenev once said that "no matter what I write my work will always take the form of a series of sketches." In his last novel, *Virgin Soil*, he tried a more ambitious approach, comparable to the grand scale of Tolstoy or Dostoyevsky. It did not work although the book has memorable passages, not least the satire of the populist "back to the people" movement of students and revolutionaries of the late 1860s and the portraits of the "liberal" noble Sipyagin and his affected wife. His most successful novels are those of character and situation, like *Rudin* and *Fathers and Children*. In them his lyrical sympathy evokes the shades of a wood in autumn, a sense of bitter-sweet melancholy and regret: hints also of the political and social turmoil of his homeland, that vast strange landscape of forest and steppe. Turgenev too had that primitive soul with which the nineteenth-century Russians captivated Europe.

This makes him a deceptive writer. His books evoke melancholy, disillusion and frustrated romance; they are often chronicles of decay, hopelessness, and futility. Charm is one of their chief attributes, together with a beguiling style, a beauty of description, a deftness of characterization. Yet, as *A Sportsman's Notebook* shows, he is also profoundly Russian, an exile from a vast and extraordinary country for which he retained a deep love in spite of his disapproval of its often brutal and unjust government. With this love came a profound concern for the social and political developments of his homeland. Turgenev refused to shut himself away with his art in the way that his friend and admirer Flaubert did. He was a stylist but not in isolation, never apart from his times.

At first glance Turgenev's "Russianness" is not so obvious as that of Tolstoy or Dostoyevsky. This is partly because his love of Russia was tempered with respect for western ideas and institutions about which he knew more than his other great Russian literary contemporaries. Fluent in several European languages, he was as at ease in the literary worlds of Paris, London and Berlin as in those of Moscow and St. Petersburg. Among his friends and admirers were Flaubert, George Sand, the Goncourt brothers, Carlyle, Monckton Milnes and Henry James. He attended the Magny dinners and the salon of the Princess Mathilde. He lived out of Russia for much of his life, with the Viardots in France or at Baden-Baden and for a brief time in London during the Franco-Prussian War.

He became a "westerner" early on, after escaping from his mother to study in Berlin. It is probable that the scorn of Potugin in "Smoke" for simplistic Slavophilism echoes the views of Turgenev himself and his fears for Russia in the years of revolutionary turmoil that followed the abolition of serfdom in 1861. Yet glib "westerners" such as Panshin in *A Nest of Gentlefolk* or the old noblemen Ivan Matveitch in "An Unhappy Girl" receive rough handling as well. In 1859 Turgenev wrote from the house of his beloved Pauline Viardot in France that "there is no happiness outside the family—and outside one's native land; everyone should stay in his own nest and put down roots into his native soil. What is the point of clinging on to the edge of someone else's nest?" Turgenev clung to the edge of someone else's nest for much of his life.

To a European reader, he is perhaps the most approachable of the great Russians. He was the first great Russian writer to attain fame in the west and seems to have appealed particularly to the climate of disenchantment and melancholy in England at the end of the nineteenth century. The early translations by Constance Garnett were admired by Arnold Bennett and Galsworthy; Henry James proclaimed him "the first novelist of the day" although he complained about the Russian's "atmosphere of unrelieved sadness." Others have found themselves moved and haunted by the stories of loss and disillusion, of failure and regret, of the often disappointing consequences of enthusiasm, of an almost timeless world where emotion and character draw gentle weak men to an inevitable doom. Most of Turgenev's men are weak, just as many of his women are strong.

Only a Russian could have portrayed such a gallery of fools, eccentrics, brutes and saints; through the great nineteenth-century Russian writers we have come to recognize these characters as typical of only one European country. Turgenev was the polite companion of the Viardots, gentle guest of the Princess Mathilde and cultivated participant in the Magny dinners. Yet he carried with him also those memories of a brutal loveless childhood, the barbarity and arbitrary power that reigned in a huge pitiless landscape where humans were bought and sold like chattels. Against this he felt often quite powerless. The achievement of *A Sportsman's Notebook* is to show how genius can have power enough of its own.

The critical tone of the book annoyed the authorities. Throughout his life they continued to look upon its author with suspicion.

After Turgenev's death in France in 1883 his body was taken back to St. Petersburg to be buried near Belinsky, his first mentor. The great European writer who had proclaimed himself to be a coward showed his influence in his homeland even from beyond the grave. The Tsar's secret police watched his funeral for signs of political demonstration, a tribute indeed to this man who had been criticised for his weakness and supposed reluctance to take sides.

                                                            Max Egremont

PREFACE

My Afghan godfather, a bristling military man, who at one time back in the 1930s held the all-India motorcycle speed record, spoke of *A Sportsman's Notebook* as one of the two or three books that formed and continued to inform his mind. I remember his copy of it lying on his bedside table, leather-bound, pocket-size, printed on onionskin paper. He cared more for horses and dogs than for books, and could in no degree be thought literary, yet he found a place of repose in Turgenev's stories, a cool refuge from a life of heat and action. The *Notebook* is that kind of book, one that appeals widely, and one that strikes deep, one that can serve sturdily through an entire life.

The *Notebook* lands at a critical stage in the development of the short story. Turgenev had the good fortune to be born and bred in the place where this poetic form, the short story, came to its highest (yet) glory—the Russia of the middle and late nineteenth century. Chekhov is Chekhov, and comparisons are odious when talking about writers of this standard and so closely aligned. Yet if Chekhov finds a sublimity unequaled by anyone, certainly *A Sportsman's Notebook* can beguile us so deeply with its descriptions of man and beast and the lord's good earth that we say, thank you for what you have done, and well done, and please do it again and again, as he does. The book passes through many rooms, and each has its deep interest. It is that unusual thing, a classic that is not pitched right down the middle. It is quirky. Coming early in the development of the short story form, it has the raw originality of youth, is bright and morning.

Turgenev's family received properties from the czars whom they served since coming over from the Golden Horde in 1440 to join the court of Grand Prince Vasili Ivanovich. Spasskoye, the name of Turgenev's principal estate, where these stories are set, comprised fifty thousand acres of good black earth. The Turgenevs held this land since the 1600s, granted to them as a reward for military service. Fifty thousand acres is not merely a farm, it's a state. There were Indian princely states—other principalities throughout history—smaller than that. That's seventy-eight square miles, or a box eight miles to a side.

Russian history—the history of those lands—is shot through with violence, right up to the present day. The callousness of the administration toward the workers sent in to clean with mop and pail the irradiated hulk of the Chernobyl reactor had roots in the violence of the earliest rulers of Russia. Peter the Great could crush a gold coin in his massive fist, but all those mad or sane rulers crushed men for sport. Absolute in her realm, Turgenev's mother, Varvara Petrovna, ruled Spasskoye with a caprice and violence rare even for the extravagantly despotic nobility of her day. She printed her own paper, weaved cloth, grew all her food, cut timber, ran sawmills, made candles. All sorts of works. If Russia had ceased to exist and Spasskoye floated in the middle of a blue sea she would have missed only the clothes she ordered from Paris—the indulgence of a *jolie laide* married to a dashing and chronically unfaithful man.

Turgenev's grandmother once beat to death a page-boy and hid the body in her embarrassment under a pile of cushions. His mother demanded that men being sent to Siberia or to serve in the army, a lifetime's banishment, parade before leaving under her living room window and thank her for her forbearance to them. As a young man Turgenev observed a little girl being abused in the courtyard of his mother's Petersburg house and realized with a start that this was his own illegitimate daughter from a Spasskoye serf woman. His mother knew of the girl's parentage and surely bound her to hardship as another of the torments she might inflict on this son that she adored and yet must hurt—as she herself had been hurt so badly in childhood, rejected by her own mother, preyed upon sexually by her stepfather.

(Turgenev took the girl to Paris and educated her and settled a substantial dowry upon her, renamed her Paulinette after the love of his
life, Pauline Viardot—one of the finest European singing voices of
her time. That is another story.)

This estate, and the hard times his mother showed him there, are
schools for this book. Had Varvara Petrovna been a better woman,
Turgenev would not have had the knowledge to write *A Sportsman's
Notebook*. These stories are as much informed by his mother's despotism as by the larger despotism of the Russian state. His personal
revolt ran parallel to a larger national political revolt. Through his
childhood and later as a man, Turgenev sought out the company of
the serfs in the kennels and kitchens of Spasskoye because among
them he found kindness. *A Sportsman's Notebook* is the fruit of those
encounters. The strength of these stories is in his portraits of these
men and women.

The *Notebook* comprises his first truly successful work. When in
1852, at the age of thirty-four, he issued the first edition, with most
of the canonical stories that are included in the present volume, he
had published a few slight pieces, nothing to suggest the brilliance
to come. The *Notebook* has the quality of work done for himself,
for love, unrestrained. Not bothering about plot too much, he drew
portraits of these men and women from the estate, took up stories
that he had heard or seen enacted. The characteristic that distin-
guishes stories about life from life itself is that life has no plot, no
meaningful plot. In most cases, as we have come to understand the
short story form, plot is imposed upon human interactions by the
writer. One great charm of these stories is that they are so unplot-
ted, some of them held together only by the framing device of the
narrator going out hunting and encountering some man or woman
or situation. More than others, Turgenev can say, in his modest offhand voice, *I made it out of a mouthful of air.*

Unusually, for a work of fiction—for any work of art—the
Notebook played an important political role in the history of Russia.
In the middle of the nineteenth century, the necessity of liberating
the serfs, who were virtually slaves, had become pressing upon an
increasingly westernized nobility. The necessity of their liberation,

and then the means and outlines of that emancipation, puzzled the nobles and most importantly, the czar—Alexander II. This constituency found it difficult to reconcile itself to the loss of their revenues and powers flowing from this emancipation in part because they knew very little about their serfs, had never paid much attention to them. They commanded obedience with banishments and the knout, and otherwise indulged themselves with serf orchestras on their estates and desperate feats of gambling and spoke French among themselves. If they gave it any thought, they would have considered it an impertinence for their serfs to have private lives.

Turgenev's stories imposed the humanity of these men and women upon their owners, showed them in all their complexity. The stories came as a revelation to their readership. Any man who's ever killed a chicken knows that it's best not to look it in the eye. Turgenev forced his fellow landowners to do that, look the serfs in the eye. Alexander II acknowledged the role these stories played in guiding him to issue the Emancipation Edict that freed the serfs in 1861.

Even today, with our different circumstances, we can benefit from this compelled awakening. In Turgenev's time a debate—which directly led to the terrible Russian Revolution—raged between those who advocated a turn to the West, and those who dreamed of a new Slavic establishment different from anything bred in Europe. It might seem that these combats, long played out, are irrelevant today. The debate about the correct direction for Russia's development, while it included the class conflict between landowners and serfs, had at its core a cultural conflict, a fundamentally Oriental Russianness pulling against European rationalism. This is in many respects the same as our present-day debate about the interpenetration between the Northern and the Southern hemispheres. Both are questions about how two cultures should marry

The *Notebook* has some particular excellencies, which I would point out to you, gentle reader, as would a host at a banquet drawing out with fork and knife a delicacy on the served platter. Turgenev is masterful in these stories of two particularly difficult arts, sketches of characters, men and women in all their complexity, and descriptions of nature. The stories are juxtapositions of these two excellencies.

He is describing the steppe, is walking across it: "Whirlwinds—sure sign of settled weather—march in tall white pillars. . . ."

I have seen many whirlwinds, but I've never before observed that, when the wind blows up twirling columns of dust and straw along a field, this means it will be fine and blue. I've taken more words to show it than he does—he is so right in these descriptions.

There are many superb passages describing landscape—I won't quote one here, you'll encounter them soon enough. No one does it better, because he observes nature so closely and because he knows it so well. The title of the book is quite accurate—these are notebooks drawn from the experiences of a passionate sportsman. The great solace of Turgenev's life was shooting, mostly birds. He was a disappointed man—disappointed first in childhood, in his mother's love. His contemporaries dismissed him as ineffectual and shapeless, and though he wrote these brilliant tales and much else, too often he was characterized simply as a *conteur.* Landscape is the refuge of the wounded spirit, and one senses behind his romantic and passionate descriptions of the Russian steppe the sad uncertainty that he felt regarding his place among men and women. The generous descriptions of men and women at Spasskoye are drawn with all the love of the hungry-hearted boy; the descriptions of nature are written from the perspective of the rootless man.

Master of description, he is also superb with endings, is quirky in this regard. Endings are the hardest part of any story, and are particularly difficult for a short story writer, among other reasons simply because he is so regularly faced with the problem of doing them right. (A novelist writes an ending only every few years.) The endings of some of these stories are so attenuated and poetically true—and true only poetically—as to leave the reader bemused and shaken. I'll walk through one of my favorites, to give you a flavor of this.

Like so many of the stories in the *Notebooks*, "The Singers" seems hardly constructed at all. A hunter, a small landowner, walks into a peasant tavern in a run-down village on a hot summer day. A highly miscellaneous group is assembled—Blinker, Muddlehead, Wild Master—these are their nicknames, and they're an odd lot, loungers and boozers, "road masters" as we call them in Pakistan, men whose main occupation is strolling up and down the village street.

It turns out that there is a contest on, a singing contest, with the prize a pot of beer. The challenger, an outsider known only as "the huckster," wins the draw and begins. He sings artfully:

> His voice was quite sweet and agreeable, though some-
> what husky; he played with it, twirled it about like a toy, with
> constant downward trills and modulations and constant re-
> turns to the top note, which he held and prolonged with a
> special effort . . . .

Gradually, he catches up his audience, enflames them.

> Encouraged by the signs of general satisfaction, the huck-
> ster fairly whirled along and went off into such flourishes,
> such tongue-clickings and drummings, such wild throat-
> play, that at length, exhausted, pale, bathed in hot sweat, he
> threw himself back, let out a last dying note—and his wild
> outburst was answered in unison by the company.

The louder part of the crowd by acclamation crowns him the winner, no contest—but cooler heads prevail and his local rival, Ya-sha, is asked to try his voice.

> His first note was faint and uneven, and came, it seemed,
> not from his chest, but from somewhere far away, as if it
> had chanced to fly into the room. . . . Seldom, I confess,
> have I heard such a voice: it was somewhat worn and had a
> sort of cracked ring; at first it had even a certain suggestion
> of the morbid; but it also held a deep, unsimulated passion,
> and youth, and strength, and sweetness, and a deliciously
> detached note of melancholy. The truthful, fervent Russian
> soul rang and breathed in it and fairly caught at your heart,
> caught straight at your Russian heartstrings.

When he finishes, the audience is silent; the innkeeper's wife, in tears, withdraws into another room. The rival singer, the huckster, goes up to Yasha. "'You. . . . It's yours. . . . You've won,' he brought out at last with difficulty and dashed from the room."

Now comes the shift, irrational and intuitive, that I find so intriguing. The narrator, the landowner, goes out of the inn, his world made strange by the music he has heard, falls asleep in a hay loft, and rises just as night has fallen. Collecting himself, he sets off home, passing the tavern, where all are drunk now and rolling around like beasts—he sees it through the window. Walking along the dark road, he hears a boy calling a name, Antropka, Antropka, over and over again.

> "Antropka! Antropka-a-a! . . ." it called, in stubborn, tearful desperation, with a long dragging-out of the last syllable.
> For a few moments it was silent, then began to call again. The voice carried clearly in the unmoving, lightly-sleeping air. Thirty times at least it had called Antropka's name, when suddenly, from the opposite end of the meadow, as if from a different world, came a scarcely audible reply:
> "What-a-a-a-at?"
> The boy's voice called at once, glad but indignant:
> "Come here you devil!"
> "What fo-o-o-r?" answered the other, after a pause.
> "Because father wants to be-ee-ee-eat you."

There it closes—leaving the strange nutty taste of this ending, which is almost unsatisfying, lingering on our palates. What does it mean?

And so that's it, or not quite. "Soft you; a word or two before you go." I make a special pleading for these stories. I am a farmer in Pakistan, in a land that surely is among the last places on earth where the condition that Turgenev describes—feudal life—still exists. I pray that this form of inequality will never again be visited upon mankind, but suspect that human folly is incapable of correction, and that someday, on Mars or on Planet X, again man will lord over man as they did in feudal Russia—and as they do in our present, sad Pakistan. I have lived, and I hope to die, in my faith in Turgenev. I speak with special knowledge. He has described this scene—this feudal scene—better than anyone—and fixed it forever.

Engage with him with love. Attach yourself to this book, it will make you larger.

—Daniyal Mueenuddin

A Sportsman's Notebook

Khor and Kalinich

ANYONE WHO HAS CROSSED FROM THE DISTRICT OF BOLKHOV into that of Zhizdra will probably have been struck by the sharp difference between the natives of the provinces of Orel and Kaluga. The peasant of Orel is short, stooping, sullen; he looks at you from under his brows, lives in flimsy huts of poplar wood, does labor-duty for his master; never goes in for trade; eats badly, wears plaited shoes. In Kaluga the peasant pays rent and lives in spacious cabins of pinewood; he is tall, with a bold gay way of looking at you, and a clean white face; he trades in oil and tar, and on feast days wears boots. In Orel—I am speaking about the eastern part of the province—the village is usually situated among ploughed fields near a ravine which peters out into a dirty pond. Except for a few willows, which are always ready to oblige, and for two or three lank birches, there is not a tree to be seen for a verst around; one hut huddles against another; the roofs have a rough thatch of rotten straw. . . . In Kaluga, on the other hand, the village is largely surrounded by forest; the huts have a freer, sturdier look and are roofed with planks, the gates are well-fitted, the wicker-work fence round the back-yard is neither tattered nor tumble-down, nor does it offer an open invitation to every pig that may come along. . . . Even the sport is better in the province of Kaluga. In Orel the remaining tracts of forest and bush will have vanished in about five years' time, and there is no question of marshes; but in Kaluga, forests where no timber may be cut stretch for hundreds of versts, and marshes for tens of versts, the blackcock (noble bird) is not yet extinct, the generous snipe abounds, and the fussy partridge cheers and startles both sportsman and dog as he flies violently up from cover.

Once, when I was shooting in the district of Zhizdra, I met in the fields, and got to know, a small landowner from Kaluga, Polutykin by name, an enthusiastic sportsman and proportionately excellent fellow. It's true that he had certain weaknesses: for instance, he had courted all the wealthy marriageable girls in the province and, being rejected and forbidden the house, he would broken-heartedly confide his sorrows to all his friends and continue to send the girls' parents presents of sour peaches and other unripe produce of his garden; he loved to repeat, over and over again, one and the same story, which, notwithstanding Mr. Polutykin's high regard for its excellence, certainly had never made anybody laugh; he admired the works of Akim Nakhimov and the story of Pinna; he stammered; he called his dog "Astronomer"; he said "aye" instead of "yes"; in his house he had introduced a French style of cooking, the secret of which, as understood by his cook, consisted in completely transforming the natural taste of every dish: meat, from the hands of this expert, tasted of fish; fish, of mushrooms; macaroni, of gun-powder; and, with it all, no carrot ever fell into the soup without taking the form of a rhombus or a trapeze. Yet, apart from these rare and unimportant failings, Mr. Polutykin was, as I have already said, an excellent fellow.

On the very first day of my acquaintanceship with him, Mr. Polutykin invited me to stay the night. "It's about five versts to where I live," he added. "It's too far to walk; let's first go and see Khor." The reader will excuse me from reproducing his stammer.

"And who may Khor be?"

"One of my peasants . . . he lives just here."

So we went to see Khor. In the middle of the forest, in a cleared and cultivated glade, stood the lonely farm where Khor lived. It consisted of several cabins of pinewood grouped together behind fences; in front of the largest hut was a lean-to roof supported on slender poles. We went in and were met by a young peasant lad of about twenty, tall and good-looking.

"Hallo, Fedya! Is Khor at home?" Mr. Polutykin asked him.

"No, Khor's gone to town," answered the lad, smiling and showing a row of snow-white teeth. "Would you like the cart harnessed?"

"Yes, my boy, we would. And bring us some kvass."

We went into the hut. There were none of your colored prints stuck to the clean boarding of the walls; in the corner, in front of the heavy icon with its crust of silver, an oil-lamp glimmered; the table of limewood had been freshly scraped and washed; between the timbers and along the jambs of the windows there were no skittish, roving bettles, no lurking, reflective cockroaches. The lad soon appeared with a big white jug full of excellent kvass, a huge hunk of wheaten bread and a dozen salted cucumbers in a wooden bowl. He set all these victuals out on the table, leant in the doorway and began to contemplate us with a smile. Before we had finished eating, a cart rattled up to the door. We went out. A boy of about fifteen, curly-headed and ruddy-cheeked, was sitting with the reins in his hand, with difficulty keeping control of a well-fed roan stallion. Round the cart stood half a dozen gigantic young men, all very much like each other and like Fedya. "The whole lot are Khor's children," observed Polutykin. "Yes, all Khor's litter,"* rejoined Fedya, who had followed us out into the porch; "and not the whole lot, either; Potap is in the forest, and Sidor has gone to town with old Khor. . . . Look here, Vasya," he continued, turning to the driver, "remember you're driving the master, and go at a good pace. Only go easy over the bumps, do you hear, or you'll damage the cart and disturb the master's digestion!"

The rest of Khor's litter chuckled at Fedya's remark. "Help Astronomer up too," cried Mr. Polutykin solemnly. Fedya gaily lifted up the dog, which wore a constrained smile, and set him down in the bottom of the cart. Vasya gave the horse its head, and off we went. "There's my estate office," said Mr. Polutykin to me suddenly, pointing to a little low house. "Shall we call in?"

"Certainly."

"It's disused now," he explained, getting down from the cart, "but it's worth looking at all the same."

---

*   Khor in Russian means "polecat." —*Translators.*

The office consisted of two empty rooms. The watchman, an old man with one eye, came running out from the back-yard.

"Good day to you, Minyaich," said Mr. Polutykin, "and where's the water?"

The one-eyed old man vanished and returned at once with a bottle of water and two glasses. "Try it," said Polutykin to me; "try my excellent spring water." We drank a glass each, the old man bowing deeply meanwhile.

"Well, now I think we might go on," observed my new friend. "In this office I sold ten acres of forest to Alliluyev the merchant, and at a good price, too."

We took our places in the cart and in half an hour were already driving into the courtyard of Polutykin's house.

"Tell me," I asked Polutykin at supper, "why does your Khor live separately from your other peasants?"

"I'll tell you: because he is the clever one among them. About twenty-five years ago his hut got burnt down; so up he comes to my late father and says: 'Nikolai Kuzmich, please may I settle on your land, in the forest beside the marsh? I'll pay you good rent.' 'But why do you want to settle beside the marsh?' 'I just do; but you, sir, Nikolai Kuzmich, please don't give me any work to do, but fix any rent you like.' 'Fifty rubles a year.' 'Certainly.' 'And no arrears, mind!' 'Of course, no arrears.' . . . So he settled beside the marsh. And since then he has been known as Khor."

"And he's done well out of it?" I asked.

"He has. Now he pays me a hundred rubles rent, and I am going to make him pay more still, I think. I have said to him several times: 'Buy your own freedom, Khor, do!' But he, the crafty brute, assures me that he could not manage it; that he has got no money . . . As if he expected me to believe him! . . ."

Next day we went out shooting as soon as we had drunk tea. As we drove through the village Mr. Polutykin told the driver to stop in front of a little low hut and called out loudly: "Kalinich!"

"Coming, sir, coming," replied a voice from the yard; "I'm just tying my shoe."

We went slowly on: outside the village we were overtaken by a man of about forty—tall, thin, with a small head, carried well in the air. This was Kalinich. His good-natured swarthy face, with pock marks here and there, appealed to me as soon as I saw it. Kalinich, as I learnt later on, accompanied his master out shooting every day, carried his bag, and sometimes his gun too, marked his birds, brought him water to drink, picked strawberries, built shelters for him, ran to fetch the drozhky; without him Mr. Polutykin could not stir a yard. Kalinich was a man of the gayest and gentlest character imaginable; he was constantly humming below his breath and throwing carefree glances in all directions; he spoke in a slightly nasal voice, smiling and screwing up his pale-blue eyes and often passing his hand over his scanty wedge-shaped beard. He walked slowly but with large strides, leaning slightly on a long thin stick. In the course of the day he and I got talking together several times, and he looked after me without a trace of servility; his attitude to his master was one of fatherly supervision.

When the unbearable midday heat compelled us to seek shelter, he led us to his bee-garden in the very depth of the forest. He opened up for us a little hut, hung with bunches of dried aromatic herbs, gave us some fresh hay to lie on, then himself put a sort of network bag over his head, took a knife, a pot and a piece of burning wood, and went off to the bee-garden to cut us some honeycomb. We washed down the warm translucent honey with spring water, and fell asleep to the monotonous humming of bees and the busy murmur of leaves. A gentle breath of wind awakened me. I opened my eyes and saw Kalinich. He was sitting on the threshold of the half-open door, fashioning a spoon with his knife. I lay and admired his face, which was gentle and serene as the evening sky. Mr. Polutykin also awoke. We did not get up at once. After a long tramp and a deep sleep it is delightful to lie motionless in the hay: a luxurious languor invades the body, the face glows with warmth, a delicious laziness closes the eyes.

At length we rose, went out, and continued our wanderings until nightfall. At supper I spoke again about Khor and also about Kalinich.

"Kalinich is a good fellow," said Mr. Polutykin: "a keen, obliging fellow. He's not much good on the land, though; I am always taking him away from it. Every day he comes out shooting with me. . . . What good that does the land, you can well imagine." I agreed with him, and we went to bed.

Next day Mr. Polutykin was obliged to go into town about some trouble which he had with his neighbor Pichukov. Pichukov had ploughed up some of Polutykin's land and, on this land, had beaten one of Polutykin's peasant women. I went out shooting alone and towards evening I paid a call on Khor. In the doorway of the hut I was met by an old man—bald, short, sturdy and broad-shouldered: Khor himself. I looked at him with curiosity. His cast of face recalled Socrates: the same high bumpy forehead, the same little eyes, the same snub nose. We went together into the hut. My friend Fedya brought me some milk and black bread. Khor sat down on a bench and, tranquilly stroking his curly beard, engaged me in conversation.

He seemed a man conscious of his own worth; slow of speech and movement, with an occasional chuckle from behind his long moustaches. I talked to him about the sowing, the harvest, about the peasant's life. . . . He always seemed to agree with me; only, when he did so, I was conscious of an uneasy feeling that I was not really right after all; our conversation had a certain strangeness about it. Some of Khor's utterances were abstruse—probably the effect of caution. Here is a sample of our conversation for you:

"Tell me, Khor," I said to him, "why don't you buy your freedom from the master?"

"And why should I buy it? As things are, I know the master and I know the rent he wants. . . . He is a good master, too."

"All the same, you would be better off if you were free," I remarked.

Khor gave me a sidelong glance. "Certainly," he said.

"Well, then, why don't you buy your freedom?"

Khor swivelled his head from side to side.

"And what am I to buy it with, sir?"

"Oh, come on, man. . . ."

"Once Khor gets in among people who are free," he continued

below his breath, as if talking to himself, "any fellow who shaves his beard would be Khor's master."

"But you could shave your own beard, too."

"What's a beard? A beard is grass; you can always cut it."

"Well, then?"

"Of course, Khor might get right in among the merchants; merchants have a good life—and they've got beards too."

"Well, don't you do a bit of trading, too?" I asked him.

"I trade in a small way, with oil and tar. . . . Now, sir, would you like me to harness the cart?"

You've got your head screwed on the right way, and a firm hold on your tongue, too, I thought. "No," I said aloud, "I don't need the cart; I shall be shooting near your place to-morrow and, if I may, I'll spend the night here in your hay-shed."

"You'll be welcome. But will you be all right in the shed? I'll tell the women to spread a sheet for you and to put out a pillow. Hey, there, women!" he shouted, rising from his place. "Come here! . . . Fedya, you go with them. Women are such fools."

A quarter of an hour later, Fedya, carrying a lantern, escorted me to the shed. I threw myself down on the sweet-smelling hay, and my dog curled up at my feet; Fedya wished me good night, and the door squeaked and slammed to behind him. For some time I couldn't get to sleep. A cow came up to the door and breathed loudly once or twice; my dog gave a dignified growl at her; a pig went past, grunting reflectively; somewhere nearby a horse began to munch hay and snort. . . .

At length I dropped off to sleep.

At dawn Fedya awoke me. I had taken a great liking to this gay, alert young fellow; he seemed to be a favorite with old Khor too, as far as I could observe. They chaffed each other in the most amiable way. The old man came out to meet me. Whether because I had spent the night under his roof, or for some other reason, at any rate Khor was much more forthcoming towards me than he had been the day before.

"The samovar's waiting for you," he told mè with a smile; "let's go and have tea."

We sat down at table. A healthy-looking peasant woman, one of Khor's daughters-in-law, brought a pot of milk. All his sons came in one after the other.

"What a tall lot you've got!" I observed to the old man.

"Yes," he replied, biting off a tiny piece of sugar. "I think that neither I nor the old woman has given them anything to complain about."

"And do they all live with you?"

"Yes. They all want to live here, so they do."

"And are they all married?"

"That rascal there won't marry," he answered, pointing at Fedya, who as before was leaning in the doorway. "As for Vaska, he's a bit young still, he has time to wait."

"What should I get married for?" rejoined Fedya. "I'm all right as I am. What good would a wife be to me? Someone to quarrel with, eh?"

"Well, you . . . I know all about you! You wear silver rings . . . you like sniffing round after servant-girls! Oh, get along with you, now!" continued the old man, imitating the voice of a serving-maid. "I know all about you, with your white hands and all!"

"But what is there that's good about a peasant woman?"

"The peasant woman is a worker," observed Khor sententiously. "She is a servant to her husband."

"And what would I want a worker for?"

"Because you like other people to pull your chestnuts out of the fire. Oh, I know you and your sort."

"Well, marry me off, if you want to. Eh? What? Why don't you say something?"

"Well, that'll do, you joker. You're disturbing the master. I'll marry you off, don't worry. . . . You mustn't mind him, sir; he's only a whipper-snapper, you see, and hasn't had time to learn any sense."

Fedya shook his head. . . .

"Is Khor in?" said a well-known voice at the door, and Kalinich came in, holding a bunch of wild strawberries which he had picked for his friend Khor. The old man welcomed him joyfully. I looked with surprise at Kalinich. I must admit, I had not expected that a peasant would be capable of such "attentions."

That day I went shooting four hours later than usual, and I spent the next three days at Khor's. I was absorbed by my new acquaintances. I can't say how I deserved their confidence, but they talked to me without constraint. I enjoyed listening to them and observing them. The two friends were not in the least similar. Khor was a positive, practical fellow, an administrator, a rationalist. Kalinich, on the other hand, belonged to the category of idealists, romantics, enthusiasts and dreamers. Khor understood reality, that is to say, he knew how to get on in the world, how to put money aside, and keep on good terms with the master and the other powers that be; Kalinich went about in plaited shoes and lived from hand to mouth. Khor was the father of a large, submissive and united family; Kalinich had once had a wife, of whom he had been afraid, but never any children. Khor saw right through Mr. Polutykin; Kalinich, on the other hand, idolized him. Khor loved Kalinich and gave him his protection; Kalinich loved and revered Khor. Khor spoke little, chuckled, and thought things out for himself; Kalinich expressed himself with warmth, although he was not one of your nightingales of eloquence, like some smart fellows of the artisan class. . . . But Kalinich was endowed with advantages which even Khor allowed him; for instance, he knew spells to cure fear, frenzy or bleeding; he could drive out worms; his bees did well, he had the right touch with them. Khor asked him, in my presence, to lead a newly-bought horse into the stable, for luck, and Kalinich carried out the request of the old sceptic with conscientious gravity. Kalinich was nearer to nature; Khor, to people, to human society. Kalinich did not like arguing and believed everything blindly; Khor had risen far enough to take an ironic view of life. He had seen a lot, he knew a lot, he taught me a lot, too. For example, from his stories I learned that every summer, just before mowing time, there appears in the country villages a small cart of unusual aspect. In the cart there sits a man in a frock-coat with scythes to sell. In cash he charges one ruble twenty-five copecks; in notes, a ruble and a half; on credit, four rubles. It goes without saying that all peasants buy from him on

credit. Two or three weeks later he appears again and demands payment. The peasant has just cut his oats, and therefore has money to
pay with; he goes with the merchant to the pot-house and there set-
tles his account. Certain landowners had the idea of buying scythes
themselves for cash and issuing them to their peasants on credit for
the same price; but the peasants showed themselves dissatisfied and
even depressed: they were deprived of the pleasure of tapping on the
scythe, listening to it, turning it in their hands and asking the crafty
vendor twenty times or so: "Well, lad, the scythe is not as good as
all that, eh?" The same tricks take place when it comes to the buying of sickles, the only difference being that then the women inter-
vene and sometimes bring the vendor himself to a point where he is
obliged to hit them—for their own good. But for the women the most
painful occasions of all are these. Purveyors of material to the paper
mills entrust the purchasing of rags to agents of a special type, who
are known in some districts as "eagles." An "eagle" receives from a
merchant two hundred rubles or so in notes and goes in search of
his prey. But, in contrast to the noble bird after which he is named,
he does not practice an open courageous method of attack: on the
contrary, the "eagle" resorts to cunning and deception. He halts his
cart somewhere in the bushes outside the village, and makes his
way on foot by back-ways and back-doors, like a casual passerby
or a common tramp. The women instinctively divine his approach
and creep out to meet him. A business deal is hurriedly completed.
For a few copper farthings the woman gives the "eagle" not only all
her unneeded rags, but often her husband's shirt too and her own
petticoat. Recently the women have found it advantageous to steal
from themselves and to dispose of their hemp in this way, which all
brings more and better business to the "eagles." Meanwhile, however, the peasants in their turn have become wise to what goes on,
and at the least suspicion, or a single distant rumor, of the appearance of an "eagle," they take swift and drastic recourse to measures
of precaution and correction. And indeed they have good grounds
for offense. Selling hemp is *their* business, and sell it they do—not
in town, for they would have to go all the way there, but to visiting hucksters, who, having no weights, reckon one pound at forty

handfuls—but you know what a handful can be, and what a palm a Russian has, especially when he gives his mind to it!

As an inexperienced man who had not lived much in the country, I listened to a good many stories such as this. But Khor didn't spend all the time telling stories, often it was his turn to question me. He discovered that I had lived abroad and this fired his curiosity. . . . Kalinich kept up with him; but he was more interested in descriptions of nature and mountains, waterfalls, unusual buildings and big cities; Khor was preoccupied by questions of administration and government. He examined everything in its right order: "Is it the same way there as it is with us, or otherwise? . . . Tell us, sir, how is it?" "Oh, Lord God Almighty!" Kalinich would exclaim as I went on; Khor remained silent, drew his shaggy brows together, and only occasionally remarked: "*This* wouldn't do here, but *that* is good—it's how it ought to be." I cannot tell you all the questions he asked, and there is no reason why I should; but from our talks I carried away a conviction which will probably surprise my readers, the conviction that Peter the Great was an essentially Russian character, and never more Russian than in his reforms. The Russian is so confident in his strength and steadfastness that he does not mind undergoing change; he cares little about his past, he looks boldly into the future. He likes what is good, he will gladly take what is reasonable, but where it comes from is all the same to him. His sound common sense enjoys a laugh at rigid minds of the German type; but the Germans, in Khor's words, are an interesting lot, and he was quite ready to learn a lesson from them. Thanks to his unusual situation, to his condition of virtual independence, Khor was able to speak to me of many things on which nothing would have extracted a word from another, not even, as peasants say, if you ground him with a grindstone.

He certainly knew where he stood. As I conversed with Khor, I heard for the first time the shrewd simple speech of the Russian peasant. He was a man of fairly wide knowledge, by his own standards, but he could not read; Kalinich, however, could. "Reading and writing come easy to this lazy rogue," observed Khor; "it's like his bees, which never die from the day they are hatched." "Haven't

you had your children taught to read and write?" Khor was silent
for a moment. "Fedya knows how to." "And the others?" "The others don't." "How is that?" The old fellow would not answer and
changed the subject. In fact, for all his shrewdness, even he was
not without prejudices and preconceived ideas. Women, for instance, he despised from the bottom of his heart, and in moments
of hilarity he enjoyed making fun of them. His wife, who was old
and shrewish, spent the whole day above the stove, grumbling and
scolding incessantly; her sons paid no attention to her, but she kept
her daughters-in-law in the fear of God. With reason does the
mother-in-law sing in the Russian folk-song:

> *You're a fine one, my son, in your family life,*
> *If you've never a touch of the stick for your wife.*

Once it occurred to me to take the part of the daughters-in-
law, and I tried to enlist the sympathy of Khor; but he calmly rejoined: "Why should you worry your head with such . . . trash? Let
'em squabble among themselves; putting them apart only makes it
worse, it's just not worth dirtying your hands."

Sometimes the old shrew climbed down from the stove, called
the dog in out of the passage, saying: "Here, doggie, here!" then
beat it over its thin back with a poker; or else she would stand in
the porch and "yap," as Khor expressed it, at everyone who went by.
Nevertheless she stood in awe of her husband and at a word from
him would retire to her perch above the stove.

But it was especially entertaining to hear the dispute that arose
between Kalinich and Khor when Mr. Polutykin's name came up.

"I won't have you touch him, Khor," said Kalinich.

"But why doesn't he have some boots made for you?" rejoined
Khor.

"Pooh, boots! . . . What should I want boots for? I'm a peasant. . . ."

"And so am I, but look . . ." As he spoke Khor lifted his foot and
showed Kalinich a boot which looked as if it had been carved out of
mammoth-skin.

"Oh—as if you were the same as the rest of us," answered Kalinich.

"Well, he might give you money for your bast shoes: look, you go out with him when he goes shooting; one day, one pair of shoes."

"He gives me money to buy them."

"Yes, last year he was so kind as to give you ten copecks."

Kalinich turned away indignantly, and Khor burst out laughing until his little eyes completely disappeared.

Kalinich had quite a pleasant voice and accompanied himself on the balalaika. Khor would listen and listen, then suddenly put his head on one side and join in in a plaintive voice. He was particularly fond of the song, "Oh, my fate, my fate." Fedya never missed the opportunity for a joke against his father: "What makes you so sorry for yourself?" But Khor propped his chin on his hand, shut his eyes and went on complaining about his fate. . . . With all this, there could be no one more active at other moments than Khor. He was eternally busy about something or other—mending the cart, fixing the fence, looking over the harness. He was no great stickler for cleanliness, however, and once answered an observation of mine by saying that "a hut ought to smell lived-in."

"But," I rejoined, "look how clean Kalinich keeps his bee-garden."

"The bees wouldn't live if he didn't, sir," he said with a sigh.

Another time he asked me: "Have you got an estate of your own?"

"Yes."

"Far from here?"

"A hundred versts."

"And do you live there, sir?"

"I do."

"But I expect you spend most of the time shooting?"

"I suppose I do."

"And quite right, too, sir; shoot blackcock to your heart's content, and change your agent every so often."

On the evening of the fourth day Mr. Polutykin sent to fetch me. I was sorry to leave the old man. Kalinich and I took our places in the cart. "Well, good-bye, Khor, look after yourself," I said. "Good-bye, Fedya."

"Good-bye, sir, don't forget us." We drove off. The sunset was just beginning to blaze. "It's going to be a glorious day to-morrow," I remarked, looking at the clear sky. "No, there is rain coming," Kalinich rejoined. "You see how restless those ducks are, and the grass smells too strong, too."

We drove into the brushwood. Kalinich began to sing under his breath as he bumped up and down on the driver's seat, and stared and stared into the sunset . . .

The following day I left Mr. Polutykin's hospitable roof.

Ermolai and the Miller's Wife

In the evening the hunter Ermolai and I went out for the "flight." . . . But perhaps there are some of my readers who do not know what I mean by this. So listen, gentlemen.

A quarter of an hour before sunset, in spring, you go into a wood, with a gun, but without a dog. You choose a place somewhere near the skirts of the wood; you have a look round; you inspect the cap; you make a sign to your companion. A quarter of an hour passes. The sun has set, but it is still light in the forest; the air is clear and translucent; the birds are chattering away; the young grass glows with a cheerful emerald brilliance. . . . You wait. Inside the forest it gradually grows dark; the scarlet light of sunset slowly slips along the roots and trunks of the trees, rises higher and higher, passes from the lower branches, still almost bare, to the motionless, sleeping tree-tops. . . . Now even the tree-tops have faded out; the ruddy sky turns to blue. The smell of the forest grows stronger; there is a faint breath of warm dampness; a breeze comes fluttering in to die away beside you. The birds go off to sleep—not all together, but according to their kinds: first the chaffinches fall silent, then, after a few moments, the robins, after them the yellow-hammers. In the forest it grows darker and darker. The trees merge into great masses that loom up ever more blackly; in the blue sky the first small stars make a timid appearance. The birds are all asleep. Only the redstarts and the small woodpeckers still give an occasional sleepy whistle. . . . Soon even they are silent. Once more there rings out above you the clear voice of the chiff-chaff; somewhere an oriole utters its mournful cry, the nightingale chuckles for the first time. Your heart grows tired of waiting, and suddenly—but only sportsmen will understand me—suddenly in the deep stillness there comes a special kind of whirr and swish, you hear the measured stroke of swift wings—and the woodcock, with his long beak drooping gracefully down, comes swimming out from a dark birch tree to meet your fire.

This is what is meant by "waiting for the flight."

So Ermolai and I set out for the "flight"; but forgive me, gentlemen: I ought first to have presented Ermolai to you.

Imagine a man of about forty-five, tall, thin, with a long sharp nose, a narrow forehead, small gray eyes, tousled hair and a wide mocking mouth. A man who went about winter and summer in a short yellowish nankeen coat of German cut, but with a belt round the waist; who wore baggy blue trousers and a round lambskin cap which had been given to him, as a joke, by a ruined landowner. From the belt hung two bags, one in front, artfully twisted into two halves—for powder and for shot; the other behind—for game; as for wads, Ermolai used to produce them from the apparently inexhaustible resources of his cap. From the money which he received in return for game he could easily have bought himself a bandolier and a game-bag; but such an idea had never even occurred to him, and he continued to load his gun as before, exciting the astonishment of all beholders by the deftness with which he avoided the danger of spilling or mixing his shot and powder. He had a single-barrelled flint-lock gun, with an ugly kick to it, so that his right cheek was permanently swollen out of all proportion to his left. How Ermolai hit the mark with this gun, even the cleverest could not guess—but he did.

He had a pointer called Valetka, a creature of surprises. Ermolai never fed him. "Why should I?" he argued. "A dog's a clever beast and ought to be able to find its own food." And he was right; although Valetka impressed even the most casual passer-by with his extraordinary leanness, he lived—and a long life into the bargain; in spite of his miserable condition, he never ran away or showed the slightest wish to desert his master. Only once, in his youth, he absented himself for two days, under the influence of love; but this was a madness which quickly left him. Valetka's most remarkable quality was his imperturbable indifference to everything in the world. . . . If I had not been talking about a dog, I would have used the word "dis-enchantment." His habit was to sit with his short tail tucked under him, frowning, shivering from time to time and never smiling. (It is well known that dogs can smile, and smile very sweetly too.) He had an extremely unprepossessing appearance, and no idle man-servant would ever miss a chance of a spiteful joke about it; but Valetka put up with all these jokes, and a few blows too, with surprising sangfroid. He gave special entertainment to cooks, who immedi-ately dropped what they were doing to rush headlong after him with shouts and curses as soon as, with a weakness not characteristic of dogs alone, he showed his hungry mug through the half-open door of a temptingly warm and succulent-smelling kitchen. In the chase his great qualities were his tirelessness and his very fine nose; but if a wounded hare happened to come his way, then he would eat it up with gusto, to the last bone, in some cool and shady spot underneath a green bush, at a respectful distance from Ermolai, who would be cursing him in all known and unknown dialects.

Ermolai belonged to one of my neighbors, a landowner of the old school—the school which does not fancy wild game and clings to its preference for domestic fowls. It is only on special occasions, such as birthdays, name days and election days, that cooks in the houses of landowners of this school set about the dressing of long-beaked game, and, working themselves into the frenzy peculiar to the Russian when he does not properly know what he is doing, in-vent such cunning sauces that the guests for the most part inspect the proffered delicacies with curiosity and attention, but cannot resolve to taste them. It was Ermolai's duty to bring to his mas-ter's kitchen once a month two brace of blackcock and two brace of partridge, but otherwise he was allowed to live where and how he pleased. His master had given him up in despair as a fellow who was good for no useful work. It goes without saying that Ermolai received no allowance of powder or shot, in virtue of exactly the same principles as those on which he himself refused to feed his dog. He was a queer fellow: carefree as a bird, talkative enough, absent-minded, and clumsy-looking; a deep drinker and a rolling stone; when he walked, he shuffled his feet and lurched from one side to the other—yet, with all his shuffling and lurching, he could cover fifty versts in twenty-four hours. He had all sorts of vicissitudes and misadventures; he would spend the night in the marshes, in a tree, on a roof, under a bridge; often he found himself sitting locked up in an attic, a cellar, or a barn, having lost his gun, his dog and the most essential parts of his wardrobe; he would be beaten hard and long—and all the same, after a while, he would return home fully clothed, complete with gun and dog. He was not what you would call of cheerful disposition, although he was almost always in pretty tolerable good spirits. In brief, he was a regular freak.

Ermolai liked a chat with a congenial soul, especially if it was over a glass, but even so it would never be for long; all of a sudden he'd be up and off. "Where are you going, you rascal—at this hour of the night?" "To Chaplino." "And what takes you to Chaplino, ten versts away?" "I'd thought of sleeping at Sofron's place there." "Why not sleep here?" "No, no, I can't." And off goes Ermolai, with Valetka after him, into the pitch-dark night, through bushes, across ravines, only to find that his friend Sofron very likely won't let him in and indeed will take him by the scruff of the neck and throw him out: "Don't you go bothering honest folk."

With it all, Ermolai had no rival in the art of catching fish in a flooded stream in spring, tickling for crayfish, smelling out game, enticing quail, training falcons, and catching nightingales with "the devil's whistle" or "the cuckoo-passage"* . . . One thing he could not do was to train dogs; he lacked the patience.

He had a wife, too. He went and saw her once a week. She lived in a miserable half-ruined hut, managed to exist somehow, never knew the day before whether she would have enough to eat on the morrow; altogether hers was a wretched lot. Ermolai, carefree and good-natured as he was, treated her roughly and harshly. When at home he took on a grim and threatening appearance—and his poor

---

* Nightingale fanciers will recognize these terms: they refer to the most beautiful modulations in the bird's song. —*Author.*

wife did not know how to please him, trembled at his glance, spent her last copeck buying vodka for him, and covered him obsequiously with her coat when he subsided majestically on the shelf above the stove and fell into an epic slumber. More than once I would observe in him the unwitting display of a sort of sullen cruelty. I did not like the expression on his face when he took a bite out of a wounded bird. But Ermolai never stayed more than a day at home; once away, he again became "Ermolka," as they called him for a hundred versts around, and as he sometimes called himself. The humblest menial felt his superiority to this vagabond—which, perhaps, was why he would treat him with friendliness: the peasants for their part began by joyfully chasing and catching him, like a hare in a field, but then they would let him go, and wish him luck; once they had got to know the queer fellow, they left him alone, even gave him bread, and enjoyed a talk with him.

This was the man that I took with me as a hunter and with whom I made my way to the "flight" in a great birch wood on the bank of the Ista.

Many Russian rivers, like the Volga, have hills on one bank and flat meadows on the other; the Ista follows the same pattern. It is a highly capricious little river, which winds like a snake, and never flows straight for more than half a verst; at some points, from the top of a steep hill, it can be seen for ten versts, with its dams, its pools, its water-mills, and orchards, bowered in willow thickets and tufted parkland. There are endless fish in the Ista, especially chub (in the heat of the summer the peasants catch them under the bushes in their hands). The little sandpipers whistle up and down the stony banks, which are enlivened here and there with springs of cold and sparkling water; wild duck swim out into the middle of the pools and look cautiously about them; herons perch in shady creeks, under the steep banks . . .

We waited for the "flight" for about an hour, shot two brace of woodcock and, wishing to try our luck again before sunrise (for one can wait for the morning flight too), decided to spend the night in the nearest mill. We came out of the wood and went down the slope. Darkly blue, the river was rolling on its way; the air was growing

heavy and charged with the vapors of the night. We knocked at
the gates of the mill. Dogs began to bark furiously in the courtyard. "Who's there?" asked a hoarse and sleepy voice. "We've been
out shooting: can we spend the night here?" There was no answer.
"We'll pay for it." "I'll go and tell the master . . . Shut up, you cursed
brutes . . . death and destruction on you!" We heard the laborer go
into the house, and soon he came back to the gates again. "No,"
he said, "the master won't let you in." "Why not?" "He's afraid,
because you've been out shooting and there's a risk of your setting
fire to the mill, what with all your powder and shot." "I never heard
such nonsense!" "We had the mill catch fire like that last year: some
cattle-dealers spent the night here and somehow or other they set
the place on fire." "Surely you wouldn't have us spend the night out
of doors?" "That's your affair." And he went off, stamping his shoes.

Ermolai wished him various evil fates. "Let's go to the village,"
he said at last, with a sigh. But the village was two versts away . . .
"Let's spend the night here," I said. "It's a warm night out of doors,
and if we offer him money the miller will send us out some straw."

Ermolai agreed without more ado. We started knocking afresh.
"What do you want now?" said the laborer's voice again. "I told you
you can't come in." We explained to him what we wanted. He went
to consult his master and the two of them came back together. The
gate opened with a squeak and the miller appeared—a big, fat-faced,
bull-necked, pot-bellied fellow. He agreed to my proposition. About
a hundred yards from the mill there was a small open shed. Beds of
straw and hay were spread for us there; the laborer set up a samovar
on the grass beside the stream, squatted down on his haunches and
started blowing heartily down the funnel. . . . The coals burst into
flame and brightly lit up his youthful face. The miller went to wake
his wife, and finally invited me to spend the night indoors; but I
preferred to stay in the open air. The miller's wife brought us milk,
eggs, potatoes, bread. Soon the samovar was boiling and we were
setting about our tea.

Mists were rising from the river and there was not a breath of
wind; corn-crakes called near by; faint sounds came from the mill-
wheels: drops falling from the blades, or water running through

between the sluices of the dam. We laid a small fire, and while Ermolai baked potatoes in the ashes I dozed off to sleep. . . . A low, discreet murmuring woke me again. I lifted my head: in front of the fire, on an up-ended tub, the miller's wife was sitting talking to my hunter. I had already placed her, by her dress, her movements and her accent, as a woman of the servant class, neither peasant nor townswoman; but it was only now that I was able to get a clear view of her features. She seemed to be about thirty; her thin, pale face still showed the traces of a remarkable beauty; I was especially taken with her large, sad eyes. Her elbows were resting on her knees and her face was propped on her hands. Ermolai was sitting with his back to me, throwing twigs on the fire.

"There's cattle disease again in Zheltukhina," said the miller's wife. "Old Ivan's cows have both got it. . . . God's mercy on us!"

"How are your pigs?" asked Ermolai after a silence.

"Still alive."

"You might at least give me a sucking-pig."

The miller's wife said nothing, then heaved a sigh.

"Who's this you are with?" she asked.

"The master from Kostomarov."

Ermolai threw a few fit-branches on to the fire; they crackled away in unison, and the thick white smoke blew straight into his face.

"Why wouldn't your husband let us come indoors?"

"He's afraid."

"The great fat lout. . . . Arina Timofeyevna, my love, bring me out a little glass of vodka."

The miller's wife got up and vanished into the darkness. Ermolai began to sing under his breath:

> *I wear my shoes out, heel and toe,*
> *So oft to see my love I go . . .*

Arina returned with a small carafe and a glass. Ermolai half-rose, crossed himself, and emptied the glass in one gulp. "That's what I like," he added.

The miller's wife sat down again on the tub.

"Well, Arina Timofeyevna—still ailing?"

"Yes."

"What's the matter?"

"My cough troubles me at night."

"I think the master's dropped off to sleep," said Ermolai after a short silence. "Don't you go to the doctor, Arina: you'll get worse."

"I wouldn't go anyway."

"But come and stay with me."

Arina looked down.

"I'll send my wife away, if you come," continued Ermolai. "Really I will."

"You'd better wake up the master, Ermolai Petrovich: look, the potatoes are done."

"Let him sleep his head off," answered my faithful retainer indifferently; "he's walked enough, and deserves it."

I turned over in the hay. Ermolai got up and came across to me.

"The potatoes are ready, sir, if you like to start on them."

I came out from the shed; the miller's wife rose from the tub and made as if to go. I kept her in conversation.

"Have you had this mill for long?"

"A year ago last Trinity."

"Where does your husband come from?"

Arina paid no heed to my question.

"Where's your husband from?" repeated Ermolai, raising his voice.

"From Belev. He's a townsman from Belev."

"Are you from Belev, too?"

"No, I'm a serf . . . or was, rather."

"Whose?"

"Mr. Zverkov's. But I'm free now."

"Which Zverkov?"

"Alexander Silyich."

"Weren't you his wife's maid?"

"However do you know that? Yes, I was."

I looked at Arina with redoubled curiosity and sympathy.

"I know your master," I continued.

"You do?" she answered in a low voice, and looked down.

I must tell the reader why I looked with such sympathy at Arina. While I was in Petersburg, chance made me acquainted with Mr. Zverkov. He held a fairly important position and passed for a man of knowledge and ability. He had a wife who was podgy, sentimental, tearful and ill-natured—a humdrum, boring creature; there was a son, too, a real mother's darling, spoilt and stupid. Mr. Zverkov's appearance was not to his advantage: in a broad, almost square face, his little mousy eyes looked slyly out above a big, sharp, protruding nose with wide-open nostrils; his close-cropped gray hair bristled up from a wrinkled forehead; his thin lips were constantly moving and shaping themselves into a sickly smile. Mr. Zverkov usually stood with his legs apart and his fat hands in his pockets. Once it so happened that I found myself alone with him in a carriage on the way out of town. We fell into conversation. As a man of experience and ability, Mr. Zverkov started to tell me "what was what."

"Allow me to observe to you," he squeaked, after a time: "All you young people—your views and opinions are all absolutely in the air. You hardly know your own country; Russia, gentlemen, to you is an unknown country—and that's the truth! . . . All you do is read German books. Now, take an instance: you tell me this and that on such and such a subject, well, say, about the servant class . . . all right, I don't dispute it, that's all very fine; but you don't know them, you've no idea what sort of people they really are." Mr. Zverkov blew his nose loudly and took a pinch of snuff. "As an instance, let me tell you a little story; it may interest you." Mr. Zverkov cleared his throat. "You know what my wife is like: I think you will agree that it would be difficult to find a kinder woman than she. The life her maids lead is no ordinary servant's existence—why, it's heaven itself made visible on earth. . . . But my wife has one firm principle: never to keep a married maid—and quite rightly, too, for no good comes of it: she has children, and so on—well, how can you expect her then to look after her mistress as she ought, and pay proper attention to her habits: she can't be bothered any longer, she has other things to think of. You've got to take human nature as you find it. Well, anyway, one

day we were driving through our village, about—let me see, when
was it exactly?—about fifteen years ago. We notice that the village
headman has a daughter, a very pretty girl, and what I call respectful-
mannered, into the bargain. My wife says to me: 'Koko'—you see,
that's what she calls me—'let's take this girl with us to Petersburg . . .
I like her, Koko. . . .' I answer: 'Let's take her, with pleasure.' The
headman of course is at our feet, he had never dreamt of such good
fortune. . . . Well, of course, the girl, like a fool, cries a little. Actually
it *must* be rather grim to begin with: leaving home and all that. . . .
There's nothing surprising about it. However, she soon gets used to
us; to begin with they put her in with the housemaids—to train her,
of course. Then what do you think happens? . . . The girl makes
astonishing progress; my wife takes a regular fancy to her, and over
the heads of all the others gives her the privilege of being her own
personal maid. . . . What d'you say to that! . . . And you've got to give
the girl her due. My wife had never had such a maid, definitely not;
obliging, modest, obedient—in short, everything you could want.
On top of it all, I've got to admit that my wife spoiled her; gave
her good clothes, fed her from our own table, let her have tea . . .
and everything else you can imagine! So there she was, employed
for ten years as my wife's maid. Suddenly, one fine morning, if you
please, in comes Arina—that was her name—without asking leave,
into my study, and falls at my feet. . . . I tell you frankly, that's one
thing I can't abide. Human beings should never forget their dignity, don't you agree? 'What do you want?' 'Alexander Silyich, sir,
please, please . . .' 'What is it?' 'Please let me get married.' I confess
to you that I was amazed. 'Why, you stupid girl, why, surely you
know your mistress has no other maid?' 'I'll serve the mistress
the same as before.' 'Stuff and nonsense! The mistress never keeps
a married maid.' 'Malanya can take my place.' 'I'll thank you not
to argue.' 'It's as you wish, sir.' . . . I must admit I was astounded.
I should explain that nothing offends me so much, I'd go so far as
to say that nothing offends me so *gravely*, as ingratitude; that's the
kind of man I am . . . Well, there's nothing more I can tell you—you
know what my wife is, an angel incarnate, her kindness is beyond
description. I think that even the worst man on earth would have

sympathized with her in this situation. I sent Arina about her business. I thought she'd be sure to come to her senses; you know, one doesn't like to believe one's fellow creatures capable of wickedness or black ingratitude. Well, what d'you think? After six months she has the impertinence to come to me again with the same request. This time, I confess, I sent her packing and no mistake. I threatened her; I swore I'd tell my wife. I was beside myself . . . But then, imagine my amazement: some time after, my wife came to me in tears, in such a state that I got quite a fright. 'Whatever's the matter?' 'It's Arina . . . you understand . . . I'm ashamed to say more.' 'It's not possible! Whoever . . . ?' 'Petrushka, the footman.' Then I blew up. I'm the sort of man that doesn't like half measures . . . Petrushka was not to blame. One could always punish him, certainly—but all the same, he, in my opinion, was not to blame. Arina—h'm—well—h'm, what more is there to say? Of course I gave orders at once that her head should be shaved, that she should be put into sackcloth and sent home to the country. My wife lost an excellent maid, but there was nothing else to be done. Say what you like, you can't have laxity in your own home. It's better to amputate the diseased limb once and for all! Now, judge for yourself—you know my wife; well, this, this . . . anyway, this angel . . . she had grown fond of Arina, and Arina knew it and yet wasn't ashamed. . . . Eh? No, honestly . . . eh? But why talk about it any more? Anyhow, there was nothing else to be done. For my own part, I felt particularly aggrieved and hurt, for a long time afterwards, by this girl's ingratitude. Whatever you may say . . . don't look for heart or feeling in these people. You can feed a wolf for all you're worth, but he'll still keep an eye on the forest. We live and learn! But I only wanted to prove to you . . ."

And Mr. Zverkov, without finishing the sentence, turned his head away and wrapped himself up more tightly in his cloak, mastering with manly self-control the violence of his feelings.

The reader will now probably understand why I looked so sympathetically at Arina.

"Have you been married to the miller for long?" I asked her eventually.

"Two years."

"Your master gave his permission?"

"No, they bought my freedom."

"Who did?"

"Savely Alexeich."

"Who's he?"

"My husband." Ermolai smiled to himself. "But did the master ever speak to you about me?" added Arina after a short silence.

I didn't know how to answer her question. "Arina!" shouted the miller from the distance. She rose and left us.

"What d'you think of her husband?" I asked Ermolai.

"Nothing."

"Have they got any children?"

"They had one that died."

"Did the miller take a fancy to her, or what? . . . Did he pay a lot for her freedom?"

"I don't know. She can read and write; in their business it's . . . well . . . it's useful. Probably he took a fancy to her."

"Have you known her for long?"

"Yes, I used to go to her master's house before. His place is not far from here."

"D'you know the footman Petrushka, too?"

"Pyotr Vasilyevich? I knew him, certainly I did."

"Where is he now?"

"He went for a soldier."

We were silent.

"It seems she is ailing?" I asked Ermolai at last.

"What else should she be? . . . Well, to-morrow there may be a good 'flight.' You could do with some sleep now."

Some wild duck came swishing over us and we heard them dropping down on to the river not far away. By now it was quite dark and growing cold; in the wood a nightingale chuckled loudly. We burrowed into the hay and went to sleep.

Raspberry Water

AT THE BEGINNING OF AUGUST THE HEAT OFTEN BECOMES UN-
bearable. At this season, from twelve until three o'clock, even a
man of the greatest decision and concentration is unable to go
shooting and even the most devoted dog begins to "clean its master's spurs," which means following him at a walk, screwing up
its eyes in pain and hanging out its tongue too far, and, in answer
to the reproaches of its master, wagging its tail humbly with an
embarrassed expression on its face, but making no move forward.
I was out shooting on just such a day as this. For a long time I
resisted the temptation to lie down in the shade, even if only for
a moment; for a long time my dog searched tirelessly through the
bushes, although it was clear that it expected no sensible result
from its feverish activity. The stifling heat at length forced me to
think of conserving our remaining strength and energy. Somehow
or other I dragged myself to the stream of the Ista, with which
my indulgent reader is already familiar, made my way down the
steep bank, and walked over the wet yellow sand in the direction
of a spring which is known in all the country round by the name
of Raspberry Water. This spring bursts from a cleft in the bank
which has gradually turned into a small but deep ravine, and after
twenty yards the water falls with a cheerful babbling rush into the
river. Oak bushes grow in all directions on the slopes of the ravine;
near the source is a green patch of short velvety grass; the rays of
the sun hardly ever touch its cold silver dewiness. I arrived at the
spring; on the grass lay a scoop of birchwood, left there by a pass-

ing peasant for the benefit of the world at large. I drank my fill, lay down in the shade and looked around.

Beside the creek where the spring flowed into the river, which for that reason was always a mass of tiny ripples, two old men were sitting with their backs towards me. One of them, tall and fairly thick-set, in a neat dark green coat and a quilted cap, was fishing; the other, who was small and thin and wore a fustian patched jacket and no cap, held on his knees a pot with worms in it and from time to time passed his hand over his small gray head, as if to protect it from the sun. I took a closer look at him and recognized Styopushka from Shumikhino. I ask the reader's permission to introduce this character to him.

A few versts away from my estate lies the big village of Shumikhino, which has a stone church raised in honor of Saints Cosmas and Damian. Opposite this church there used to stand a fine big manor house, surrounded by various dependencies, outbuildings, workshops, stables, coach-houses, bath-houses and temporary kitchens, guest-wings, agents' houses, conservatories, swings for the servants' amusement, and other more or less useful constructions. In this mansion lived a rich landowner's family and everything went swimmingly—when suddenly one fine morning the whole pleasant seat was burnt down to the ground. The owners flitted to another nest and the property fell into neglect. The great expanse of waste ground became a kitchen garden, cluttered up here and there with piles of bricks, which were all that remained of the old foundations. From the surviving timbers a hut had been hastily knocked together, roofed over with planks which had been bought ten years earlier for the construction of a pavilion in the Gothic manner, and in it were settled the gardener Mitrofan with his wife Axinya and their seven children. Mitrofan had instructions to provide his master's table— one hundred and fifty versts away—with vegetables and garden produce; Axinya was entrusted with the care of the Tyrolean cow which had been bought in Moscow for a large sum, but had unfortunately lacked all capacity for reproduction and had therefore since the time of its purchase given no milk; she was also entrusted with the tufted smoke-colored drake, the only bird of "feudal" status; the children were too small to have any special duties assigned to them, which did not prevent them from growing as lazy as could be.

On two occasions I had spent the night in the gardener's hut; whenever I passed by I would collect cucumbers which, God knows why, impressed you even in summer by their size, their unpleasant watery taste, and their thick yellow skin. It was here that I saw Styopushka for the first time. Apart from Mitrofan and his family and Gerasim the deaf old sacristan, who lived on charity in a little cabin belonging to a one-eyed soldier's wife, there was not a single serving-man left in Shumikhino, for Styopushka, with whom I propose to make the reader acquainted, could be regarded neither in general as a man, nor in particular as a servant.

There is no man who does not have some sort of status in society, some sort of human ties; there is no servant who does not receive either his wages or at least some so-called equivalent in kind; whereas Styopushka certainly had no means of subsistence, was related to nobody, and nobody knew how he existed. He didn't even have a past; no one spoke about him; when the census was taken they hardly bothered to count him. There were dark rumors abroad that he had once been employed somewhere as a valet; but who he was, where he came from, whose son he was, how he came to be one of the serfs of Shumikhino, in what manner he acquired the fustian coat which he had worn from time immemorial, where and on what he lived—no one had the slightest idea and, to tell the truth, no one cared either. Even grandfather Trofimich, who knew the family tree of all the Shumikhino retainers as far back as the fourth generation, even he had been known to mention only once that, as he remembered, Styopushka had been related to a Turkish woman whom the late master, Brigadier-General Alexei Romanich, had been pleased to bring back in the baggage-train after one of his campaigns. Even on feast days, days of universal treating and regaling with bread and salt, with buckwheat pies and green spirits, in the old Russian manner—even on these days Styopushka never appeared when the tables and barrels were set out, never made his bow, never came to kiss his master's hand, never drank a glass in one draught under the master's eye and to the master's health, a glass which had been filled by the greasy hand of the factor; at best, some good-natured soul might run into the poor fellow and give him a half-eaten pie-crust. On Easter Sunday he got the three traditional kisses, but he never turned up his greasy sleeve, never pulled out from his back pocket a red-painted egg, never brought it, panting and blinking, to the master's children or to the lady herself. In summer he lived in a shed behind the chicken-house and in winter in the porch of the bath-house; if the frost was heavy he spent the night in the hay-loft. People were used to seeing him; sometimes they went so far as to give him a friendly kick, but no one ever fell into conversation with him; indeed he seemed never to have opened his mouth from birth. After the great fire this outcast creature took shelter with or, as the Orel people say, "leant against," the gardener Mitrofan. The gardener left him alone, never offered him a roof, but never drove him out either. And Styopushka in fact did not live at the gardener's; he wandered about the garden and made it his home. His walk and his movements were noiseless: he sneezed and coughed into his hand as if afraid to break the silence; he was for ever hurrying silently about like an ant; and the object of the whole thing was food, just food. And indeed, had he not busied himself from morning to night with matters of subsistence, my friend Styopushka would have died of hunger. It is a sorry fate not to know in the morning how you are going to fill your belly before the day is done. Sometimes Styopushka sits under a fence and gnaws a radish, or sucks a carrot, or scatters round him the shreds of a dirty cabbage stalk; sometimes he groans under the weight of a pail of water which he is carrying away; sometimes he gets a small fire going under a pot, into which he throws black morsels which he brings out from under his coat; sometimes in his little den he can be heard knocking with a piece of wood, driving in a nail, putting up a shelf on which to keep his bread. He does it all in silence, as though peeping round the corner; one look from you and he has vanished. Then suddenly he disappears for a couple of days; it goes without saying that no one notices his absence. Next time you look, he is back again, and somewhere near the fence he has furtively built a fire out of odd splinters. He has a small face, little yellow eyes, hair down to his eyebrows, a sharp nose, enormous transparent ears like a bat's, and what appears to be two weeks' growth of beard, never more nor less. This was Styopushka as I met him on the bank of the Ista sitting beside another old man.

I went up to them, exchanged greetings and sat down beside them. In Styopushka's companion I recognized another acquaintance: this was a liberated serf of Count Pyotr Ilyich——, by name Mikhailo Savelyev, commonly known as Tuman.* He lived in Bolkhovo, with the consumptive innkeeper with whom I had fairly often stayed. Young officials or other idle travellers passing along the main road to Orel—(merchants, sunk deep inside their striped quilts, never spare the time to look)—can still to this day observe not far from the large village of Troitskoye a huge two-storied wooden house, completely derelict, with its roof fallen in and windows boarded up, thrusting right out on to the roadside. At midday, in clear sunny weather, it is impossible to imagine a sorrier spectacle than this ruin. It was once the home of Count Pyotr Ilyich, a rich magnate of the old days who was famous for his hospitality. The time had been when all the province assembled in his house, danced and made merry in famous style, to the deafening strains of a home-taught orchestra, to the crackling of fireworks and of Roman candles; and, probably, more than one old lady, driving past the now deserted halls of the Boyar, heaves a sigh and recalls times gone by and the days of her youth. For long years the Count continued to give banquets and to walk about with a welcoming smile among the throng of obsequious guests. But, alas, his fortune was not enough to outlast his lifetime. Ruined beyond repair, he went place-hunting in St. Petersburg and died in an hotel bedroom before he knew the result of his quest. Tuman had been his butler and received his freedom while the Count was still alive. He was a man of about seventy, with an agreeable, regular face. He wore an almost constant smile, the sort of smile that is now seen only on the faces of survivors from the days of Catherine the Great; a smile that is both benign and stately; when he spoke, his lips parted and came together again

---

* "Fog." —*Translators*.

slowly, his eyes narrowed amiably and the words came out with a slightly nasal tone. His manner of blowing his nose or taking snuff was equally unhurried, as of a man engrossed in serious business.

"Well, Mikhailo Savelyich," I began; "what luck with the fish?"

"Look at my basket, sir, if you will. I've caught two perch, and five roach. . . . Show them, Styopushka."

Styopushka held the basket out to me.

"How are you, Styopushka?" I asked him.

"Oh . . . oh . . . oh . . . all right, sir, not so bad," answered Styopushka, stammering as though he was rolling weights on his tongue.

"Is Mitrofan well?"

"Well, sir . . . why, yes."

The poor fellow turned away.

"They're not taking," said Tuman. "It's much too hot; the fish are all tucked away under the bushes, fast asleep . . . Put a new worm on, Styopushka." Styopushka took out a worm, laid it on the palm of his hand, tapped it once or twice, put it on the hook, spat on it and handed it to Tuman. "Thank you, Styopushka . . . but you, sir," he continued, addressing himself to me, "you have been shooting?"

"As you see."

"Quite so . . . And is that dog that you have with you from England—or from *Fourland*?" The old man enjoyed showing off when he had the chance, as if to say, "We too have lived in the great world!"

"I don't know what breed he is, but he's a good dog."

"Quite so . . . and do you hunt with hounds too?"

"Yes, I have two packs."

Tuman smiled and shook his head. "That's just how it is. One gentleman is dead keen on hounds and another would not take them as a gift. That's how it is, to my simple way of thinking. A gentleman ought to keep hounds more for the sake of appearances than for anything else, if you take my meaning. And everything ought to be in its proper style: horses in style, whippers-in in style, and everything else too. His late Lordship—may God rest his soul!—was not a born huntsman, it is true, but he kept his hounds, and hunted them about twice a year. The huntsmen would muster in the courtyard, in their red coats trimmed with braid, blowing their horns; out comes his Lordship, his horse is led up; his Lordship mounts, and the head huntsman puts his feet into the stirrups, takes the cap off his head and hands the reins in his cap to his Lordship. His Lordship gives his whip a good crack, the huntsmen cry 'halloo,' and off they go. A groom rides behind his Lordship, leads his master's two favorite dogs on a silken lead, and keeps a sharp eye on them, too, you may be sure. . . . And there he sits, this groom-fellow, way, way up on a Cossack saddle. A red-cheeked fellow with great big rolling eyes. . . . Well, of course, there were guests there, too, for the occasion. And great fun it was, and everything as it should be. . . . Oh, he's got away, the *Chinaman!*" he added suddenly, giving his rod a twitch.

"They say the Count had quite a time of it in his day?" I asked.

The old man spat on the worm and made a cast.

"He certainly lived like a lord. I dare say that all the leading people from Petersburg came out to see him. There they all were in their blue ribbons, sitting at table feasting. And he was certainly a master-hand at entertaining, too. He used to call me: 'Tuman,' he says, 'I need live sterlets for to-morrow; order them to be sent, do you hear?' 'Very good, your Lordship.' Embroidered coats, wigs, canes, perfumes, *Lady-Cologne* of the finest quality, snuff-boxes, great big pictures like this—everything ordered straight from Paris. He would give a banquet and, Lord God Almighty! the fireworks, the drives there would be! They would even shoot off cannons. The musicians alone were forty strong. There was a German conductor, but he got too big for his boots; he wanted to eat at the master's table; so his Lordship sent him packing: 'Even without him,' he says, 'my musicians understand their business.' Of course, the master's word was law. They would start dancing—and dance until sunrise; they'd mostly dance the *acossaise-matrador* . . . Eh . . . eh . . . our friend is hooked!" The old man drew a small perch out of the water. "Here you are, Styopushka. The master was everything a master should be," continued the old fellow, making another cast.

"And he had a good heart too. He might beat you—but before
you could look round he would have forgotten all about it. There
was one thing, though: he kept *may-tresses*. Oh, those *may-tresses*,
merciful God! It was they who ruined him. For choice, strange to
say, he liked a common sort of girl. You would have thought that
they would have had all they wanted—but no, they must have everything that's most expensive in the whole of Europe! Of course
you can say, why shouldn't the master live as he wants to—it's his
own business . . . but he shouldn't have gone and ruined himself.
There was one of them in particular, by name, Akulina; she is dead
now—may she rest in peace! She was a simple sort of girl, daughter
of the village policeman at Sitovo, but what a shrew! She used to
smack his Lordship in the face. She had him properly bewitched.
She had my nephew's head shaven because he had spilled chocolate
on her new dress, and he wasn't the only one either. But they were
good old days, all the same!" added the old man, with a deep sigh;
then he looked down and said no more.

"You had a strict master, I see," I began, after a few moments of
silence.

"That was the fashion then, sir," rejoined the old man, shaking
his head.

"Things are different now," I observed, looking at him keenly.
He gave me a sidelong glance.

"No doubt things are better now," he muttered, and cast his line
far out into the stream.

We were sitting in the shade; but even there the heat was stifling; the heavy sultry air was without a breath; your burning face
longed for a breeze, but no breeze came. The sun was fairly beating
down from the sombre blue sky; right in front of us on the opposite
bank was the yellow blaze of an oatfield, broken here and there by
patches of wormwood, and not a single ear was stirring. A little
farther downstream a peasant's horse was standing up to its knees
in the water, lazily swishing a wet tail; now and then, beneath an
overhanging bush, a big fish came to the surface, let off a stream
of bubbles and quietly sank again to the bottom, leaving a faint
ripple behind. Grasshoppers chirruped in the rust-colored grass;

quails called with a reluctant note; hawks floated smoothly above the fields and often stopped dead, with wings working at full speed and tails fanned out.

We sat there motionless, overcome by the heat. Suddenly we heard a noise behind us in the ravine; someone was coming down to the spring. I looked round and saw a peasant of about fifty, covered in dust, wearing a shirt and plaited shoes, with a basket-work satchel and a coat slung over his shoulders. He came across to the source, drank thirstily and rose to his feet again.

"Hey, Vlas!" exclaimed Tuman, after taking a good look at him. "Hallo, boy. Where have you come from?"

"Hallo, Mikhailo Savelyich," said the peasant, walking over to us. "I've come from miles away."

"Where have you been all this time?" Tuman asked him.

"I walked to Moscow to see the master."

"Why?"

"I went to ask him something."

"What did you want to ask him?"

"To lower my rent, or to move me, or let me work instead of paying . . . Since my son died I can't manage on my own any more."

"Your son died?"

"Yes. He lived in Moscow," added the peasant, after a silence; "he was a cabman; he used to pay my rent for me."

"But *do* you pay rent these days?"

"Yes."

"And what did your master say?"

"What did he say? He threw me out. He said: 'How dare you come straight to me? That's what the factor's for,' he says, 'and you ought to report to him first . . . and where can I move you to, anyway? You pay your own arrears first,' he says. He got very angry."

"So now you've walked all the way back again?"

"Yes. I went to find out whether my boy hadn't left any belongings behind, but I couldn't make head or tail of it. I told his master that I was Philip's father, but he says to me: 'How should I know? Besides, your son left nothing; he still owed me money,' he says. So I came back again."

The peasant told us the whole story with a grin, as if talking about someone else; but in his little shrunken eyes a tear hovered, and his lips twitched.

"What are you doing now—going home?"

"Where else? Of course I'm going home. I expect that by now my wife is whistling in her fist with hunger."

"But you could . . . well . . ." began Styopushka suddenly, then grew confused, broke off, and began fumbling in his pot.

"Will you go to the factor?" Tuman continued, after a surprised glance at Styopushka.

"What should I go to him for? . . . Even so, I've got my arrears to pay. My son was sick for about a year before he died and could not even pay his own rent . . . but it's all the same to me: there's nothing they can take from me. . . . No, my friend, however clever you are, you won't catch me, I haven't got a farthing." The peasant burst out laughing. "However sharp he may be, that fellow Kintilyan Semyonich, all the same . . ."

Vlas began to laugh again.

"What? That's bad, Vlas," said Tuman slowly.

"What's bad? It's not . . ." Vlas's voice broke off. "What a scorching day," he went on, wiping his face with his sleeve.

"Who is your master?" I asked.

"Count——, Valeryan Petrovich."

"The son of Pyotr Ilyich?"

"Yes," answered Tuman. "Pyotr Ilyich, his late Lordship, while he was still alive, gave his son the village where Vlas lives."

"Is he alive and well?"

"Yes, praise be to God," rejoined Vlas. "He's got so red in the face, he's all sort of mottled."

"That's how it is, sir," continued Tuman, turning to me. "If it had been near Moscow, it wouldn't have been so bad, but he's been settled *here* and has to pay rent."

"What are you assessed at?"

"Ninety-five rubles," muttered Vlas.

"Well, you see how it is: there's very little land, and what there is is under timber for the master."

"And even that has been sold, they say," observed the peasant.

"Well, that's how it is . . . Styopushka, give us a worm. . . . Hey, Styopushka, have you dropped off to sleep, or what?" Styopushka started up. The peasant sat down beside us. We fell silent again. On the other bank someone started singing, but such a melancholy song . . . My poor friend Vlas grew sadder and sadder.

Half an hour later we parted.

The Country Doctor

ONE AUTUMN, ON THE WAY BACK FROM AN OUTLYING PROPERTY, I caught a heavy chill. Luckily I was in the local markettown, at the inn, when the fever came on. I sent for the doctor. After half an hour he appeared, a shortish, thinnish man, with black hair. He prescribed the usual sudorific, ordered a mustard-plaster to be applied, deftly tucked my five-ruble note away up his sleeve—meanwhile coughing loudly, it is true, and averting his gaze—and was on the point of going home, when somehow or other he got talking and stayed on. I was oppressed by my fever; I foresaw a sleepless night and was glad to have the chance of a talk with the good man. We had tea served. My friend the doctor let himself go. The little fellow was no fool. He had a lively and rather amusing way of expressing himself. It's strange how things happen in life: you live with someone for a long time, you are on the best of terms, yet you never once speak to them frankly and from the heart; with someone else, you've hardly even got acquainted—and there you are: as if at confession, one or other of you is blurting out all his most intimate secrets. I do not know what I did to deserve the confidence of my new friend—anyway, for no particular reason, he got going, as they say, and told me a rather remarkable story, which I will relate here for the benefit of my courteous reader. I will try to express myself in the doctor's own words.

"You don't happen to know," he began, in a voice that had grown suddenly faint and trembling (such is the effect of unadulterated "birch" snuff), "you don't happen to know our local judge, Pavel

Lukich Mylov? You don't? . . . Well, it doesn't matter." He cleared
his throat and wiped his eyes. "Anyway, this is the story. Let me see,
now—to be exact, it was in Lent, at the time of the thaw. I was sitting at the judge's, playing Preference. Our judge is a capital fellow
and a great hand at Preference. Suddenly"—this was a word that
the doctor often used—"a message comes that someone is asking
for me. I say, 'What does he want?' 'He's brought a note'—doubtless
from a patient. 'Give me the note,' I say. Yes: it's from a patient. . . .
Well, all right—you know, it's our daily bread. . . . The note is from
a landowner's widow; she says: 'My daughter is dying, for God's
sake come, I've sent horses to fetch you.' Well, that's all right . . . but
the lady lives twenty versts from town, and night's upon us, and the
roads are in such a state, my word! and the lady herself is not so well
off as she was; two silver rubles is the most you can expect, and even
that is doubtful. Perhaps all that I shall get out of it will be a piece of
linen and a little flour. . . . However, duty first, you know: someone's
dying. At once I pass my hand to Councillor Kalliopin and return
home. I see a small cart standing outside my porch; real peasant's
horses—enormous pot bellies, and woolly hair as thick as felt; and a
coachman sitting bareheaded, as a sign of respect. Well, my friend,
I think, it's plain that *your* masters don't eat off gold plate. . . . You,
sir, may well smile, but I tell you: we are poor men in our profession and we have to notice all these things. . . . If the coachman sits
up like a prince and doesn't take off his cap, if he sniggers at you
in his beard and toys with his whip—you can rely on a couple of
five-ruble notes. But this turn-out here is a very different pair of
shoes. Well, I think, it can't be helped: duty first. I grab the essential medicines, and off I go. Believe me, it was all we could do to
get there. The road was hellish: streams, snow, mud, ravines, then,
suddenly, a burst dam. Chaos! At last I'm there. A little house with
a thatched roof. The windows are lit up: they must be waiting for
me. A dignified little old lady in a cap comes to meet me. 'Save
her,' she says, 'she is dying.' I say: 'Pray calm yourself. . . . Where
is the patient?' 'Here, please come this way.' I see a small, clean
room, an oil-lamp in the corner, on the bed a girl of about twenty,
unconscious, heat fairly blazing from her, breathing heavily: a high

fever. There are two other girls there, too, her sisters—badly scared, and in tears. 'Yesterday,' they say, 'she was perfectly well and had a good appetite; this morning she complained of a headache, then suddenly in the evening she became like this.' I repeat again, 'Pray calm yourselves'—it's part of the doctor's job, you know—and I set to work. I bleed her, I order mustard-plasters, I prescribe a mixture. Meanwhile I look at her. I look and look; my goodness, never have I see such a face before . . . an absolute beauty! I feel so sorry for the girl, it fairly tears me to pieces. Such lovely features, such eyes. . . . At last, thank God, she gets more comfortable; she begins to sweat, partly recovers consciousness; looks around, smiles, passes her hand over her face . . . The sisters bend over her and ask: 'What's the matter?' 'Nothing,' she says, and turns her head away. . . . I look—she's dropped off to sleep. 'Well,' I say, 'now we must leave the patient in peace.' We all tiptoe out; only the maid stays behind in case of emergencies. In the sitting-room the samovar's on the table and a bottle of rum beside it: in our job we can't get along without it. They gave me tea; they asked me to stay the night. I accepted: where else could I go at that hour! The old lady keeps up a steady groaning. 'What's the matter?' I ask. 'She'll live; calm yourself and go to bed: it's two o'clock.' 'You'll have me woken up if anything happens?' 'Of course I will.' The old lady retired and the girls went to their room; a bed was put up for me in the drawing-room. I lay down—but couldn't get to sleep, strangely enough. You'd have thought that I'd worried my head enough already. I couldn't get my patient out of my head. Finally I could stand it no longer and all of a sudden I got up; I thought I'd just go and see how she was. Her bedroom adjoined the drawing-room. Well, I got up, and quietly opened the door, and my heart was fairly beating away. I saw the maid asleep, with her mouth open, snoring away like an animal, and the patient lying with her face towards me, her arms moving restlessly, poor girl! I went up to her . . . and suddenly she opened her eyes and stared at me. 'Who are you?' I felt awkward. 'Don't be afraid,' I said; 'I am the doctor; I've come to see how you feel.' 'You're the doctor?' 'Yes, I am . . . your mother sent for me from town; we've bled you, and now, please, you must rest, and in two days, with

God's help, we shall have you up and about.' 'Oh, yes, yes, doctor, don't let me die . . . please, please.' 'Good Heavens, whatever next!' But, I thought to myself, the fever is on her again; I felt her pulse: yes, I was right. She looked at me—and suddenly she took me by the hand. 'I'll tell you why I don't want to die, I'll tell you . . . now that we're alone: only not a word, please . . . listen . . .' I bent over her; her lips moved right against my ear, her hair touched my cheek—I admit, my head went round in circles—and she began to whisper. . . . I didn't understand a word. . . . Oh, of course, she must be delirious. She whispered and whispered, but so quickly, as if in a foreign language, and when she had done she shuddered, dropped her head on the pillow and raised a finger at me. 'Listen, doctor, not a word.' . . . Somehow or other I calmed her, gave her a drink, woke the maid and went out."

The doctor took another violent pinch of snuff and sat stock-still for a moment.

"Anyhow," he continued, "next day, contrary to my expectations, the patient was no better. I thought and thought and suddenly decided to stay on, although I had other patients waiting for me. . . . You know, one shouldn't neglect them: it's bad for one's practice. But, in the first place, the girl was really desperately ill; and secondly, to tell the truth, I felt myself strongly attracted to her. Besides, I liked the whole family. Although they were very hard up, they were extraordinarily cultivated people. . . . The father had been a scholar, a writer; he died a poor man, of course, but he'd managed to give his children an excellent education; he left them a lot of books, too. Whether it was because I put my whole heart into looking after the patient, or whether there were other reasons, anyway, I'd go so far as to say that they came to love me in that house like one of the family. . . . Meanwhile the thaw got worse and worse: communications were completely broken, I could hardly even get medicines sent out from town. . . . The girl got no better . . . day after day, day after day . . . but then . . . well . . ." The doctor paused. "The truth is that I don't know how to explain to you . . ." He took another pinch of snuff, sneezed, and swallowed a gulp of tea. . . . "I'll tell you straight out, my patient . . . how shall I put it? . . . fell in love with me, I suppose . . . or rather, she wasn't exactly in love . . . but anyway . . . it's certainly . . ." The doctor looked down and blushed.

"No," he continued with some animation, "'Love' is the wrong word. One must see oneself at one's own worth, after all. She was a cultivated, intelligent, well-read girl, and I, well, I'd even forgotten my Latin, more or less completely. My figure, too"—and the doctor looked at himself with a smile—"is nothing to boast about, I think. But God didn't make me a fool either: I don't call white black; I've got a mind that works at times. For instance, I understood very well that what Alexandra Andreyevna—that was her name—felt towards me was not love, but affection, so to speak, regard, or what not. Although she herself probably misread her feelings towards me, her condition was such, as you can imagine . . . Anyhow," added the doctor, who had uttered all these disjointed statements without drawing breath, and with obvious embarrassment, "I think I've let my tongue run away with me . . . and the result is that you won't understand what happened . . . so I'll tell you the story in its proper order."

He finished his glass of tea and resumed in a calmer voice.

"This is how it was. My patient continued to get worse and worse. You, my good sir, are not a doctor; you have no idea of what goes on inside a doctor's head, especially in his early days, when it dawns on him that a patient's illness is defeating him. All his self-assurance vanishes into thin air. I can't tell you how scared he gets. It seems to him that he's forgotten everything he ever knew, that his patient has no confidence in him, that other people are beginning to notice that he's out of his depth, and don't want to describe the patient's symptoms, that they are looking at him strangely, and whispering . . . oh, it's terrible! He feels there must be some way of treating the case if only it could be found. Perhaps this is it? He tries—no, wrong after all. He leaves no time for the treatment to take its proper effect. . . . He snatches first at one method, then at another. He takes up his book of prescriptions . . . here it is, he thinks, this is it! To be quite honest, sometimes he opens the book at random: this, he thinks, must be the hand of fate. . . . Meanwhile there is someone dying; someone whom another doctor would have saved. I must have another opinion, you think; I won't take the whole responsibility myself. But what a fool you look on such occasions! Well, as time goes on, you get used to it, you say to yourself: never mind. The patient has died—it's not your fault; you only followed the rules. But what disturbs you still more is this: when other people have blind confidence in yourself, and all the time you know that you're helpless. It was exactly such confidence that all Alexandra Andreyevna's family felt towards me: they no longer even thought of her as in danger. And I, on my side, was assuring them that there was nothing to worry about, but really my heart was in my boots. To make things even worse, the thaw became so bad that the coachman spent whole days fetching medicines. Meanwhile I never left the patient's room; I simply couldn't tear myself away. I told her all sorts of funny stories; I played cards with her; I spent the nights at her bedside. The old lady would thank me with tears in her eyes; but I thought to myself: I don't deserve your gratitude. I confess to you frankly—there is no reason why I should conceal it now—I was in love with my patient. And Alexandra Andreyevna grew fonder and fonder of me: she would allow no one into her room except me. We would get talking; she would ask me where I studied, what sort of life I led, and about my parents and my friends. And I felt that we shouldn't be talking, but to stop her, stop her really firmly, was more than I could do. I would bury my head in my hands: what are you doing, scoundrel? . . . And then she would take my hand and hold it, look at me for a long, long time, turn away, sigh and say: 'How good you are!' Her hands were so feverish, her eyes so big and languid. 'Yes,' she would say. 'You're a good, kind man. You're not like our neighbours . . . you're quite, quite different. . . . To think that I never knew you until now!' 'Alexandra Andreyevna, calm yourself,' I'd say. 'Believe me, I appreciate it; I don't know what I've done to . . . only calm yourself, for Heaven's sake, calm yourself . . . everything will be all right; you'll get quite well again.' By the way, I must tell you," added the doctor, leaning forward and lifting his eyebrows, "they had little to do with their neighbors, because the smaller people weren't up to them, and they were too proud to get to know the richer ones. I tell you, it was an extraordinarily cultivated family; so that, for me, it was quite flattering. Alexandra would only take her medicine from my hands . . . the poor girl would lift herself up, with my help, swallow the medicine and gaze at me . . . and my heart would fairly turn over. But all the time she was getting worse and worse: she will die, I thought, she will surely die. Believe me or not, I would gladly have lain in the coffin instead of her; but there were her mother and sisters watching me, looking into my eyes, and I could feel their confidence on the wane. 'Well, how is she?' 'Nothing to worry about, nothing at all'—but what did I mean, 'nothing at all'? My head was in a daze. There I was, one night, alone, as usual, sitting at the bedside. The maid was sitting in the room too, snoring for all she was worth . . . well, one couldn't find fault with the poor girl, she too was quite exhausted. Alexandra had been feeling very bad the whole evening; the fever gave her no rest. Right up to midnight she had been tossing away; at last she seemed to fall asleep; at any rate she stopped moving and lay still. The oil-lamp was burning in the corner in front of the icon. I sat there, my head dropped forward, you know, and I too dozed off. Suddenly it was as if someone had given me a push in the ribs; I looked round . . . God Almighty! Alexandra was staring at me wide-eyed . . . her lips parted, her cheeks aflame. 'What is it?' 'Doctor, am I going to die?' 'For Heaven's sake!' 'No, please, doctor, please, don't tell me that I'm going to live . . . don't tell me that . . . if only you knew . . . listen, for God's sake don't try to hide my condition from me.' I noticed how quickly she was breathing. 'If I can know for sure that I am going to die . . . then I can tell you everything I have to say.' 'Alexandra Andreyevna, for mercy's sake!' 'Listen, I haven't slept a wink, I've been looking and looking at you . . . for God's sake . . . I trust you, you're kind, you're honest, I implore you by everything that's holy on earth—tell me the truth! If only you knew how much it matters to me. . . . Doctor, tell me, for God's sake, am I in danger?' 'What *can* I tell you, Alexandra Andreyevna?' 'For God's sake, I beseech you to tell me.' 'Alexandra Andreyevna, I can't hide the truth from you—you *are* in danger, but God is merciful . . .' 'I'm going to die, I'm going to die . . .' And it was as if she was overjoyed at the thought, her face lit up so; I was fairly terrified. 'Never fear, never fear, death has no terror for me.' All of a sudden she raised herself on one elbow. 'Now . . . well, now I can tell you that I'm grateful to you from all my heart; that you're good and kind; that I love you.' . . . I looked at her like a man possessed; I can tell you, I had quite a creepy feeling. . . . 'Listen to me. I love you.' 'Alexandra Andreyevna, what have I done to deserve this?' 'No, no, you don't understand me, my dear one . . .' And suddenly she reached out, took my head in her hands and kissed me. Believe me or not, it was all I could do not to cry out loud. . . . I fell on my knees and hid my head in the pillow. She said nothing; her fingers trembled on my hair; I could hear her crying. I began to comfort her, to assure her. . . . I really don't know what I said to her. 'You'll wake the maid . . . believe me when I say . . . how grateful I am . . . and calm yourself.' 'Don't . . . don't,' she kept repeating. 'Never mind any of them, let them wake, let them come—it doesn't signify: I'm dying anyway. . . . Why are you so shy and timid? Lift your head . . . Or can it be that you don't love me, that I was mistaken? . . . If that is so, please forgive me.' 'What are you saying? . . . I love you, Alexandra Andreyevna.' She gazed at me, straight in the eyes, and opened her arms. 'Then, put your arms around me.' . . . I tell you honestly: I don't understand how I got through that night without going out of my mind. I knew that my patient was killing herself; I saw that she was half delirious; I also understood that if she had not believed herself on the point of death, she would never have given me a thought; but, say what you like, there must be something appalling about dying at twenty-five without ever having loved; that was the thought that tormented her, that was why, in despair, she seized on me. Now do you see it all? She still held me tightly in her arms. 'Have pity on me, Alexandra Andreyevna, have pity on us both,' I said. 'Why?' she answered, 'what is there to pity? Don't you understand that I've got to die?' She kept on repeating this phrase. 'If I knew that I was going to live and turn into a well-brought-up young lady again, I should be ashamed, yes, ashamed . . . but, as it is? . . .' 'And who told you that you were going to die?' 'Oh, no, enough of that, you can't deceive me, you don't know how to lie, just look at yourself.' 'You will live, Alexandra Andreyevna; I will cure you; we will ask your mother for her blessing . . . nothing will part us; we shall be happy.' 'No, no, I have your word that I must die . . . you promised me . . . you told me I must . . .' It was a bitter moment for me, bitter for many reasons. You know, sometimes small things can happen: they amount to nothing, but they hurt all the same. It occurred to her to ask me my name, my Christian name, I mean. Of course it would be my ill-luck to be called Trifon.* Yes, sir; Trifon, Trifon Ivanich. In the house, all the family called me doctor. Well, there was nothing for it, so I answered: 'Trifon.' She screwed her eyes up, shook her head and whispered something in French—oh, it was something unflattering, and she laughed unkindly, too. Well, like this, I spent almost the whole night with her. At dawn I went out, like one possessed; it was midday when I returned to her room, after taking tea. God Almighty! You couldn't recognize her: I've seen prettier sights laid out in the coffin. Upon my word, I don't know to this day, I simply don't know how I stood the ordeal. For three days and three nights my patient's life still flickered on . . . and what nights they were! What things she told me! . . . On the last night of the three—just fancy—I was sitting beside her, praying now for one thing only: O, God, take her quickly, and take me as well . . . when suddenly the old lady, her mother, burst into the room. . . . I had already told her the day before that there was little hope, that things were bad, and that it would be as well to send for the priest. As soon as she saw her mother, the sick girl said: 'I'm glad that you've come . . . look at us, we love each other, we are pledged to each other.' 'What's she saying, doctor, what's she saying?' I went pale as death. 'She's delirious,' I said, 'it's the fever.' But then, from Alexandra: 'Enough of that, just now you spoke to me quite differently and accepted my ring. . . . Why pretend? My mother is kind, she will forgive, she will understand, but I am dying—why should I lie? Give me your hand.' I jumped up and ran from the room. Of course, the old lady guessed the whole story.

"Anyway, I won't attempt to bore you further, and, what's more, to tell you the truth, it hurts me to remember. The following day my patient passed away. May God rest her soul!" added the doctor hur-

---

* "Trifon" is roughly the equivalent of "Cuthbert." —*Translators*.

riedly, with a sigh. "Before she died, she asked that everyone should go out and leave me alone with her. 'Forgive me,' she said. 'Perhaps I've acted wrongly towards you . . . it's my illness . . . but, believe me, I've never loved anyone more than you . . . don't forget me . . . treasure my ring. . . .'"

The doctor turned away; I seized him by the hand.

"Och!" he said, "let's talk about something else, or perhaps you'd like a little game of Preference for low stakes? You know, in our profession we should never give way to such exalted sentiments. In our profession all we should think about is how to stop the children from yelling and the wife from nagging. For, since then, I have gone in for holy matrimony, as they call it . . . with a vengeance . . . I married a merchant's daughter: seven thousand rubles dowry. Her name is Akulina; it's on a par with Trifon. A spiteful hag, I must say, but luckily she sleeps all day. . . . What about that game of Preference?"

We got down to Preference for copeck stakes. Trifon Ivanich won two and a half rubles from me—and went home late, very pleased with his victory.

My Neighbor Radilov

IN THE AUTUMN, WOODCOCK ARE OFTEN TO BE FOUND IN THE old type of lime-tree plantation. We have quite a number of such plantations in the province of Orel. Our forefathers, when choosing places to live in, never failed to plant five acres of good ground with orchards and avenues of lime. After fifty or often seventy years, these seats, these "gentle homes," have gradually vanished from the face of the earth. The houses rotted away or were sold for scrap, the stone outbuildings were reduced to heaps of rubble, the apple-trees died and were sawn up into firewood, the hedges and fences were obliterated. Only the limes went on growing in their pristine glory and, now surrounded by ploughed fields, they speak to this feather-headed generation of "our fathers and forefathers that went before us." This old lime is a splendid tree. . . . It is spared even by the Russian peasant's ruthless axe. Its leaves grow delicately, its mighty branches spread out far and wide and beneath them there is perpetual shade.

One day, roaming the fields with Ermolai after partridges, I found myself beside one of these neglected plantations and made my way towards it. As soon as I came up to the fringe of it, a woodcock rose noisily from a bush, I fired, and at the same moment, from a few paces away, there came a cry, the frightened face of a young girl looked out from behind the trees and immediately disappeared again. Ermolai came running up to me. "What are you shooting here for? There's a gentleman lives here." There was not time for me to answer him, nor for my dog, with noble self-importance, to bring me the dead bird, when hurried steps were heard and a tall man with moustaches emerged from the brushwood and came to a halt in front of me, wearing an expression of displeasure. I made such excuses as I could, said who I was, and offered him the bird which had been shot on his property.

"Very well," he said with a smile, "I'll accept your bird, but only on condition that you stay and dine with us."

I confess that I was not overjoyed by his suggestion, but it would have been impossible to refuse. "This is my land. I am your neighbor Radilov—you may have heard of me," continued my new acquaintance. "To-day being Sunday, there ought to be a decent dinner at home, otherwise I wouldn't have invited you."

I answered as one does on such occasions, and set off at his heels. A path which had recently been cleared soon led us from the lime-grove up to a kitchen-garden. Between ancient apple-trees and overgrown gooseberry-bushes, cabbages displayed their round, pale-green, mottled heads; hop tendrils wound their way round tall stakes; the borders were closely studded with brown stakes, lost in a mass of withered peas; great flat pumpkins lay about on the ground; yellow cucumbers were revealed underneath their dusty angular leaves; along the fence tall nettles waved; in two or three places there grew bushes of tartar, honeysuckle, elder, and dog-rose—remnants of former shrubberies. Close to a small pond, full of slimy reddish water, was a well, surrounded by puddles; ducks were splashing and waddling fussily about in them; in an open space a dog, trembling all over and screwing up its eyes, was gnawing a bone; close at hand a piebald cow was lazily browsing the grass, with an occasional flick of her tail against her bony back. The path took a turning, and behind a thick clump of willows and birches a small, gray old house with a wooden roof and a crooked porch peeped out at us. Radilov halted.

"By the way," he said, looking me full in the face, with a good-natured expression, "it's just occurred to me that perhaps you don't feel at all like coming in; in that case . . ."

I didn't let him finish, but assured him that on the contrary I would be delighted to dine with him.

"Well, it's as you wish."

We went into the house. A young fellow in a long coat of thick blue cloth met us in the porch. Radilov at once told him to give Ermolai a drink of vodka. My hunter bowed respectfully towards the back of the munificent donor. From a hall adorned with various brightly-colored pictures and hung with check curtains, we went into a small room—Radilov's study. I took off my shooting gear and put my gun in the corner. The boy in the long-skirted coat fussed around brushing me.

"Well, now let's go into the drawing-room," said Radilov agreeably; "I want to introduce you to my mother."

I followed him. In the drawing-room, on a sofa in the middle of the room, sat a little old lady in a brown dress and a white bonnet, with a kind, thin face, and a timid, sad expression.

"Mother, let me introduce our neighbor."

The old lady half-rose and bowed to me without loosening the grip of her bony hands on her bulging, sack-shaped worsted reticule.

"Have you been in our part of the country for long?" she asked in a low, faint voice, blinking her eyes.

"No, not for long."

"Do you think of staying here for some time?"

"Until winter, I think."

The old lady said nothing.

"Now," interposed Radilov, drawing my attention to a tall thin man whom I hadn't noticed as I came into the drawing-room, "this is Fyodor Mikheich. . . . Well, Fedya, show our guest your skill. Why are you hiding in the corner?"

Fyodor Mikheich at once rose from his chair, took a rickety violin from the window-sill, grasped the bow, not correctly by one end, but by the middle, propped the violin against his chest, shut his eyes, and went off into a dance, humming the tune and scraping away at the strings. He looked about seventy; his long nankeen coat hung sadly on his thin bony limbs. He danced; now he would perform a dashing jig, now sway his little bald head from side to side with a swooning motion and stick out his lean neck; he stood and stamped his feet; sometimes, with obvious difficulty, he flexed his knees; from his toothless mouth came a senile quavering. Radilov must have guessed from my expression that Fedya's "skill" was giving me no particular satisfaction.

"Thanks, old fellow, that will do," he said. "You can go and get your reward." Fyodor at once put down his violin on the windowsill, bowed, first to me, as a guest, then to the old lady, then to Radilov, and went out of the room.

"He was a landowner, too," went on my new friend, "and a rich one, but he ruined himself—and here he is, living with me. . . . In his day he was the biggest rake in the province; he ran off with two people's wives, kept his own singers, sang and danced like a master. . . . But won't you have some vodka? Dinner's on the table."

A young girl, the same one I had seen for a flash in the garden, came into the room.

"Ah, and here is Olga!" remarked Radilov, with a slight turn of his head. "Let me recommend her to your kindness. . . . Well, let's go and dine."

We went into the dining-room and sat down. While we were passing in from the drawing-room and taking our places, Fyodor, whose "reward" had made his eyes sparkle and his nose slightly red, sang: "*Let Vict'ry's thunder sound!*" A separate place had been laid for him in a corner, on a little table without a napkin. The poor old man couldn't boast of cleanliness, and was therefore always kept at a certain distance from the company. He crossed himself, sighed, and began to eat with a shark-like voracity. The dinner was indeed not a bad one and, the day being Sunday, it didn't fail to include a quivering jelly and the sweet dish known as "Spanish puffs." At table Radilov, who had served ten years in an infantry regiment of the line and had campaigned in Turkey, started telling stories; I listened to him with attention and kept a furtive eye on Olga. She was not particularly pretty, but her calm, decisive expression, her broad, white forehead, her thick hair, and especially her brown eyes, which, though small, were clear and full of intelligence and life, would have struck anyone else in my place. She fairly hung on every word of Radilov's; it was not just interest, it was a passionate concentration which expressed itself in her face. In years, Radilov could have been her father. He addressed her in the second person singular, but I guessed at once that she was not his daughter. In the course of conversation he mentioned his late wife. "Her sister," he added, indicating Olga. She blushed swiftly and lowered her eyes. Radilov fell silent, then changed the subject. The old lady didn't utter a word all through dinner; she hardly ate at all, and did not press me to do so either. Her features breathed that air of timorous, hopeless expectancy, that senile melancholy, which lays such a painful hand on the heart of the beholder. At the end of dinner, Fyodor was starting to "toast" his hosts and their guest, but Radilov glanced at me and begged him to be silent; the old man passed his hand over his lips, blinked, bowed, and sat down again, but this time on the very edge of his chair. After dinner, Radilov and I made our way to his study.

In people who are intensely and continuously preoccupied with a single thought or a single passion, one can detect an element in common, a certain external likeness of manner, however much they may differ in qualities, capability, position in the world, or education. The longer I observed Radilov, the more strongly I became convinced that he belonged to this class of people. He spoke about farming, harvesting and haymaking, about war, local gossip, and the approaching elections. He spoke without constraint, and indeed with concern, then suddenly he would sigh, sink back in his chair, like a man exhausted by heavy labor, and pass his hand over his face. His whole good, warmhearted nature seemed penetrated through and through and saturated by a single feeling. I had already been surprised by my failure to find any passion on his part, either for food, drink, shooting, nightingales from Kursk, epilepsy in pigeons, Russian literature, trotting horses, Hungarian jackets, cards, billiards, *soirées* with dancing, trips to the provincial or national capitals, paper-mills, sugar-beet factories, painted summerhouses, tea, the progress of viciousness in side-horses, or even for fat coachmen, with belts right up under their armpits, those magnificent coachmen with whom, heaven knows why, every movement of the neck is accompanied by a roll and a bulge of the eyeballs. . . . "He's a queer sort of landowner, anyway," I thought. But, with it all, he made no pretence of moroseness or dissatisfaction with his lot; on the contrary, he fairly radiated undiscriminating goodwill, affability, and an almost irritating disposition to make friends with anyone and everyone he met. It was true that at the same time you felt he was incapable of making really close friends with anyone, not because he never needed other people's society, but because for a time his whole life had been directed inwards. As I gazed at Radilov, I couldn't begin to imagine him happy, either then or at any other time. He was no beauty, either, but in his glance, in his smile, in his whole being, there lurked—lurked in the true sense of the word—something extraordinarily seductive. It made you feel that you wanted to get to know him better and to love him. Of course sometimes the steppe landowner bobbed up in him, but all the same he was really a very fine man.

We were beginning to talk about the new Marshal of Nobility of the district, when suddenly in the doorway we heard Olga's voice: "Tea is ready."

We went into the drawing-room. As before, Fyodor was sitting in his corner, between the window and the door, with his legs modestly drawn in beneath him. Radilov's mother was knitting a stocking. Through the open windows there came from the garden a breath of autumn freshness and the smell of apples. Olga was busy pouring out tea. I looked at her now with closer attention than I had at dinner. She spoke very little, as is usually the way with girls of provincial society, but at any rate I failed to detect in her any desire to say something clever, accompanied with an agonizing sense of emptiness and helplessness; with her there were no sighs, as if from an overflow of indescribable emotions, no upward rolling of the eyes, no vague and dreamy smiles. Her gaze was calm and equable, as of someone who rests after great happiness or great anxiety. Her gait and her movements were free and resolute. I took a great liking to her.

Radilov and I got talking again. I no longer remember by what path we came to the familiar observation that so often the most insignificant things produce more of an impression on people than the most important ones.

"Yes," said Radilov, "I have had that experience myself. I used to be married, as you know. Not for long . . . three years; my wife died in childbirth. I thought that I would never survive her; I was terribly distressed, broken, but the tears would not come—I just went about as if I were out of my mind. She was duly dressed and laid out on the table—here in this room. The priest came, the deacons came too and began to sing and pray and to burn incense; I bowed right down to the ground, but couldn't shed a single tear. My heart seemed to have turned to stone, my head, too; and my whole body had become a heavy weight. And so the first day went by. Will you believe me? That night I even managed to sleep. The next morning I went in to look at my wife—it was summer, and the sun shone on her from head to foot and so brightly, too. Suddenly I saw"—here Radilov gave an involuntary shudder—"what do you think? Her eyes was not properly closed, and on it a fly was walking. . . . I dropped like a sheaf of corn, and, as soon as I came to myself again, began to weep and weep—there was just no stopping me. . . ."

Radilov paused. I looked at him, then at Olga. . . . Never shall I forget the expression on her face. The old lady put down the stocking on her knee, took a handkerchief out of her bag and furtively wiped away a tear. Fyodor suddenly got up, seized his violin, and struck up a song in a strange, hoarse voice. He probably wanted to cheer us up; but we all shuddered at his first note and Radilov begged him to be quiet.

"Anyhow," he continued, "what's gone is gone; there is no going back to the past, and, in the end . . . everything is for the best in this world, as Voltaire—wasn't it?—observed," he added hurriedly.

"Yes," I rejoined, "of course. What's more, every misfortune can be endured and there's a way out of every bad situation."

"Do you think so?" said Radilov. "Who knows, perhaps you are right. I remember, I was lying in hospital in Turkey, more dead than alive, I had marsh-fever. Well, the quarters were nothing to boast about—it was wartime, of course—but, just the same, they might have been worse. And all of a sudden they bring in more patients—and the question is where to put them. The doctor rushes up and down—there's no room. So up he comes to me and asks the dresser: 'Is he alive?' The dresser answers: 'He was, this morning.' The doctor bends down and listens: he hears my breathing. This was more than the good doctor could stand. 'Look how stupid nature is,' he said. 'Look, here is a man dying,

dying for certain, but he has still got a squeak in him, he's still dragging on, he's just taking up a place and keeping the others out.' Well, I thought to myself, it looks bad for you, Mikhailo Mikhailich . . . But all the same, I got better and am still alive to-day, as you may have been good enough to observe. So you're right."

"Whatever happened, I would have been right," I answered. "Even if you had died, it would have got you out of the fix that you were in."

"Yes, to be sure," he rejoined, thumping his hand loudly on the table. "It's just a question of making up one's mind. . . . What's the point of being in a fix? What's the good of lingering, dragging on? . . ."

Olga got up quickly and went out into the garden.

"Well, Fedya, give us a dance!" exclaimed Radilov.

Fyodor jumped up, crossed the room with the special mincing step of the man who plays "giddy goat" in front of a tame bear, and began to sing: "*While before our gates* . . ."

From the porch we heard the sound of a racing drozhky, and in a few moments there came into the room a tall, burly, broad-shouldered old man. This was Ovsyanikov the freeholder . . . But Ovsyanikov is such a remarkable and original character, that with the reader's permission we will describe him in the next story. For the moment I will only add, on my own account, that on the next day Ermolai and I went out shooting at daybreak, that after shooting we returned home; that a week later I again called at Radilov's, but found neither him nor Olga at home, and that two weeks later still I learned that he had suddenly vanished, left his mother and gone off with his sister-in-law. This incident caused much excitement and discussion throughout the province, and it was only then that I finally understood Olga's expression while Radilov was telling us his story. At that moment her face was not just alive with sympathy: it was on fire with jealousy.

Before leaving the country, I visited Radilov's old mother. I found her in the drawing-room; she was playing a game of "idiots" with Fyodor Mikheich.

"Have you heard from your son?" I asked her eventually.

The old lady burst into tears. I asked her no more questions about Radilov.

Ovsyanikov the Freeholder

PICTURE TO YOURSELF, DEAR READER, A TALL, STOUT MAN OF
about seventy, with a face rather reminiscent of Krylov's,* clear intelligent eyes beneath overhanging brows, a dignified bearing, a
measured speech, and a deliberate gait: there you have Ovsyanikov.
He wore a capacious long-sleeved blue coat, buttoned right up, a
lilac-colored silk handkerchief round his neck, and brilliantly pol-
ished boots with tassels, and in general had something of the look of
a well-to-do merchant. His hands were well-shaped, soft and white:
often, in the course of conversation, he would play with the buttons
of his coat. With his dignity and immobility, his intelligence and
indolence, with his straight-forwardness and his obstinacy, Ovsyanikov reminded me of the Russian boyars of the period of Peter the
Great. The traditional Russian attire would have suited him well.
He was one of the last survivors from the good old days.

All his neighbors had an extraordinary respect for him and considered his acquaintance an honor. His fellow-freeholders practically said their prayers to him, started fingering their hats as soon
as they caught sight of him in the distance, and regarded him as
their pride. Generally speaking it is difficult to distinguish the
Russian freeholder from the peasant. His standard of farming is
hardly higher than the peasant's, his calves never budge from the
buckwheat field, his horses have little life in them, their harness is
made of string. Although he was not known as a man of means,

---

* The well-known writer of fables.—*Translators.*

Ovsyanikov was an exception to the general rule. He lived alone with his wife in a neat and cozy little house, he kept a few servants, he dressed them in the Russian manner and referred to them as "hands." It was in fact they who ploughed his land. He never pretended to be a nobleman, never posed as a landowner, never, as they say, "forgot himself," never sat down unless invited to do so, and when a new guest arrived would never fail to rise from his place, but with such dignity, such majestic grace that the guest involuntarily bowed to him all the lower for it. Ovsyanikov kept up the old-fashioned ways, not from superstition (for he was a reasonably open-minded man), but from habit. For example, he disliked carriages with springs, because he found them unrestful, and he travelled either in a racing drozhky or in a neat little cart with a leather cushion. He drove his good bay trotting-horse himself. (He kept only bay horses.) His coachman, a red-cheeked peasant lad, with hair cropped round a basin, in a plush overcoat and a low hat and with a strap round his waist, sat respectfully at his side. Ovsyanikov always slept after dinner, went to the bath-house on Saturdays, read nothing but religious works (for which he would solemnly fix a pair of round silver spectacles on his nose), rose and retired early. He wore no beard, however, and his hair was cut in the German manner. He gave his guests a joyful welcome, but never made them a deep bow, never fussed over them, never pressed preserves or pickles on them. "Wife!" he would say slowly, not rising from his place, but slightly turning his head in her direction: "Bring the gentlemen something tasty." He considered it a sin to sell corn, since it was the gift of God, and in the year '40, at the time of the great famine and the terrible rise in prices, he distributed all his store to the landowners and peasants of the district; in the following year they gratefully repaid him their debt in kind.

Ovsyanikov's neighbors often appealed to him with requests to decide their disputes and make peace between them, and almost always took his advice and bowed to his decision. Thanks to him, many neighbors finally reached agreement on the boundaries of their land. But after two or three encounters with female landowners, he announced his decision never to mediate between disputants of the opposite sex. He could not stand the flurries, the restless bustle, the old-wives' chatter, the fuss.

Once, somehow or other, his house caught fire, and one of his hands rushed up to him at full speed, crying, "Fire, fire!" "Well, what are you shouting about?" said Ovsyanikov calmly. "Give me my hat and stick . . ." He was fond of training horses himself. Once a fiery steed bolted with him downhill into a ravine. "Well, that will do, that will do, young colt—or you'll kill yourself," Ovsyanikov said to him good-naturedly and, a moment later, he was flying into the ravine, complete with his racing drozhky, the boy who sat behind him, the horse and all. Luckily there were piles of sand lying at the bottom of the ravine. No one was hurt, only the horse put its leg out. "Well, you see," continued Ovsyanikov in a calm voice as he got up from the ground, "I told you so."

He had found a wife after his own heart. Tatyana Ilyinichna Ovsyanikova was a tall, dignified, silent woman, with a brown silk handkerchief permanently tied over her head. She had a chilling presence, although no one had ever accused her of severity. On the contrary, many beggars called her "mother" and "kind soul." Her regular features, her big dark eyes, her fine lips, still testified to a once famous beauty. Ovsyanikov had no children.

As the reader already knows, I made his acquaintance at Radilov's, and two days later I went to call on him. I found him at home. He was sitting in a large leather armchair, reading *The Lives of the Saints*. A gray cat was purring on his shoulder. He received me in his usual manner, warmly and with dignity. We fell into conversation.

"Tell me, Luka Petrovich," I said in the course of our talk, "things were better, weren't they, in the old days, in your time?"

"Some things were certainly better, I should say," rejoined Ovsyanikov. "We had a quieter life; things were easier, certainly . . . but all the same, it is better now; and for your children it will be better still, please God."

"And I was so expecting you to sing me the praises of the good old days."

"No, I have no special reason for praising the good old days.

Now take yourself, for example. You're a landowner to-day, as your late grandfather was, but you've nothing like the same power, and you're not the same sort of man, either. Even to-day there are other gentlemen who make life difficult for our sort; but evidently that can't be avoided. First you grind the corn and then you get flour. No, I shall never again see the sort of things that I saw when I was young."

"But what, for example?"

"Well, take your grandfather's case again. A hard man he was. Did much harm to fellows like us! You may know—of course you will, as it is your own land—the wedge-shaped piece of ground between Chepligin and Malinin? . . . You've got it under oats at the moment . . . Well, it's ours—the whole piece, as it stands, is ours. Your grandfather took it away from us; he rode out, pointed with his hand, and said: 'My property,' and his property it became. My late father (Heaven rest his soul!) was a just man, and a hot-tempered one too; he wouldn't take it lying down—indeed who *is* keen on losing his property?—and he made a petition to the court. He did so by himself, as the others wouldn't support him—they were frightened. So they told your grandfather: 'Pyotr Ovsyanikov is putting in a complaint against you, sir, on the grounds that you have taken away his land.' . . . Your grandfather at once sent his huntsman Bausch to our home with a whole troop of fellows. . . . And they took my father and carried him off to your estate. I was a little boy then, I ran after him barefoot. What next? They brought him to your home and flogged him right under the windows. And your grandfather stands on the balcony and looks on; and your grandmother sits in the window and looks, too. My father cries out: 'Marya Vasilyevna, gracious lady, save me—*you* at least should have pity on me.' But all she does, d'you see, is sit up straight and look on. Well, they made my father promise to give up his claim to the land, and then made him say thank you for having been left off with his life. So the land stayed with you. Go and ask your peasants what the land is called. It's called 'cudgel field,' because it was taken away with the cudgel. That's the sort of reason why we simple folk don't miss the old ways too badly."

I didn't know how to answer Ovsyanikov and I didn't dare look him in the face.

"Then we had another neighbor on our hands about that time—Komov, Stefan Niktopolionich. He fairly drove my father to death—first in one way, then in another. He was a drunken fellow and liked entertaining others, but when after a drop or two he would come out in French with '*say bon*' and lick his lips—it was more even than a saint could bear. He'd send out and summon all his neighbors. He'd have a troika standing ready and if you didn't come at once he'd pay you a surprise visit himself. . . . What a strange fellow he was! When he was sober he didn't tell lies but, as soon as he'd had a drink, he'd begin to tell you that he had three houses on the Fontanka in Petersburg: one, red, with one chimney; another, yellow, with two chimneys; the third, blue, with no chimneys; and three sons (and he never so much as married): one in the infantry, one in the cavalry, and the third *all on his own* . . . And he'd say that he had a son living in each house, and that the eldest entertained admirals, the second entertained generals, and the youngest entertained Englishmen only! Then up he'd get and say: 'To the health of my eldest son, he's the best son of the lot!' and he'd begin to cry. And woe betide anyone who wouldn't drink with him. 'I'll shoot you!' he'd say, 'and I won't let them bury you either!' Then he'd jump up and shout: 'Dance, good people, dance for your own entertainment and my consolation!' Well, you'd have to dance, even if it killed you, you'd have to dance. He gave his serf girls terrible trouble. They had to be singing choruses all the livelong night and the one who raised her voice the highest would get a prize. But if they started to get tired he would put his head in his hands and feel sorry for himself: 'Oh, fatherless orphan that I am! They're dropping me, like the poor little thing that I am!' The grooms would at once put fresh heart into the girls. He took a liking to my father, and there was nothing to be done about it . . . he nearly drove him to his grave, and would have done so quite, but luckily he died first himself. He fell down from a dovecote when he was drunk. That's the sort of nice neighbors we used to have."

"How the times have changed," I observed.

"Yes, yes," agreed Ovsyanikov. "But, there's the other side, too. In the olden days the nobility lived on a grander scale. Not to mention the real magnates; I saw plenty of them in Moscow. I've heard that now they've died out, even there."

"You have been in Moscow?"

"Yes, long, long ago. I'm now seventy-two, and I went to Moscow when I was fifteen."

Ovsyanikov sighed.

"Whom did you see there?"

"I saw any number of great magnates—everybody did; they lived openly, in a blaze of glory and admiration. But there was not one of them to touch Count Alexei Grigoryevich Orlov-Chesmensky. I often saw Alexei Grigoryevich; my uncle served as his steward. The Count lived by the Kaluga Gates, on the Shabolovka. There was a real magnate for you! Such presence, such graciousness of manner, not to be imagined or described. His size alone was something extraordinary, and his strength, his expression! Until you knew him, you would be too shy and frightened to enter his house; but once you went in, he would warm you like the sun and all your spirits would rise. He was accessible to everyone, and very open-minded. At the races he drove himself and was ready to take on anybody. And he would never overtake them at once, he'd never hurt their feelings or pull them up short, but he'd just pass them at the very end; and so nice about it, too—he'd console his opponent and praise his horse. He kept tumbler-pigeons of the very best breed. Sometimes he'd go out into the courtyard, sit down in an armchair and order the pigeons to be let out; and all around, on the roof, would be men standing with guns to keep the hawks off. At the Count's feet they'd put a big silver bowl full of water; he'd look into the water, too, to see the pigeons play in it. The poor and needy lived by hundreds on his charity . . . and what fortunes he gave away! When he was angry, it was like a thunderclap. It was terrifying—but nothing really to cry about; you'd look again—and already he'd be smiling. He would give a feast—and make all Moscow drunk . . . And what a brain he had! Look how he beat the Turk. He liked wrestling, too; they brought him champions from Tula, from Kharkov, from

Tambov, from all over the place: the ones he threw he'd reward; but if any one threw him, he'd load him with presents and kiss him on the mouth. . . . While I was in Moscow, he gave a party the like of which had never been seen in Russia. He invited to his house all the sportsmen in the whole country, and fixed a day three months ahead. So they all assembled, they brought with them their dogs and huntsmen—why, it was an army, a whole army, that arrived! First of all they feasted in proper style, then they went out to the gates. The people came swarming together! . . . And what d'you think happened? . . . Your grandfather's dog came in first of the lot."

"Not Milovidka?" I asked.

"Yes, Milovidka. . . . So the count started asking your grandfather to sell him his dog: 'Take what you like,' says he. 'No, Count,' says your grandfather, 'I am no merchant: I am no seller of unwanted trash; for honor's sake I would be ready even to yield up my wife, only not Milovidka. . . . I'd sooner give my own self up into captivity.' Alexei Grigoryevich praised him: 'That's what I like to hear,' he says. Your grandfather took Milovidka back in his carriage; and when Milovidka died, he gave her a funeral with music in his park—he gave the bitch a funeral and set up a headstone with an inscription over her body."

"Well, your Alexei Grigoryevich certainly gave offence to nobody," I observed.

"Yes, it's always the same way: it's the small chap that picks the quarrels."

"And what was this fellow Bausch like?" I asked, after a pause.

"How is it that you've heard of Milovidka and not of Bausch? . . . He was your grandfather's head huntsman and whipper-in. Your grandfather loved him as much as he loved Milovidka. He was a desperate fellow, and whatever your grandfather ordered, he would carry out in the twinkling of an eye—even if it meant climbing on to a knife. And what a halloo he would give: the whole forest would fairly ring with it. And then he'd suddenly set his jaw, dismount, and lie down . . . and the moment the hounds no longer heard his voice, the game was up! They'd drop the hottest scent, they'd not run farther for anything in the world. Eh, how angry your grand-

father would get! 'Don't let me live a moment longer if I can't hang
the lazy rascal! I'll turn the devil inside out! I'll drag the scoundrel's
heels out through his throat!' But it'd all end by his sending to find
out what Bausch wanted and why he wasn't hallooing, and Bausch
would then generally ask for a drink, swallow it, get up, and start
tally-hoing again for all he was worth."

"You're fond of hunting, too, Luka Petrovich, I think?"

"I might have been, certainly—but not now: now my day is
over—but when I was young . . . though, you know, it's awkward,
because of my standing. It isn't right that fellows like us should ape
the nobility. It is true, you may find one of our kind, some drunken
idiot who becomes a hanger-on of the gentry . . . and what a time
he has! . . . all he does is make a fool of himself. They give him a
rotten, stumbling horse; they keep on knocking his cap off on to the
ground; they give him a stinging blow with the whip and pretend
it was meant for the horse; and all the time it's his job to laugh and
make the others laugh too. No, I'll tell you: the humbler your station, the stricter the watch you must keep on yourself if you want to
avoid the mud.

"Yes," continued Ovsyanikov, with a sigh. "Plenty of water has
flowed under the bridges since I've been in the world: the times have
changed indeed. I see a specially big change among the nobility. The
small landowners have all either gone into the Government service,
or else don't stay at home; and as for the bigger fellows, they're not
the same men any more. I've seen enough of them, your big landowners, in these boundary cases, and I'm bound to tell you: it delights my heart to see how amiable and obliging they are. The only
thing that surprises me is this: they have learned all the sciences,
they talk so eloquently that it fairly melts your heart, but they make
no sense out of the business in hand, they're not even conscious of
their own interest; any clerk, their own serf, can bend them any
way he wants, like so many longbows. You perhaps know Korolev,
Alexander Vladimirich. A nobleman through and through, handsome, rich, been to those universities abroad even, I believe, fluent
and modest of speech, shakes hands with us all. You know him? . . .
Well, listen, then. Last week we all assembled at Berezovka at the

invitation of Nikifor Ilyich, the arbitrator. And Nikifor Ilyich the arbitrator says to us: 'Gentlemen, we must demarcate our land, it's shameful, our district is so badly behind-hand. Let's get busy.' So we did. As usual, there was arguing and quarrelling; our attorney started to be tiresome. But it was Porfyry Ovchinnikov who began the trouble. . . . And what about? . . . He himself does not own a square foot of land: he's acting on his brother's behalf. He shouts: 'No, you can't cheat *me*! No, you're up against someone of a different kind! Give the plans here! Send the surveyor to me, send the Judas here!' 'Well, after all this, what are you claiming?' 'D'you think I'm such a fool as that, eh? Do you think that I am going to tell you what my claim is, just like that? . . . No, give the plans here, that's what I say!' and he bangs on the plans with his fists. Marfa Dmitryevna takes mortal offense. She cries: 'How dare you defame my reputation?' He answers: 'I wouldn't have your reputation even for my bay mare.' They had to pour madeira down her throat. When he calmed down, the others started making trouble instead. Alexander Vladimirovich Korolev, the dear sweet fellow, was sitting in a corner, biting the knob of his cane, and just shaking his head. I felt so ashamed of the whole business, I could stand it no longer, and wanted to run away. What on earth could he be thinking of us? All of a sudden my friend Alexander Vladimirovich gets up and shows that he wants to speak. The arbitrator starts fussing about and says: 'Gentlemen, gentlemen, Alexander Vladimirovich wishes to speak.' And, to give the gentlemen their due, they all fell silent at once. So Alexander Vladimirovich begins and says: 'I think we have forgotten the reason for our assembly: although it's true that demarcation of boundaries is to the advantage of the landowners, what is its real purpose? It is to make things easier for the peasant, to make his work handier for him and his taxes easier to pay; at present he does not know his own land and often walks five miles to do his ploughing—so that you cannot ask too much from him.' Then Alexander Vladimirovich said that it was wicked for a landowner not to care about the welfare of his peasants, that, in the long run, if you look at it in the right way, the peasants' interests are exactly the same as ours; if he does well, so do we, if he does badly so do we . . . and therefore it is both wicked and ill-considered not to reach agreement because of trifles . . . and he went on and on . . . and how he spoke! He fairly gripped your heart . . . all the gentlemen hung their heads; and as for me, well, I practically burst into tears. Upon my word, you won't find language like his in any old books. But what was the end of it all? He himself refused to give up or sell ten acres of moss-hags. He said: 'I am going to drain this marsh with my own labor and I am going to start a cloth factory there, an *improved* cloth factory. I have already chosen the site: I have got my own plans for it. . . .' And had it been fair, it would have been another matter, but the plain truth is that Anton Karasikov, Alexander Vladimirovich's neighbor, had been too mean to give Alexander's agent a bribe of a hundred rubles. So we all went our ways without settling our business. And Alexander Vladimirovich still considers himself in the right and goes on talking about his cloth factory, only he does nothing about draining the marsh."

"And how does he manage his estate?"

"He's always introducing new methods. His peasants don't like it—but it is no use listening to them. Alexander Vladimirovich is quite right."

"How is that, Luka Petrovich? I thought you were all for conservatism?"

"My own feelings are a different question. I'm not a nobleman, I'm not a landowner. What do my ideas on farming matter? Anyhow I don't know how to do otherwise. I try to do what is right and just, with God's help. The younger gentry don't like the old ways: I can't blame them. . . . It's high time people sat down and thought things out. There is only one thing that's a pity: they're all so terribly clever. They treat the peasant like a doll: they turn him this way and that, they break him and throw him away. And the agent, who's a serf, or the bailiff, who's of German origin, gets the peasant into his clutches once more. And if only just one of these young gentlemen would give an example and show how things ought to be done! . . . What will be the end of it? Must I really die without seeing any new system in action? . . . It's a strange thing when the old order passes and there's no new one to take its place!"

I did not know how to answer Ovsyanikov. He looked around, leaned closer to me and continued in an undertone: "Have you heard about Vasily Nikolaich Lyubozvonov?"

"No, I haven't."

"It's an extraordinary story which you may be able to explain to me. I can't grasp it at all myself. His own peasants told the story but I can't make any sense of what they said. He's a young fellow, you know, and inherited from his mother not long ago. Well, he arrives at his place. The peasants have assembled to have a look at their master. Vasily appears before them. What on earth is it that they see? A master who comes before them in velveteen pantaloons like a coachman, and in boots with trimmings on them: he wears a red shirt, and a coat which is also like a coachman's; he has let his beard grow, and on his head such a queer little hat, and such a queer face too. Not that he is drunk, but just not in his right mind. 'Good day to you, my lads; God bless you.' The peasants give him a deep bow—but in silence, for he has made them feel shy. And he himself seems to feel shy, too. He begins to make them a speech. 'I am Russian,' he says, 'and you are Russian, too; I love everything that's Russian. . . . My soul is Russian and so is my blood.' . . . Then suddenly he gives them an order: 'Well, my lads, go on, sing me a Russian folk-song.' The peasants' knees were all of a tremble; they were knocked quite silly. One stout fellow struck up a song, then dropped down at once and hid behind the others. . . . And this is the surprising thing: we have had strange landowners before, gentlemen-desperadoes, regular rakes, certainly: they dressed up as coachmen, I dare say, danced, played the guitar, sang and drank with their own serving-folk, and feasted with the peasants; but this chap Vasily is like a pretty girl: all the time reading books, or writing them, or, if not that, reciting verse aloud—talks to no one, is shyness itself, walks in the garden alone, as if he's bored or sad. The former agent had been quite scared to begin with. Before Vasily's arrival, he ran around the peasants' back-yards, and bowed to them all. Clearly, as they say, the cat had smelt whose meat he had eaten! The peasants were full of hope; they thought to themselves: 'No more of your tricks, my friend. Now you'll have to answer for what you've done; now you'll have to dance all right, you mean old rascal! . . .' But instead of that, it turned out—how can I explain it to you?—the Lord himself could not make out what happened! Vasily sends for the agent, talks to him, blushes, you know, and gasps out: 'I want you to be just and not to oppress anybody—d'you hear?' And from that day forward he never even sent for him! He lives on his own estate as though he was a stranger there. Well, the agent heaved a sigh of relief, and, as for the peasants, they don't dare to approach Vasily: they're afraid to. And, look, here is another surprising thing: the master bows to them and gives them friendly looks—but their stomachs fairly turn from fear. What an extraordinary story, sir! Eh? . . . Or perhaps I've grown old and stupid or something, and don't understand."

I answered Ovsyanikov that Mr. Lyubozvonov was probably ill.

"Ill! Why he is fatter across than he is tall, and such a great sprawling face, my word, you'd never think he was a young man. . . . But of course, who can tell—except God?" And Ovsyanikov sighed deeply.

"Well, enough of the gentry," I began. "What have you got to tell me about the freeholders, Luka Petrovich?"

"No, there I must ask to be excused," he said hastily. "It is true, I could tell you. . . . But what's the use?" Ovsyanikov waved his hands. "We'd better have tea. Peasants we are, just ordinary peasants; besides, what else should we be?" He paused. Tea was served. Tatyana Ilyinichna rose from her chair and sat down again closer to us. In the course of the evening she had several times noiselessly gone out and no less quietly returned. Silence reigned in the room. Ovsyanikov, with slow-moving dignity, drank cup after cup.

"Mitya was here to-day," observed Tatyana Ilyinichna in a low voice.

Ovsyanikov frowned.

"What did he want?"

"He came to beg your pardon."

Ovsyanikov shook his head.

"There you are," he went on, turning to me. "What's a man to do with his relations? He can't just drop them, can he? Take my case: a nice little nephew God has rewarded me with. A head on his shoulders, a smart lad, there's no question of that; quite a scholar—and yet no good's ever likely to come out of him. He was in the Government service—then threw it up: promotion was not fast enough for him, if you please. . . . Does he think he is a nobleman, or what? Even *they* don't get promoted to generals at once. Anyway, now he's without a job. . . . And as if that wasn't bad enough, he's become a tale-bearer too! He composes petitions for the peasants, writes reports, instructs the village spokesmen, shows up surveyors at their tricks, crawls around the pot-houses, rubs shoulders with townsfolk and yard-sweepers in every tavern. In short, he's heading for a bad end. The police have warned him more than once. Luckily he knows how to crack a joke: he makes them laugh, then gets them into hot water too. . . . Why, I bet he's sitting in your little den, isn't he?" he added, turning to his wife. "*I* know you, you're so soft-hearted— you've taken him under your wing."

Tatyana Ilyinichna dropped her head, smiled and blushed.

"So it's like that, is it?" continued Ovsyanikov: "You mollycoddler! Well, tell him to come in—let it pass. I'll forgive the silly boy for the sake of our dear guest. . . . Well, call him, call him . . ."

Tatyana Ilyinichna went to the door and called: "Mitya!"

Mitya, a lad of about twenty-eight, tall, well-built and curlyheaded, came into the room, and, catching sight of me, halted on the threshold. He was dressed in the German fashion, but you'd only to look at the unnaturally high padding of the shoulders to see clearly that his clothes had been cut by the most Russian of tailors.

"Well, come on, come on," said the old man, "what are you ashamed about? You must thank your aunt you are forgiven . . . Here, sir, let me introduce him," he continued, pointing at Mitya, "my own nephew, but the two of us don't see eye to eye. I've come to the end of my patience!" Mitya and I bowed to each other. "Well, tell me, what sort of a scrape are you in now? Tell me what they've got against you this time!"

Mitya was clearly reluctant to explain and justify himself in front of me.

"Later on, uncle," he murmured.

"No, not later on, but now," persisted the old man. "I know

you're ashamed to speak in front of this gentleman, all the better—it's a punishment for you. Come on, tell us. . . . We'll hear what you have to say."

"I've nothing to be ashamed of," began Mitya vehemently, and he shook his head; "please, uncle, judge for yourself. The freeholders of Reshetilovo come and ask for my help. 'What is the matter?' I ask. 'Here's the matter: our grain-sheds are all in order, they could not be better than they are. Suddenly there comes to us an official and says he's got orders to inspect the sheds. He inspects them and says our sheds are in bad order, seriously neglected, he must report it to his superiors. But how are they neglected, pray? *I* know how, he says. We got together and decided to grease his palm in the usual way, but old Prokhorich prevented us, he said we would only sharpen his appetite; why, hadn't we any means of redress? . . . We took the old man's advice, but the official was annoyed and made a complaint and wrote a report. And now we're called on to answer him.' 'And are your sheds really in order?' I asked. 'Before God, they are indeed; and there's as much grain there as the law prescribes. . . .' 'Well,' I say, 'you've nothing to be afraid of, then,' and I wrote them out a paper . . . and it's not known yet which way the case has gone . . . But as for the complaint that's been made to you about it all, it's as clear as day: everyone has got his own axe to grind."

"Everyone except you apparently," said the old man, in a low voice. . . . "And what are the tricks you have been up to with the peasants of Shutolomovo?"

"How d'you know about that?"

"I just know."

"There too I was in the right—please judge again for yourself. The peasants of Shutolomovo had ten acres of their land ploughed up by their neighbor Bespandin. 'It's my land,' he says. The Shutolomovo people pay rent, their master's away abroad—tell me yourself, who is there to help them? But there's no question of it, the land is theirs, they've been serfs on it since time immemorial. So they come to me and ask me to write a petition, and I do. But Bespandin finds out and starts threatening, and says: 'I'll take this little Mitya and

I'll pull the backs of his shoulder-blades out, or else I'll take his head right off his shoulders.' We'll see whether he does. So far my head is safe and sound."

"Well, don't boast: your head will come to a bad end," said the old man, "raving lunatic that you are."

"But, uncle, didn't you tell me yourself?"

"I know, I know what you are going to say to me," Ovsyanikov interrupted him. "Exactly: a man must live justly and ought to help his neighbor. Certainly there are times when a man shouldn't spare himself . . . but do *you* always live up to those principles? Don't they take you to pot-houses, eh? and stand you drinks? and bow to you, eh? and say: 'Dmitry Alexeich, sir, help us, and we will prove to you how grateful we are,' and don't they slip a silver ruble or a note from under their coat skirts into your hand? eh? Isn't that what happens? Tell us, isn't it, eh?"

"There I'm certainly guilty," answered Mitya, lowering his head. "But I don't accept money from the poor and I don't act against my conscience."

"You don't accept from them now, but once things go badly for you, then you will. You don't act against your conscience. Get along with you! I suppose you're always on the side of the angels! . . . Why, have you forgotten Boris Perekhodov? Who was it who fussed about him? Who was it who took him under his wing, eh?"

"Perekhodov deserved his fate, certainly . . ."

"He embezzled Government money. . . . Nothing more than that!"

"But, uncle, just imagine his poverty, his family . . ."

"Poverty . . . he was a drunkard and a gambler—that's what he was."

"It was his troubles that started him drinking," observed Mitya, lowering his voice.

"Troubles, indeed! Well, you could have helped him, if you're so warm-hearted, but without sitting around in pot-houses with a drunkard like that, dazzled by his fine words, as though you'd never heard the like."

"He was the kindest of men . . ."

"According to you, everyone is kind. . . . By the way," continued Ovsyanikov, turning to his wife, "did you send him . . . well, *you* know?"

Tatyana Ilyinichna nodded.

"Where have you been, these days?" said the old man.

"In town."

"Playing billiards, I suppose, and drinking tea, and strumming on the guitar, skipping round the offices, writing petitions in back rooms, and prancing about with the sons of merchants? Am I right? . . . Tell us!"

"That's about right," said Mitya, with a smile. "Ah yes, I'd almost forgotten: Anton Parfenich Funtikov invites you to dine with him next Sunday."

"I shan't go to see that pot-belly. He'll give us an expensive fish and then put rancid butter on it. Good luck to him!"

"And then I met Feodosya Mikhailovna."

"Which Feodosya d'you mean?"

"The one who belongs to Garpenchenko, the landowner, the one who bought Mikulino by auction. This Feodosya is from Mikulino. She lived in Moscow on quit-rent, worked as a sempstress, and paid her rent regularly, 182½ rubles a year. And she knows her job, too; she got good orders in Moscow. But now Garpenchenko has sent for her and just keeps her here, and won't give her any definite duties. She'd be ready to buy herself out, and has told the master so, but he won't let her know his decision. You, uncle, know Garpenchenko—couldn't you have a word with him about it? . . . Feodosya would pay a good price for her freedom."

"At your expense, eh? Well, all right, I will speak to him, yes. Only I don't know," continued the old man with an expression of disfavor. "This Garpenchenko—may the Lord forgive me—is a sharper: he buys up bills of exchange, and lends out money at interest: he acquires properties under the hammer . . . What ill wind brought him to our part of the world, I'd like to know? Oh, I've had enough of these birds of passage! It's no easy matter to get sense out of him—but anyway we'll see."

"Do your best, uncle."

"All right, I will. But you look out, look out, there! Don't argue . . . God's mercy on you! . . . But just look out in future. Look out or else, by God, you'll come to no good—by God, you'll come to a bad end. I can't carry you on my shoulders all the time. . . . It's not as if I were a man of influence. Well, you can go now, and God bless you."

Mitya went out. Tatyana Ilyinichna followed behind him.

"Give him a good drink of tea, you mollycoddler," Ovsyanikov called after her. "The boy's no fool," he continued, "and he's got a good heart, only I'm worried about him. . . . But I'm sorry to have bored you for so long with trifles."

The door from the hall opened. A little gray-haired man in a velvet coat came in. "Ah, Franz Ivanich!" exclaimed Ovsyanikov; "good day to you! Is God in his mercy treating you well?"

Allow me, dear reader, to introduce this gentleman to you.

Franz Ivanich Lejeune, a landowner of Orel province and a neighbour of mine, had reached the honorable degree of Russian nobleman by a somewhat unusual path. He was born of French parents in Orleans and had set out with Napoleon for the conquest of Russia in the capacity of drummer-boy. At first everything went as smoothly as a knife through butter, and our Frenchman entered Moscow with his head held high. But on the way back poor Monsieur Lejeune, half-frozen and without his drum, fell into the hands of the peasants of Smolensk. The peasants of Smolensk shut him up for the night in an empty clothmill, and on the next morning brought him to a hole cut in the ice beside the weir, and began to request the drummer *de la Grrrande Armée* to oblige them by diving under the ice. Monsieur Lejeune was unable to agree to their suggestion and, in his turn, began to urge the peasants of Smolensk, in the French tongue, to let him go back to Orleans. "*Messieurs*," he said, "I have a mother living there, *une tendre mère*." But the peasants, probably through ignorance of the geographical situation of the city of Orleans, continued proposing to him an underwater journey down the stream of the sinuous river Gniloterka, and had already begun to urge him forward with gentle blows on the vertebrae of his neck and spine, when suddenly, to Lejeune's indescribable joy, the sound of sleigh-bells was heard, and there drove out across the dam an enormous sledge with the brightest of rugs over its unusually high back-seat and with three roan horses harnessed to it. In the sledge sat a stout, ruddy-faced gentleman in a wolf-skin coat.

"What are you doing there?" he asked the peasants.

"We are drowning a Frenchman, sir."

"Oh," replied the gentleman indifferently, and turned away.

"Monsieur! Monsieur!" exclaimed the poor wretch.

"Ah, ah," said the wolfskin-coat reproachfully. "You marched on Russia, you and your twelve tongues, you burnt Moscow—damn you—you dragged down the cross from Ivan the Great and now—*monsyor, monsyor!* Now you have got your tail between your legs. The punishment fits the crime. . . . Go on, Filka-a!"

The horses started off.

"No, stop!" added the landowner. "Hey, you, *monsyor*, d'you know *musik?*"

"*Sauvez-moi, sauvez-moi, mon bon monsieur*," insisted Lejeune.

"There's a fine people for you! Not one of them knows even any Russian. *Musik, musik, savay musik voo? Savay?* Well, answer me! *Comprenay? Savay musik voo? Savay jooay piano?*"

Lejeune at last understood what the landowner was driving at and nodded his head affirmatively: "*Oui, monsieur, oui, oui, je suis musicien, je joue tous les instruments possibles! Oui, monsieur . . . Sauvez moi, monsieur!*"

"Well, you're a lucky devil," rejoined the gentleman. "Let him go, lads, here's twenty copecks to buy yourselves a drink."

"Thank you, sir, thank you kindly. Take him, by all means."

Lejeune was installed in the sledge. He choked for joy, wept, trembled, bowed, thanked the gentleman and his driver and the peasants. He was wearing nothing but a green vest with pink ribbons, though it was a day of crackling frost. The gentleman glanced silently at his numb blue limbs, wrapped the poor wretch in his own fur coat and drove him home. There was a scurrying of serving-folk. The Frenchman was soon warmed, fed, and dressed. The gentleman took him to see his daughters.

"Here, children," he told them. "I have found a teacher for you. You were always nagging at me to have you taught music and French, well here is a Frenchman for you. He plays the piano too. Well, *monsyor*," he continued, pointing at the cheap little piano he'd bought five years before from a Jew, who was really a seller of eau-de-Cologne, "show us your skill. *Jooay!*"

Lejeune sat down with a sinking heart; he had never touched a piano in his life.

"Go on, *jooay, jooay*," repeated the gentleman.

The poor wretch struck the keys in desperation, as he would have done a drum, and played away at random. . . .

"I thought," he used to say afterwards, "that my savior would seize me by the scruff of the neck and throw me out of his house." But, to the extreme amazement of the reluctant improviser, the gentleman, after waiting a moment, patted him approvingly on the shoulder. "Good, good," he said. "I see you can play; go and have a rest now."

Two weeks later Lejeune passed on from this gentleman to another, who was rich and cultivated, and took a fancy to him for his gay and gentle ways. Lejeune married his ward, entered the Government service, became a nobleman, married his daughter to a landowner of the Orel province named Lobyzanyev, a retired dragoon and a writer of verses, and came to settle in Orel province himself. This Lejeune, or, as he is now known, Franz Ivanich, was the gentleman I saw arriving to visit his friend Ovsyanikov.

But perhaps the reader is tired of sitting with me at Ovsyanikov's, and I shall therefore lapse into eloquent silence.

Lgov

"Let's go to Lgov," Ermolai, who is already known to the reader, said to me one day. "We'll shoot all the duck we want there."

Although wild duck present no special attraction to a real sportsman, the temporary lack of other game (it was the beginning of September: the woodcock had not yet arrived, and I was tired of tramping the fields after partridges) led me to take the advice of my hunter and to make my way to Lgov.

Lgov is a big village in the steppe with a very old single-domed stone church and two mills on the marshy stream of the Rosota. Five versts from Lgov this stream turns into a broad pond with thick rushes covering the banks and growing here and there in the middle. This pool, its creeks, and the still depths of its rushes, were the hatching-place and haunt of a countless multitude of duck of every possible kind: mallard, half-mallard, pintail, teal, pochard, and so forth. Small flights were continually circling and hovering over the water, but a shot would put up such clouds that the sportsman involuntarily held his hat with his hand and let out a long-drawn "phew!"

Ermolai and I walked along the pool, but, in the first place, the duck, which is a canny bird, keeps well away from the bank, and secondly, even if some straggling inexperienced teal should expose itself to our fire and fall a victim, our dogs would not have been able to fetch it from the thick rushes: even with the noblest degree of self-denial, they would have been able neither to swim nor to walk on the bottom, but would only have cut their precious noses to no purpose on the sharp edges of the reeds.

"No," said Ermolai at last. "It won't work, we must get a boat. . . . Let's go back to Lgov."

We set off. We had gone only a few paces when we were met by a rather mongrelly pointer which came dashing out of a willow thicket, followed by a man of middle height in a threadbare blue coat, canary waistcoat and *gris de laine* or *bleu d'amour* trousers, the ends of which were carelessly stuck into a pair of leaky boots, with a red handkerchief round his neck, and a single-barrelled gun over his shoulder.

While our dogs, with the Chinese ceremonial which is the special custom of their kind, exchanged sniffs with their new acquaintance, who in evident alarm had lowered his tail, thrown back his ears, and kept circling rapidly round, with knees stiff and teeth bared, the stranger came up to us and made us an extremely polite bow. He looked about twenty-five; his long reddish hair, which was fairly soaked in kvass, stuck out in solid tufts, his small brown eyes had a friendly twinkle in them, his whole face, which was bound up in a black handkerchief as though from toothache, was set in the sweetest of smiles.

"Allow me to introduce myself," he began in a soft wheedling voice. "I am Vladimir, a sportsman of these parts. . . . Hearing of your arrival, and learning that you were bound for the banks of our pool, I decided that, if you had no objection, I would offer you my services."

Vladimir's turn of language was exactly that of a young actor who plays the part of leading man in the provinces. I accepted his offer and, while still on the way to Lgov, managed to find out his history. He was a house-serf who had been given his freedom. In tender youth he had learned music, had then served as a valet, knew his alphabet, had read—so far as I could make out—a few trashy books, and now lived, as so many do in Russia, without a farthing in his pocket, with no steady employment, more or less subsisting on manna from on high. He expressed himself with extreme refinement and was clearly enchanted with his own manners; he was doubtless also a terrible flirt and, in all probability, a successful one, too: Russian girls like fine language. Amongst other things, he gave me to understand that from time to time he visited the neighboring landowners, went calling in town, played Preference, and had friends in the capital. He was a master of the most different types of smile; what suited him best was the modest, restrained one which played on his lips when he was listening to someone else. He would hear you out, agree with you absolutely, but all the same he would never lose the sense of his own dignity and it was as if he wished to let you know that he too, on occasion, had his own opinion to give. Ermolai, like the none too well-educated and in no way subtle fellow that he was, began to address him in the second person singular. You should have seen the mocking smile with which Vladimir said to him: "You, sir . . ."

"Why do you wear a handkerchief round your face?" I asked him. "Have you got toothache?"

"No, sir," he replied. "It's something more serious, the result of carelessness. I had a friend, a good man, sir, but, as some people are, he was far from being a sportsman. Well, sir, one day he says to me: 'My dear friend, take me out shooting, I'm curious to find out wherein the fun of it lies.' As a matter of course, I didn't want to say no to my friend: I myself found him a gun and took him out shooting. Well, sir, we duly had our shooting and finally we decided to take a rest. I sat beneath a tree, but he, on the contrary, started fooling about with his gun and taking aim at myself. I begged him to desist, but he had too little experience to take my advice. A shot rang out, and I lost my chin and the index finger of my right hand."

We had reached Lgov. Vladimir and Ermolai had both decided that it would be impossible to go shooting without a boat.

"Suchok has a punt," observed Vladimir; "but I don't know where he has hidden it. I must run around to see him."

"Who is he?" I asked.

"A man who lives here, nicknamed Suchok."

Vladimir and Ermolai set off to find Suchok. I told them that I would wait for them by the church. As I was looking at the gravestones in the churchyard, I came across a square and blackened urn

with the following inscriptions: CI-GIT THÉOPHILE-HENRI, VI-
COMTE DE BLANGY; on the second side: BENEATH THIS STONE IS
BURIED THE BODY OF A FRENCH SUBJECT, COUNT BLANGY; BORN
1737, DIED 1799, AGED 62; on the third side: PEACE TO HIS DUST;
and on the fourth:

> BENEATH THIS STONE LIES A FRENCH ÉMIGRÉ;
> A MAN OF TALENT AND ILLUSTRIOUS BIRTH.
> MOURNING THE MASSACRE OF WIFE AND FAMILY,
> HE FORSOOK HIS COUNTRY, THE PREY OF TYRANTS;
> REACHING THE SHORES OF RUSSIA,
> HE FOUND A HOSPITABLE ROOF FOR HIS OLD AGE:
> HE TAUGHT THE YOUNG AND SOOTHED THE OLD . . .
> THE SUPREME JUDGE LAID HIM HERE TO REST.

My reflections were interrupted by the arrival of Ermolai, Vladimir, and the man of the strange nickname, Suchok.

Suchok, a bare-legged, shock-headed tatterdemalion, was, I
thought, probably a retired house-serf, aged about sixty.

"Have you got a boat?" I asked.

"Yes," he answered in a hoarse and broken voice. "But it's a very
bad one."

"How so?"

"It's come unstuck; the bolts have come out of their sockets."

"That's nothing," Ermolai put in. "You should caulk it with
oakum."

"One could, of course," agreed Suchok.

"And what do you do?" I asked.

"I am the master-fisherman."

"How is it that you are a fisherman and have a boat in such bad
repair?"

"Because there are no fish in our river."

"Fish don't like brackish marsh water," observed my hunter importantly.

"Well," I said to Ermolai. "Go and find some oakum and mend
the boat for us, only be quick about it."

Ermolai went off.

"So we are likely to go to the bottom, it seems," I said to Vladimir.

"God's mercy on us," he answered. "In any event we may presume that the pool is not deep."

"No, it is not deep," observed Suchok, who had a strange sleepy way of talking. "There's slime and grass at the bottom, it's all covered in grass. There are pot-holes, too, of course."

"But if the grass is so thick," observed Vladimir, "it won't be possible to row."

"And who rows a punt? You have to pole it. I'll go with you, I have got a pole there—or you could use a spade as well."

"It's awkward with a spade, as I suppose that often you can't reach the bottom," said Vladimir.

"It's certainly awkward."

I sat on a tombstone and waited for Ermolai. Vladimir went a little way off, for correctness' sake, and sat down too. Suchok continued to stand where he was, hanging his head, his hands folded behind his back in the traditional attitude.

"Tell me," I began, "have you been a fisherman here for long?"

"It will soon be seven years," he answered, with a start.

"And what was your job before?"

"I was a coachman before."

"And who reduced you from the rank of coachman?"

"The new lady."

"What lady?"

"The lady who bought us. You don't know her, sir: Alena Timofeyevna, a stout lady . . . and not young."

"What gave her the idea of making you into a fisherman?"

"God knows. She came to us from her own estate in Tambov, called the whole staff together and came out to speak to us. First we went and kissed her hand, and she was all right: she didn't get cross . . . Then she began to ask us one after the other what we did and what our jobs were. My turn came, and she asked me what I was. 'A coachman,' I said. 'A coachman? Why, what sort of coachman are you, just look at yourself, what sort of coachman are you? It's not right for you to be a coachman; you must shave your beard

and be my fisherman. When I come, you must provide me with
fish for my table, do you hear? . . .' So since then I have counted as
a fisherman. 'And see that you keep my pond in order.' . . . But how
am I to do that?"

"Whose were you before?"

"We belonged to Sergei Sergeich Pekhterev. He inherited us. He
was not our master for long, either, only six years altogether. It was
with him that I was a coachman. . . . Not in town—he had other
coachmen there, but in the country."

"Had you been a coachman since you were young?"

"No, indeed. I became a coachman under Sergei Sergeich. Before that I was a cook—not a town cook, either, but just in the
country."

"Whose cook were you?"

"My former master's, Afanasy Nefeditch, the uncle of Sergei
Sergeich. He bought Lgov, Afanasy Nefeditch did, and Sergei Sergeich inherited it from him."

"From whom did he buy it?"

"From Tatyana Vasilyevna."

"Which one?"

"The one who died last year near Bolkhovo. . . . That's to say, near
Karachev. She died an old maid . . . she never married. Did you not
know her, sir? We came to her from her father, Vasily Semyonich.
She had us for a long time. . . . Twenty years or so."

"You were her cook?"

"Yes, first I was cook, and then I became coffee-server."

"You became what?"

"Coffee-server."

"What kind of job is that?"

"I don't know, sir. I stood by the sideboard and was called Anton
instead of Kuzma. It was the mistress's order."

"Your real name is Kuzma?"

"Yes."

"And you were coffee-server all the time?"

"No, not all the time: I was an *achtyeur* too."

"Indeed?"

"Certainly I was . . . I acted in the theater. Our mistress had a private theater."

"What sort of parts did you play?"

"I beg your pardon, sir?"

"What did you do in the theater?"

"Oh, don't you know? They would take me and dress me up; then I would walk, all dressed up, or stand, or sit, as the case might be. They'd tell me what to say—and I'd say it. Once I played the part of a blind man. . . . They put a pea under each of my eyelids . . . Yes, that's how it was."

"And what were you after that?"

"Then I became a cook again."

"Why did they make you a cook again?"

"Because my brother ran away."

"And what were you when you were with the father of your first mistress?"

"I had various jobs. First I was a page, then I was a postilion, then a gardener, then a whipper-in."

"A whipper-in? . . . and you went out hunting, too?"

"Yes, I did, and I hurt myself badly: I was thrown and damaged my horse. Our old master was very strict; he had me beaten, and sent me to a cobbler in Moscow to learn a trade."

"How was that? You couldn't have been a child when you became a whipper-in?"

"I was twenty-something at the time."

"Fancy teaching you a trade at that age."

"It must have been all right, it must have been possible, if the master ordered it. Luckily he soon died and they brought me back to the country."

"And when did you learn your skill as a cook?"

Suchok raised his thin, yellowish face and chuckled: "What, lessons for that, too? . . . Why, even women can cook!"

"Well," I said. "You've seen a thing or two, Kuzma, in your time. What are you doing now as fisherman, if you haven't got any fish?"

"I don't complain, sir. In fact it's a mercy that they have made me a fisherman. Why, the mistress ordered them to put another old chap like me—Andrei Pupyr—into the paper factory as a pulper. It's wicked, she says, to eat bread without working for it. And Pupyr had hoped for some special favor: he had a young cousin who worked as a clerk in the mistress's office, and promised to speak to the mistress about him and to remind her of him. And a fine way he reminded her! . . . And with my own eyes I had seen Pupyr going down on his knees to this cousin of his."

"Have you a family? Did you get married?"

"No, sir, I did not. The late Tatyana Vasilyevna—may God rest her soul!—allowed none of us to marry. 'God forbid,' she used to say. 'Don't I live unmarried? What's all the fuss about? Whatever do they want to get married for?'"

"What d'you live on now? D'you get any wages?"

"Wages? Certainly not, sir . . . they give me food—and I am quite content, thank God. May God give the mistress a long life!"

Ermolai returned.

"The boat is mended," he announced sulkily. "Go and get the pole, you! . . ."

Suchok ran off for the pole. Throughout my conversation with the poor old man, the sportsman Vladimir had been gazing at him with a contemptuous smile.

"A stupid old man," he said, when Suchok had left us. "Completely uneducated, a peasant and nothing more, sir. . . . Not fit to be called a house-serf . . . and yet how he boasted. . . . Just fancy him as an actor! I ask you! You need never have bothered with him, sir, or troubled to talk to him!"

Within a quarter of an hour we were sitting in Suchok's punt. (We had left the dogs in a hut in the care of Yegudil the coachman.) We were not very comfortable, but sportsmen are an uncomplaining race. Suchok stood in the blunt stern-end and "poled"; Vladimir and I sat on the thwart; Ermolai installed himself forward, right in the bows. In spite of the oakum, water soon appeared under our feet. Luckily it was a calm day and the pond lay as if asleep.

We made fairly slow progress. The old man had difficulty in pulling his long pole out of the sticky mud, as it was all tangled with green strands of water-grass; masses of round water-lily leaves further hindered the course of our boat. Eventually we reached the rushes, and the fun began. The duck rose noisily and fairly wrenched themselves from the surface, startled by our unexpected appearance in their realm; shots rang out together after them, and it was fun to see the short-tailed fowl turn a somersault in the air and come splashing down heavily on to the water. We did not manage to pick up all the duck we had shot, of course: the lightly wounded ones dived away; others, killed outright, fell so deep in the rushes that even the lynx eyes of Ermolai could not make them out; but all the same, by dinner-time, our boat was filled to the gunwales with game.

Much to Ermolai's satisfaction, Vladimir shot far from well and, after every miss, expressed astonishment, inspected his gun, blew through it, looked perplexed, and finally explained to us why he had missed. Ermolai, as he always did, shot triumphantly; I, fairly badly, as usual. Suchok looked at us with the eyes of a man who has been in domestic service since his youth, occasionally shouted: "Look, look there's another one!"—and constantly scratched his back—not with his hand, but with a wriggle of his shoulders. The weather remained splendid; round white clouds floated quietly past overhead and were clearly mirrored in the water; the reeds rustled around us; here and there the pond glittered like steel in the sun. We were on the point of turning back to the village when suddenly something rather unpleasant happened. For some time we had noticed that the water was slowly rising inside the boat. Vladimir had been given the task of bailing it out with a scoop which my far-sighted hunter had spirited away, against possible emergencies, from an unsuspecting peasant woman. All went well, so long as Vladimir remembered his duties. But at the end of our shoot, as if by way of farewell, the duck began to rise in such masses that we hardly had time to load. In the heat of the fusillade we paid no attention to the condition of our punt—until suddenly, at a violent movement by Ermolai, who was trying to reach a dead bird and leaning across the gunwale with all the weight of his body, our ancient vessel listed over, took a plunge, and solemnly went to the bottom, luckily not in deep water. We shouted, but it was already too late: within a moment we were standing with water up to our throats, surrounded by the floating bodies of dead duck. To this day I cannot remember without a chuckle the pale, startled faces of my companions (probably my own face was not particularly ruddy at that moment either); but, at the time, I confess that it never occurred to me to laugh. Each of us held his gun over his head, and Suchok, doubtless from a habit of copying his masters, lifted his pole in the air. The first to break the silence was Ermolai.

"The devil and all!" he muttered, spitting into the water. "That's a fine thing to happen! And you, you old scoundrel!" he added with feeling, turning to Suchok, "what sort of boat is this of yours?"

"I'm sorry," whispered the old man.

"And you're a good one, too," continued my hunter, turning in Vladimir's direction. "What were you looking at? Why weren't you bailing? . . . you . . ."

But Vladimir was in no state to reply: he was trembling like a leaf, his teeth chattered without meeting, and he wore a completely witless smile. What had become of all his eloquence, his feeling for the finer shades of decency, his sense of his own importance?

The wretched punt wobbled feebly beneath our feet. . . . In the moment of shipwreck the water seemed to us extremely cold, but we soon became used to it. When the first shock had passed, I looked round; on all sides, ten paces from us, the reeds began; in the distance, over their tops, the bank could be seen. It looks bad, I thought.

"What shall we do about it?" I asked Ermolai.

"Well, we'll see; this is no place to spend the night," answered he. "Here, you, hold the gun," he said to Vladimir.

Vladimir obeyed without demur.

"I'll go and look for a ford," continued Ermolai confidently, as if a ford was bound to exist in every lake—took the pole from Suchok, and set off in the direction of the bank, carefully sounding the bottom as he went.

"Can you swim?" I asked him.

"No, I can't," came his voice from behind the rushes.

"Very well, then, he'll drown," observed Suchok indifferently.

From the beginning he had been afraid, not of the danger, but of our wrath, and now, completely reassured, simply let out a puff from time to time and, so it seemed, felt in no way impelled to change his situation.

"And will perish to no avail," added Vladimir mournfully.

Ermolai did not return for more than an hour. That hour seemed to us an eternity. At first we and he exchanged cries with a good heart; then he began to answer our shouts less often, and finally he was completely silent. In the village the bells were ringing for evening service. We didn't talk, and tried not to look at each other. Duck flew over our heads, some prepared to settle beside us, but suddenly shot straight up into the air, quacked and flew away. We began to feel numb. Suchok blinked as though he was getting ready to go to sleep.

Finally, to our indescribable joy, Ermolai returned.

"Well?"

"I got to the bank; I found the ford. Let's go."

We were all for setting off at once; but first Ermolai put his hand under the water, brought a line out of his pocket, made the dead duck fast to it by the legs, took both ends of the line between his teeth and set off ahead, with Vladimir behind him, and me behind Vladimir. Suchok brought up the rear. It was about two hundred yards to the bank and Ermolai went boldly and unhesitatingly forward (so well had he made out the way), with only an occasional cry of "Keep to the left—there's a pothole on the right!" or "Keep to the right, you'll sink in if you go to the left." . . . At times the water rose to our throats and twice poor Suchok, who was shorter than the rest of us, choked and gave off bubbles. "Hey, hey, hey!" Ermolai shouted at him menacingly, and Suchok scrambled and floundered and jumped and somehow escaped to a shallower place, but even in these extremities could not make up his mind to take hold of the skirts of my coat. Exhausted, dirty, dripping, we reached the bank at last.

Two hours later, having dried ourselves to the best of our ability, we were all sitting in a big hay-shed preparing to have supper. Yegudil the coachman, an extremely slow, phlegmatic, deliberate,

sleepy fellow, stood in the gateway and diligently plied Suchok
with snuff. (I have noticed that in Russia coachmen very soon make
friends with each other.) Suchok sniffed with frenzy, to vomiting
point: he spat and coughed and was clearly enjoying himself. Vladimir looked sad, leant his head on one side, and said little. Ermolai
was cleaning our guns. The dogs were wagging their tails at top
speed, in anticipation of their groats; the horses were stamping and
neighing in the shed. . . . The sun was setting; its last rays ran out in
broad crimson stripes; the sky was full of golden clouds that grew
ever more fine-drawn, like a rinsed and combed-out fleece . . . From
the village came the sound of singing.

Bezhin Meadow

IT WAS A BEAUTIFUL JULY DAY, ONE OF THOSE DAYS WHICH COME only after long spells of settled weather. From the earliest morning the sky is clear; the dawn does not blaze and flame, but spreads out in a gentle blush. Instead of the flaming incandescence that goes with sultriness and drought, or the dark crimson that precedes the storm, the sun has a bright and friendly radiance, as it swims peacefully up from behind a long, narrow cloud, shines out briskly, and then veils itself in the lilac-colored mist. The tenuous upper edge of the spreading cloud sparkles with a serpentine brilliance, like that of beaten silver. But now the dancing beams come shooting out again—and gaily, grandly, as if on wings, the mighty luminary emerges. About midday there usually appears a multitude of high, round clouds, golden-gray, with edges of tender white. Like islands, scattered across a boundless and brimming river, which surrounds them with deep, translucent expanses of an even blueness, they scarcely stir; farther off, towards the horizon, they concentrate, crowd together, there is no more blueness to be seen between them; but the clouds themselves are of the same azure as the heaven, they are penetrated through and through with light and warmth. The color of the horizon, a pale and floating lilac color, remains unchanged the whole day, and uniform all around; there is no darkening or deepening to foretell a storm; sometimes, here and there, there are bluish shafts falling down, betokening the passage of a hardly perceptible shower. Towards evening, these clouds vanish; the last of them, blackish and vague as smoke, lie with a pink curling face turned to the setting sun; over the place where it disappears, as quietly as it rose into the heavens, a scarlet radiance stands for a while over the darkening earth, and, trembling gently, like a carefully carried taper, the evening star begins to burn. On such days, all colors are softened; they are clear, but not brilliant; they are tinged with a gentleness that is somehow touching. Such days may be scorching-hot, and the steam may rise from the sloping fields; but the wind disperses and breaks up the accumulated sultriness, and whirlwinds—sure sign of settled weather—march in tall white pillars along the tracks across the plough-land. In the dry, clean air there is a smell of wormwood, of rye-harvest, and of buckwheat; even an hour before nightfall you feel no dampness. This is the weather that the husbandman needs to gather in his crop. . . .

Once, on just such a day as this, I was shooting blackcock in the district of Chern, in the government of Tula. I had found and shot a fair quantity of game; a bulging game-bag cut mercilessly into my shoulder; but the sunset glow was already dying down, and in the air, still light, although no longer flushed with the rays of the vanished sun, cold shadows were beginning to deepen and to spread, when at last I decided to return home. At a quick pace I passed through a long brake of undergrowth, climbed a hill and, instead of the familiar plateau which I expected, with a clump of oaks to the right and a little white church in the distance, I saw a completely different, unknown landscape. Below my feet ran a narrow valley; immediately opposite, a dense wood of poplar rose in a steep wall. I stopped in perplexity and looked around. . . . Aha! I thought, I've come out in quite the wrong place, I've struck too far to the right; and, amazed at my own mistake, I went swiftly down the hill. I was immediately enveloped in a disagreeable, stagnant dampness, as if I had passed into a cellar; the thick tall grass at the bottom of the valley, dripping wet, made a pale, even tablecloth all round; walking over it was somehow an eerie business. I scrambled out to the other side with all speed and struck off to the left along the poplar wood. Bats were already flitting above the sleeping treetops, wheeling mysteriously and quivering against the dim radiance of the sky; a belated hawk flew briskly past on his straight, high course, hurrying back to his nest. As soon as I come out at that corner, I thought to myself, I shall strike the track at once; but I've gone a good mile out of my way.

Eventually I reached the corner of the wood, but found no sign of any track there: stunted, straggling undergrowth stretched far and wide before me, and behind it, away in the distance, could be seen an empty plain. I halted again. What an extraordinary thing. . . . Where on earth was I?—I began going over again in my mind the course I had taken during the day. . . . "Oh! This must be Parakhin spinney," I exclaimed at last. "Yes! and over there must be Sindeyev wood . . . However did I manage to get here? So far out of my way? . . . Very odd! Now I must bear to the right again."

I went to the right, through brushwood. Meanwhile night approached and grew on me like a storm-cloud; it was as if darkness was welling up from the ground on all sides, with the mists of evening, and streaming down from above at the same time. I fell in with a rough, overgrown path, and went along it, keeping a sharp look-out ahead. Soon it was all dark and still around me—there was only the call of quails from time to time. A small night-bird, flying low on soft and soundless wings, almost knocked into me and shied off to one side. I came to the end of the brushwood and continued along the edge of a field. It was already difficult to distinguish distant objects; the field made a white blur around me; beyond it was a gloomy, towering mass of darkness which looked nearer every moment. My footfalls sounded muffled in the stagnant air. The sky, which had become drained of color, began to grow blue again—but, this time, with the blue of night. Against it, little stars were stirring and twinkling.

What I had taken for a wood turned out to be a dark, round hillock. "Then where on earth am I?" I repeated again, aloud, halted for the third time, and looked inquiringly at my piebald-yellow gun-dog Dianka, decidedly the cleverest of all the four-legged creation. But the cleverest of all the four-legged creation only wagged its tail, gave a sad twinkle of its tired eyes and had no sort of practical advice to offer. I felt ashamed in front of it, and set off ahead in desperation, as if I had suddenly guessed which way to go, skirted the hill, and found myself in a gentle hollow in the midst of cultivation. A strange feeling immediately came over me. The hollow was like an almost symmetrical cauldron with sloping sides. At the bottom of it rose, bolt upright, several large white stones, which seemed to have crept down there for a secret conclave, and the whole place had such a deaf-and-dumb feeling, the sky hung so flatly and gloomily above it, that my heart shrank. Some little creature was squeaking faintly and plaintively among the stones. I hastily came out again on to the hillock. Hitherto I had not given up all hope of finding the way home; but here I finally convinced myself that I was completely lost and, no longer attempting to recognize the surrounding landscape, which was almost completely sunk in darkness, boldly set a straight course by the stars. . . . I went on in this way for about half an hour, plodding forward with difficulty. It seemed to me that I had never been in such a desert in all my life; there was not a twinkle of light to be seen, not a sound to be heard. One sloping hill succeeded another, fields stretched endlessly one after another, bushes fairly started up from the earth under my nose. I was still walking, and already preparing to lie down somewhere until morning came, when suddenly I felt myself on the edge of a fearful precipice.

I quickly withdrew my foot in mid-air, and, through the hardly penetrable darkness of the night, I made out, far below me, an enormous plain. A broad river bounded it in a receding arc; steely gleams of water, flashing faintly here and there, marked its course. The hill on which I was standing dropped sharply in an almost perpendicular cliff; its massive outline showed up blackly against the bluishness of the airy void, and just below me, in the angle of cliff and plain, beside the river, which at this point stood in a dark and motionless mirror, right at the foot of the hill, two fires close beside each other were blazing redly and smoking. Around them, people were stirring, shadows were swaying, and sometimes the front half of a curly head was brightly illuminated. . . .

At last I recognized where I was. This field rejoices, in our neighborhood, in the name of Bezhin meadow. . . . But to return home was quite impossible, especially by night; my legs were foundering beneath me from exhaustion. I decided to go down to the fires and, in company with the people whom I had seen, and took to be drovers, to wait for the dawn. I got safely down, but had not yet let go of the last branch I had seized, when suddenly two big white shaggy dogs hurled themselves at me, barking evilly. The ringing voices of children sounded from around the fires; and two or three boys rose quickly from the ground. I shouted back in answer to their questioning cries. They ran towards me, at once calling off the dogs, who were particularly surprised by the sight of my Dianka, and I went up to them.

I was wrong in taking the people sitting round the fires for drovers. They were just peasant-lads from the neighboring village, who were minding horses. In the hot summer weather it is the custom in our part of the world to turn the horses out at night to graze in the fields: in daytime the flies and bluebottles would give them no peace. Taking the horses out towards evening time, and driving them back at dawn, is a great treat for the peasant-lads. Sitting bareheaded and in old coats on the liveliest nags, they dash off with gay shouts and cries, waving arms and legs, jumping high in the air and laughing at the tops of their voices. The light dust rises in a yellow pillar and blows along the road; from afar you can hear the jolly clatter of hooves, the horses gallop with ears pricked; in front of them all, with tail up, continuously changing his pace, gallops a shaggy sorrel with his tangled mane full of burrs.

I told the boys that I had lost my way, and sat down beside them. They asked me whence I had come, grew silent and made room for me. We talked for a while. I lay down beneath a bush which had been eaten bare, and began to look around me. It was a marvellous picture: around the fires a circle of reddish, reflected light trembled and seemed to die away into the darkness; at times the flame blazed up and scattered swift gleams beyond the edges of the circle; a thin tongue of light licked the bare willow-twigs and disappeared in a flash—long, sharp shadows, bursting in for a moment in their turn, ran right up to the fires: it was the war of darkness with light. Sometimes, when the flame burnt lower and the circle of light narrowed, from the nearer darkness there would suddenly emerge a horse's head, a bay head with crooked markings, or a plain gray one, and would give us an attentive, dull look, while busily munching the long grass, then would drop back again and immediately vanish. But one could still hear the horse munching and snorting away. From the lighted circle it was difficult to make out what was happening in the shadows, and therefore everything close at hand seemed hidden by a blackish curtain; but farther off, towards the horizon, long shapes could be discerned dimly as hills and woods. The clear, dark sky stood, solemn and immeasurably high above us, in all its mysterious magnificence. It caught one deliciously at the heart to breathe that unmistakable, languorous, cool breath—the breath of a summer night in Russia. Around us there was hardly a sound to be heard . . . only sometimes, from the nearby river, the sudden loud splash of a big fish, and the low murmuring of the rushes on the bank, hardly stirred by the touch of a ripple . . . only the fires crackling away faintly.

The boys sat round them, and with them the two dogs which had so much wanted to eat me up. They were still unable to reconcile themselves to my presence, and, sleepily narrowing their eyes and looking sideways at the fire, gave an occasional growl which had an extraordinary accent of self-importance, began with a growl and finished with a faint whine, as if regretting the impossibility of doing as they wished. The boys were five in all: Fedya, Pavel, Ilyusha, Kostya, and Vanya. (I learned their names as they talked, and propose now to make the reader acquainted with them.)

The first, and eldest of them all, Fedya, seemed to be about fourteen. He was a well-built lad, with handsome, fine, smallish features, fair, curly hair, bright eyes, and a permanent smile that was half-jolly, half-absent. By all appearances he came of a well-to-do family and had ridden out to the field, not because he had to, but just for the fun of it. He wore a gay cotton shirt with a yellow pattern; a small, new overcoat, thrown on carelessly, stayed with difficulty on his narrow shoulders; from his blue belt hung a comb. His boots, with very low tops, were really his—not his father's. The second boy, Pavel, had a shock of black hair, gray eyes, broad cheek-bones, a pale, pock-marked face, a large but regular mouth, an enormous pot-head, and an awkward, stocky body. He was an unprepossessing lad, there were no two ways about it, but all the same I liked him: he had an intelligent, direct look, and there was a note of strength in his voice. His dress was nothing to be proud of: it consisted simply of a plain blouse and a patched pair of trousers. The face of the third, Ilyusha, was rather nondescript: hook-nosed, long, short-sighted, it expressed a certain dull, sickly concentration; his tight lips never moved, his contracted brows never parted—he seemed all the time to be keeping his eyes narrowed against the fire. His yellow, almost white, hair stuck out in sharp tufts from beneath a low felt cap, which now and again he took in both hands and rammed down on his ears. He wore a new pair of rope-slippers and leggings; a stout cord, wound three times round his waist, elaborately fastened his neat black smock. He and Pavel looked no more than twelve. The fourth lad, Kostya, was about ten, and excited my curiosity by his sad and thoughtful look. His face was small, thin, freckled, sharp-chinned as a squirrel's; I could hardly make out his lips; but a strange impression was produced by his big, black, liquidly brilliant eyes; it was as if they wanted to say something for which no tongue—or at least not his—had any words. He was small and punily built and rather poorly dressed. The last one, Vanya, I had at first not even noticed; he was lying on the ground, quietly curled up under a sheet of matting, and only occasionally stuck out from beneath it his reddish, curly head. This lad was no more than seven.

So I lay under a bush to one side and looked at the boys. A small pot hung over one of the fires; in it potatoes were cooking. Pavel was keeping an eye on them and, on his knees, was prodding with a splinter in the boiling water. Fedya lay propped on his elbow, with the skirts of his coat thrown open. Ilyusha sat beside Kostya, his eyes still narrowed and intense; Kostya, with slightly drooping head, was gazing far away into the distance. Vanya never stirred beneath his matting. I pretended to be asleep. Gradually the boys got talking again.

At first they chatted of this and that, of to-morrow's duties, of the horses; but suddenly Fedya turned to Ilyusha, and, as if resuming an interrupted conversation, put a question to him.

"Well, so you really did see the ghost?"

"No, I never saw him; you can't see him," answered Ilyusha, in a low, hoarse voice, the sound of which went to perfection with the expression on his face. "But I heard him, and I wasn't the only one, either."

"But where does he walk?" asked Pavel.

"In the old paper-mill."

"Do you really work in a paper-mill?"

"Certainly we do. My brother Avdyushka and I work in the pulping-rooms."

"I say!—factory workers! . . ."

"Well, how was it that you heard him?" asked Fedya.

"It was like this. It happened to me and my brother Avdyushka and Fyodor from Mikheyev and Squinting Ivashka and the other Ivashka, the one from Red Hills, and Ivashka from Sukhorukov, too—and other boys were there as well; there were about ten of us boys altogether—the whole shift, all complete. Well, it happened that we spent the night in the paper-mill, that is, it didn't happen just like that, but Nazarov, the foreman, kept us in: 'What's the use,' he says, 'of you traipsing all the way home, my lads? There's plenty of work to-morrow, so you'd better not go home.' So we stayed and all lay down together, and Avdyushka started off and said: 'Well, boys,' he says: 'suppose the ghost comes? . . .' and he didn't finish saying it, Avdyushka didn't, when suddenly somebody started walking, over our heads; we were lying downstairs, and he was walking up aloft by the wheel. We listen: he walks, the planks fairly bend and creak beneath him; he passes over our heads; suddenly the water beside the wheel begins to ripple and ripple and knock and knock against the wheel and the wheel begins to turn; and yet the flanges of the water-inlet were closed. We were amazed—who could have lifted them and let the water through? Anyway the wheel turned and turned and then stopped. Then *he* walked again, to the door up aloft, and started coming downstairs, down he came, as if there was no hurry about it; the treads fairly groaned beneath him, too; well, he came up to our door, and waited and waited—then suddenly the door flew wide open. We started up, and stared—there was nothing there. Suddenly, look, the net on one of the tubs began to move, came up, dropped and floated and floated about in the air as if someone was stirring with it, then went back to its place. Then the hook of another tub came off its nail, then went back on to the nail again. Then someone seemed to go to the door and suddenly started coughing and sort of bleating, like a sheep, and quite loud, too. . . . We had all fallen into a heap together and each of us was trying to get underneath the others . . . Goodness, how scared we were!"

"Just fancy!" said Pavel. "Why did he start coughing, though?"

"I don't know; perhaps because of the damp."

They were all silent for a while.

"Well," asked Fedya, "are the potatoes done?"

Pavel felt them.

"No, they're not done yet. . . . Do you hear the splash?" he added, turning his face in the direction of the river. "Must be a pike. . . . There was a shooting star."

"Now I'll tell you a story, boys," said Kostya in his little tiny voice. "Listen to the story that I heard father tell the other day."

"Well, we're listening," said Fedya with a protective, condescending look.

"You know Gavrila, the village carpenter?"

"Yes."

"But d'you know why he is always so glum and silent? This is why he is so glum; once he went, father said, he went into the forest, to gather nuts, so he went into the forest to gather nuts, and lost his way. He walked on and on, boys—but no, he couldn't find the way; and night was already on him. So he sat down under a tree; all right, he said, I'll wait for the morning—he sat down and dozed off to sleep. So he dozed off to sleep, and suddenly he heard someone calling him. He looked—there was nobody. He dozes off to sleep again—and again they call him. He looks again, he looks; and in front of him on a branch sits a water-fairy, swinging, and calling him, and laughing, and dying of laughter, and the moon was shining bright, so bright and clear it shone, that you could see everything. So she called him, and she was so bright as she sat on the branch,

and so white, like a dace or a gudgeon—or is it a carp, which is
that whitish, silvery color? And so, boys, Gavrila the carpenter fairly
died of fright, but she, why, she just laughed and went on beckoning
him to her with her hand. So Gavrila got up and started to do as the
water-fairy said, but God must have warned him: he made the sign
of the Cross. . . . But how difficult that was for him to do! It seemed
that his hand was just like stone and would not stir. . . . Oh, it was
the devil and all! . . . Well, when he made the sign of the Cross, the
fairy stopped laughing and suddenly began to cry. She cried, boys,
she wiped her eyes with her hair, and her hair was as green as hemp.
So Gavrila looked and looked at her and began to ask her: 'What are
you crying for, you green thing of the forest?' And the water-fairy
said to him: 'If you hadn't crossed yourself,' she says, 'you would
have lived with me merrily for ever; but I am crying and grieving
because you crossed yourself; and I won't grieve alone, either: you
too shall grieve for ever.' Then she vanished, and Gavrila understood
at once how to get out of the forest. And ever since then he has been
going about all glum."

"Well!" said Fedya after a short pause. "But how could such an
evil thing of the forest harm a Christian soul—after all, he didn't
obey her?"

"Yes, you well may ask," said Kostya. "And Gavrila said that she
had a thin, sad little voice, like a toad's."

"Did your father tell that story himself?" continued Fedya.

"Yes. I was lying on the shelf and heard it all."

"What a strange thing! Why should he be glum? . . . She must
have liked him, since she called him."

"She liked him all right," agreed Ilyusha. "Of course, she wanted
to tickle him, that's what she wanted. That's their way, these water-
fairies."

"There ought to be water-fairies here, too," observed Fedya.

"No," answered Kostya; "not in a wholesome, open spot like
this. The only thing is, though, that the river is near."

They were all silent. Suddenly, away in the distance, came a
drawn-out, ringing, almost plaintive sound, one of those mysterious night-sounds which issue out sometimes from the depth of si-

lence, rise, hang in the air and slowly die away at last. You listen more intently—there is nothing there, but the resonance remains. It seemed that someone had cried out, far, far away, right under the horizon, and that then someone else answered from the forest with a thin, sharp laugh, and that a low whistle went hissing down the river. The boys exchanged glances, and trembled.

"The power of the Cross be with us!" whispered Ilyusha.

"Oh, you lot of crows!" exclaimed Pavel. "What are you jumping at? Look, the potatoes are done." They all went up to the pot and began to eat the steaming potatoes. Only Vanya never stirred. "What's the matter with you?" said Pavel.

Still Vanya never stirred from under his matting. The pot was soon quite empty.

"Have you heard, boys," began Ilyusha, "what happened with us the other day at Varnavitsy?"

"At the dam?" asked Fedya.

"Yes, yes, at the broken dam. There's a haunted place for you—haunted, and airless, too. All around it is broken ground, and the ravines are full of snakes."

"Well, what happened? Tell us. . . ."

"This is what happened. You may not know it, Fedya, but there's a drowned man buried there. He was drowned long, long ago, when the pool was still deep; only his grave still shows, and even that, hardly: just a little mound. . . . Well, the other day, the agent sends for the kennelman Ermil, and says: 'Go to the post office, Ermil.' Ermil is always driving to the post; his dogs all starve to death: somehow or other he can't keep them alive—never could, and yet he's a good kennelman, everybody says so. So Ermil went to the post and stayed too long in town and, when he drove back, he was tight. It was night, and bright moonlight. . . . So Ermil rides across the dam: that's how his way took him. He rides across, Ermil the kennelman does, and sees, on the drowned man's grave, a pretty, curly, white lamb, walking. So Ermil thinks: well, I'll take him—why should he be left like that? So he goes down and takes the lamb in his arms. And the lamb doesn't mind a bit. So Ermil comes up to his horse, but the horse shies away from him, and snorts, and shakes his head; but he quietens him down, mounts with the lamb, and rides off holding the lamb in front of him. He looks at the lamb, and the lamb looks him straight in the eyes. Ermil the kennelman feels there is something uncanny about him. Why, he thinks, I don't ever remember a lamb looking a chap in the eyes like that; but never mind; and he begins to stroke the fleece, and say: 'Baa-lamb, baa-lamb!' But then the lamb suddenly bares his teeth and answers him back: 'Baa-lamb, baa-lamb. . . .'"

The story-teller had hardly uttered this last word, when suddenly both dogs leapt up and with a burst of barking rushed away from the fire and vanished into the darkness. The boys all jumped with fright. Vanya sprung up from under his matting, and Pavel darted off shouting after the dogs. Their barking quickly grew more distant. . . . We could hear the restless hooves of frightened horses. Pavel shouted loudly: "Gray! Beetle!" After a few moments the barking stopped. Pavel's voice could be heard, already some way off. . . . A little time went by; the boys exchanged puzzled glances as if expecting something to happen. . . . Suddenly came the sound of a galloping horse; it stopped sharp at the very fireside and, holding on by the mane, Pavel jumped nimbly down. The two dogs came darting into the circle of firelight as well, and sat down at once with their red tongues hanging out.

"What was it? What was the matter?" asked the boys.

"Nothing," answered Pavel, waving his hand at the horse. "The dogs just scented something. I thought it was a wolf," he added in an indifferent voice, breathing quickly and full-chestedly.

I found myself involuntarily admiring Pavel. He was splendid at that moment. His ugly face, animated by the gallop, blazed with cool audacity and firm resolution. Without a stick in his hand, at night, he had ridden out alone after a wolf, without turning a hair. . . . That's a fine boy, I thought, as I looked at him.

"Well, did you see them, the wolves?" asked Kostya the coward.

"There are always lots of them about here," answered Pavel, "but they're only troublesome in winter."

He settled down again in front of the fire. Sitting on the ground, he propped his hand on the shaggy neck of one of the dogs and for a while the delighted animal never moved its head, but looked sideways at Pavel with grateful pride.

Vanya huddled up again under the matting.

"But that's a terrible story you told us, Ilyusha," said Fedya, who, as the son of a well-to-do peasant, was the right one to call the tune (while saying little himself, as if afraid of cheapening his dignity). "And some evil spirit made the dogs bark like that. . . . I'd certainly heard that the place was haunted."

"Varnavitsy? . . . I should say it is! the old master is supposed to have been seen there more than once—the late master. They say he walks in a coat with long skirts and groans all the time and looks for something on the ground. Grandfather Trofimich met him once, and asked him: 'What is it, Ivan Ivanich, sir, that your worship is looking for on the ground?'"

"He asked him?" interrupted Fedya in astonishment.

"Yes, he did."

"Well, Trofimich is a stout fellow to have done that! And what answer did he get?"

"'I am looking for saxifrage,' he says: and he says it in such a flat, flat voice: 'saxifrage.' 'But, Ivan Ivanich, sir, what do you want with saxifrage?' 'The grave presses hard on me, Trofimich,' he says. 'I want to get out and away. . . .'"

"Fancy that!" remarked Fedya. "As if he hadn't lived enough."

"That's very strange!" said Kostya. "I thought you could only see the dead on All-Hallows day."

"You can see the dead at any hour of the day or night," asserted Ilyusha with conviction. So far as I could observe, he seemed to know all the village lore better than his fellows . . . "But on All-Hallows day you can see a living man too whose turn it is to die in the same year. All you have to do is to sit at night at the porch of the church and keep on looking at the road. The people who go past you on the road are those who are going to die in the same year. Ulyana in our village sat up like that last year."

"Well, and did she see anybody?" asked Kostya curiously.

"Certainly she did. First of all she sat for a long, long while and never saw or heard anyone; she only thought she heard a dog barking, barking away somewhere the whole time . . . Suddenly she looks, and along the road comes a boy wearing nothing but a shirt; she looks closer, and it's Ivashka Fedoseyev going by . . ."

"The one who died in the spring?" Fedya interrupted.

"Yes, that's the one. He was walking along without lifting his head. But Ulyana recognizes him. . . . And then she looks—a woman is walking past. She looks and looks—and good Lord!—it's she herself, Ulyana herself, walking along the road."

"Really herself?" asked Fedya.

"Yes, by God, herself."

"Well, what about it? She still hasn't died."

"The year isn't up yet. But you just look at her. Her soul only just hangs on to her body."

They all fell silent again. Pavel threw a handful of dry twigs on the fire. They showed up sharp and black against the sudden blaze of flame, crackled, smoked, and started to shrivel and lift their charred ends. Flickering and trembling, the reflection of the blaze struck out in all directions, especially upwards. Suddenly, out of nowhere, a white pigeon flew straight into this reflection, pulled up in fright, hovered, all suffused with the warm glow, and vanished with a whirr of wings.

"He must have escaped from home," observed Pavel. "Now he'll fly until he strikes something, and wherever he does he'll stay until daybreak."

"Why, Pavel," said Kostya, "wasn't that a just soul flying to heaven?"

Pavel threw another handful of twigs on the fire. "Perhaps," he said at length.

"But tell me, Pavel," began Fedya, "in your village, too, in Shalamovo, did you see the heavenly portent?"*

"When the sun hid itself? Of course we did."

"I suppose you were frightened, too?"

"Yes, and we were not the only ones. Our master, although he told us beforehand that there would be a portent, yet, when it got

---

* This is what the peasants in our part of the country call an eclipse. —*Author.*

dark, it seems he got so scared himself, you wouldn't believe it. And in the servants' quarters, as soon as it got dark, the cook went and broke all the pots in the oven with the oven-fork: 'Who's going to eat now,' she says, 'now the end of the world has come?' So the soup was all spilled. And in our village they were saying that white wolves would run about the earth and eat people up, and birds of prey would fly about, and that we would see Trishka* himself."

"Who is Trishka?" asked Kostya.

"Don't you know?" took up Ilyusha excitedly. "Where do you come from, not to know about Trishka? They must all be stay-at-homes in your village, that's what they must be! Trishka's a marvellous sort of man who's going to come one day; such a marvellous sort of man that you won't be able to take hold of him or do anything to him, such a marvellous man he'll be that some Christian folk will want to get hold of him, they'll go at him with sticks, they'll surround him, but he'll lead their eyes astray, so that they'll start beating each other. Say they put him in prison, he'll ask for a drink of water in a bowl; they'll bring him the bowl, and he'll dive into it and vanish right away. They'll throw him in chains, but he'll clap his hands and the chains'll just fall off him. Well, this Trishka will walk in village and town; and this Trishka, the sly fellow that he is, will tempt Christian folk. . . . But there'll be nothing that you can do to him. That's the sort of marvellous, sly fellow he'll be."

"Yes," continued Pavel in his unhurried voice, "that's how he'll be. We were expecting him, too. The old people told us that as soon as the heavenly portent started, Trishka would come. Well, the portent started. Everyone went out into the road and into the fields and waited for what would happen next. Round us, you know, the country is clear and open. They looked, and suddenly down from the village on the hill came an odd sort of man with a marvellous sort of head . . . and everybody shouted: 'Oy, Trishka is come! Oy, Trishka is come!' And everyone hid where they could. The village elder crept into a ditch; his wife got stuck under the gate and screamed for all

---

* The superstition about "Trishka" probably derives from the legend of Antichrist. —*Author*.

she was worth, and gave the dog in her yard such a fright that it snapped its chain and went off through the fence into the forest; and Kuzka's father, Dorofeich, jumped into a field of oats, sat down, and started calling like a quail: 'Surely,' he thought, 'a *bird* ought to be safe from him, fiend and destroyer though he is!' That's how scared we all were! . . . And all the time it was our barrelmaker, Vavila: he'd bought himself a new jug, and had put the empty jug over his head."

All the boys laughed, and again fell silent for a moment, as often happens when people are talking in the open air. I looked round: night reigned in all the majesty of its empire; the moist freshness of late evening had given place to the dry warmth of midnight, which would lie for some while yet, in a soft veil, over the sleeping fields; we were still a long time from the first murmur, the first rustlings and swishings of dawn, the first dewdrops of daybreak. There was no moon in the heavens; it was the period of late moonrise. The numberless golden stars, twinkling in rivalry, seemed all to be floating gently in the direction of the Milky Way, and, indeed, looking at them, you felt yourself vaguely aware of the earth's purposeful, unceasing course . . . A strange, sharp, ailing cry sounded, suddenly, twice together, from above the river and, after a few moments, it came again from farther in the distance. . . .

Kostya shuddered . . . "What was that?"

"It was a heron calling," rejoined Pavel calmly.

"A heron," repeated Kostya. "But, Pavel, what was it that I heard yesterday evening?" He added after a pause: "You may know . . ."

"What did you hear?"

"This is what I heard. I was going from Stone Ridge to Shashkino; first I went right along our hazel-wood, then across the meadow—you know the place where it comes out at the corner of the ravine—well, there, you know, there's a dewpond; it's all overgrown with reeds; well, I was walking past this dewpond, when suddenly, from out of it, someone sort of groaned, and so sadly, so sadly: 'u—u . . . u—u . . . u—u! . . .' Such a fright took hold of me: it was late, and the voice sounded so ill. It was enough to make you cry yourself. . . . What could that have been, eh?"

"In that dewpond, the summer before last, Akim, the forester, was drowned by thieves," observed Pavel. "So perhaps it's his soul complaining."

"Well, there you are, boys," rejoined Kostya, widening his eyes, which were anyway huge enough. "I never even knew that Akim was drowned in that dewpond: if I'd known, I'd have been ever so frightened."

"Or else, there are tiny little frogs, so they say," continued Pavel, "which call out sadly like that."

"Frogs? No, it wasn't frogs . . . it wasn't frogs that made that noise."

A heron called again from over the river: "Ooh, there he is!" said Kostya involuntarily. "Like a wood-goblin calling."

"The wood-goblin doesn't call, he's dumb," asserted Ilyusha. "He can only clap his hands and rattle! . . ."

"I suppose you've seen him?" Fedya interrupted, in a mocking voice.

"Certainly not, and heaven preserve me from doing so: but others have. Why, the other day, he led one of our peasants astray: took him round and round in the forest, all the way round the same clearing. . . . He hardly got home before dawn."

"Did he see him?"

"Yes, he said he was a great big dark fellow, all muffled up, he seemed to be hiding behind a tree; you couldn't make him out clearly, he seemed to be hiding from the moon, and he looked and looked with his great eyes, and twinkled and twinkled away with them. . . ."

"Ugh!" exclaimed Fedya, trembling slightly and shuddering at the shoulders. "Phew!"

"And what's this pest doing walking the earth?" observed Pavel. "What does he think he's doing?"

"Don't curse him: look out, or he'll hear you," said Ilyusha.

Silence fell again. "Look, look, boys," came suddenly Vanya's childish voice. "Look at God's little stars—like bees swarming." He stuck out his fresh little face from under the matting, leant on his fist and slowly raised his big, calm eyes aloft. All the boys gazed up to the sky and didn't look down for quite a while.

"Well, Vanya," began Fedya tenderly, "is your sister Anyutka well?"

"Very well," answered Vanya, slightly slurring the "r."

"Tell her to come and see us; why doesn't she come?"

"I don't know."

"Tell her to come."

"I will."

"Tell her that I'll give her a present."

"And me too?"

"Yes, you too."

Vanya sighed.

"Well, no, I don't need one. Better give it to her, she's so good and kind."

Vanya rested his little head on the ground again. Pavel stood up and took the empty pot in his hands.

"Where are you going?" Fedya asked him.

"To the river, to draw water: I feel like a good drink of water."

The dogs rose and went after him.

"Mind you don't fall into the river," Ilyusha called after him.

"Why should he fall?" said Fedya. "He'll take care."

"Yes, he'll take care. But anything may happen. Say he bends down and begins to draw water, and the water-goblin takes him by the hand and pulls him under. Afterwards they'll say the lad fell into the water. . . . Fell in, indeed! . . . There, he's gone down into the rushes," he added, listening hard.

There came the rustle of parting reeds.

"Is it true," asked Kostya, "that crazy Akulina went off her head when she fell into the water?"

"Yes. . . . Just look at her now! . . . But they say that she used to be beautiful. The water-goblin spoilt her. I suppose he didn't expect that they'd pull her out so soon. So he spoilt her, down there at the bottom where he lives."

(I had met this Akulina more than once. Covered in rags, dreadfully thin, with a face as black as coal, a clouded look and teeth ever-bared, she would stamp for whole hours on the same spot on the road, tightly pressing her bony hands to her breast and slightly shifting her weight from one leg to the other, like a wild creature in a cage. She understood not a word of what was said to her, but only laughed convulsively from time to time.)

"But, they say," continued Kostya, "that Akulina threw herself into the river because her lover played her false."

"Yes, that was why."

"D'you remember Vasily?" added Kostya suddenly.

"What Vasily?" asked Fedya.

"The one who was drowned," answered Kostya. "In this very same river. What a fine chap he was! Oh, what a fine chap! His mother, Feklista, how she loved him! It was as if she felt, Feklista did, that his death would come by water. Vasily used to come with us in summer to bathe in the river—and she'd get all of a fluster. The other mothers didn't care a bit, they'd walk past with their wash-pails, they'd waddle by, but Feklista would put her pail down and start calling him. 'Come back, come back,' she'd say, 'come back, light of my eyes! Oh, come back, my little eagle!' And how he came to drown, Lord alone knows. He was playing on the bank, and his mother was there too, raking hay, and suddenly she heard what sounded like someone blowing bubbles under water—she looked, and there was only Vasily's cap floating in the water. Well, since then, Feklista, too, hasn't been right in the head. She comes and lies at the place where he drowned; there she lies, boys, and starts to sing—d'you remember, Vasily always used to sing a song—well that's the one she sings, too, and cries and cries, and complains bitterly to God . . ."

"Here comes Pavel," said Fedya.

Pavel came up to the fire with a full pot in his hand.

"Well, boys," he began after a silence, "there's something bad."

"What?" asked Kostya hurriedly.

"I heard Vasily's voice."

Everyone shuddered.

"What's that you say?" whispered Kostya.

"So help me God. I'd just begun to bend down to the water, and suddenly I heard my name being called, in Vasily's voice, like it was from under the water: 'Pavel, Pavel, come here!' I went away. I got the water, though."

"Good Lord!" said the boys, crossing themselves.

"That was a water-goblin calling you, Pavel," added Fedya. "And we were just talking about Vasily."

"Oh, that's an evil sign," said Ilyusha, with deliberation.

"Well, never mind, forget about it!" said Pavel resolutely, and sat down again. "You can't escape your fate." The boys became quieter. It was clear that Pavel's story had made a deep impression on them. They began to settle down in front of the fire, as if preparing to sleep.

"What's that?" asked Kostya suddenly, lifting his head.

Pavel listened intently.

"That's curlews flying past and whistling."

"Where are they flying to?"

"To the country where there's supposed to be no winter."

"Is there really such a country?"

"Yes, there is."

"Far away?"

"Far, far away, beyond the warm seas."

Kostya sighed and closed his eyes. More than three hours had passed since I had been in company with the boys. At last the moon rose; I didn't notice her at once, so small and thin she was. The moonless night seemed still as magnificent as before. . . . But many stars, which, not long ago, had stood high in the heavens, were now stooping towards the earth's dark rim; everything was perfectly silent all around, with the special silence that usually falls towards daybreak: everything was sunk in the heavy, immobile sleep that precedes the dawn. There was no longer the same strong scent in the air—moisture seemed to be distilled in it afresh. Oh, the short nights of summer! . . . The boys' talk had died down with the fires. . . . Even the dogs were dozing; the horses, as far as I could make out, in the hardly-discernible, feebly pulsing light of the stars, were lying down too, with sunken heads. . . . A gentle drowsiness came over me and merged into slumber.

A flood of freshness coursed over my face. I opened my eyes—the day was breaking. There was still no flush of dawn, but a growing pallor in the East. I could vaguely make out my surroundings. The pale-gray sky was growing light, and cold, and blue; the stars twinkled feebly or went out; the earth had grown damp, the leaves dripped, from somewhere came sounds of life, and voices, and the damp breath of dawn was already abroad, hovering above the earth. My body answered it with a faint thrill of exhilaration. I rose quickly and went across to the boys. They were all sleeping like the dead around the dying fire; only Pavel half-raised himself and stared fixedly at me. I nodded to him and went my way along the steaming river. I had not gone two versts when, around me in the broad water-meadow and ahead on the deepening green of the hills, from wood to wood, and behind me over the long dusty track, over the flushed sparkling bushes, and along the river, which was of a timid blue below the thinning mist—flowed scarlet, then red, then golden torrents of youthful, blazing light. . . . The world began to rustle, awoke, began to sing, to murmur, to speak. On all sides the heavy dewdrops flashed into blazing diamonds; to meet me, pure and clear, as if they too had been washed in the coolness of morning, came the sounds of a church bell, and suddenly, driven by my friends the boys, the herd of horses, fresh from sleep, galloped past me. . . .

With sorrow I must add that Pavel died before the year was out. He was not drowned, but killed by a fall from a horse. A pity, he was a splendid lad!

Kasyan from Fair Springs

I WAS DRIVING BACK FROM SHOOTING IN A JOLTING CART AND, overcome by the stifling heat of an overcast day in summer (in such weather the heat can of course be more unbearable even than on fine days, and especially so when there is no wind), I was dozing and swaying, submitting my whole person with a sullen patience to the nagging attentions of the fine white dust which rose constantly off the broken track from beneath our cracked and lurching wheels, when suddenly my notice was attracted by an unwonted restlessness, a certain fidgety uneasiness on the part of my coachman, who up to that moment had been dozing away even more soundly than myself. He tightened his reins, began fussing about on his seat and shouting at the horses, meanwhile gazing somewhere away to one side. I looked round. We were driving across a wide, cultivated plain; low hills, also cultivated, merged into it in gentle rolling undulations; the eye could embrace at least some five versts of open country: in the distance, small birch-copses were all that broke the almost straight line of the horizon, with the rounded tracery of their treetops. Narrow paths stretched across the fields, disappeared into folds in the ground, wound over hillocks, and on one of them, which was due to intersect our track about five hundred yards ahead of us, I could make out some sort of procession. It was at this that my coachman was gazing.

It was a funeral. In front, in a cart drawn at walking pace by a single nag, rode the priest; a deacon sat beside him and drove: behind the cart, four peasants, with heads bared, carried a coffin covered in a white cloth; two peasant women walked behind the coffin. The thin, plaintive voice of one of them suddenly came to my ears. I listened intently: she was wailing for the dead. Her song came cheerlessly over the empty fields, warbling, monotonous, mournful, without hope. My coachman urged on his horses so as to pass ahead of the procession. To meet a dead man on the road is an evil omen. He was indeed successful in hurrying past before the dead man could reach the track; but we had not gone a hundred yards farther, when suddenly our cart gave a violent jolt, listed to one side and almost overturned. The coachman halted the horses, which had made as if to bolt, threw up his hand and spat.

"What's the matter?" I asked.

My coachman got down in silence and without haste.

"But what is it?"

"The axle's broken—burnt through," he answered morosely, and suddenly straightened the harness on the side-horse with such indignation that the horse almost toppled right over, managed to stand its ground, snorted, trembled, and began tranquilly nibbling its foreleg below the knee. I got down and stood for a while on the track, oppressed by a vague and disagreeable feeling of bewilderment. The right wheel had almost completely collapsed under the cart and now seemed to be lifting its hub aloft in dumb despair.

"What are we going to do now?" I asked at length.

"That's whose fault it is!" said my coachman, pointing with his whip at the procession, which had now turned on to the track and was approaching us. "I've always noticed that," he continued; "it's a sure sign, when you meet a dead man."

He began again to worry the side-horse, which, sensing his ill-humored and grim mood, decided to stand motionless, with only an occasional modest flick of its tail. I walked a few paces up and down and halted again in front of the wheel.

Meanwhile the dead man had come up with us. Quietly turning off the track on to the grass, the sad procession made its way past our cart. My coachman and I took off our caps, bowed to the priest and exchanged glances with the coffin-bearers. They were stepping out ponderously, their broad chests bulging. Of the two women following the coffin, one was very old and pale; her motionless features, cruelly disfigured by grief, preserved an expression of dour and solemn dignity. She walked in silence, occasionally raising a bony hand to her thin, sunken lips. The other, a young woman of about twenty-five, had red, tearful eyes and her whole face was swollen with weeping; as she came level with us, she interrupted her wailing and covered her face with her sleeve. . . . By now the dead man had passed us and had got back on the track and the woman's plaintive, heartbreaking song burst out again. After silently following with his eyes the measured swaying of the coffin, my driver turned to me:

"That's Martin the carpenter they're burying," he said: "the one from Ryaba."

"How do you know?"

"I recognized the women. The old one's his mother, the young one's his wife."

"Was he ill, or what?"

"Yes . . . the fever. . . . The day before yesterday the bailiff sent for the doctor, but the doctor was out. . . . He was a good carpenter; he took a drop now and then, but he was a good carpenter. You can see how badly his wife has taken it. . . . Well, yes, of course it's true that women's tears don't cost a thing. Women's tears are the same as water . . . yes."

And he bent down, ducked under the side-horse's traces and took hold of the shaft-bow in both hands.

"Anyway," I remarked, "what are we going to do?"

My coachman first pressed his knee against the shoulder of the shaft-horse, shook the shaft-bow twice, straightened the strap, then ducked again under the side-horse's trace, and, knocking the horse's face as he passed, went up to the wheel; then, without taking his eyes off it, slowly brought out a snuff-box from beneath the skirts of his coat, slowly pulled the top off by its strap, slowly inserted his two thick fingers into the snuff-box (and there was hardly room for both of them, at that), rubbed and rubbed away at the snuff, gave his nose an anticipatory twist, sniffed with deliberation, accompanying every intake with a prolonged grunt; then, screwing up and blinking his tear-filled eyes, as if in pain, he plunged into a profound reverie.

"Well, what about it?" I said at length.

My coachman carefully put the snuff-box away in his pocket, jerked his hat forward on to his forehead, without the help of his hands, just with a flick of his head, and reflectively climbed on to his seat.

"Where are you off to?" I asked him, not without astonishment.

"Please to take your place," he answered calmly, and picked up the reins.

"But how are we going to go on?"

"We'll go on all right."

"But the axle . . ."

"Please to take your place."

"But the axle is broken."

"It's broken, yes, but we can get as far as the hamlet . . . at a walk, that is. It's over there behind the wood to the right: it's called Yudiny."

"D'you think we'll get there?"

My coachman did not vouchsafe me a reply.

"I'd better walk," I said.

"As you please, sir . . ."

He waved his whip and the horses started off.

We did indeed reach the hamlet, although the right fore-wheel hardly stayed on, and turned in the strangest way. On one hill it practically came off, but my coachman shouted in a furious voice and we got safely down to the bottom.

The hamlet of Yudiny consisted of six little low cabins, which had already managed to take a list to one side, although they had probably not been standing long; some of the back-yards were not even fenced-in. As we drove into the hamlet, we met not a single living soul. There was not even a fowl to be seen, not even a dog—or rather only one, a black dog, with a docked tail, which jumped up hurriedly in front of us out of a completely dry trough where it had no doubt been driven by thirst, and at once, without a bark, dashed headlong under a gate. I went up to the first cabin, opened the door, and called for the master and mistress. No one answered me. I called again; the hungry mewing of a cat sounded from behind the inner door. I pushed it with my foot; a thin cat darted past me, with a flash of green eyes in the darkness. I put my head into the room and looked around it. It was dark, smoky, and empty. I made my way to the yard and found nobody there either. . . . Behind a fence a calf lowed; a lame gray goose limped away to one side. I crossed to the second cabin and there too found not a soul. I went to the yard . . .

Right in the middle of the yard, in broad daylight, in the full blaze of the sun, lay, with his face to the ground and his head covered with a coat, what I took for a boy. A few paces away from him stood a wretched little cart in a thatched lean-to shed, with a bony nag in ragged harness beside it. The sunlight streaming through the narrow interstices of the decrepit roof fell in small pools of light on its shaggy sorrel-brown coat. Up aloft was a boxful of starlings, chattering and looking down with tranquil curiosity from their airy abode. I went up to the sleeper and set about waking him . . .

He raised his head, saw me, and at once jumped to his feet. "Why, what is it? What's the matter?" he mumbled sleepily.

I didn't answer him at once: such was the impression made on me by his appearance. Imagine a dwarf of about fifty, with a swarthy, wrinkled little face, sharp little nose, brown, hardly perceptible little eyes, and thick curly black hair sticking out on all sides of a tiny head like the hat on top of a mushroom. His whole body was extremely thin and puny and I find it quite impossible to convey in words the utter strangeness of his expression.

"What is it?" he asked me again.

I explained to him what the matter was and he listened to me without taking his slowly blinking eyes off me.

"You couldn't let us have a new axle?" I asked at length. "I'd be glad to pay for it."

"But who are you? A sportsman, eh?" he asked, sizing me up from head to foot.

"Yes."

"You shoot the birds of the heaven, I'll be bound? . . . and the creatures of the forest? . . . But isn't it a sin to kill God's birds and to shed the blood of the innocent?"

The strange little man spoke with a pronounced drawl. His tone also astonished me. Not only had it no hint of infirmity, but it was surprisingly sweet and young and had an almost feminine tenderness in it.

"I have no axle," he added, after a slight pause. "That thing there is no use." He pointed to his cart. "I suppose you've got a big cart?"

"Can't I find an axle in the village?"

"Village, indeed! . . . No one here has got one. No one is at home either, they're all at work. Be off with you!" he said suddenly, and lay down again on the ground.

I had in no wise expected this conclusion.

"Listen, old fellow," I said, touching his shoulder, "be kind, and help me."

"Be off, and good luck to you! I'm tired; I've been into town," he told me, and drew his coat over his head.

"But, please help me," I continued. "I . . . I'll pay you."

"I don't need your money."

"Now look here, old fellow . . ."

He half got up, and sat with his thin little legs crossed.

"I could take you, if you like, to the clearing. Some merchants have bought our wood—may God be their judge. They're cutting down the wood, and they've built an office. May God be their judge. You could order an axle there, from them, or buy one ready-made."

"Splendid!" I exclaimed joyfully. "Splendid! . . . Let's go."

"An oaken axle, a good one," he continued, not rising from where he sat.

"Is it far to the clearing?"

"Three versts."

"Oh, well, we could drive there in your cart."

"Oh, no. . . ."

"Well, let's go," I said. "Let's go, old fellow! My coachman's waiting in the road."

The old man got up reluctantly and followed me out into the road. My coachman was in a mood of irritation. He had tried to water the horses, but there turned out to be extremely little water in the well, and what there was had a bad taste, which is what matters most, so coachman say. . . . At the sight of the old man, however, he grinned, nodded several times, and exclaimed: "Ah, Kasyan! Good day!"

"Good day, Erofei, you man of righteousness!" answered Kasyan in a cheerless voice.

I lost no time in conveying his proposal to my coachman; Erofei expressed agreement and drove into the yard. While he was unharnessing the horses, with an air of busy deliberation, the old man stood with his shoulder propped against the gate and looked gloomily first at him, then at me. He seemed perplexed, and, as far as I could make out, not overjoyed by our sudden visitation.

"So they've transferred you, too?" Erofei asked him suddenly, while taking off the shaft-bow.

"Yes."

"Ugh!" said my coachman through his teeth. "Martin, you know, the carpenter . . . of course you know Martin from Ryaba?"

"I do."

"Well, he's dead. We've just passed his coffin."

Kasyan started.

"Dead?" he said, and looked down.

"Yes, dead. Why didn't you cure him, eh? They say that you can cure people, that you're a healer."

My coachman was evidently amusing himself at the old man's expense.

"Is that your cart, eh?" he added, indicating it with his finger.

"Yes."

"Well, it's certainly a cart . . . a cart!" he repeated, and taking it by the shafts he practically overturned it. . . . "A cart, indeed! . . . But what horse are you going to take to the clearing? . . . You'll never manage to harness one of our horses between these shafts: our horses are too big for this sort of a contraption."

"I don't know," answered Kasyan. "No, you'll get there on this beasty here, perhaps," he added, with a sigh.

"This one?" interjected Erofei, and, going over to Kasyan's nag, he prodded it contemptuously in the neck with the third finger of his right hand. "Oho," he added reproachfully, "the old crow's asleep!"

I asked Erofei to hurry up and harness the horse. I was keen to go myself with Kasyan to the clearing: it ought to be a good place for blackcock. When the cart was ready, and I had somehow installed myself with my dog inside the back of its body, and Kasyan, curled up into a ball, with the same cheerless expression still on his face, had sat down on the raised part in front, Erofei came up to me and whispered, with a mysterious air: "You're quite right, sir, to go with him. He's one of these cranky fellows; they call him the Flea. I don't know how you got any sense out of him . . ."

I wanted to remark to Erofei that, so far, Kasyan had struck me as a most judicious fellow, but my coachman at once went on in the same tone: "But just keep an eye on where he takes you. And please choose the axle yourself, sir; choose the soundest one that you can see. Well, Flea," he added loudly, "can I get a crust of bread here?"

"Have a look; maybe you'll find some," answered Kasyan; he gave a twitch of the reins and off we went.

To my unfeigned surprise, his nag went very tolerably. All the way Kasyan maintained a stubborn silence and answered my questions disjointedly and with reluctance. We soon reached the clearing, and there found the office, a lofty cabin standing by itself at the top of a small ravine, which not far off was blocked by a dam and spread out into a pond. In the office I found two young merchant-clerks, with snow-white teeth, and suavity in their glance, in their ready speech and their shrewd smiles. I compounded with them for my axle, and set off for the clearing. I thought that Kasyan would stay with his horse and await me there, but he suddenly approached me.

"Well, are you going shooting birdies?" he said. "Eh?"

"Yes, if I find any."

"I'll go with you . . . may I?"

"Certainly you may."

So off we went. The clearing stretched for about a verst. I confess that I paid more attention to Kasyan than to my dog. He was not called the Flea for nothing. His black capless noddle (for that matter his hair was the equal of any cap) fairly bobbed up and down among the bushes. He walked extremely fast, hopped as he went, and kept stooping down to pick herbs, stuffing them in his bosom, mumbling something to himself and looking at me and my dog with a strange questioning glance. In the brushwood, in the small scrub, and in clearings, you will often find little gray fowl constantly flitting from one tree to another and whistling and suddenly swooping as they fly. Kasyan imitated them and conversed with them; a young quail flew up chirruping from under his feet, and he chirruped back at it. A lark dropped towards him, singing loudly, with wings a-quiver— Kasyan took up its song. He still avoided conversation with my-self. . . .

The weather was magnificent, even better than earlier on; there was no break in the sweltering heat. In a clear sky, there floated a few high, almost motionless, clouds, yellowish-white, like remnants of snow in spring-time, with a long, flattened shape, like lowered sails. The pattern-work of their edges, which were soft and downy as cotton-wool, altered slowly but perceptibly as the moments went by: they were dissolving, these clouds, and they cast no shadow. For a long while Kasyan and I tramped around the clearing. Young saplings, not more than two feet high, surrounded the low and black-ened tree-trunks with their slender, smooth stems; round, jagged, gray-bordered growths, the sort from which touchwood is made, clung to these trunks, and the wild strawberry stretched its pink tendrils over them. Close at hand mushrooms sat tightly in families. Our feet kept getting caught and tangled in the long grass, which was wilting under the blazing sun; on all sides our eyes were dazzled by the sharp, metallic flickering of young, reddish leaves on the trees; on every hand were the gleaming blue berries of enchanter's night-shade, the celandine's bright golden bells, and the purple and yellow flowers of the wild pansy; here and there, beside overgrown tracks, on which wheel marks showed up as stripes of fine red grass, stood piles of timber, blackened by wind and rain, and stacked in lengths; slanting rectangles of faint shadow fell from them, otherwise there was not a shadow to be found. The light breeze rose and fell: a sud-den burst of it blows straight into your face, and all around there is a cheerful rustling and nodding and movement, a gracious swaying of the supple fern-tops, and your heart rejoices . . . then suddenly it dies away again and all grows still. Only the grasshoppers chatter away together like mad—and how oppressive is their interminable, harsh, dry sound. It goes well with the nagging heat of noon; it seems born of the heat, evoked by it from the incandescent earth.

Without having put up a single bird, we came at length to a new clearing. Here, lately-felled poplars lay sadly on the ground, crushing the grass and undergrowth beneath them; on some of them, dead but still green leaves drooped limply from the rigid branches; on others, the leaves were already dried up and shrivelled. Fresh, golden-white splinters, lying in piles beside the damp, bright-colored trunks, gave out their special, strong, bitter-sweet scent. From farther off, near the edge of the wood, came the dull thudding of axes, and from time to time, solemnly and serenely, as if bowing and opening its arms, down fell a leafy-headed tree. . . . For a long time I found no sport; at last, from a spreading oak-bush densely entwined with wormwood, a corncrake flew up. I hit him; he turned a somersault in the air and dropped. Hearing the shot, Kasyan quickly covered his eyes with his hand and never stirred until I had re-loaded my gun and picked up the bird. When I had set off again, he went up to the spot where the dead bird had dropped, bent over the grass, which was spattered with a few drops of blood, shook his head, and gave me a frightened look. . . . Afterwards I heard him whispering: "Sinful! . . . That's what it is—sinful! . . ."

At length the heat compelled us to go into the wood. I threw myself down under a lofty hazel-bush, above which a slender young maple graciously extended its floating branches. Kasyan sat down on the stout butt-end of a sawn-down birch. I looked across at him. High above us, leaves were faintly trembling, and their liquid green shadows slipped gently backwards and forwards over his frail body, muffled up in its dark coat, and over his little face. He never lifted his head. Bored by his taciturnity, I lay on my back and began to admire the peaceful play of the intricate leafage against the bright, distant sky. It is a strangely enjoyable occupation to lie on one's back in the forest and look upwards. You seem to be looking into a bottomless sea, extending far and wide beneath you; the trees seem not to rise from the ground, but, like the roots of huge plants, to drop perpendicularly down into those glass-clear waves, and the leaves on the trees are now translucent as emeralds, now opaque with a goldish, almost blackish, green. Somewhere far, far away, at the end of its slender twig, a single leaf stands motionless against a blue patch of pellucid sky, and beside it another one sways with a movement like the play of a fish on a line, a movement that seems spontaneous and not produced by the wind. Like fairy islands under the sea, round wide clouds float quietly up and quietly away—and suddenly the whole sea, the radiant air, the sun-drenched branches and leaves, all begin to ripple and tremble with a transitory brilliance, and there comes a fresh, thrilling murmur, like the interminable faint splashing that follows the rising of a sudden swell. You gaze without stirring, and no words can express the gladness and peace and sweetness that catch at your heart. You look—and that deep, clear azure calls to your lips a smile as innocent as itself; like the clouds in the sky, and as it were in company with them, happy memories pass before you in slow procession, and you feel your gaze passing farther and farther into the distance, drawing you after it into that peaceful, radiant gulf, and you have no power to tear yourself away from its height, from its depth . . .

"Master, I say, master!" said Kasyan suddenly, in his tuneful voice.

I half-rose, in surprise; hitherto he had hardly answered my questions and now he had suddenly addressed me himself.

"What is it?" I asked.

"Why did you kill that birdie?" he began, looking me straight in the face.

"How do you mean, why? . . . A corncrake is game: you can eat him."

"That's not why you killed him, master, as if you were going to eat him! You killed him for your sport."

"But I'll warrant that you yourself eat goose, or chicken, for example."

"Those are fowls set apart by God for man; but a corncrake is a free fowl, a fowl of the woods. And he is not the only one; there are many of them—every kind of creature of the woods and the fields and the rivers and the marshes and the meadows and the air and the earth—that it's a sin to kill; you should let them live their allotted span on earth. Other food is reserved for man: other food, other drink; bread, which is God's blessing, and the waters of the heaven, and the creatures that were tamed by our forefathers before us."

I looked at Kasyan in surprise. His words flowed freely; he did not search for them, he spoke with quiet inspiration and gentle dignity, occasionally closing his eyes.

"Then you think it sinful to kill fish, too?"

"The fish is a cold-blooded creature," he rejoined, with conviction, "the fish is a dumb creature. He knows not fear or joy; he is a speechless creature. He has no feeling. Even his blood is not alive. Blood," he continued after a pause, "a sacred thing is blood! Blood sees not God's sun, blood hides away from the light. . . . A deadly sin it is, to show blood to the light—a deadly sin and horror . . . deadly indeed!"

He sighed and sank his head. I confess that I looked at the strange old fellow in complete amazement. His speech was not that of a peasant. No simple folk talk like that, not even those with the gift of speech. This language, of such a deliberate solemnity and strangeness . . . I had never heard anything like it.

"Tell me, Kasyan," I began, not moving my gaze from his slightly flushed face: "What do you live by?"

He did not at once answer my question. His gaze travelled restlessly round for a moment.

"I live as the Lord ordains," he said at last; "but as for what I live by—why, by nothing. I have been a feckless creature, ever since I was a boy; I work when I can—but I am a bad workman. So there I am! My health is bad, and my hands are clumsy. Well, in spring I trap nightingales."

"You trap nightingales! . . . Then how is it that you just said that we ought not to touch any creature of the woods and fields, and so forth?"

"We ought not to kill them, certainly. Death takes his due without that. Take Martin the carpenter: Martin lived, lived a while, and died; now his wife is weeping for her husband and her little children. . . . There is no man, no creature that can cheat death. Death runs not, nor is there any running from him; but neither should we help him. . . . I kill no nightingales—God forbid! I trap them, not to torment them, or to do them to death, but for man's pleasure, for his joy and his delight."

"Do you go to Kursk to trap them?"

"I go to Kursk, and farther, too, if need be. I spend my nights in the marshes and in the woods, alone in the fields, in the solitary places: where the sandpiper whistles, the hare calls, the drake quacks. . . . At evening-time I'm on the look-out, in the morning I listen, in the twilight I spread my net over the bushes. . . . There are some nightingales that sing so sadly, so sweetly . . . so sadly, too."

"And you sell them?"

"I give them away to good folk."

"And what else do you do?"

"How d'you mean, do?"

"How do you occupy yourself?"

The old man was silent.

"I have no occupation. . . . I'm a bad worker. I can read and write, though."

"You can?"

"Yes. Thanks to the help of God, and of some good folk, too."

"Have you got a family?"

"No."

"Why . . . are they all dead?"

"No; but that was not the answer that life gave. It's all under Providence, we all move under Providence; man must be righteous—that's all! as God would have us, that's to say."

"And have you no kin?"

"Yes . . . I have . . . but . . ." The old man became confused.

"Tell me," I began, "I overheard my coachman asking you why you didn't heal Martin; are you a healer, too?"

"Your coachman is a righteous man," Kasyan replied reflectively, "but he too is not without sin. They call me a healer . . . a fine healer indeed! Why, who can heal? All that comes from God. Healing is only possible as a gift from God. But there are . . . there are grasses

and flowers that help, certainly. Take the marigold, for instance—
there is a herb that is good for man; there is plantain, too; there is
no shame in speaking of that: they are wholesome herbs, herbs of
God. There is another sort as well: they help, too, but it is sinful; it
is sinful even to speak of them, except may be with prayer. . . . And,
of course, there are also certain words . . . But he who believes shall
be saved," he added, lowering his voice.

"Did you give Martin nothing?" I asked.

"I heard of it too late," answered the old man. "But what of it?
It's foreordained for us all at birth. Martin the carpenter was not
meant to live, not meant to live on earth; that's how it was. No, if
a man is not meant to live on earth, the sun does not warm him
as it does his fellow, and bread gives him no sustenance—it is as if
something was calling him away . . . yes; Lord rest his soul!"

"Is it long since you were transferred to these parts?" I asked,
after a short silence.

Kasyan gave a start.

"No, not long; four years. In the old master's time we all lived
in our former homes, but then his executors transferred us. Our old
master was a gentle soul, a man of peace—may the Kingdom of
Heaven be his! Of course, the executors decided rightly; it clearly
had to be so."

"Where did you live before?"

"We come from Fair Springs."

"Is that far from here?"

"A hundred versts."

"Were you better off there?"

"Yes . . . better off. It's open country there, a country of rivers,
our own home-country; but here it is all cramped and dried up . . .
we are like orphans here. At home, at Fair Springs, you go up a hill,
you go up—and, good Lord, what is it that you see, eh? . . . River
and meadow and forest; here a church, over there, meadows again.
You can see far, far away. You look, and look, and there's no end to
it. Well, the land is certainly better here, it is clay, good clay soil,
so the peasants say; anyway, there is corn growing for me in plenty
everywhere."

"But tell me, I dare say you'd like to visit your home-country?"

"Yes, to have a look at it. All the same, I'm well off anywhere. I have got no family, I'm a rolling stone. Why! you cannot sit at home for ever, eh? So when you go off, when you go off," he repeated, raising his voice, "your heart grows lighter, indeed it does. And the sun shines down on you, and God can see you better, and singing comes easier to you. You see a herb growing; you mark it, and pick it. There may be water flowing—for instance, spring water, from the source, holy water; you drink your fill—you mark it, too. The birds of the heaven sing . . . And then, beyond Kursk, come the steppes, the steppe-country, the surprise of it, the joy to your heart, the spaciousness of it, the blessing of God! Why, the steppes run, so they say, right to the warm seas, where lives the Gamayun bird with the sweet voice, and the leaves never fall from the trees in winter, nor in autumn, and golden apples grow on silver branches, and all men live in joy and righteousness . . . and that's where I'd be fain to go. . . . I have done my fair share of travelling! I've been to Romyon, and to Simbirsk, the noble city, and right to Moscow of the golden domes; I've been to Oka the life-giver, to the kindly Tsna, and to mother Volga; I've seen many good Christian folk and I've been in fine cities. . . . Well, I'd be fain to go there . . . so I would . . . and I, poor sinner that I am, I'm not the only one. There are plenty of Christian folk going round in rope shoes, wandering the face of the earth, seeking the truth . . . yes! . . . What is there to stay at home for, eh? There is no righteousness inside man's heart—and that's the truth. . . ."

These last words Kasyan pronounced rapidly, almost inaudibly: then he said something more which I couldn't distinguish at all, and his face took on such a strange expression that I couldn't help remembering his nickname, "the crank." He lowered his head, cleared his throat, and seemed to come to himself again.

"Look at the sun!" he said in an undertone. "Look at the Lord's blessing! Look at the warmth inside the forest!"

He moved his shoulders, fell silent, looked vaguely around, and began to sing quietly. I could not catch all the words of his long drawn-out song; I made out the following:

> *Kasyan is my name,*
> *My nickname is the Flea . . .*

"Aha!" I thought, "so he makes verses . . ."

Suddenly he started and fell silent, looking fixedly into the undergrowth of the forest. I turned and saw a little peasant girl of about eight, in a blue dress, with a check handkerchief over her head and a wicker basket over her bare sunburnt arm. She had probably never expected to meet us; she had stumbled on top of us and stood motionless in a green hazel-thicket on a shady patch of grass, looking timorously at me with her black eyes. I had hardly caught sight of her when she darted behind a tree.

"Annushka, come here, don't be afraid," called the old man tenderly.

"I *am* afraid," came her thin little voice.

"Don't be afraid, don't be afraid, come to me."

Annushka slowly abandoned her hiding-place, walked quietly around, her little feet hardly rustling in the thick grass, and came out of the bushes beside the old man. This was no girl of eight, as I had thought at first, judging by her small size, but one of thirteen or fourteen. Her whole body was small and thin, but trim and graceful, and her pretty little face was strikingly like Kasyan's own, although Kasyan himself was no beauty. She had the same sharp features, the same strange expression, at once cunning and trustful, reflective and penetrating, and the same movements. . . . Kasyan looked her over; she was standing beside him.

"Well, have you got some mushrooms?" he asked.

"Yes, some mushrooms," she answered, with a timid smile.

"Have you found plenty of them?"

"Yes, plenty." She looked quickly at me and smiled again.

"Some white ones, too?"

"Yes, white ones, too."

"Show me, do. . . ."

She lowered the basket from her arm and half-lifted a broad burdock leaf which covered the mushrooms.

"Oh," said Kasyan, stooping over the basket, "what fine ones! Well done, Annushka!"

"Is she your daughter, Kasyan, eh?" I asked. Annushka's face showed a slight blush.

"She's a sort of relation," said Kasyan, with assumed carelessness.

"Well, Annushka, off you go," he added at once; "off you go, and good luck to you. And be careful . . ."

"But why should she walk?" I interrupted him. "We could give her a lift. . . ."

Annushka flushed the color of a poppy, clutched with both hands at the string handle of her basket, and looked anxiously at the old man.

"No, she'll get there all right," he rejoined in the same indifferent, casual voice. "Why should we? . . . She'll get there all right. . . . Be off with you."

Annushka went nimbly off into the forest. Kasyan looked after her, then lowered his gaze and smiled. In this long smile, in the few words which he had said to Annushka, in the very tone of his voice when he spoke to her, there was more passionate love and tenderness than language can express. He looked again in the direction in which she had vanished, smiled again, wiped his face, and nodded his head several times.

"Why did you send her off so quickly?" I asked him. "I should like to have bought some of her mushrooms. . . ."

"Why, it does not matter to you, you can buy them at home whenever you like," he answered me, using the formal "you" for the first time.

"Well, you've got a pretty one there."

"No . . . well . . . there it is . . ." he answered, as if reluctantly, and from that moment he relapsed into his earlier mood of silence. Seeing that all my efforts to engage him again in conversation were proving vain, I went off to the clearing. Meanwhile it had grown slightly less hot; but my ill-success continued, and I returned to the hamlet with only one corncrake besides my new axle. As we were driving up to his yard, Kasyan suddenly turned to me: "Master, I say, Master," he began. "I'm sorry for what I did to you; you see, it was I who called all the birds away from you."

"What do you mean?"

"It's my trick. That's a clever dog you have, and a good one, but all the same there was nothing he could do. . . . When you come to think of it, what are men? Here's an animal, too, and what have they made of him?"

It would have been futile to try to convince Kasyan of the impossibility of "putting spells" on game, and therefore I gave him no answer. Meanwhile we had turned through the gates.

Annushka was not in the cabin; she had already been there and left the mushrooms. Erofei fixed the new axle, after first submitting it to a harsh and unjust appraisal; within an hour I drove off, leaving some money with Kasyan, who at first refused to take it, but then, after thinking and holding it in the palm of his hand, put it into his bosom. During this hour he had uttered hardly so much as a word. As before, he stood leaning against the gates, without answering the reproaches of my coachman. He took leave of me very coldly.

As soon as I had returned, I had at once observed that my Erofei was again in a gloomy mood. . . . In fact he had found nothing to eat in the village and the water for the horses was brackish. We drove off. With dissatisfaction expressed even at the back of his head, he sat on the box, wanting desperately to talk to me; but while awaiting my first question he limited himself to faint grumblings under his breath and to words of instruction addressed to the horses, but sometimes venomously expressed. "Village!" he muttered. "Village, indeed! Why, I tried asking for kvass and they haven't even got that. . . . Good Lord! and as for the water, it's just filth!" He spat loudly. "No cucumber, no kvass, nothing. Well, you," he added loudly, turning to the right side-horse, "I know you, you fraud, you! You like pretending, to be sure. . . ." He struck the horse with the whip. "He's become an utter rascal, and yet he used to be such an obedient beast. . . . Well, just you look out!"

"Tell me, Erofei," I began, "what sort of fellow is this Kasyan?"

Erofei didn't answer at once: he was always a man of reflection and deliberation; but I guessed at once that my question had pleased and calmed him.

"The Flea?" he said at length, changing his grip on the reins. "A queer fellow: a regular crank, a queer fellow whose like you wouldn't find in a hurry. You see, he's exactly like this horse of ours; he has become quite unmanageable, too . . . so far as making him work goes. Well, of course, he's no use as a worker—he's hardly got any body for his soul to hang on to—well, anyway . . . You see, he's been the same ever since he was a boy. First of all, he went into the driving business with his uncles; they drove in troikas; then, of course, he got bored and chucked it. He started living at home, but even at home he couldn't sit still, such a restless chap he is—a proper Flea. Luckily he happened to have a good master who didn't make him do anything, and since then he has done nothing but wander about like a stray sheep. And such a strange fellow he is, God knows. Sometimes still as a stock, then suddenly he starts talking—and what it's all about, God knows. What sort of manners is that? No sort of manners at all. He makes no sense, and that's the truth. He sings well, though, solemn and well."

"Is it true that he is a healer?"

"Healer, indeed! . . . Whatever next? A fellow like him! All the same he did cure me of jaundice. . . . A stupid fellow if ever there was one," he added, after a silence.

"Have you known him for long?"

"Yes. We were neighbors at Sychovka, near Fair Springs."

"But this girl who met us in the forest—Annushka—is she anything to do with him?"

Erofei looked at me over his shoulder and smiled all over his face. "Ho . . . yes, they're related. She's an orphan: no mother, no one knows who her mother was. But she must be a relation of his: she's so like him. . . . Anyway, she lives with him. She's a smart girl; she's a good girl. And you won't believe this, but, if you please, he's had the idea of teaching his Annushka to read and write. That's just like him. He's such an extraordinary fellow. Such a flighty chap, with such big ideas, too . . . eh, eh, eh!"

My coachman suddenly interrupted himself and, holding the

horses, bent over sideways and started sniffing the air. "Isn't there a smell of burning? I thought so! Oh, these new axles! . . . I was right to give it a good greasing . . . I must get some water: luckily, here's a pond."

Erofei slowly dismounted from the box, untied the bucket, went to the pond, and, returning, listened, not without enjoyment, to the hissing of the wheel-hub under the sudden shock of water. . . .

Six times in some ten versts he had to drench the overheated axle. The evening was already far advanced when we returned home.

The Bailiff

FIFTEEN VERSTS AWAY FROM MY PROPERTY THERE LIVES AN ACquaintance of mine, a young landowner, a retired Guards officer, by name Arkady Pavlich Penochkin. There is plenty of game on his land, his house is built to the plans of a French architect, his servants are dressed in the English manner, he gives excellent dinners, receives his guests amiably, yet all the same one goes to his house with reluctance. He is a judicious, steady fellow, he had what is considered an excellent education, served in the army, moved in the best society, and now devotes himself to agriculture with a great deal of success. Arkady Pavlich, to use his own words, is strict but just, has the good of his serfs at heart, and punishes them—for their good. "One must treat them like children," he says on such occasions. "Illiteracy, *mon cher, il faut prendre cela en considération.*" He himself, when "the painful duty" impels him, avoids sharp or abrupt movements, dislikes raising his voice, and prefers to slide his hand out, adding calmly: "But I asked you to, my good fellow," or "What is the matter with you, my friend? Wake up," and this with only a slight clenching of the teeth and a twist of the mouth to one side. He is of small stature, neat of build, not at all bad-looking, with carefully kept hands and nails; his red lips and cheeks fairly breathe good health. He has a ringing, carefree laugh, accompanied by an attractive narrowing of his clear brown eyes. He dresses excellently and with taste. He gets French books, illustrations, and papers sent to him, but he is not a great reader. It was all he could do to plough through "The Wandering Jew." At cards, he plays a masterly game.

All in all, Arkady Pavlich is considered one of the most cultured
gentlemen and eligible bachelors of our province; the ladies are mad
about him, and particularly admire his manners. He conducts himself extremely well, is as careful as a cat, and has never in all his life
been mixed up in any trouble; although, on occasion, he likes to
throw his weight about and to embarrass and snub the timid. He
resolutely spurns low company—from fear of compromising himself; all the same, in his moments of high spirits, he declares himself
for a devotee of Epicurus, though his general opinion of philosophy
is poor, and he describes it as the "cloudy sustenance of the Teutonic
mind," or sometimes, simply, as "twaddle." He loves music; at cards,
he sings through his teeth, but with feeling; he remembers a few
airs from *Lucia di Lanunermoor* and *Somnambula*, but sings them
all slightly sharp. In the winter he goes to Petersburg. His house is
remarkably well-ordered; even the coachmen have felt his influence
and not only clean the harness and their own coats every day, but
wash their own faces. Arkady Pavlich's house-serfs have, it is true, a
somewhat sidelong look—but in Russia it is never possible to distinguish the surly from the merely sleepy. Arkady Pavlich speaks in a
soft and pleasant voice, with deliberation, as if it gave him pleasure
to pass his words one by one through his handsome, scented moustache. He also uses plenty of French expressions like: *"Mais c'est im-
payable! Mais comment donc!"* and so on. With it all, I, for one, am
never overkeen to visit him, and if it weren't for the blackcock and
the partridge I should probably have lost sight of him altogether.
A strange uneasiness takes hold of you in his house; even the comfort gives you no pleasure, and every time, in the evening, when a
footman with curled hair, in a blue livery with heraldic buttons,
appears before you and begins obsequiously pulling your boots off,
you feel that if, instead of his pale, lean figure, there could suddenly
bob up in front of you the enormous wide cheekbones, the improb-
able snub-nose, of a sturdy young peasant-lad, only just taken by his
master from the plough, but already successful in having burst at a
dozen places the seams of his new nankeen coat, you would be quite
overjoyed, and would eagerly submit yourself to the danger of having your leg pulled right off from the hip-bone with the boot.

Notwithstanding my aversion for Arkady Pavlich, I once stayed the night in his house. Early the following morning I ordered my carriage to be harnessed, but he refused to let me go without taking breakfast in the English manner, and led me into his study. We were served with tea, cutlets, soft-boiled eggs, butter, honey, cheese, and so forth. Two footmen in clean white gloves swiftly and silently forestalled our slightest wish. We were sitting on a Persian divan. Arkady Pavlich was wearing wide silk trousers, a black velvet jacket, a handsome fez with a blue tassel, and yellow heelless Chinese slippers. He drank tea, laughed, inspected his nails, smoked, tucked cushions under his side, and in short was in an excellent humor. After breakfasting amply and with evident satisfaction, Arkady Pavlich poured himself out a glass of red wine, lifted it to his lips, and suddenly frowned.

"Why is the wine not warmed?" he asked one of the footmen, in a fairly sharp voice.

The man became confused, halted as if rooted to the ground, and turned pale.

"I am asking you a question, my good fellow," continued Arkady Pavlich calmly, without shifting his gaze from him.

The unhappy footman fidgeted where he stood, twisted his napkin, and said not a word. Arkady Pavlich lowered his head and looked thoughtfully at him from under his eyebrows.

"*Pardon, mon cher,*" he said with an agreeable smile and a friendly touch of his hand on my knee, and stared again at the footman. "Well, you can go," he added, after a short silence, lifted his eyebrows, and rang.

A man came in, a stout, swarthy fellow with black hair and a low forehead and eyes completely buried in fat.

"About Fyodor . . . the necessary steps," said Arkady Pavlich, in a low voice and with complete self-possession.

"Very good, sir," answered the fat one and went out.

"*Voilà, mon cher, les désagréments de la campagne,*" remarked Arkady Pavlich gaily. "But where are you off to? Wait, sit down again for a bit longer."

"No," I answered. "It is time for me to go."

"Always shooting! Oh, you shooting men! But where are you going now?"

"To Ryabovo. Forty versts away."

"Ryabovo? Goodness me, why in that case I'll come with you. Ryabovo is at most five versts from my place at Shipilovka, and it is ages since I was last there: I could never find a moment to go. This is a piece of luck: you shoot at Ryabovo to-day, and in the evening you come to my place. *Ce sera charmant.* We will dine together—we will take the cook with us, and you will stay the night with me. Splendid!" he added, without waiting for me to answer. "*C'est arrangé.* Hey there! Tell them to harness the carriage for us, and be quick about it. You've never been to Shipilovka? I would have been ashamed to suggest that you should spend the night in my bailiff's cabin, but I know you're not fussy and wouldn't have minded spending the night at Ryabovo in a hay-shed. . . . Let's go, let's go!"

And Arkady Pavlich began to sing a French love-song.

"You may not know," he continued, swaying from one leg to the other, "that my peasants there are rent-paying. It's that Constitution—and there's nothing one can do about it. All the same, they pay their rent regularly, or of course I would have transferred them to labor-duty long ago, but there is so little land! Even as it is, I am surprised at the way they make both ends meet. Anyhow, *c'est leur affaire.* The bailiff I have there is a stout fellow, *une forte tête*, a born administrator! You'll see. . . . Well, what a piece of luck this is!"

There was nothing for it. Instead of leaving at nine o'clock in the morning, we left at two. Sportsmen will imagine my impatience. Arkady Pavlich loved, as he put it, to make a fuss of himself when he got the chance, and took with him an immense supply of linen, victuals, liquor, perfumes, pillows, and dressing-cases of all sorts, such as would have lasted a careful, self-denying German for a whole year. Every time we went downhill Arkady Pavlich treated the coachman to a short but vehement lecture, from which I was able to conclude that my acquaintance was a thorough poltroon. Our journey went off without a hitch; except that on a recently mended bridge the cook's cart broke down and the cook's belly got bruised by the back wheel.

Seeing the mishap to his home-trained Karem, Arkady Pavlich got a bad fright and at once sent to ask if his hands were all right. Receiving an affirmative answer, he calmed down at once. What with all this, we had spent a long time under way; I sat in the carriage with Arkady Pavlich and towards the end of the journey I became bored to death, the more so because, as the hours went by, he talked himself out and even got round to liberalism. At last we came, not to Ryabovo, but straight to Shipilovka; it just happened that way. In any case, it would have been too late for me to go shooting that day, so I contained myself and submitted to my fate.

The cook had arrived a few minutes before us and evidently had already managed to take the necessary steps and warn those concerned, for at the very moment when we crossed the village boundary we were met by the headman (the son of the bailiff), a sturdy, red-headed peasant, seven feet high, on horse-back, capless, and wearing a new overcoat, unbuttoned. "But where is Sofron?" Arkady Pavlich asked him. The headman first jumped nimbly from his horse, bowed deeply to his master, and said: "Good day, father Arkady Pavlich," then raised his head, pulled himself together, and announced that Sofron had gone to Perov, but that they had already sent to fetch him. "Well, come along after us," said Arkady Pavlich. The headman led his horse respectfully to one side, clambered on to it, and trotted after the carriage, holding his cap in his hand. We drove through the village. A few peasants in empty carts were driving towards us; they were coming from the threshing-floor and singing songs, beating time with their bodies and waving their legs in the air; but, when they saw our carriage and the headman, they suddenly fell silent, took off their winter caps (it was in fact summer) and sat up as if expecting orders. Arkady Pavlich gave them a gracious bow. A mood of anxious excitement spread visibly through the village. Peasant women in check skirts threw bits of wood at dogs who were slow in the uptake or over-zealous; a lame old man, with a beard which began immediately under his eyes, snatched a horse which had not finished drinking away from the well, struck it on the side for no apparent reason, and only then made his bow. Little boys in long blouses ran wailing to the cabins, lay on their stomachs on the high thresholds, hung down their heads, threw their legs in the air, and thus disappeared with great agility behind doors into dark passages from which they did not reappear. Even the chickens made off under the gates at a rapid trot; one bold cock, with a black chest like a satin waistcoat and a red tail which came curling right up to his crest, made as if to stay in the road and was just preparing to crow, but suddenly became self-conscious and ran off too. The bailiff's cabin stood away from the others in the middle of a thick green hempyard. We halted in front of the gates. Mr. Penochkin got up, threw off his cloak with a picturesque gesture and alighted from the carriage, casting a friendly glance around. The bailiff's wife welcomed us with low curtsies, then came up and kissed her master's hand. Arkady Pavlich let her kiss away to her heart's content and then went up to the porch. Inside the passage, in a dark corner, stood the headman's wife and she curtsied too, but didn't dare kiss hands. In the so-called "cold room"—to the right of the passage—two other women were already busy; they were carrying out all kinds of junk, empty jugs, sheepskin coats that had gone stiff, greasy pots, and a cradle containing a heap of rags and a mottle-faced baby, and were sweeping up the dust with bathbrooms. Arkady Pavlich sent them packing and installed himself on the bench under the icons. His coachmen began to carry in trunks, chests, and other accessories, while doing everything possible to deaden the sound of their heavy boots.

Meanwhile, Arkady Pavlich was questioning the headman about the harvest, the sowing, and other farm topics. The headman answered adequately, but with a certain dull awkwardness, like a man buttoning up a coat with frozen fingers. He was standing in the doorway, constantly looking over his shoulder and making way for the swift-footed valet. Behind his powerful frame I managed to get a glimpse of the bailiff's wife quietly beating another woman in the passage. All at once a cart rattled up and halted in front of the porch, and the bailiff came in.

This "born administrator," to quote Arkady Pavlich, was a short, broad-shouldered, squat, gray-haired man with a red nose, little blue eyes, and a fan-shaped beard. Let us remark in passing that in all her history Mother Russia has never known a man make good and grow rich without a substantial beard; a man may have worn a meagre goatee all his days, then suddenly you see him enveloped on all sides in a kind of halo—wherever can all the hair come from! The bailiff must have taken a drop in Perov: his face was quite bloated, and he smelt of drink, too.

"Oh, sir, father, benefactor," he began in a sing-song voice, and with such emotion in his face that you expected the tears to start at any moment. "At last you have done us the honor! . . . Your hand, sir, your hand," he added, sticking out his lips in anticipation.

Arkady Pavlich satisfied his wish.

"Well, Sofron, my friend, how are things with you?" he asked in a kind voice.

"Oh, father!" exclaimed Sofron. "How could they be but well? For you, our father, sir, our benefactor, have done us the honor of brightening our village with your presence, and have made us happy to the end of our days! Praise be to the Lord, Arkady Pavlich, praise be to the Lord! All is well, thanks to your goodness."

Here Sofron fell silent, looked at his master, and, as if carried away again by a wave of emotion (added to which the drink inside him was claiming its due), begged leave to kiss his hand for a second time and began again with a more pronounced singsong than before.

"Oh, sir, father, benefactor . . . and what besides! Goodness me, I've gone quite off my head from joy. . . . Goodness me, I can't believe my eyes. . . . Oh, father! . . ."

Arkady Pavlich looked at me, laughed, and asked: "*N'est-ce pas que c'est touchant?*"

"But, sir, Arkady Pavlich," continued the irrepressible bailiff, "how comes it? You have quite distressed me, sir; you never warned me of your visit. Where will you spend the night? Look at all the dirt and dust here. . . ."

"Never mind, Sofron, never mind," answered Arkady Pavlich with a smile. "It's all right here."

"But, father—all right for who? All right for peasants like me; but for you, you. . . . Oh, father, benefactor, oh, father mine! . . . Forgive me, I'm a fool, I've gone off my head; goodness me, I have gone all silly."

Meanwhile supper was served and Arkady Pavlich fell to. The old man dismissed his son. "You're spoiling the air," he said.

"Well, have you got the boundaries settled, gaffer?" asked Mr. Penochkin, in an evident attempt at a peasant's way of talking, and with a wink at me.

"Yes, sir—all thanks to your goodness. The day before yesterday they signed the whole story. To begin with, the Khlynovo folk made difficulties . . . they did, father, they did indeed. They asked . . . and asked . . . God knows what they didn't ask; they're such fools, sir, such a stupid lot. But we, sir, thanks to your goodness, we offered a little something to Nikolai Nikolaich, who was the arbitrator, and satisfied him; we followed your instructions closely, sir; we did exactly what you were good enough to tell us, and Egor Dmitrich knows just what we did."

"Egor reported to me fully," observed Arkady Pavlich pompously.

"Of course, sir, of course he did."

"Well, I suppose you're satisfied now?"

Sofron was waiting just for this. "Oh, father, oh, benefactor!" he began to intone again. "Forgive me . . . you see, we pray to the Lord God day and night for you, father. . . . Of course we've so little land . . ."

Penochkin interrupted him. "Well, all right, all right, Sofron, I know what a faithful servant you are. But tell me, how is the yield?"

Sofron sighed.

"Well, the yield is not too good, sir. Let me tell you, Arkady Pavlich, sir, about something that has happened." Here he spread out his arms, came closer to Mr. Penochkin, bent down, and narrowed one eye. "A dead body was found on our land."

"How so?"

"I can't make head or tail of it, sir, father: an enemy must have had a hand in it. Yes, luckily it was found near the boundary; but on our land, all the same—it's no good denying it. I at once gave orders for it to be dragged off to the neighbor's bit of land while that was still possible, and posted a sentry on it and told my people to hold their tongues. But, to take no risks, I reported it to the district police officer. 'This is the way things are,' I told him; and I gave him a cup of tea and a little something besides. . . . Well, sir, what do you think? It's ended up round somebody else's neck: a dead body is just a matter of two hundred rubles—and that's all there is to it."

Mr. Penochkin laughed heartily at his bailiff's ruse, and said to me several times, pointing at him with his head: *"Quel gaillard, ah?"*

Meanwhile it had grown quite dark out-of-doors; Arkady Pavlich ordered the table to be cleared and straw to be brought. The valet made our beds and arranged the pillows; we lay down. Sofron retired, after receiving his orders for the following day. Arkady Pavlich, while dropping off to sleep, still had quite a lot to say about the excellent qualities of the Russian peasant, and at the same time observed to me that, since Sofron had been in charge, the peasants of Shipilovo had not been a farthing in arrears. . . . The watchman hammered on his board; a child, who had evidently not yet succeeded in acquiring a fitting sense of self-abnegation, cried somewhere in the cabin. . . . We fell asleep.

Next day we rose fairly early. I was preparing to leave for Ryabovo, but Arkady Pavlich wanted to show me his estate and induced me to stay. I was in fact not reluctant to verify in practice the excellent qualities of that born administrator, Sofron. The bailiff appeared. He wore a blue overcoat girt with a red belt. He had much less to say than the day before, he met his master's gaze with a sharply attentive stare and answered him coherently and to the point. We set off with him for the threshing-floor. Sofron's son, the seven-foot headman, who showed every sign of extreme stupidity, followed us as well, and we were also joined by the village constable Fedoseich, an ex-soldier with huge moustaches and the peculiar expression of a man who very long ago had been extremely surprised at something and had never recovered since. We inspected the threshing-floor, the threshing-barn, the drying-barns, the cartshed, the windmill, the cow-byre, the winter-fields, the hemp-yards;

everything was in fact extremely well-kept: only the sad faces of the peasants caused me a certain perplexity. Sofron's care was not purely utilitarian but covered the amenities as well: he had planted willows round all the ditches, he had made paths between the ricks leading to the threshing-floor and sprinkled sand on them; on the windmill he had fixed a weather-vane in the shape of a bear with open jaws and a red tongue; he had adorned the brick cow-byre with something in the nature of a Grecian pediment and under the pediment he had written in white letters: BILT IN THE VILLEGE OF SHIPILOVO IN THE YEAR ONE THOWSEND AIT HUNDRID FORTY. THIS COW-BIRE. Arkady Pavlich grew quite sentimental and let himself go in an explanation to me in French of the advantages of the rent-system, observing that labor-duty was the more advantageous system for the landowner—but that that wasn't everything . . . He began to give his bailiff advice on how to plant potatoes, how to prepare fodder for cattle, and so on. Sofron listened to his master's dissertation attentively, gave him an occasional rejoinder, but no longer dignified Arkady Pavlich with the title of father or benefactor, and kept on stressing that they had so little land and that there was no reason against some more.

"Why, buy away," said Arkady Pavlich. "Buy in my name. I don't mind."

Sofron gave no answer to this but simply stroked his beard.

"But now it wouldn't do us any harm to ride to the forest," observed Mr. Penochkin. Horses were immediately brought for us to ride, and we proceeded to the forest. Here we found dense undergrowth and lots of game, for which Arkady Pavlich praised Sofron and patted him on the shoulder. Mr. Penochkin adhered to the Russian school of forestry, and took the opportunity of telling me what he called a very amusing instance of how a practical joker of a landowner had made his forester see the light by pulling out about half his beard to prove that cutting timber down doesn't make it grow any thicker. In other respects, however, neither Sofron nor Arkady Pavlich was afraid of innovation. When we returned to the village, the bailiff led us to inspect the winnowing-machine which he had recently ordered from Moscow. The machine certainly functioned well, but, if Sofron had known what an unpleasant incident awaited him and his master on this last bit of their tour, he would probably have stopped with us at his home.

This is what happened. As we came out of the shed, we saw the following spectacle. A few paces away from the door, beside a muddy pond, in which three ducks were splashing about without a care in the world, two peasants were kneeling. One was an old man of about sixty, the other a youth of about twenty. Both wore patched and crumpled shirts, with bare legs and belts of cord. The constable Fedoseich was fussing busily around them and would probably have induced them to go away if we had stayed longer in the shed, but, seeing us, he went all taut and remained rooted to the spot. Near him stood the headman with open mouth and fists hanging down undecidedly. Arkady Pavlich frowned, bit his lip, and went up to the petitioners. They both bowed at his feet in silence.

"What do you want? What is your request?" he asked, in a strict, slightly nasal voice. The peasants exchanged glances and said not a word, but only narrowed their eyes as if against the sun, and began to breathe more quickly.

"Well, what is it?" continued Arkady Pavlich, and immediately turned to Sofron. "From what family?"

"From the Toboleyev family," answered the bailiff slowly.

"Well, what is it?" began Mr. Penochkin again. "Have you no tongues, or what? Tell me, you, what d'you want?" he added, motioning his head towards the old man. "Don't be afraid, you fool."

The old man stuck out his dark brown, wrinkled neck, opened his bluish lips crookedly, and pronounced hoarsely: "Defend us, my lord!" And he again struck his forehead on the earth. The young peasant bowed too. Arkady Pavlich gazed with dignity at the backs of their necks, threw his head back, and planted his legs farther apart.

"What is it all about? Of whom are you complaining?"

"Have mercy on us, my lord! Give us a chance to breathe . . . We're being plagued to death." The old man spoke with difficulty.

"Who has been plaguing you?"

"Why, Sofron Yakovlich, sir."

Arkady Pavlich was silent.

"What is your name?"

"Antip, sir."

"And who is this?"

"My son, sir."

Arkady Pavlich was silent again and worked his moustaches.

"Well, in what way has he been plaguing you?" he began, look-ing at the old man through his moustaches.

"Sir, he's utterly ruined us. He's sent two of my sons out of their turn to join the army, and now he is taking the third one away too. Yesterday, sir, he took my last cow out of my yard and he beat my old woman—that was *his* kind work." He pointed at the headman.

"H'm," said Arkady Pavlich.

"Don't let him finish us right off, kind sir."

Mr. Penochkin frowned.

"What is the meaning of all this?" he asked the bailiff, in a low voice and with an expression of displeasure.

"He's a drunkard, sir," answered the bailiff, using the respectful form for the first time. "He won't work. He's not been out of arrears for the last five years, sir."

"Sofron Yakovlich paid the arrears for me, sir," continued the old man. "It's five years now since he paid them—and ever since then he's made a slave of me, sir, that's what he's done. . . ."

"But how comes it that you have been in arrears?" asked Mr. Penochkin threateningly. The old man hung his head. "I suppose you like getting drunk, hanging around the pot-houses?"

The old man began to open his mouth.

"I know you," continued Arkady Pavlich, his temper flaring up. "All you think of is drinking and lying over the stove, and then the good peasant has to answer for you."

"He's a rude fellow, too," the bailiff interjected while his master was still speaking.

"Well, that goes without saying. It's always the same way; I've noticed it more than once. He spends the whole year in debauchery and impertinence and now he throws himself at my feet!"

"Arkady Pavlich, sir," began the old man desperately. "Have

mercy on me, protect me—how have I been rude? The Lord be my witness, it's more than I can bear. Sofron Yakovlich doesn't like me, for some reason or other—the Lord be his judge! he's ruining me for good, sir . . . this is the last of my sons . . . and him too . . ." In the old man's yellow, puckered eyes a teardrop twinkled. "Have mercy, my lord, protect me . . ."

"And we aren't the only ones," the young peasant was beginning.

Arkady Pavlich suddenly burst out: "And who is asking you, eh? No one, so you keep quiet. . . . What sort of behavior is this? Keep quiet, I tell you, keep quiet! . . . My goodness! this is sheer sedition. No, my friend, I don't advise sedition on my land, on my land . . ." Arkady Pavlich stepped forward, then probably remembered my presence, turned away, and put his hands in his pockets. . . . "*Je vous demande bien pardon, mon cher,*" he said with a forced smile and a significant lowering of his voice. "*C'est le mauvais côté de la médaille.* . . . Well, all right, all right," he continued, without looking at the peasants. "I shall give suitable orders. All right, you may go." The peasants remained kneeling. "All right, I tell you. . . . You can go. I shall give suitable orders, I tell you."

Arkady Pavlich turned his back on them. "Perpetual discontent," he said through his teeth, and returned home with long strides. Sofron followed behind him. The constable opened his eyes wide, as if he was preparing for a very long jump. The headman chased the ducks away from the puddle. The petitioners stayed where they were, looked at each other and then trudged away without looking round.

Two hours later I was at Ryabovo and prepared to go out shooting with Ampadist, a peasant of my acquaintance. Right up to the moment of my departure, Penochkin had kept Sofron in disgrace. I started a conversation with Ampadist about the peasants of Shipilovo and about Mr. Penochkin and asked whether he knew the bailiff there.

"Sofron Yakovlich? . . . I should think I do!"

"What sort of a man is he?"

"A dog, not a man: a dog such as you won't find between here and Kursk."

"But how so?"

"Why, Shipilovo is supposed to belong to, what's his name, Penkin; but he's not the master: Sofron's the master."

"Really?"

"He's the master, and treats it like his own property. The peasants all round are in his debt, they work for him as if they were his own laborers; some he sends off with the waggons, some he sends off somewhere else. He chases them about properly."

"They haven't got much land, I think?"

"Not much? Why, in Khlynovo alone he farms two hundred acres, and three hundred in our village—five hundred acres in all. And land is not his only interest: he trades in horses, cattle, tar, pitch, oil, hemp, and all the rest of it. . . . He's clever, damned clever, and rich, too, the beast! The worst thing is the way he knocks them about. He's an animal, not a man. It's well known: a dog; a dirty dog, if ever there was one."

"But why don't they complain about him?"

"Ho! What does it matter to the master? There are no arrears, so what does he care? If you go and complain," he added, after a short pause, "he'll, he'll . . . treat you like he did that other fellow. . . ."

I remembered about Antip and told him what I had seen.

"Well," said Ampadist, "he'll be eating him up now, eating the fellow alive. The headman will be giving him such a beating now. Poor, unlucky wretch, just fancy! And what's he suffering for? Because he quarrelled with him at a meeting, with this bailiff-fellow, probably he couldn't put up with it any longer. . . . A fine thing! That's how he got his knife into Antip. Now he'll finish the job off. He's such a dog, such a dirty dog—may God forgive my sins—he knows who to fasten on. He doesn't touch any of the older people who have got a bit of family or money, he doesn't touch them, the crafty devil, but with that Antip he's really let himself go. You see, he's sent Antip's sons to the army out of their turn, the wicked rogue, the dog—may God forgive me my sins."

We set off to shoot.

The Estate Office

IT WAS AUTUMN. I HAD SPENT SEVERAL HOURS ROAMING THE fields with my gun, and would probably not have returned before evening to the inn on the Kursk highway where my troika was awaiting me, if the remarkably fine, cold rain which had been chasing me around since early morning, like a tireless and determined spinster, had not finally forced me to seek at any rate a temporary shelter somewhere close at hand. While I was still considering which way to go, my gaze lighted unexpectedly on a low hut beside a field of peas. I went up to the hut, peered under the thatched eaves, and saw an old man in an advanced state of decrepitude which at once reminded me of the dying goat found by Robinson Crusoe in a cave on his island. The old man was squatting down, with his dim little eyes screwed up, and, busily but carefully, like a hare (the poor fellow had not a tooth in his head), was chewing a hard, dry pea and constantly shifting it from one side of the mouth to the other. He was so absorbed in this occupation that he didn't notice my arrival.

"Grandfather, I say, grandfather!" I exclaimed.

He stopped chewing, arched his brows and with an effort opened his eyes.

"What?" he mumbled in a husky voice.

"Where is the nearest village?" I asked.

The old man resumed his chewing. He hadn't heard what I said. I repeated my question louder than before.

"Village? . . . Why, what do you want?"

"I want to shelter from the rain."

"What?"

"To shelter from the rain."

"Oh!" He scratched the nape of his sunburned neck. "Well, there, that's the way to go," he said suddenly, with a confused wave of his hands. "Then, when you've passed the wood—that's how you go—you'll see a track; you leave it, the track, and all the time keep to the right, keep to the right, keep to the right . . . well, there you'll find Ananyevo. Or else you'd be at Sitovka."

I had difficulty in following the old man. His moustache got in the way, and his tongue did its duty badly.

"Where are you from?" I asked him.

"What?"

"Where are you from?"

"From Ananyevo."

"What do you do here?"

"What?"

"What do you do here?"

"I sit and keep watch."

"What do you watch?"

"The peas."

I could not help laughing.

"But for goodness' sake, how old are you?"

"God knows."

"I suppose you don't see so well?"

"What?"

"You don't see so well, I suppose?"

"No. And sometimes I don't hear anything either."

"Then how can you keep watch, for goodness' sake?"

"Ask my elders and betters."

Elders and betters! I thought, and looked with pity at the poor old man. Fumbling, he took from inside his coat a piece of dry bread and began to suck it like a child, laboriously drawing in his cheeks, which were anyway sunken enough.

I went off in the direction of the wood, turned to the right, kept on bearing to the right as the old man had directed me, and finally reached a big village with a stone church in the new taste, that's to say with columns, and a big manor house, also with columns. From some way off, through the fine net of the rain, I noticed a cabin with a wooden roof and two chimneys, larger than the others, probably the home of the headman of the village. I went towards it, in the hope of finding there a samovar with tea, sugar, and some not completely sour cream. Accompanied by my shivering dog, I went up to the porch and into the passage, opened a door, but saw, instead of the usual appointments of a cabin, tables piled with papers, two red cupboards, bespattered ink-wells, heavyweight pewter sand-boxes, the longest possible quills, and so on. At one of the tables sat a youth of about twenty, with a puffy, unhealthy face, tiny little eyes, a greasy forehead, and side-locks of unconscionable length. He was decently dressed in a gray nankeen coat which had worn shiny round the collar and over the stomach.

"What can I do for you?" he asked me, with a jerk of the head, like a horse which never expected to be taken hold of by the mouth.

"Does the factor live here . . . or? . . ."

"This is the head office of the estate," he interrupted me. "I am the clerk on duty. . . . Did you not see the notice outside? That's what it's put there for."

"Where can one dry oneself here? Has anyone in the village got a samovar?"

"Of course there are samovars," replied the youth in the gray coat, with dignity. "You can go to Father Timofei or failing that to the servants' cabin, or failing that to Nazar Tarasich, or failing that to Agrafena the hen-woman."

"Who are you talking to, you blockhead? You're spoiling my sleep!" came a voice from the next room.

"Here's a gentleman has come and is asking where he can dry himself."

"What gentleman?"

"I don't know. He's got a dog and a gun."

A bed creaked in the next room. The door opened and in came a man of about fifty, stout, short, bull-necked, pop-eyed, very round-cheeked, and with a face that shone all over.

"What do you require?" he asked me.

"I want to dry myself."

"This isn't the place for it."

"I didn't know that this was an office; but, by the way, I'm ready to pay. . . ."

"I suppose it *could* be done here," rejoined the stout one. "Won't you come this way?"

He led me into another room, which was not the one from which he had come himself.

"Will you be all right here?"

"Yes. . . . You couldn't get me some tea with cream?"

"Certainly, at once. If you'll take your things off and rest your-self, tea will be ready in a moment."

"Whose estate is this?"

"It belongs to Elena Nikolaevna Losnyakova."

He went out. I looked round: along the partition dividing my room from the office stood a huge leather sofa, and two chairs, also of leather and with extremely high backs, were planted on both sides of the only window, which looked out on the village street. On the walls, which were papered in green with a pink design, hung three huge pictures painted in oils. One of them depicted a spaniel with a blue collar, on which was written: "This is my Joy." At the dog's feet was a river, and on the opposite bank, underneath a pine tree, sat a hare of disproportionate size with one ear pricked. The second picture showed two old men eating a water-melon: behind the water-melon could be seen in the distance a Grecian portico with the inscription: *The Temple of Content*. The third pic-ture represented a half-nude woman in a recumbent attitude, fore-shortened, with red knees and enormous heels. My dog, without an instant's delay, got himself under the sofa, by supernatural exer-tions, and there apparently found a lot of dust, because he began to sneeze his head off. I went to the window. Boards had been laid obliquely across the street from the manor house to the office: a very useful precaution, since all round, thanks to our black soil and the prolonged rain, the mud was terrible. Outside the manor house, which stood with its back to the street, was a scene typical enough in such a setting: maids in faded print dresses were darting backwards and forwards; house-servants were strolling about in the mud, halting and reflectively scratching their backs; the constable's tethered horse was slowly swishing its tail and tossing its head and gnawing at the fence; hens were clucking, consumptive-looking turkeys gobbling away at each other. On the porch of a dark, decrepit building, probably a bath-house, sat a sturdy lad with a guitar singing, not without gusto, the well-known ditty:

> *Away to the desert I'm bound to go,*
> *From this enchanted spot.*

The fat fellow came into the room.

"Your tea's just coming," he told me with an agreeable smile.

The young man in the gray coat, the duty-clerk, set out, on an old card-table, a samovar, a tea-pot, a glass with a broken saucer, a bowl of cream, and a string of Bolkhovo biscuits, which were hard as flint. The fat fellow went out.

"Who is that?" I asked the duty-clerk. "The factor?"

"No, sir: he used to be the head cashier, but now he has been promoted head clerk."

"Haven't you got a factor?"

"No, sir, we have a bailiff, Mikhailo Bikulov, but no factor."

"D'you have an agent?"

"Certainly, a German, Lindamandol, Karlo Karlich; only it's not he who gives the orders."

"Who does, then?"

"The lady herself."

"So that's how it is? . . . Well, have you got many people working in the office?"

The young man reflected.

"Six altogether."

"Who are they all?" I asked.

"Well, first there is Vasily Nikolaich, the head cashier; then,

Pyotr the clerk; Pyotr's brother Ivan, also a clerk; another Ivan who
is a clerk, too; Koskenkin Narkizov, also a clerk; and me—there's
no end of us."

"I suppose your lady has a lot of house-servants?"

"Not so many as all that."

"Well, how many?"

"I dare say there are a hundred and fifty or so."

We were both silent.

"Well, are you a good handwriter?" I began again.

The lad smiled proudly, nodded, went into the office, and brought
back a sheet of paper covered with writing.

"This is my hand," he said, still smiling.

I looked; on the quarto sheet of grayish paper, in a fine large
hand, was written the following:

ORDER

From the Head Office of the Ananyevo Estate
to the Bailiff Mikhailo Bikulov. No. 209.

Immediately on receipt of this present, you are hereby instructed to
ascertain who it was that last night went past the English garden
in a state of intoxication, singing indecent songs, awakening
and alarming the French governess Madame Enzhenie, what
the nightwatchmen were up to, and which of them was on duty
in the garden and permitted such dastardly behaviour. You are
instructed to inquire into all particulars of the foregoing and to
report to the office forthwith.

> *Nikolai Khvostov,*
> *Head Clerk.*

Affixed to the order was an enormous armorial seal with the
legend, "Seal of the Head Office of the Ananyevo Estate," and below it was added a minute: "To be carried out to the letter. Elena
Losnyakova."

"The lady wrote that herself, did she?" I asked.

"Certainly she did, sir: she always does it herself. Otherwise the order can't take effect."

"Well, so you'll send the bailiff this order?"

"No, sir, he'll come himself and read it—that's to say, it will be read to him; you see, he can't read."

The duty-clerk paused again. "Well, sir," he added, smiling, "d'you like my writing?"

"I do."

"I admit it wasn't I who drafted it. Koskenkin is the masterhand at that."

"What? . . . Do you actually have your orders drafted first?"

"Of course, sir. It would never do to go straight to the fair copy."

"What salary d'you get?" I asked.

"Thirty-five rubles, and five rubles shoe-money."

"And you're satisfied?"

"Yes, certainly. It's not everyone who can get into the office. In my case, of course, it was the hand of God; my uncle's the butler."

"And you're all right?"

"Yes, sir. To tell the truth," he continued with a sigh, "working for merchants, for instance, we clerks are better off. Working for merchants, we clerks do very very well. Why, last night we had a visit from a merchant from Venyovo—so his man told me. . . . Well-off, there are no two ways about it."

"You mean that a merchant pays a higher salary?"

"Good Lord, no! He'd chuck you out if you asked him for a salary. No, if you work for a merchant, you live on faith and fear. He gives you food and drink and clothes and so on. If you serve him well, he'll give you even more. . . . Salary! you don't need one at all . . . and a merchant will live simply, in the good old Russian way: you take the road with him—he drinks tea and so do you; what he eats, you eat too. The merchant . . . is a happy-go-lucky fellow; it's not like working for a gentleman. There are no fads about your merchant; if he's angry with you, he beats you and the thing's done with. None of your nagging, none of your sly digs. . . . But working for a gentleman is dreadful! Nothing's ever right: this is badly done, that's all wrong. You give him a glass of water or some food—'Ah, the water stinks! Ah, the food stinks!' You take it away; you wait behind the door, bring it back again, 'Well, now it's all right, now it doesn't stink any more.' And as for ladies, well, as for ladies! . . . And as for young ladies, what's more! . . ."

"Fedyushka!" came the voice of the fat man from the office. The duty-clerk hurried out. I drank my glass of tea, lay down on the sofa, and went to sleep. I slept for two hours. Wakening, I meant to get up, but laziness won the day; I shut my eyes, but didn't fall asleep again. Behind the partition, in the office, a discreet conversation was in progress. Involuntarily I began to listen.

"Just so, just so, Nikolai Eremeich," said one voice. "Just so. We have got to take that into account; certainly we have got to. . . . H'mm!"

The speaker coughed.

"You can take my word for it, Gavrila Antonich," rejoined the voice of the fat man. "You can judge for yourself whether or not I know the way things are here."

"Of course you do, Nikolai Eremeich. One might say that you are the top man here. Well, how shall it be?" continued the voice that was unknown to me. "What shall we decide on, Nikolai Eremeich, if you don't mind my being curious?"

"Yes, what shall we decide on, Gavrila Antonich? It depends on you, so to speak; you don't seem very keen."

"Good heavens, Nikolai Eremeich, whatever d'you mean? It's our job to trade and do business; it's our job to buy. That's the very ground we stand on, Nikolai Eremeich, as you might say."

"Eight rubles," said the fat one with deliberation.

I could hear a sigh.

"Nikolai Eremeich, it's an awful lot that you're asking."

"Gavrila Antonich, I swear before God that it's the only course I can take."

Silence reigned.

I raised myself softly and looked through a crack in the partition. The fat fellow was sitting with his back to me. Opposite him sat a merchant, a man of about forty, thin and pale, looking as if he had been anointed with Lenten oil. He kept wagging his beard and blinking away busily and twitching his lips.

. "The winter fields this year are tip-top, as you might say," he began again. "I have been admiring them as I drove along. Tip-top, they were, all the way from Voronezh—first-class, one might say."

"They're certainly not bad," answered the head clerk. "But as you know, Gavrila Antonich, autumn proposes and spring disposes."

"Just so, Nikolai Eremeich: everything is as God wills it; it's absolutely true, what you've just said. . . . Your guest won't have woken up?"

The fat one turned around . . . listened . . .

"No, he's asleep. All the same, maybe that . . ."

He went to the door.

"No, he's asleep," he repeated, and returned to his place.

"Well, how shall it be, Nikolai Eremeich?" began the merchant again: "We must conclude our business. Let's have it like this, Nikolai Eremeich. Let's have it like this," he continued, blinking away the whole time. "Two gray notes and a white one for your good self and six and a half rubles for over there." He nodded towards the manor house. "Shall we shake hands on it?"

"Four gray ones," answered the clerk.

"Three, then."

"Four gray ones and no white ones."

"Three, Nikolai Eremeich."

"Three and a half and not a farthing less."

"Three, Nikolai Eremeich."

"Don't waste your breath, Gavrila Antonich."

"What a stubborn fellow," muttered the merchant. "Why, I could get a better deal direct with the lady."

"As you like," answered the fat one. "You could have done that long ago. I really don't know what all the fuss is about. . . . You'd get a much better deal."

"Oh, all right, Nikolai Eremeich, all right. How you flew into a rage! Why, I was just talking, like that."

"No, I really don't know . . ."

"It's all right, I tell you . . . I tell you, I was joking. . . . Well, take your three and a half, there's nothing else to be done with you."

"I ought to have taken four, but, like a fool, I was in too much of a hurry," grumbled the fat one.

"So it's six and a half over there, at the house, Nikolai Eremeich—the price of the corn is six and a half."

"Six and a half was what we said."

"Well, then, let's shake hands on it, Nikolai Eremeich." The merchant spread out his fingers and struck them against the clerk's palm. "And now with God's speed!" The merchant rose. "Now, sir, Nikolai Eremeich, I will go to the lady, and send my name in, and say to her: 'Nikolai Eremeich has agreed to sell for six and a half, madam.'"

"That's right."

"And now please take this."

The merchant handed the clerk a small wad of notes, bowed, shook his head, took his hat in two fingers, twitched his shoulders, and, with a rippling movement of his person, went out, his shoes squeaking decorously. Nikolai Eremeich crossed to the wall, and, as far as I could observe, began to sort the notes which the merchant had handed to him. Around the door appeared a red head with thick side-whiskers.

"Well?" asked the head, "everything in order?"

"Everything in order."

"How much?"

The fat fellow waved a hand irritably and pointed towards my room.

"Oh, all right," rejoined the head, and disappeared.

The fat fellow went to the table, sat down, opened a book, took up an abacus, and began to sling the beads backwards and forwards, using not the fore-finger but the third finger of his right hand: it looks more decorous.

The duty-clerk came in.

"What do you want?"

"Sidor has come, from Golopleky."

"Oh! well, bring him in. No, wait . . . first go and look whether the strange gentleman there is still asleep or whether he's woken up."

The duty-clerk came cautiously into my room. I had put my head on the game-bag which served me as a pillow and closed my eyes.

"He's asleep," whispered the duty-clerk, returning to the office. The fat fellow mumbled something through his teeth.

"Well, call Sidor," he said finally.

I sat up again. A peasant came in, an enormous fellow of about thirty, hale, red-cheeked, fair-haired, with a smooth, curling beard. He prayed before the icon, bowed to the head clerk, took his hat in both hands, and straightened himself out again.

"Good day to you, Sidor," said the fat one, rattling the abacus.

"Good day, Nikolai Eremeich."

"Well, how's the road?"

"All right, Nikolai Eremeich. A bit muddy." The peasant spoke slowly and softly.

"Is your wife well?"

"Well enough."

The peasant sighed and put one foot forward. Nikolai Eremeich set his pen behind his ear and blew his nose.

"Well, what have you come for?" he continued, putting his check handkerchief away in his pocket.

"It's like this, Nikolai Eremeich, they want carpenters from us."

"Well, haven't you got any, or what?"

"Of course we have, Nikolai Eremeich: we are right in the forest, no question of that. But it's the working-time, Nikolai Eremeich."

"The working-time! Tck, tck, you're dead keen to work for anyone else, but when it comes to working for your own master, you don't like it. . . . It's all the same work."

"The same work, certainly, Nikolai Eremeich . . . but . . ."

"Well?"

"The pay is very . . . that is . . ."

"I never did! You're thoroughly spoiled. Get along with you!"

"Well, there's more to it, Nikolai Eremeich. The work is supposed to be for a week, all told, but it takes a month to get through. Either the materials aren't there, or else they send us into the garden to sweep the paths."

"I never did! It's orders from the lady herself, so there's nothing for you and me to say about it."

Sidor said nothing and began shifting his weight from one leg to the other. Nikolai Eremeich twisted his head to one side and rattled away busily at his beads.

"Our . . . peasants . . . Nikolai Eremeich," began Sidor finally, hesitating over every word, "have sent me to present . . . here . . . there's . . ." and he thrust his enormous hand inside his overcoat and began to pull out a rolled-up towel with a red pattern on it.

"What's the matter, you fool, have you gone off your head, or what?" the fat one interrupted him suddenly. "Get along to my cabin," he continued, practically pushing out the astonished peasant. "Ask the wife . . . she will give you tea, and I'll be over straight away, so be off with you. Get along with you, I say."

Sidor went out.

"You . . . bear!" muttered the head clerk after him, and he shook his head and applied himself again to his abacus.

Suddenly there were cries of "Kuprya, Kuprya! You can't do down Kuprya!" coming from the street and from the porch, and a few moments later there came into the office a short, consumptive-looking man with an extremely long nose, great, immobile eyes, and a very arrogant manner. He wore an old, tattered coat of the color known as Adelaide (or, in our part of the world, "odelloid"), with a velveteen collar and tiny buttons. He was carrying a bundle of faggots on his shoulder. Around him jostled five house-servants, shouting: "Kuprya! You can't do down Kuprya! Kuprya's the new boiler-man, boiler-man!" But the man in the coat with the velveteen collar paid not the slightest attention to the uproar of his companions and kept an absolutely straight face. With measured steps he crossed to the stove, threw down his burden, straightened himself, brought a snuff-box out of his back pocket, opened his eyes wide and took a large pinch of grated trefoil mixed with ashes.

At the entry of this noisy mob, the fat fellow had begun by frowning and rising from his seat; but, on seeing the cause of the commotion, he smiled and merely told them not to shout, as there was a sportsman asleep in the next room.

"What sportsman?" asked two people at once.

"A gentleman."

"Oh!"

"Let them shout their heads off," said the man in the velvet collar, spreading out his hands. "What do I care, so long as they keep their hands off me? I'm the new boiler-man."

"Boiler-man! Boiler-man!" the mob repeated joyously.

"It was the lady's orders," he continued, shrugging his shoulders. "But just you wait . . . you'll be swineherds yet. But the fact that I'm a tailor, a good one, apprenticed to the best master-tailors in Moscow, and that I've made uniforms for generals—*that* no one can take away from me. What are *you* so proud of, anyway? . . . Eh? You're just so many drones, so many sluggards, that's all you are. If I get my freedom, I shan't die of hunger, I shan't fall by the wayside. If I get my passport, I shall pay in a good rent and satisfy my masters. But what will happen to you? You'll fall by the wayside, you'll just die like flies, and that's the truth!"

"That's a fine story," interrupted a pock-marked, white-lashed youth with a red cravat and tattered elbows. "You've been out on a passport, but the masters have never seen a copeck of rent from you and you've never earned so much as half a copeck for yourself: it was all you could do to drag yourself back home, and you've worn the same little coat ever since."

"Well, what of it, Konstantin Narkizich?" rejoined Kupryan. "A man falls in love and then he's dead and done for. You just live as long as I have before you judge me."

"And what have you chosen to fall in love with? A proper monster!"

"No, don't say that, Konstantin Narkizich."

"Who are you talking to, anyway? Why, I saw her; last year, in Moscow, I saw her with my own eyes."

"Last year she was a bit under the weather, and that's a fact," observed Kupryan.

"No, gentlemen, listen," said, in an offhand casual voice, a tall, thin man with a pimply face and curled, oiled hair, doubtless a valet. "Just let Kupryan Afanasich sing us his song. Now, Kupryan Afanasich, begin away!"

"Yes, yes!" took up the others. "Quite right, Alexandra!—That's finished Kuprya off, hasn't it just? . . . Sing, Kuprya! . . . Good for Alexandra!" (Serving folk often use feminine forms in an endearing sense when talking about a man.) "Sing!"

"This is no place for singing," rejoined Kupryan firmly, "this is the Estate Office."

"What has that to do with you? Are you aiming at becoming a clerk yourself?" answered Konstantin roughly, with a laugh. "That must be it."

"Everything depends on the masters' pleasure," observed the poor fellow.

"You see, you see what he'd like to become, you see the sort of chap he is! Ooh! ooh! ah!"

They all burst out laughing and some of them started jumping about. The one who roared loudest of all was a lad of about fifteen, probably the son of some aristocrat of the servant world: he wore a waistcoat with bronze buttons and a lilac-colored cravat and had already managed to grow a pot-belly.

"But listen, tell us, Kuprya," began Nikolai Eremeich complacently; he was evidently amused and mollified: "It's no fun to be boiler-man? It isn't, eh?"

"Well, Nikolai Eremeich," said Kupryan, "you're now head clerk, certainly; there's no question about that, admittedly; but even *you* have been in disgrace in your time and lived in a peasant's cabin."

"You be careful and don't forget yourself in front of me," the fat man interrupted him irritably. "They're laughing at you for the fool that you are; a fool like you ought to appreciate it, and be thankful, when anyone takes notice of—a fool like you."

"The words just slipped off my tongue, Nikolai Eremeich. I'm sorry . . ."

"Even if they did . . ."

The door opened and a page ran in.

"Nikolai Eremeich, the lady wants to see you."

"Who is with the lady?" he asked the page.

"Axinya Nikitishna and a merchant from Venyovo."

"I shall come at once. But you, my friends," he continued in a voice that carried conviction, "you'd better go somewhere else with your newly-promoted boiler-man, otherwise the German might turn up and he'd complain at once."

The fat fellow straightened the hair on his head, coughed in his hand, which was almost completely hidden by the sleeve of his coat, buttoned up his coat, and set off to see the lady, straddling his legs widely as he walked. After waiting a moment, the whole throng moved away after him, Kupryan with them. Only my old acquaintance the duty-clerk remained behind. He made as if to trim some pens, but dropped off to sleep where he sat. Some flies immediately took advantage of the opportunity and crawled over his mouth. A mosquito sat on his forehead, spread out its legs methodically, and slowly plunged the whole length of its sting into the soft flesh. The same red-whiskered head as before again appeared round the door, stared hard, then entered the office, with a tolerably hideous body attached to it.

"Fedyushka! always asleep!" said the head.

The duty-clerk opened his eyes and got up from his chair.

"Has Nikolai Eremeich gone to see the lady?"

"Yes, Vasily Nikolaich, he has."

Oho! I thought, here he is, the head cashier.

The head cashier began to pace up and down the room, in fact he prowled rather than paced, and his whole demeanor resembled a cat's. From his shoulders hung an old black frock-coat, with very narrow tails; he kept one hand at his breast, but with the other he fidgeted away at his high, tight horsehair cravat, and turned his head intently from side to side. He wore goatskin shoes without a squeak in them and stepped out very softly.

"Yagushkin the landowner was asking after you to-day," added the duty-clerk.

"H'm, he was, was he? What did he say, exactly?"

"He said that he was coming to Tyutyurev this evening and would wait for you there. He said he wanted to talk with Vasily Nikolaich on business, but on what business he didn't say. Vasily Nikolaich will know, he said."

"H'm!" rejoined the head cashier, and went over to the window.

"Hey, is Nikolai Eremeich in the office?" said a loud voice in the passage, and a tall man, evidently angry, with irregular but expressive, bold features, and reasonably tidily dressed, strode across the threshold.

"Isn't he here?" he asked with a quick look around.

"Nikolai Eremeich is with the lady," answered the cashier. "Tell me what I can do for you, Pavel Andreich; you can tell me. . . . What do you want?"

"What do I want? You want to know what I want?" The cashier gave a nervous nod.

"I want to teach him a lesson, the worthless pot-belly, the low tale-bearer that he is. . . . I'll teach him to tell tales!"

Pavel threw himself down in a chair.

"What on earth is the matter, Pavel Andreich? Calm yourself. . . . Aren't you ashamed? Don't forget who you are speaking about!" whispered the cashier.

"Who, indeed? What do I care if they have made him head clerk? A fine fellow, indeed, they've found for the job! They've let the goat loose among the cabbages, with a vengeance!"

"That'll do, Pavel, that'll do! Enough of that . . . what nonsense are you talking?"

"So Foxy Sly-Boots is wagging his tail, is he! . . . I'll wait for him," said Pavel with feeling, and he thumped his hand on the table. "Ah, here comes his worship," he added, looking out of the windows. "Talk of the devil. And welcome back!" He got up.

Nikolai Eremeich came into the office. His face radiated satisfaction, but at the sight of Pavel he showed a certain confusion.

"Good day, Nikolai Eremeich," said Pavel significantly, moving slowly to meet him. "Good day."

The head clerk made no answer. In the doorway appeared the face of the merchant.

"Why don't you do me the favor of answering?" continued Pavel. "Anyway, no . . . no . . ." he added. "That's not the way; you'll gain nothing by shouting and cursing. You'd do much better to tell me civilly, Nikolai Eremeich, what you're chasing me around for, and why you're out to ruin me. Well, speak, man, speak out."

"This is not the place for an explanation between us," rejoined the head clerk, not without agitation. "Nor the time either. But I'm certainly surprised at one thing: what has given you the idea that I am out to ruin you or that I am chasing you round? And anyway, how could I do so? You don't work with me in the office."

"No, indeed," answered Pavel. "That would be the last straw. But what's the point of pretending, Nikolai Eremeich? You understand what I mean."

"No, I don't."

"You do."

"Before God, I don't."

"Taking God's name in vain into the bargain. If it comes to that, tell me: have you no fear of God? Then, why don't you let the poor girl alone? What d'you want from her?"

"Who are you talking about, Pavel Andreich?" asked the fat one in feigned astonishment.

"Oho, he doesn't know, eh? I'm talking about Tatyana. You should fear God—and not seek revenge. You ought to be ashamed of yourself—you, a married man with children of my own size, whereas I am not after anything else. . . . I want to get married: I am going about it the honorable way."

"But how am I to blame, Pavel Andreich? The lady doesn't allow you to get married; she is our mistress, and that's her will! How do I come into it?"

"How do you come into it? I suppose you have never come to any agreement with that old witch of a housekeeper? I suppose you have never told her any tales, eh? You've not brought up every kind of trumped-up story against a defenseless girl? I suppose it had nothing to do with your kind help that she was moved from the laundry to the scullery? That she was beaten, and punished by being made to wear slops? . . . You ought to be ashamed of yourself, an old man like you! Why, a palsy might take you at any moment. . . . You'll have to answer for it to God."

"That's right, Pavel Andreich, roar your head off. . . . Are you going to go on roaring like that for much longer, do you think?"

Pavel exploded.

"What? you dare to threaten me?" he said furiously. "You think I am afraid of you? No, my friend, you're not dealing with anyone like that! What have I got to be afraid of? . . . I can earn my bread anywhere. But it's a different story with you! All you can do is live here and tell tales and steal. . . ."

"He's got a fine idea of himself," interrupted the clerk, who was also beginning to lose patience. "A plain hospital orderly, a wretched little medico; but to listen to him—phew! what an important person he must be!"

"Yes, a hospital orderly, but without him your worship would now be rotting in the graveyard. . . . And an evil spirit it was that made me cure him," he added, through his teeth.

"So you cured me? No, you wanted to poison me, you made me drink aloes," asserted the clerk.

"What of it, if aloes were the only thing which could have an effect on you?"

"Aloes are forbidden by the Board of Health," continued Niko-lai. "I'll lodge a complaint against you yet. . . . You wanted to do me in, and that's the truth! But the Lord didn't let you."

"That'll do, gentlemen, that'll do," began the cashier.

"Hold your tongue!" shouted the clerk. "He wanted to poison me! D'you understand what I say?"

"As if I needed to. . . . Listen, Nikolai Eremeich," began Pavel desperately. "I'm asking you for the last time . . . you've driven me further than I can bear. Leave us alone, d'you hear? or else, by God, no good will come of it to one or the other of us, I can promise you that."

The fat one lost all control. "I'm not afraid of you," he shouted: "Do you hear, you milk-sop! I've settled accounts with your father in my time; I broke his horns too—let that be an example to you, and look out for yourself!"

"Don't you start on my father, Nikolai Eremeich, don't you start on that!"

"Get out! Who are you to lay down the law to me?"

"I tell you, don't you start on that!"

"But I tell you, don't you forget yourself. . . . However necessary you may think you are to the lady, if she has got to choose between us two—it won't be you that keeps his place, my little dove! No one has got the right to sedition, so look out!" Pavel was trembling with fury. "And as for the girl Tatyana, it serves her right. . . . You wait, there's more trouble coming to her yet!"

Pavel threw himself forward with fists raised, and the clerk fell heavily to the floor.

"Put him in irons, put him in irons," groaned Nikolai Eremeich. . . .

I will not take it upon myself to describe the end of this scene. Even as it is, I am afraid I may have offended the reader's feelings.

The same day I returned home. A week later, I learned that Mrs. Loznyakova had kept both Pavel and Nikolai on in her service, but sent away the girl Tatyana: it seemed that her services were not required.

The Bear

ONE EVENING I WAS RETURNING ALONE FROM SHOOTING IN MY racing drozhky. I was still eight versts from home; my good trotting mare was going smartly along the dusty road, snorting and fidgeting her ears from time to time; my tired dog maintained a position within a pace of the rear wheels, as if fastened to them. A thunderstorm was approaching. Ahead of me a huge lilac-colored storm-cloud slowly rose from behind a forest; long gray clouds floated above me and towards me; there was an anxious stir and murmur among the willows. The stifling heat suddenly gave way to a moist chill; swiftly the shadows gathered. I flicked the horse with the reins, went down into a ravine, crossed a dry stream-bed, completely overgrown with willow bushes, climbed a hill, and entered a forest. Ahead of me the road wound between thick clumps of hazel, already plunged in darkness; I made progress with difficulty. The drozhky jolted over the hard roots of hundred-year-old oaks and limes, which kept on intersecting the deep ruts left by cartwheels; my mare began to stumble. All of a sudden, high above me, a strong wind whistled, the trees swayed violently, heavy rain-drops splashed and smacked sharply on the leaves, lightning flashed, and the storm burst. Rain fell in rivers. I drove on at a walk, and was soon compelled to stop: my mare was stuck, and I could see not an inch ahead of me. Somehow or other I found shelter under a spreading bush. Huddled together, with my face covered, I was patiently awaiting the end of the downpour, when, suddenly, in a flash of lightning, I thought I saw a tall figure on the road. I began staring that way—and the figure started right up out of the ground beside my drozhky.

"Who's there?" asked a resonant voice.

"Who are *you*?"

"I'm the forester here."

I told him my name.

"Oh, I know! Are you on the way home?"

"Yes. But what a storm! . . ."

"A storm, certainly," answered the voice.

A white lightning-flash lit up the forester from head to foot; a short, crackling thunder-clap followed immediately after. The rain came sluicing down with redoubled force.

"It'll be some time passing," continued the forester.

"What can I do about it?"

"If you like, I'll show you the way to my cabin," he said abruptly.

"I'd be much obliged."

"If you'll keep your seat . . ." He went to the mare's head, took hold of the bridle, and pulled. We began to move. I held on to the cushion of the drozhky, which was tossing like a coracle on the high seas, and called my dog. The poor mare splashed heavily about in the mud, slithered, and stumbled; in front of the shafts, the forester swayed about to right and to left like a spectre. We drove on for some way; at length my guide halted. "Here we are, sir, we're home," he said calmly. A gate squeaked, and several puppies set up a friendly barking. I lifted my head, and saw, illuminated by the lightning, a small cabin in the middle of a spacious yard surrounded by a fence. From the one little window a light glowed faintly. The forester led the mare up to the porch and knocked on the door. "Coming, coming!" said a faint little voice; there was a patter of bare feet, a bolt screamed, and a girl of about twelve, in a little shift tied together with list, appeared on the threshold with a lantern in her hand.

"Light the way for the gentleman," he said to her, "and I will put the drozhky into the shed."

The girl glanced at me and went into the cabin. I followed her in.

The forester's cabin consisted of a single room, soot-blackened, low, and empty, without any smaller chambers or partitions. A tattered sheepskin coat hung on the wall. On a bench lay a single-barrelled gun, in a corner was an untidy pile of rags; two big pots stood beside the stove. A splinter of wood burned on the table, flaring and dying lugubriously. Right in the middle of the cabin hung a cradle attached to the end of a long pole. The girl put out the lantern, sat down on a tiny stool, and began with her right hand to swing the cradle and with her left to trim the splinter. I looked round and my heart sank within me: visiting a peasant's cabin at night is cheerless indeed. The child in the cradle was breathing heavily and fast.

"Are you alone here?" I asked the girl.

"Yes, alone," she pronounced, in a hardly audible voice.

"Are you the forester's daughter?"

"Yes, the forester's," she murmured.

The door squeaked, and the forester, stooping his head, strode across the threshold. He lifted the lantern from the floor, went to the table, and lighted the wick. "I dare say you're not used to a splinter-light?" he said with a shake of his curly head.

I looked at him. Rarely have I seen such a sturdy fellow. He was tall, broad-shouldered, and admirably built. Through his wet shirt his powerful muscles stood out in relief. A black, curly beard half-covered his stern, masculine face; from under his wide brows, which met in the middle, small, brown eyes looked boldly out. He rested his hands lightly on his sides and came to a halt in front of me. I thanked him and asked him his name.

"My name is Foma," he answered. "But they call me the Bear."

"Oh! *you're* the Bear!"

I looked at him with redoubled curiosity. From my friend Ermolai, and from others, I had often heard stories about the Bear, whom all the peasants of the neighborhood feared like death. According to them, there had never been in the world such a master of his craft. "He won't let you take away so much as a faggot; whatever the time may be, even if it's midnight, he'll swoop down on you, like snow on your head. And there's no hope of resisting—he's as strong and neat-handed as the devil himself. . . . And there's no way of getting at him: neither drink, nor money; there's no bait at all to catch him. There's good folk have tried to do him in, more than once, but no— there's no catching him." Such were the terms in which the peasants of the neighborhood spoke of the Bear.

"So you're the Bear," I repeated. "I've heard of you, my friend, they say you let no one get past you."

"I do my duty," he answered solemnly. "It isn't right to eat the master's bread without earning it."

He took a hatchet from his belt, sat down on the floor, and began to cleave a splinter.

"You have no wife?" I asked him.

"No," he answered, with a mighty blow of the hatchet.

"Is she dead, then?"

"No . . . yes . . . she's dead," he added, and turned away.

I was silent. He raised his eyes and looked at me.

"She ran off with a fellow from the town who happened to be passing," he pronounced with a savage smile. The girl lowered her head; the baby woke up and began to cry; the girl went to the cradle. "Well, feed him," said the Bear, pushing into her hand a dirty feeding-bottle. "She chucked *him*, too," he continued in a low voice, pointing at the baby. He went to the door, halted, and turned around. "I suppose that you, sir," he began, "wouldn't want to eat our bread, but bread is all that I . . ."

"I'm not hungry."

"Well, as you like. I would have got the samovar going for you, but I have no tea. I'll go and see how your mare is."

He went out and slammed the door. I looked around again. The cabin seemed to me even sorrier than before. The sharp smell of stale smoke oppressed my lungs. The girl never stirred from where she sat or lifted her eyes; from time to time she gave the cradle a push, or shyly pulled the shift on to her shoulder when it had slipped. Her bare legs hung motionless.

"What's your name?" I asked.

"Ulita," she said, holding her sad little face even lower than before.

The forester came in and sat on the bench.

"The storm is passing," he observed, after a short silence: "If you wish, I'll see you out of the forest."

I got up. The Bear took his gun and examined the trigger.

"What's that for?" I asked.

"They're up to their tricks in the forest. They're cutting down a tree in Mare's Valley," he added, in answer to my inquiring glance.

"Can you hear it from here?"

"You can hear it from the yard."

We went out together. The rain had stopped. In the distance, heavy cloud masses were still banking up, and long lightning flashes burst out from time to time. But, over our heads, here and there we could already see the dark-blue heaven, and stars twinkled through thin, scurrying clouds. The outlines of trees, raindrenched and wind-stirred, were beginning to loom up out of the darkness. We listened. The forester took off his cap and lowered his head. "Th—there," he said suddenly, and stretched out a hand. "You see what a night he's chosen." I heard nothing except the rustling of leaves. The Bear led the horse out of the shed. "Like this, maybe," he added aloud, "I won't catch him."

"I could come with you . . . if you like?"

"All right," he answered, and backed the horse in. "We'll catch him in no time, and then I'll see you on your way. Let's go."

We set off, the Bear in front and I behind him. God knows how he found the road, but he only halted occasionally, and then just to listen for the sound of the axe.

"There," he murmured through his teeth. "D'you hear? D'you hear?"

"But where?"

The Bear shrugged his shoulders. We went down into a ravine, the wind dropped for a moment—and the sound of measured blows fell clearly on my ears. The Bear looked at me and motioned with his head. We went on through wet bracken and nettles. There was a dull, prolonged crashing . . .

"He's felled it . . ." murmured the Bear.

Meanwhile the sky continued to clear. In the forest it was just light. We made our way at last out of the ravine. "Wait here," the forester whispered to me; he bent down, and, holding up his gun, vanished among the bushes. I listened intently. Through the continuous noise of the wind I thought I could catch faint sounds from not far off; cautious blows of an axe on branches, the squeaking of wheels, the snorting of a horse. . . . "Where are you going? Stop!" roared the Bear's iron voice all of a sudden. Another voice called plaintively, like a hare's . . . A fight began. "Oh, no, you don't," insisted the Bear breathlessly. "You're not going to get away. . . ." I dashed in the direction of the noise and arrived, stumbling with every step, at the scene of battle. On the ground, beside a felled tree, the forester was busily engaged. He held the thief under him and was twisting his arms behind his back with a belt. I went up to them. The Bear rose and set him on his feet. I saw a peasant, dripping wet, in rags, with a long dishevelled beard. A wretched nag, half-covered under a sheet of matting, stood close by, together with a rudimentary sort of cart. The forester uttered not a word; the peasant also kept silence, and simply shook his head.

"Let him go," I whispered in the Bear's ear. "I'll pay for the tree."

The Bear silently took the horse by the forelock in his left hand: with his right he held the thief by the belt. "Well, look sharp, you scoundrel," he said sternly.

"Take the axe, over there," murmured the peasant.

"Yes, why leave it behind?" said the forester, and picked up the axe. We set off. I walked behind . . . Rain began spitting again and was soon falling in torrents. With difficulty we got back to the cabin. The Bear left the captured nag in the middle of the yard, led the peasant into the room, loosened the knot in the belt, and made him sit down in a corner. The girl, who had gone to sleep beside the stove, jumped up and looked at us in silent terror. I sat down on the bench.

"Look at it, how it's pouring," remarked the forester. "We'll have to wait till it's over. Wouldn't you like to lie down for a while?"

"No, thank you."

"I'd have shut him up in the closet for your honor," he continued, indicating the peasant, "but, you see, the bolt . . ."

"Leave him where he is, don't touch him," I interrupted the Bear.

The peasant gave me a sidelong look. I promised myself that, whatever happened, I would set the poor wretch free. He sat motionless on the bench. In the light of the lantern I could make out his lean, wrinkled face, his overhanging, yellow eyebrows, his restless eyes, his thin limbs. . . . The girl lay down on the floor right at his feet and went to sleep again. The Bear sat at the table, his head propped on his hand. A cricket chirruped in the corner . . . the rain rattled on the roof and slid down the windows; we were all silent.

"Foma Kuzmich," began the peasant suddenly, in a dull broken voice. "Foma Kuzmich."

"What d'you want?"

"Let me off."

The Bear didn't answer.

"Let me off . . . It's hunger that . . . let me off."

"I know you," rejoined the forester morosely. "Your village are all the same—one thief on top of another."

"Let me off," repeated the peasant. "The agent . . . ruined . . . that's what we are . . . let me off!"

"Ruined! . . . No one has the right to steal."

"Let me off, Foma Kuzmich . . . That chap of yours will gobble me up, you know he will, and that's the truth."

The Bear turned away. The peasant was twitching as if at the onset of fever. He kept shaking his head, he breathed irregularly.

"Let me off," he repeated with mournful desperation. "Let me off, for God's sake do! I'll pay, really I will, by God. By God, it was hunger that . . . with children to feed, you know what it is. It's hard, and that's the truth."

"All the same, you shouldn't go out stealing."

"My horse," continued the peasant; "let the horse go, if only that . . . that's the only animal I've got . . ."

"I tell you, I can't. I'm not my own master, either; they'll make me pay. It's not for me to spoil you, anyway."

"Let me off! It's want, Foma Kuzmich. It's want that does it . . . let me off!"

"I know you."

"But let me off."

"Oh, what's the use of arguing with you; sit quiet, d'you hear, or else . . . Can't you see the gentleman, eh?"

The poor wretch sank his head. The Bear yawned and put his head down on the table. The rain still went on. I waited to see what would happen next.

The peasant suddenly sat up. His eyes began to blaze and a flush spread over his face.

"Well, then, eat away, and choke yourself," he began, screwing up his eyes and dropping the corners of his mouth. "You damned murderer, drink the blood of Christian folk, drink away."

The forester turned around.

"I'm talking to you . . . you bloodsucking Tartar, you!"

"Are you drunk, to start swearing like this?" said the forester in astonishment. "Have you gone off your head, eh?"

"Drunk! On your money, I suppose, you damned murderer, you brute, you!"

"You . . . I'll give it you!"

"What do I care? I'm done for anyway; where can I go without my horse? Kill me—it's one way of finishing; whether it's hunger, or that—it's all the same. Do them all in: wife, children—let the whole lot die like animals . . . but we'll get you, just you wait!"

The Bear half-rose.

"Beat away," repeated the peasant savagely. "Beat away."

The girl hurriedly got up from the floor and stared at him.

"Beat away."

"Be quiet!" roared the forester, and took two steps forward.

"That'll do, Foma," I exclaimed. "Leave him alone . . . the poor devil."

"I won't be quiet," continued the unfortunate. "It's always the same—dying like animals. You murderer, you brute, there's no end to the harm you do . . . but wait, your reign won't be for long! They'll get you by the throat, just you wait!"

The Bear seized him by the shoulder . . . I dashed to the peasant's rescue.

"You keep out, sir," the forester shouted at me.

I would not have feared his threats and had already put out

my hand, when, to my astonishment, he jerked the belt from the peasant's elbows in a single turn, seized him by the scruff of the neck, rammed his cap down over his eyes, opened the door, and threw him out.

"Go to the devil, and your horse, too!" he shouted after him. "But look, the next time I catch you . . ."

He came back into the cabin and started rummaging in a corner.

"Well, Bear," I said at last, "you surprise me; I see you're a good sort."

"Oh, no more of that, sir," he interrupted me crossly; "not a word about it, please. And now I'd better see you on your way," he added. "I don't suppose you'll be waiting till the rain is over."

In the yard the wheels of the peasant's cart rattled. "There he goes, sneaking off," he muttered. "I'll give it him! . . ."

Within half an hour he parted from me at the forest's edge.

Two Landowners

I HAVE ALREADY HAD THE HONOR TO PRESENT TO YOU, INDUL-
gent readers, some of the gentlemen of my neighborhood; allow me
now, in passing (for us writers, everything is "in passing"), to acquaint you with two more landowners on whose land I have often
shot; highly-respected, well-intentioned gentlemen, enjoying the
universal esteem of several districts.

First I shall describe for you Major-General (retired) Vyacheslav
Ilarionovich Khvalinsky. Imagine a tall man, once well-built, now
a bit run to fat, but far from decrepit, indeed not even touched by
age, a man of mature years, right in his prime. True, his once regular and still agreeable features have somewhat changed, his cheeks
hang, crowded wrinkles have taken up a position radiating out
from his eyes, some of his teeth are no longer with him (such was
Sadi's phrase, if Pushkin is to be believed); his fair hair, or at least
that part of it that remains intact, has turned to a lilac color, thanks to
a compound bought at Romyon horse-fair from a Jew professing to be
an Armenian; but Vyacheslav Ilarionovich steps out briskly, laughs
resonantly, jingles his spurs, twirls his moustaches, and sooner or
later refers to himself as an old cavalryman, whereas it is well
known that really old men never refer to themselves as old at all. He
is usually dressed in a coat buttoned right up, a high cravat with a
starched collar, and pepper-and-salt trousers of military cut; he
wears his hat down over his eyes, leaving the whole of the back of
his head uncovered. He is a capital fellow, but has somewhat strange
principles and habits. For example, he can never treat gentlemen

who are poor, or have no official position, as his own equals. In conversation with them, he generally looks at them sideways, leaning his cheek heavily on his stiff white collar, or suddenly goes and flashes at them a bright, unblinking stare, but says nothing, and moves the whole skin of his head underneath the hair; he even pronounces words differently and, for instance, instead of saying, "Thanks, Pavel Vasilich," or "Come along, Mikhail Ivanich," addresses them as, "ks, Pall'Asilich," or "C'long, Mikhall'Vanich." With people lower down the social scale he behaves even more strangely: he never looks at them at all, and, before explaining to them his wishes or giving them orders, he repeats several times over, with a preoccupied, dreamy look: "What's your name? . . . What's your name?" emphasizing heavily the first word "*what*," but pronouncing the rest very fast, so that the whole phrase acquires a resemblance to the call of the cock-quail. He is fussy, terribly mean, does badly out of his land: he employs as steward a retired sergeant-major, a Little-Russian, a man of unusual stupidity. Incidentally, in agricultural matters none of us has yet outdone an important official from Petersburg who, seeing from his agent's reports that the barns for drying crops on his land were subject to frequent fires, which caused the loss of a great deal of grain, gave the strictest instructions that in future no sheaves were to be put into the drying-barn until the fire had been completely extinguished. The same dignitary had the idea of sowing all his fields with poppies, in view of what appeared a very simple calculation: poppies are dearer than rye, therefore it's better business to sow poppies. He it was, too, who told his women-serfs to wear *kokoshniks* on a pattern sent from Petersburg; and indeed, to this day, the peasant women on his lands wear this head-dress . . . only on top of their own. . . . But let us return to Vyacheslav Ilarionovich. He is a great fancier of the ladies, and has only to see a pretty face in the main street of the local market-town, to dash off after her at once, at the same time—and that is the remarkable circumstance—starting to limp. He likes playing cards, but only with people of lower station; they call him "Your Excellency," and he blows them up and ticks them off to his heart's content. When he happens to be playing with the Governor or with some official personage, an extraordinary transformation takes place in him: he smiles, he nods, he looks them in the eye—honey fairly flows from him . . . He even loses without complaining. He reads little and, while doing so, keeps up a constant working of his moustaches and eyebrows, as if from the upward passage of a wave across his face. This wavelike movement on the face of Vyacheslav Ilarionovich is especially noticeable when he happens (in the presence of guests, of course) to be running through the columns of the *Journal des Débats*. At election-time he plays a fairly important rôle but refuses, from meanness, the honorable estate of Marshal of the Nobility. "Gentlemen," he will say to noblemen who may approach him on the subject, speaking in a voice of patronage and heavy self-sufficiency, "I am greatly obliged for the honor; but I am resolved to devote my leisure to retirement," and, having said these words, he moves his head several times to right and left, and then with a dignified movement presses his chin and his cheeks against his cravat. In his youth he served as adjutant to some important Personage, whom he never refers to except by his Christian name and patronymic; the story goes that he discharged not only the functions of adjutant, but that, for example, having donned full parade-dress, having even done up the hooks, he had been wont to give his chief a good steam-bath—but one can't believe all the rumors that one hears. General Khvalinsky himself doesn't like to speak of his military career, which on the whole is somewhat strange; it seems moreover that he never saw active service. General Khvalinsky lives alone in a small house. He has had no experience of married bliss, and therefore still considers himself marriageable, and highly eligible too. As to his housekeeper, a woman of about thirty-five, black-eyed, black-browed, plump, fresh, and moustached, she goes about on weekdays in starched dresses, and on Sundays adds a pair of muslin sleeves. Vyacheslav Ilarionovich is a good man at the big dinner-parties given by landowners in honor of Governors and other potentates; there he is, you might say, absolutely in his element. On such occasions he usually sits, if not on the Governor's right, at any rate not far from him; at the beginning of dinner he is very conscious of his own importance and, throwing himself back, but without turning his head, sweeps a sidelong glance down the round pates and stand-up collars of the guests; however, towards the end of the meal, he becomes gayer, begins to smile in all directions (in the Governor's direction he has been smiling since dinner started), and sometimes even proposes a toast to the honour of the fair sex—the adornment of our planet, to use his own words. General Khvalinsky is not bad, either, on solemn and public occasions, examinations and church functions; he is also a master-hand at receiving ceremonial benedictions. At cross-roads, ferries, and other such places, the servants of Vyacheslav Ilarionov-ich never shout or bawl; on the contrary, in making people give way for him or in calling forward his carriage, they say in a pleasant, throaty baritone: "Make way, please, make way, please and let General Khvalinsky pass"; or, "General Khvalinsky's carriage" . . . True, Khvalinsky's carriage is of fairly antiquated type; the lackeys and footmen wear fairly shabby livery (it's of course hardly necessary to mention that it is gray with red facings); the horses, too, are getting on and have seen service in their time, but Vyacheslav Ilarionovich has no pretensions to foppishness and, indeed, doesn't think it suit-able to his station to throw dust in people's eyes. Khvalinsky has no special command of language, or, perhaps, has no occasion to show his eloquence, because he tolerates no argument, no objection even, and studiously avoids all long conversations, especially with the young. That's certainly the safer course; indeed the pity is that peo-ple nowadays are losing the habit of obedience and forgetting all respect. In the presence of his superiors, Khvalinsky is silent most of the time, but with his inferiors, whom he seems to despise but who are nevertheless his only familiars, he holds forth abruptly and to the point, caustically using expressions like the following: "What you say is absolutely non-sens-ical!" or, "I find myself at last obliged, m'dear sir, to make it clear to you," or, "All the same, you ought to know to whom you are speaking," and so on. He is the special ter-ror of postmasters, permanent delegates, and station-inspectors. At home he never entertains, and lives, so one hears, the life of a miser. With it all, he is a splendid type of landowner. "An old campaigner, an irreproachable character, a man of principles, a *vieux grognard*," so his neighbours describe him. Only the Public Prosecutor of the province allows himself to smile, when mention is made in his presence of Khvalinsky's capital, solid qualities—but there are no lengths to which envy will not go! . . .

Now let us pass on to another landowner.

Mardary Apollonich Stegunov is not in the least like Khvalinsky; he can hardly have seen service and has never passed as handsome. He is an old man, short, podgy, bald, with a double chin, soft hands, and a fair-sized belly. He is a famous host and joker; he lives for his pleasure, as the saying goes; goes about winter and summer in a striped, quilted dressing-gown. In one respect only he resembles General Khvalinsky: he too is a bachelor. He has five hundred serfs. Mardary Apollonich occupies himself rather superficially with his estate; ten years or so ago, in order to keep in the swim, he bought a threshing-machine at Butenop's in Moscow, locked it up in a barn, and worried no more. On a fine summer's day he will even order his racing drozhky to be harnessed and drive into the fields to have a look at the crops and pick cornflowers. He lives entirely in the good old style. His house is of old-fashioned construction: in the hall there is the proper smell of kvass, tallow candles, and leather. On the right is a sideboard with pipes and towels; in the dining-room are family portraits, flies, a big pot of geraniums, and an ill-tuned piano; in the drawing-room, three sofas, three tables, two looking-glasses, and a wheezing clock, with blackened enamel and hands in carved bronze; in the study, a table covered with papers, bluish screens stuck with pictures cut out of various works of the last century, cupboards full of musty books, spiders and black dust, a bulging armchair, an Italian window, and a firmly nailed-up door to the garden . . . In a word, everything is as it should be. Mardary Apollonich has crowds of serving-folk, all dressed in the old-fashioned style: long blue coats with high collars, drab-colored pantaloons and short yellowish waistcoats. They address guests as "father" . . . The management of his land is in charge of a bailiff, one of his own peasants, with a beard that quite covers his sheepskin coat. His house is run by a wrinkled, mean old woman with a brown kerchief over her head. Mardary Apollonich has in his stables thirty horses of miscellaneous calibre; he drives out in a heavyweight home-made carriage. He loves receiving guests and entertains them lavishly, that's to say, thanks to the stupefying qualities of Russian cooking, he deprives them, right up to nightfall, of any capacity to attend to anything but Preference. He himself has no occupations and has even stopped reading "The Dream Book." But in Russia there are still fairly many landowners of this type; it will be asked, why, and with what object, I have started to speak of him. Well, allow me, instead of answering, to tell you about one of my visits to Mardary Apollonich.

I arrived at his house at about seven o'clock on a summer evening. The evening service was just over and the priest, a young man who was evidently very timid and just out of the seminary, was sitting in the drawing-room near the door on the very edge of his chair. As was his custom, Mardary Apollonich gave me the warmest of welcomes; he was unfeignedly glad to see any guest, and he was anyway the kindest of men. The priest got up and took his hat.

"Wait, Father, wait," said Mardary Apollonich, without letting go of my hand. "Don't go away . . . I've ordered some vodka for you."

"I don't drink, sir," murmured the priest, with embarrassment, and he blushed to the ears.

"What nonsense! Not drinking, in your profession!" answered Mardary Apollonich. "Mishka! Yushka! Vodka for the Father!"

Yushka, a tall, lean old man of about seventy, came in with a glass of vodka on a black-painted tray with flesh-colored spots on it.

The priest began by refusing.

"Drink, Father, drink; don't make such a fuss, it isn't right," observed the landowner in a tone of reproach.

The poor young man obeyed.

"Well now, Father, you may go."

The priest started bowing.

"Well, all right, all right, off you go. . . . A capital fellow," continued Mardary Apollonich, looking after him. "I'm very pleased with him, but the only thing is that he's a bit young. Preaches sermons all the time and then doesn't drink. But how are you, my dear friend? How *are* you? Let's go on to the balcony—it's such a glorious evening."

We went out on to the balcony, sat down, and began to talk. Mardary Apollonich looked down, and suddenly became terribly agitated.

"Whose are those hens? Whose are those hens?" he shouted. "Whose are those hens in the garden? . . . Yushka, Yushka! Go and find out at once whose they are; how many times have I forbidden it, how many times have I told them!"

Yushka ran off.

"That's a fine state of things!" declared Mardary Apollonich. "It's frightful!"

The unfortunate hens—I remember them still, two speckled ones and a white one with a crest—were continuing to walk about under the apple-trees with the utmost calmness, from time to time expressing their feelings by a prolonged clucking, when suddenly Yushka, capless and with a stick in his hand, and three other serving-folk, all of whom had reached the years of discretion, darted at them simultaneously. Then the fun started. The hens squawked, flapped their wings, jumped, and clucked fit to deafen you; the servants ran, stumbled, fell; the master shouted from the balcony like a mad-man: "Catch them! catch them catch them! . . . Whose are they, whose are they?" Finally one of the servants succeeded in seizing the crested hen, catching it between his chest and the ground, when at the same moment, through the garden fence from the road, jumped a girl of about eleven, dishevelled and with a long switch in her hand.

"Oh, that's whose they are!" exclaimed the landowner trium-phantly. "Ermil, the coachman's! He sent his Natalka to chase them . . . of course he hasn't sent Parasha," added the landowner in a low voice, and with a significant grin. "Hey, Yushka! Leave the chickens. Catch Natalka for me."

But before the breathless Yushka could reach the terrified girl, the housekeeper, arriving from nowhere, caught her by the hand and slapped the poor girl several times on the back . . .

"That's the way, that's the way," asserted the landowner. "There, there, there! . . . Take the chickens away from her, Avdotya," he added loudly, and turned to me with a radiant face: "What a chase, eh? Why, look, I'm all of a sweat."

And Mardary Apollonich burst out laughing.

We stayed on the balcony. It was indeed an unusually fine evening.

We were served with tea.

"Tell me," I began, "Mardary Apollonich, are those outlying farm-buildings yours, over there on the road beyond the ravine?"

"Yes . . . what of it?"

"But how can you allow it, Mardary Apollonich? Why, it's shameful. The huts assigned to the peasants are mean and cramped; there's not a tree to be seen around, not even a pond either, there's one well, but even that is no use at all. Couldn't you really find another site? . . . And they say that you've even taken away the old hempyards that were there?"

"But what can you do, when your boundary is fixed by agreement?" answered Mardary Apollonich: "I'm fed right up to here with the whole business." He pointed to the back of his neck. "And I foresee no good from it, either. But as for my taking away their hempyard, and not digging the pond for them there—well, my friend, I know all about that. I'm a simple chap and I go about things in the old-fashioned way. As I see it, the master is the master, and the peasant is the peasant . . . and that's all there is to it."

There was of course nothing to be said in answer to such a clear and convincing argument.

"And anyway," he continued, "they're a bad lot of peasants, they're in disgrace. There are two families there in particular; even my late father, God rest his soul in peace, couldn't stand them at any price. But I tell you, I believe in the saying that if the father's a thief, the son's a thief too; you can say what you like . . . it's blood that counts. I tell you frankly, from those two families, I have sent men to the army out of turn and I have scattered them about all over the place. But they don't change, and what can you do about it? They are great breeders, too, curse them."

Meanwhile the air had grown completely still. Only occasionally a breeze rippled past and, finally dying away around the house, brought to our ears the sound of measured blows, sounding from the direction of the stable. Mardary Apollonich had just lifted to his lips a full saucer and was already dilating his nostrils, without which, as is well-known, no true Russian can imbibe tea, but he stopped, listened, nodded, gulped, and, putting the saucer down on the table, pronounced, with the kindest of smiles, as if involuntarily echoing the blows: "Chooky-chooky-chook! Chooky-chooky-chook!"

"What's that?" I asked in amazement.

"That's a naughty boy being punished on my instructions. D'you know my butler Vasily?"

"Which is he?"

"The one who served us at dinner the other day. He goes about with big side-whiskers like this."

The fiercest indignation could not have resisted the clear and gentle gaze of Mardary Apollonich.

"What's the matter, young man, what's the matter?" he said, shaking his head. "D'you think I'm a brute, eh, that you are staring at me like that? Whom he loveth, he chasteneth—*you* know."

A quarter of an hour later I took my leave of Mardary Apollonich. Driving through the village, I saw Vasily the butler. He was walking along the road munching nuts. I told my driver to stop the horses and called to him. "Well, my lad, so you were punished today?" I asked him.

"How d'you know?" rejoined Vasily.

"Your master told me."

"The master himself?"

"Why did he have you punished?"

"It was quite right, sir, quite right. We don't get punished for nothing; there's none of that sort of thing with us—no, certainly not. Our master is not that sort, our master . . . you won't find another master like him in the whole province."

"Go on!" I said to the driver. There's the old Mother Russia for you, I thought on my way home.

Lebedyan

ONE OF THE CHIEF ADVANTAGES OF SHOOTING, MY DEAR READERS, is that it involves you in a constant change of scene, which, for an idle fellow, is a most agreeable condition. True, sometimes (particularly in rainy weather) there's not much fun in roaming the byways, "keeping right on," stopping every peasant you meet with the question: "Hey, my friend, what's the best way to Mordovka?" then in Mordovka cross-examining some dull-witted peasant-woman (the men all being away working in the fields) about how far it is to the inn on the high road, and how to get there—and, after covering ten versts, instead of the inn, finding oneself in the ruined manor-village of Khudobubnov, to the extreme amazement of a whole herd of pigs who are up to their ears in dark brown mud right in the middle of the road and very far indeed from expecting any such interruption. It is no fun, either, to cross breath-takingly insecure foot-bridges, to clamber down into ravines, to ford marshy streamlets; it's no fun driving for twenty-four hours on end over the greenish waves of the high road or—Heaven protect us from it—bogging down for several hours in front of a gaily-colored mile-post with the figure 22 on one side and the figure 23 on the other; it's no fun living for weeks on eggs, milk, and the much-vaunted rye bread. But all these discomforts and setbacks are redeemed by advantages and satisfactions of another order. Anyway, let us get on to our story.

After the above remarks I need not explain to the reader how it was that, five years ago, I chanced to arrive in Lebedyan when the horse-fair was in full swing. We sportsmen can easily drive out from our more or less ancestral homes on a fine morning with every intention of returning in the evening of the following day, and then, by easy stages, without ceasing to shoot snipe, finish up on the blessed banks of the Pechora; moreover, every sportsman of the gun-and-dog variety is a passionate admirer of the noblest animal in the world—the horse. So it was that I arrived in Lebedyan, put up at the inn, changed my clothes, and went out to the fair. (The waiter, a tall gaunt youth of twenty or so, who spoke in a sweet nasal tenor, had already had time to inform me that his Highness Prince N——, Remount Officer of the —— Regiment, was staying in the inn, that many other gentlemen had arrived, that in the evenings the gypsies were singing and there were performances of "Pan Tvardovsky" in the theater, that horses were fetching a decent price and that anyway there were some good ones to be seen.) On the fair-ground stood endless rows of carts and, behind them, horses of every possible kind: trotters, stallions, cart-horses, draught-horses, coach-horses, and plain peasant-nags. Some, well-fed and sleek, of matched colors, covered with blankets of various hues, tethered short to tall racks, gave anxious sidelong glances at the too familiar whips of their lords the dealers; gentlemen's horses, sent by steppe-landowners from a couple of hundred versts away under the supervision of some decrepit coachman and two or three thick-skulled grooms, waved their long necks, stamped their hooves, and gnawed the fences out of sheer boredom; two little roan mongrel horses jostled each other closely; majestically immobile, like lions, the broad-cruppered trotters stood, with wavy tails and shaggy fetlocks, gray-roan, black, and bay. Fanciers paused respectfully in front of them. In the lanes between the carts people of every class, age, and appearance were jostling each other; horse-copers in blue coats and tall caps looked out knowingly as they waited for buyers; pop-eyed, curly-headed gypsies dashed backwards and forwards like a house on fire, looking horses in the teeth, lifting their hooves and tails, shouting, quarrelling, acting as go-betweens, drawing lots, or pressing round some remount officer in his forage-cap and beaver-trimmed military overcoat. A huge cossack sat on a lean gelding with a deerlike neck and offered to sell him "all-in," that's to say, with saddle and bridle. Peasants in sheepskin coats torn under the arms pressed their way desperately through the crowd and swarmed in their dozens into a cart harnessed to a horse which needed "trying out" or, away to one side, with the help of a shifty gypsy, bargained themselves silly, struck each other's hands a hundred times, each insisting on his price, while the subject of their dispute, a wretched little nag covered with a piece of warped matting, just blinked as if it had nothing to do with him . . . and indeed it made no difference to the horse who was going to beat him! Landowners with wide foreheads, dyed moustaches, and pompous expressions, wearing confederate caps and camlet coats put on by one sleeve only, chatted condescendingly with fat-bellied merchants in pot-hats and green gloves. The place was alive with officers of different regiments; a long cuirassier of German extraction coolly asked a lame dealer "how much he wished to receive for that sorrel horse." A little fair-haired hussar of about nineteen was trying to find a side-horse to match a lean pacer; a postilion, wearing a low hat with a peacock's feather wound round it and a brown coat with leather gauntlets thrust under his narrow green belt, was looking for a shaft-horse. Coachmen plaited their horses' tails, wetted their manes and gave gentlemen respectful pieces of advice. Those who had completed a deal hurried off to the inn or the pot-house, according to their condition. . . . And the whole crowd—hustling, shouting, fussing, quarrelling, and making it up again, cursing and laughing, were up to their knees in mud.

I wanted to buy three passable horses for my britzka: my own were getting past their work. I found two, but couldn't see a third to match them. After a dinner which I will not undertake to describe (did not Æneas know how disagreeable it is to recall past griefs?), I made my way into the so-called coffee-house, which was a meeting-place every evening for remount officers, horse-breeders and other visitors. In the billiard-room, flooded with leaden waves of tobacco smoke, were a score or so of people. There were dandified young landowners in Hungarian jackets and gray trousers, with long side-whiskers and oiled moustaches, looking proudly and gallantly around them; other gentlemen in frock-coats, with extremely short necks and eyes sunk in fat, wheezed painfully; merchants sat about in corners, so to say, on edge; officers conversed easily among themselves. At the billiard-table was Prince N——, a young man of about twenty-two, with a gay, somewhat contemptuous face, wearing his coat unbuttoned, a red silk shirt, and baggy velvet trousers. He was playing with Ensign (retired) Viktor Khlopakov.

Viktor Khlopakov, a lean, swarthy little fellow of about thirty, with black hair, brown eyes and blunt, upturned nose, is an untiring visitor to elections and fairs. He walks with a hop, throws his elbows out in a swaggering gesture, wears his hat at an angle and turns up the sleeves of his military coat, which is lined with dove-colored calico. Mr. Khlopakov has a talent for making up to well-to-do young bucks from Petersburg, smokes, drinks and plays cards with them, and addresses them in the second person singular. Why they accept him is hard enough to understand. He is not clever, he is not funny: even his jokes are no good. True, they treat him with friendly indifference, like a good-hearted but insignificant fellow; they hobnob with him for two or three weeks, then suddenly cut him, and he starts cutting them, too. Ensign Khlopakov specializes in employing continuously for a whole year, sometimes for two, a single expression, which is not always to the point, and is in no way amusing, but which, goodness knows why, makes everyone laugh. Eight years ago, he used to say at every step: "My respects to you and humblest thanks"—and every time his current protectors died of laughter and made him repeat "my respects." Then he began to use a tolerably complicated expression: "Cross my heart, *kess-kersay*, that's a bit of all right"—and with the same brilliant success. Two years later he thought out a new pleasantry: "*Ne voo fuss-ay pas*, you jolly good chap, in your sheepskin wrap"—and so forth. Well, these phrases, simple though they may be, are his meat, drink, and raiment. (He long ago ran through his own fortune and lives entirely at his friends' expense.) Observe that he has absolutely no other agreeable qualities; true, he smokes a hundred pipes of Beetle mixture a day, lifts his right foot above his head at the billiard-table, and, when taking aim, rubs his cue furiously with his hand—but it is not everybody who appreciates these accomplishments. He is a fair drinker, too . . . but in Mother Russia it is hard to achieve distinction on that score. . . . In short, I find his success a complete enigma. . . . There is one thing about him, though: he is cautious, never lets a quarrel go further, or says a bad word about anyone.

Well, I thought when I saw Khlopakov, what is his present catchword?

The prince hit the white.

"Thirty-love," sang out the marker, a consumptive-looking fellow with a dark face and leaden rings below the eyes.

The prince put the yellow ball into the end pocket with a bang.

"Ho!" came an approving, full-bellied wheeze from a fat merchant sitting in a corner at a rickety one-legged table—a wheeze that dwindled into a fit of shyness. But luckily no one had noticed him. He sighed and stroked his beard.

"Thirty-six to a duck's egg!" called the marker through his nose.

"Well, what about it, my friend?" the prince asked Khlopakov.

"What about it? Why, it is a rrrrapssscallion, of course, a real rrrrapsscallion."

The prince burst out laughing.

"What, what? Say it again?"

"A rrapssscallion!" repeated the retired ensign complacently.

So that's the new slogan, I thought.

The prince put the red into the pocket.

"Hey! don't do that, prince, don't do that," came a sudden murmur from a little blond officer with bloodshot eyes, a tiny nose and the face of a sleepy child. "Don't play it like that . . . you ought to have . . . not like that!"

"How then?" asked the prince over his shoulder.

"You ought to have . . . gone for a triplet."

"Indeed?" muttered the prince through his teeth.

"I say, prince, are you going to the gypsies this evening?" continued the young man hastily, in some embarrassment. "Steshka is going to sing . . . and Ilyushka."

The prince didn't even answer him.

"Rrrrapsscallion, old boy," said Khlopakov, with a sly wink of his left eye.

The prince burst out laughing.

"Thirty-nine love," intoned the marker.

"Love, love . . . just look what I'm going to do to the yellow . . ."
Khlopakov jiggled the cue on his hand, took aim, and missed.

"Oh, rrapscallion," he exclaimed in disgust.

The prince laughed again.

"What? What?"

But Khlopakov refused to repeat his slogan; a little coquetry
never does any harm.

"You missed it, sir," observed the marker. "Kindly put some
chalk on. . . . Forty to a duck's egg!"

"Gentlemen," began the prince, turning to the company in general, but looking at no one in particular, "you know, in the theater
this evening we must call for Verzhembitskaya."

"Certainly, certainly, of course," shouted several gentlemen in
emulation, remarkably flattered by this opportunity of answering
the princely remark: "Verzhembitskaya."

"Verzhembitskaya is a first-rate actress, much better than Sopnyakova," squeaked from the corner a seedy little fellow with side-
whiskers and glasses. Poor wretch! he was secretly head-over-heels
in love with Sopnyakova, but the prince didn't think him worth so
much as a glance.

"Waiter, hey, get me a pipe!" shouted, through his cravat, a tall
gentleman with regular features and a noble bearing—and all the
characteristics of a sharper.

The waiter ran for a pipe and, returning, announced to his Highness that the coachman Baklaga was asking for him.

"Oh! tell, tell him to wait, and give him some vodka."

"Very good, sir."

Baklaga, as I learned afterwards, was a young, good-looking,
extremely spoilt coachman; the prince loved him, gave him horses,
rushed round with him, spent whole nights in his company . . . To-
day you would never recognize this same prince for the gay spend-
thrift that he was. . . . What scented, corseted haughtiness! What
preoccupation with official duties—and, above all, what sagacity!

The tobacco smoke was beginning to eat my eyes out. After listening once more to Khlopakov's exclamation and the prince's laugh,
I went to my room, where my man had already made my bed on

the narrow broken-down horsehair sofa with its tall, curving back.

The following day I went to look at the horses in the various yards and began with the well-known dealer Sitnikov. I passed through the gate into the sand-sprinkled yard. In front of the wide-open door of the stable stood the master himself, a tall, stout, middle-aged man in a hareskin coat with its collar turned up and tucked inwards. When he saw me, he moved slowly over to meet me, held his cap above his head in both hands and said in a sing-song voice: "My compliments to you. Would you like to see some horses?"

"Yes, that's what I have come for."

"What sort exactly, if I may ask?"

"Show me what you've got."

"With pleasure."

We went into the stable. Several white mongrels rose from the straw and ran up to us, wagging their tails; an old goat with a long beard went away to one side in displeasure; three grooms in stout but greasy sheepskins bowed to us in silence. To right and left, in specially constructed stalls, stood some thirty horses, groomed and combed to perfection. Above the joists, pigeons fluttered and cooed.

"What d'you want the horse for: driving, or stud?" Sitnikov asked me.

"Both."

"I see, sir, I see," pronounced the dealer with deliberation. "Petya, show the gentleman Ermine."

We went out into the yard.

"Wouldn't you like a seat brought out from inside? . . . No? . . . As you please."

There was a clatter of hooves on boards, the crack of a whip, and Petya, a fellow of about forty, pockmarked and swarthy, sprang out from the stable with a gray, rather imposing stallion, made him rear, ran with him twice round the yard and mounted him neatly at the best place for showing him off. Ermine stretched himself, gave a whistling snort, threw up his tail, tossed his head, and squinted at us.

You're a wily bird! I thought.

"Give him his head, give him his head," said Sitnikov and stared at me. "What d'you think of him, sir?" he asked at length.

"Not a bad horse; the fore-legs aren't all one could wish."

"They're capital legs!" rejoined Sitnikov with conviction. "But his quarters . . . have a look, sir . . . they are broad as a stove, you could fairly sleep on them."

"He's long in the pasterns."

"Long, indeed—have a heart! Run him round, Petya, let him trot, let him trot . . . don't let him gallop."

Petya went round the yard again on Ermine. We were all silent.

"Well, take him back," said Sitnikov, "and let's see Falcon."

Falcon, a lean, beetle-black, Dutch-bred stallion with drooping quarters, proved rather better than Ermine. He was the type of horse known to the fancier as "bumpers and borers," that is, with an action which throws the fore-legs out in all directions, but does not make much direct headway. Middle-aged merchants have a weakness for horses of this type: their action resembles the swaggering gait of a smart waiter; they are all right on their own, for an after-dinner drive: prancing and caracoling, they will eagerly pull a lumbering drozhky, loaded high with a coachman who has gorged himself stupid, an over-fed merchant who is having twinges of heartburn, and his puffy wife in a blue silk mantle with a lilac kerchief over her head. I turned Falcon down too. Sitnikov showed me several more horses. . . . One, at last, a gray roan stallion of military antecedents, took my fancy. I could not refrain from giving him an appreciative pat on the withers. Sitnikov at once feigned indifference.

"Well, does he go all right?" I asked. (You say "go" when speaking of a trotter.)

"He does," answered the dealer calmly.

"Can I see? . . ."

"Of course you can, sir. Hey, Kuzya, harness Dogonyai to the drozhky."

Kuzya, the jockey, who was a master of his craft, drove past us three times along the road. The horse went well, without stumbling, or throwing up his quarters; he had a free action, carried his tail well up.

"What are you asking for him?"

Sitnikov opened with an unheard-of price. We were starting to bargain where we stood in the road, when suddenly, from around the corner, thundered a team of three magnificently matched horses which halted smartly in front of the gates of Sitnikov's house. In this rakish, fancier's equipage sat Prince N——, with Khlopakov beside him. Baklaga was driving, and how he drove! The rascal could have driven through an earring. The side-horses were lively little bays with black eyes and black legs, keen as mustard; you had only to whistle and they were gone. The shaft-horse, a dark bay, stood throwing his neck back, like a swan, chest well forward, legs like arrows, head tossing, eyes arrogantly narrowed. . . . Fine! A turn-out fit for Tsar Ivan on Easter Day!

"Your Highness! Welcome!" shouted Sitnikov.

The prince jumped down. Khlopakov climbed slowly out on the other side.

"Good day to you, my friend. Got any horses?"

"I have always got horses for your Highness. Please come in . . . Petya, let's see Peacock! and tell them to get Superb ready. As for you, sir," he continued, turning to me, "we will finish our business another time. . . . Fomka, bring a seat for his Highness."

They brought Peacock out from a separate stable which I had not noticed at first. The powerful dark bay flew right up into the air with all his legs. Sitnikov looked away and screwed up his eyes.

"Ooh rrrrapscallion!" pronounced Khlopakov. "*Zhemsa!*"

The prince burst out laughing.

They had some difficulty in holding Peacock; he fairly pulled the groom around the yard; finally they got him up against the wall. He snorted, shivered, collected himself, and Sitnikov teased him with a wave of his whip.

"What are you gaping at? Wait till I show you! ooh!" said the dealer, with fond menace, admiring the horse in spite of himself.

"How much?" asked the prince.

"For your Highness, five thousand."

"Three."

"Impossible, your Highness, upon my word! . . ."

"Three, did you hear? Rrrrapscallion," repeated Khlopakov.

I went off without awaiting the end of the deal. At the furthest corner of the road I noticed a big sheet of paper stuck to the gates of a little gray house. At the head of it was an ink drawing of a horse with a trumpet-shaped tail and an interminable neck, and under the horse's hooves were the following words, written in an old-fashioned hand:

"For sale, horses of various breeds, brought to Lebedyan fair from the well-known steppe-country stud of Anastasei Ivanich Chornobai, landowner of Tambov. Horses of excellent antecedents, fully broken, and nice-mannered. Purchasers kindly ask for Anastasei Ivanich himself, or, in his absence, for his coachman Nazar Kubyshkin. Gentlemen customers, pray do an old man the honor of a visit!"

I halted. I thought I would have a look at the horses of the well-known steppe-country breeder, Mr. Chornobai. I tried to go through the gate, but, contrary to usual practice, found it locked. I knocked.

"Who's there? . . . A customer?" squealed a woman's voice.

"Yes."

"Coming, sir, coming."

The gate opened. I saw a peasant woman of about fifty, bare-headed, in shoes and with a sheepskin thrown loosely on.

"Please, kind sir, come in, and I'll go and tell Anastasei Ivanich at once. . . . Nazar, hey, Nazar."

"What?" muttered a septuagenarian voice from the stable.

"Get the horses ready; a customer has come."

The old woman ran into the house.

"A customer, a customer," muttered Nazar, by way of answer to her. "I haven't washed all their tails yet."

Oh, Arcadia! I thought.

"Good day, sir, and welcome," said a pleasant, slow, fruity voice behind my back. I looked round; in front of me, in a long-skirted blue overcoat, stood an old man of middle height, with white hair, a friendly smile, and beautiful blue eyes.

'Horses? Please, sir, please . . . But wouldn't you like to come and take tea with me first?"

I thanked him and declined.

"Well, as you please. You must forgive me, sir: you see, I am old-fashioned." Mr. Chornobai spoke unhurriedly and with a broad country accent. "Everything is simple and straightforward with me. Nazar, hey, Nazar," he added, drawlingly, and without raising his voice.

Nazar, a little, wrinkled old chap with the nose of a hawk and a triangular beard, appeared on the stable threshold.

"What sort of horses do you want, sir?" continued Mr. Chornobai.

"Not too dear, well-broken, for carriage-work."

"Certainly, I have some like that, certainly . . . Nazar, show the gentleman the gray gelding, you know, the one at the end, and the bay with the bald spot—no, the other bay, the one by Krasotka, you know?"

Nazar returned into the stable.

"Just bring them out on the halter," Mr. Chernobai shouted after him. "My ways, sir," he continued, looking straight at me with his clear, mild eyes, "are not those of the dealers—devil take them! They go in for all sorts of ginger, salt, bran.* God forgive them, anyway! . . . But with me, be pleased to note, everything is open-handed and above board."

The horses were brought out. I didn't like them.

"Well, take them back," said Anastasei Ivanich. "Show us some more."

They showed us some more. Eventually I chose one of the cheaper ones. We began to bargain. Mr. Chornobai remained cool, spoke so judiciously, with such dignity, that I could not fail to "honor the old man": I paid a deposit.

"Well now," said Anastasei Ivanich, "allow me, in the old-fashioned way, to hand the horse over to you from coat-tail to coat-tail. . . . You'll be grateful to me. . . . He's as fresh as a nut . . . unspoiled. Straight from the steppes! He'll go in every kind of harness."

He crossed himself, took his coat-skirt in his hand, grasped the halter, and handed the horse over to me.

"He's yours now, and good luck to you. You still won't take tea?"

"No, thank you very much indeed: I must go home."

---

* Horses grow fat quickly on bran and salt.—*Author.*

"As you please. . . . Shall my coachman lead the horse after you now?"

"Yes, now, if he will."

"Certainly, my dear sir, certainly. . . . Vasily, hey, Vasily, go with the gentleman; lead the horse and take the money. Well, good-bye, sir, and God bless you."

"Good-bye, Anastasei Ivanich."

The horse was led home for me. The very next day he proved broken-winded and lame. I tried putting him in harness: he backed away, and when I struck him with the whip, he balked, bucked, and lay down. I at once set off to see Mr. Chornobai. I asked if he was at home.

"Yes."

"How is this!" I said. "Why, you've sold me a broken-winded horse."

"Broken-winded? . . . Heaven preserve us."

"And lame into the bargain, and a jibber as well."

"Lame? I don't know, your coachman must certainly have hurt him somehow . . . but I, before God . . ."

"Really, Anastasei Ivanich, you ought to take him back."

"No, sir, no, I'm sorry; once he's out of my yard, the deal is done. You should have been good enough to look at him first."

I understood what I was up against, submitted to my fate, laughed, and went off. Luckily I hadn't paid too dear for my lesson.

Two days later I departed, but returned to Lebedyan a week afterwards on the way back. In the coffee-house I found almost the same faces and caught Prince N——at billiards again. But Mr. Khlopakov's fortunes had already suffered one of their usual vicissitudes. The little fair-haired officer had replaced him in the prince's favors. The poor Ensign (retired) tried once more in my presence to put in his catch-word—surely, he thought, it will work as it did before—but the prince not only failed to smile, he actually frowned and shrugged a shoulder. Mr. Khlopakov looked down, shrank into himself, crept away into a corner, and began quietly filling his pipe. . . .

Tatyana Borisovna and Her Nephew

GIVE ME YOUR HAND, DEAR READER, AND COME WITH ME. THE weather is glorious; the May sky is a tender blue; the smooth young willow leaves shine as if they had been washed; the wide, even highway is all covered with that fine, red-stemmed grass which sheep crop with such enjoyment; to right and left, on the long slopes of the gentle hills, a peaceful ripple passes over the green rye; over it glide in faint outline the shadows of small clouds. In the distance are green forests, glittering pools, yellow villages; larks rise in their hundreds, sing, drop like plummets, and sit with necks outstretched on tussocks; rooks halt on the road, look at you, bow down to the earth, let you drive by, and, after a couple of hops, fly ponderously away; on the hill across the ravine there is a peasant ploughing; a roan foal, dock-tailed and wild-maned, runs on unsteady legs after his mother; you can hear his faint whinnying. We drive into a birchwood; the strong, cool smell holds you breathless with delight. We have come to a village-boundary. The coachman gets down, the horses snort, the side-horses look round, the shaft-horse flicks his tail and leans his head against the shaft-bow . . . the gate opens with a squeak. The coachman takes his seat . . . Off we go! In front of us is the village. After passing five back-yards, we turn to the right, go down into a hollow and drive out over a dam. Beyond a small pond, behind round-topped apple-trees and lilacs, we can see a wooden roof that was once red, and two chimneys; the coachman turns to the left along the fence and, to the whining, throaty barking of three aged mongrels, drives through open gates, wheels smartly

around a wide courtyard, past a stable and a barn, bows gallantly
to an old housekeeper who has just stepped sideways over the high
threshold into the open larder-door, and stops at last before the
porch of a dark little house with gleaming windows . . . We are at
Tatyana Borisovna's. And here she is herself, opening a casement
and nodding her head at us . . .

Good day to you, madam!

Tatyana Borisovna is a woman of about fifty, with large, protruding gray eyes, a bluntish nose, red cheeks, and a double chin.
Her face radiates warm-heartedness and affection. Once upon a
time she was married, but she early became a widow. Tatyana Borisovna is a very remarkable woman. She never leaves her little estate,
hardly knows her neighbors, entertains and loves young people only.
She was born of a family of very poor landowners and never received
any education, that's to say, she doesn't speak French; she has never
been to Moscow—and, notwithstanding all these deficiencies, she
is so simple and good, so free in feeling and thought, so little in-
fected with the usual ailments of the ladies of the smaller gentry,
that it is really impossible not to admire her . . . And, indeed, a
woman who lives the whole year round in the country, at the back
of beyond—and neither gossips, nor squeaks, nor drops curtsies, nor
has fits of agitation or choking, nor gets the shivers from curiosity—
such a woman is a regular portent! She usually wears a gray taffeta
dress and a white bonnet with lilac-colored ribbons hanging from
it; she likes food, but there is no gluttony about her; she leaves jam-
making, drying, and pickling to her housekeeper. Then what does
she do all day? you will ask. Read?—no, she doesn't read; to tell
the truth, books are not printed for the likes of her. . . . If she has
no company, my friend Tatyana Borisovna sits alone at the window and knits a stocking—in winter, that is; in summer she walks
in the garden, plants and waters her flowers, plays for whole hours
with her kittens, feeds her pigeons . . . She has little to do with the
management of her land. But if someone calls, some young neighbour, whom she likes, Tatyana Borisovna becomes quite animated;
she makes him sit down, serves him with tea, listens to his stories,
laughs, sometimes pats his cheek, but speaks little herself; in mis-

fortune or grief she will have comfort and good advice to give. How
many people have confided in her the secrets of their homes and
hearts, how many have wept on her shoulder! Sometimes she sits
opposite her visitor, leans quietly on one elbow and looks him in the
eyes with such sympathy, smiles with such affection, that the visitor thinks in spite of himself: You're a wonderful woman, Tatyana
Borisovna! let me tell you all that's in my heart. In her small, cozy
rooms it is comfortable and warm; the weather in her house is always fine, if I may so express it. Tatyana Borisovna is a marvellous
woman, and yet no one marvels at her: her common sense, her firmness and frankness, her burning sympathy in the joys and sorrows
of others, all her good qualities, in a word, seem to have been born
with her and to have cost her no pain or trouble. . . . It would be
impossible to imagine her otherwise; therefore there can be nothing
to thank her for. She particularly likes looking on at the pranks and
games of the young; she folds her arms below her breasts, throws
back her head, screws up her eyes, and sits there smiling, then suddenly sighs and says: "Oh, you children, my children!" . . . So, at
times, you want to go up to her, take her by the hand and say to
her: "Listen, Tatyana Borisovna, you don't know your own worth;
with all your simplicity and lack of book-learning, you're a remarkable being." Her very name has something familiar and welcoming
about it, one likes pronouncing it, it excites an affectionate smile.
Often, for instance, I have chanced to ask a passing peasant how
to get, say, to Grachevka. "Ah, sir, you go first to Vyazovoye, and
from there to Tatyana Borisovna's, and from Tatyana Borisovna's
anyone will be able to show you the way." And at the name Tatyana
Borisovna the peasant has a special shake of the head. In keeping
with her means, she has few servants. Her house, laundry, larder,
and kitchen are under the charge of Agafya the housekeeper, her old
nurse, an excellent, tearful, toothless creature; two hale and hearty
girls, with firm, dove-colored cheeks like Antonov apples, serve under her direction. The functions of footman, majordomo, and butler
are discharged by a seventy-year-old man-servant named Polikarp,
a freak if ever there was one—a well-read fellow, a retired violinist
and devotee of Viotti, a personal enemy of Napoleon, or, as he calls

him, "Bonapartishka," and a passionate trapper of nightingales. He always has five or six of them in his room. In early spring he sits for whole days beside the cages, waiting for the first "roll" and, when his vigil is over, covers his face with his hands and groans, "Oh, dear, dear me!" and bursts into floods of tears. Polikarp is assisted by his grandson Vasya, a curly-headed, quick-eyed lad of twelve; Polikarp loves him to distraction and grumbles at him from morning to night. He also occupies himself with his education. "Vasya," he says, "say 'Bonapartishka is a rascal.'" "And what will you give me, grandfather?" "What will I give you? . . . I'll give you nothing. . . . Look here, what are you? Are you a Russian?" "I'm an Amchanian, grandpa: I was born in Amchensk.*" "You stupid! and where is Amchensk?" "And how should I know?" "Amchensk is in Russia, stupid!" "What if it is in Russia?" "What if it is? Why, Bonapartishka was driven off Russian soil by his Grace the late prince Mikhailo Ilarionovich Kutuzov of Smolensk, with the help of God. That's when they made up the song:

> *Bonaparte's forgot his paces*
> *Since he went and lost his braces . . .*

"D'you understand: he liberated your native land." "But what's that got to do with me?" "Oh, you stupid, stupid boy. Look, if his Grace Prince Mikhailo Ilarionovich had not driven Bonapartishka out, some *Moussieu* would be hitting you on the noddle with a stick. He would come up to you, see, and say to you: *'Coman voo portay voo?'*—and then, rap-rap." "But I'd punch him in the pot." "And he'd say to you: *'Bonzhur, bonzhur, venay ici'*—and he'd pull you by the hair." "But I'd get him by the legs—by the spring-onions." "Quite right, their legs *are* like spring-onions. . . . But supposing he began to tie your hands?" "I wouldn't let him; I'd call Mikhei the coachman to help me." "Why, yes, Vasya, the Frenchman wouldn't be able to stand up against Mikhei, would he?" "Stand up against him, indeed!

---

* Dialect version of "Mtsensk," the name of a town in Orel province. —*Translators*.

Why, Mikhei's as strong as a horse." "Well, and what would you do to him?" "We'd give it to him on the back, we would . . ." "But he would shout: *'Pardon, pardon, sivooplay!'*" "And we would answer him: 'None of your *sivooplay*, you Frenchman, you!'" "Well done, Vasya! . . . Well, shout it out, then: 'Bonapartishka is a rascal!'" "And you give me some sugar!" "There's a lad for you!"

Tatyana Borisovna has few dealings with the ladies of the neighborhood; they are not fond of visiting her and she is unskilful at entertaining them, drops off to sleep to the murmur of their conversation, then starts up, struggles to open her eyes, and drops off to sleep again. On the whole, Tatyana Borisovna doesn't like women. One of her friends, an excellent and quiet young man, had a sister, an old maid of thirty-eight and a half, a very good creature, but warped, overstrung, and given to enthusiasms. Her brother used often to tell her about their neighbor. One fine morning my old maid—just like that, out of the blue—ordered her horse to be saddled and set off to Tatyana Borisovna's. In her long dress, with a hat on, a green veil, and straying curls, she entered the hall and, passing the astonished Vasya, who took her for a fairy, rushed into the drawing-room. Tatyana Borisovna, startled, tried to get up, but her legs gave way. "Tatyana Borisovna," began the visitor, in a voice of entreaty, "forgive my boldness. I am the sister of your friend Alexei Nikolaevich K——, and I've heard so much about you from him, that I've decided to make your acquaintance." "Very much honored," murmured her stupefied hostess. The visitor threw off her hat, shook her curls, sat down beside Tatyana Borisovna, took her by the hand. . . . "So this is she," she began thoughtfully, with a catch in her voice. "This is that good, serene, noble, holy being! This is she, that woman so simple and at the same time so profound! What a joy, what a joy! What friends we are going to be! I can breathe at last! . . . Just as I imagined her," she added in a whisper, gazing into the eyes of Tatyana Borisovna. "You're not angry with me, you good kind soul?" "Not at all, I am very pleased . . . won't you have some tea?" The visitor smiled condescendingly. *"Wie wahr, wie unreflectirt,"* she murmured, as if to herself. "Let me kiss you, you dear creature!"

The old maid sat on at Tatyana Borisovna's for three hours,

without even a moment of silence. She tried to explain to her new acquaintance just what her significance was. As soon as the unexpected guest had left, the poor lady took a bath, had a good drink of lime tea, and went to bed. But the next day the old maid returned, sat for four hours and left with a promise to visit Tatyana Borisovna every day. She had determined to put the finishing touches to the evolution and development of what she described as such a richly-endowed nature. And indeed she would probably have finished her off completely if, in the first place, she hadn't been thoroughly disillusioned about her brother's friend before two weeks were up, and secondly, if she hadn't fallen in love with a young student who was passing by and with whom she at once embarked on an energetic correspondence; in her epistles, she sent him the customary blessings for the holiness and beauty of his life, offered "to sacrifice her whole being," asked him just to call her sister, went off into descriptions of nature, referred to Goethe, Schiller, Bettin, and German philosophy, and ended by landing the poor young man into a state of black despair. But youth claimed its own: one fine morning he woke up in such a frenzy of hatred for his "sister and best friend" that he almost killed his servant in the heat of the moment, and for a long time afterwards he practically snapped at the slightest allusion to pure and exalted love. . . . But from that time on Tatyana Borisovna began to avoid contacts with the ladies of the neighborhood even more decidedly than before.

Alas! There is nothing durable on earth. All that I have told you about the good lady's way of life is a thing of the past; the peace that reigned in her house is broken for ever. For more than a year she has had living with her a nephew, an artist from Petersburg.

Eight years ago there lived at Tatyana Borisovna's a lad of twelve, an orphan, little Andrei, the son of her late brother. Little Andrei had big, bright, dewy eyes, a tiny little mouth, a straight nose, and a fine high forehead. He spoke in a sweet, gentle voice, conducted himself in a neat and orderly fashion, was charming and attentive with guests, and kissed his aunt's hand with all the sensibility of an orphan. You had hardly time to appear before, lo and behold, he would be bringing you a chair. He never got into any sort of mischief: he never made a noise; he would sit by himself in a corner with a book, and so quietly and modestly, he wouldn't even lean against the back of the chair. A visitor would come in—and up Andrei would get, with a respectful smile and a blush; the visitor would leave—down he would sit again, bring out of his pocket a little brush and looking-glass, and tidy his hair. From his earliest years he had been fond of drawing. If a scrap of paper came his way, he would at once ask Agafya the housekeeper for a pair of scissors, carefully cut out of the paper an exact square, put a border round it, and get to work: he would draw an eye with an enormous pupil, or a Grecian nose, or a house with a chimney and a spiral of smoke, a dog *"en face"* looking like a bench, or a tree with two pigeons, and underneath he would write: "Drawn by Andrei Belovzorov, on such and such a date in such and such a year, in the village of Malye Bryki." For the two weeks before Tatyana Borisovna's name-day he was at work with a special zeal: he was the first to appear with good wishes, and brought a little scroll tied up in pink ribbon. Tatyana Borisovna kissed her nephew on his forehead and undid the knot. The scroll opened and the curious gaze of the beholder fell on a round frame in bold shading, with pillars and an altar in the middle; on the altar was a burning heart and a wreath and above, on a twisted banderole, was written in bold letters: "To his aunt and benefactress Tatyana Borisovna Bogdanova from her respectful and loving nephew, as an expression of his deepest affection." Tatyana Borisovna kissed him again and gave him a silver ruble. All the same, she felt no great attachment towards him: little Andrei's obsequiousness did not altogether please her. Meanwhile Andrei was growing up; Tatyana Borisovna began to feel anxious about his future. An unexpected development delivered her from her perplexity. . . .

This is what happened: one day, eight years ago, she received a visit from a certain Mr. Pyotr Mikhailich Benevolensky, a Collegiate Councillor and Cavalier of an Order. Mr. Benevolensky had once held a Government appointment in the nearest provincial town and had been assiduous in his visits to Tatyana Borisovna; then he had been transferred to Petersburg, entered a Ministry, reached a fairly important position, and on one of his frequent tours on official business had remembered his old acquaintance and turned up to see her, with the intention of resting for two days from the cares of office in the bosom of the peaceful countryside. Tatyana Borisovna received him with her usual cordiality, and Mr. Benevolensky . . . but before we proceed with our story, allow me, amiable reader, to acquaint you with this new character. Mr. Benevolensky was a stoutish, soft-looking man of medium build, with short legs and podgy little hands. He wore a voluminous and extremely neat frock-coat, a high, wide cravat, snow-white linen, a gold chain on his silk waistcoat, a ring with a stone in it on his index finger, and a blond wig; he spoke quietly and with authority, walked noiselessly, had a pleasant smile, a pleasantly roving eye, and a pleasant way of sinking his chin in his cravat: he was an altogether pleasant person. He had also been endowed by the Lord with an excellent heart: he was easily moved to tears or enthusiasm; in addition to which he burnt with a disinterested passion for the arts, a really disinterested one, because the truth was that in matters of art Mr. Benevolensky understood not the first thing. It is a mystery, from what quarter, in virtue of what secret and incomprehensible laws, this passion had gained its hold on him. He gave the impression of being a matter-of-fact, indeed a humdrum sort of man . . . in fact his type is fairly well represented in Mother Russia. . . .

Their love for art and artists gives these people an indescribable, cloying sweetness; acquaintance or conversation with them is excruciating: they are bores of a honeyed variety. For instance, they never call Raphael Raphael, or Correggio Correggio. "The Divine Sanzio, the inimitable de Allegris," they say, in a voice which is invariably affected. Every home-bred, self-satisfied, over-subtilized, mediocre talent becomes a genius for them: the blue sky of Italy, the lemons of the south, the scented mists of Brenta's banks never leave their tongue. "Ah, Vanya, Vanya," or: "Ah, Sasha, Sasha," they say to each other with emotion: "We ought to be off to the South, to the South . . . you and I are Greeks at heart, ancient Greeks." They are to be observed at exhibitions, before certain works of certain Russian painters. (It must be remembered that for the most part these gentlemen are impassioned patriots.) Now they take two steps back and put their heads to one side, now they go up to the picture again; their eyes are veiled in oily moisture . . . "Phew, my goodness me," they say at last, in a voice broken with emotion, "what soul, what soul! . . . look, what heart, what heart! He's put his soul into it!—his very soul! . . . And the composition! The masterly composition!" And the pictures that hang in their own drawing-rooms! The artists that go to their evening parties, drink their tea, listen to their discourses! The offerings they receive, the perspectives of their own rooms with a brush in the right foreground, a pile of dirt on a glossy floor, a yellow samovar on a table by the window, and the master himself in a dressing-gown and skull-cap, with a sharp highlight on his cheek! What long-haired nurselings of the Muses visit them, and with what feverishly superior smiles! What pale-green young ladies whine at their pianos! For such is the custom in Mother Russia: a man cannot devote himself to a single art,—he must take on the whole lot. So it is not at all surprising that these gentlemen-amateurs also extend their vigorous protection to Russian literature and in particular to the drama. . . . It is for them that works like *Jacob Sanazar* are written. The thousand-times depicted struggle of unrecognized talent against society, against the whole world, shakes them to the bottom of their soul. . . .

The day after Mr. Benevolensky's arrival, at tea, Tatyana Borisovna told her nephew to show the visitor his drawings. "So he draws, does he?" said Mr. Benevolensky in some surprise, and he turned to little Andrei with interest. "Certainly, he does," rejoined Tatyana Borisovna. "He's so keen! and all on his own too, without any teacher." "Oh, show me, show me," repeated Mr. Benevolensky. Blushing and smiling, Andrei produced his sketch-book for the visitor. Mr. Benevolensky began to turn over the pages with the air of a connoisseur. "Well done, young man," he pronounced at last. "Very well done," and he stroked Andrei's head. Andrei kissed his hand in mid-air. "There's talent for you! I congratulate you, Tatyana Borisovna, I do indeed." "You know, Pyotr Mikhailich, I can't find him a teacher here. To get one from the town is expensive, my neighbors the Artamonovs have a painter, an excellent one, I understand, but the lady of the house forbids him to give lessons outside, she says it will spoil his taste." "Hmm, hmm," pronounced Mr. Benevolensky; he reflected, and gave a sidelong look at Andrei. "Well, we'll talk it over," he added suddenly, and rubbed his hands. The same day he asked Tatyana Borisovna if he could speak with her alone. They were closeted together. Half an hour later they called for little Andrei. Little Andrei went in. Mr. Benevolensky was standing in the window, slightly flushed, and radiant-eyed. Tatyana Borisovna was sitting in a corner drying her tears. "Well, little Andrei," she began at length, "say thank you to Pyotr Mikhailich: he is going to take you under his guardianship and carry you off to Petersburg." Andrei was fairly rooted to the spot. "Tell me honestly," began Mr. Benevolensky in a voice of dignity and condescension. "Do you want to be an artist, young man, do you feel a holy vocation to art?" "Yes, I want to be an artist, Pyotr Mikhailich," rejoined little Andrei tremulously. "Well then, I am very glad. You will, of course," continued Mr. Benevolensky, "find it painful to leave your revered aunt; you should feel the liveliest gratitude towards her." "I adore my aunt," Andrei interrupted him, and began to blink. "Of course, of course, that's very understandable and does you much credit; all the same, imagine what joy when you succeed. . . ." "Kiss me, Andrei," whispered the good lady. Little Andrei threw himself on her neck. "Well, now say thank you to your benefactor . . ." Little Andrei put his arms round Mr. Benevolensky's stomach, stood up on tiptoes, and managed to reach his hand, which the benefactor permitted, certainly, but without any undue enthusiasm. . . . After all, he must console and gratify the child, well, yes, and also pander to his own vanity a bit. Two days later Mr. Benevolensky departed, taking with him his new charge.

During the first three years of his absence, little Andrei wrote fairly often and sometimes appended drawings to his letters. Occasionally Mr. Benevolensky added a few words from himself, approbatory for the most part; then the letters got fewer, and finally broke off altogether. For a whole year there was no word from the nephew; Tatyana Borisovna was beginning to grow anxious, when suddenly she received a note of the following tenor: "Dear Aunt, three days ago my protector, Pyotr Mikhailich, passed away. A cruel paralytic

stroke bereft me of this last support. Of course, I am already nineteen; in the last seven years I have made considerable progress; I
have great hope of my talent, and can live by it; I am not despon-
dent, but all the same, if you can, send me by the first opportunity
250 rubles in notes. I kiss your hand and remain, etc."

Tatyana Borisovna sent off the 250 rubles to her nephew. Two
months later he asked for more; she collected what she could and
sent it off. Six weeks after this second despatch, he asked for money
a third time, saying that it was for paints for a portrait ordered from
him by Princess Tertesheneva. Tatyana Borisovna refused. In that
case, he wrote to her, he intended to come and stay with her in the
country in order to restore his health. And so indeed, in May of the
same year, Little Andrei returned to Malye Bryki.

At first Tatyana Borisovna did not recognize him. Judging by
his letter, she expected a thin, sickly fellow, but what she saw was a
sturdy-shouldered lad with a broad, red face and curled, oily hair.
Thin, pale little Andrei had turned into a stalwart Andrei Ivanich
Belovzorov. It was not only his appearance which had altered. The
punctilious timidity, precision, and neatness of previous years had
given place to a careless joviality and an unbearable slovenliness; he
had a rolling gait, threw himself into armchairs, collapsed over the
table, sprawled about, yawned his head off; he was rude to his aunt
and to the servants. I, he seemed to say, am an artist, a free Cossack! This is how we are! Sometimes he would not take a brush in
his hand for days on end; but when the so-called inspiration overcame him, he would strut about like a man in a daze, heavy-footed,
awkward, noisy; his cheeks would blaze with a coarse flush, his eyes
would be bleary; he would go off into discourses about his talent,
his successes, his development, his progress . . . It appeared in fact
that his skill hardly ran to passable portrait-sketches. He was an
utter dunce, read nothing, indeed what has an artist to gain by reading! Nature, freedom, poetry—these are his element. All he need
do is shake his curls, sing like a nightingale and smoke himself silly
with Beetle mixture! The devil-may-care Russian touch is all very
well, but it only suits a few; untalented, second-rate exponents of it
are unbearable. Our friend Andrei Ivanich settled in at his aunt's:

free food evidently suited his palate. On visitors he inflicted mortal boredom. He would sit down at the piano (for Tatyana Borisovna actually had one) and begin strumming "The Dashing Troika" with one finger; he would strike a chord, hammer away at the keys; for whole hours he would painfully howl his way through Varlamov's songs: "The Lonely Pinetree" or "No, Doctor, come not," and all this with his eyes sunk in fat and his cheeks as shiny as a drum. . . . Then suddenly he would roar out: "Die away, ye Throbs of Passion" . . . Tatyana Borisovna would fairly jump out of her skin.

"It's a strange thing," she remarked to me one day, "how all the songs written to-day are sort of desperate; in my time they used to write them differently: there were sad songs too, but all the same they were pleasant to listen to. . . . For instance:

> Come, come to me in the meadow;
> Where I wait for you in vain;
> Come, come to me in the meadow
> Where I shed tears like the rain.
> Alas, when you come to me, I fear
> That all too late 'twill be, my dear.

Tatyana Borisovna smiled slyly.

"I su-u-ffer, I su-u-ffer," bawled her nephew in the next room.

"That's enough, Andrei."

"Parting makes the soul despo-o-ond," continued the irrepressible singer.

Tatyana Borisovna shook her head. "Oh, these artists!"

A year has passed since then. Belovzorov is still living with his aunt and still preparing to move to Petersburg. In the country he has grown as fat as he is tall. His aunt—would you believe it?—dotes on him, and girls of the neighborhood fall in love with him . . .

Many of her former acquaintances have stopped visiting Tatyana Borisovna.

Death

I HAVE A YOUNG NEIGHBOR, A FARMER AND A SPORTSMAN. ONE fine July morning I rode over to see him with the suggestion that we should go out together after blackcock. He agreed. "Only," he said, "let's go to my bit of brushwood at Zusha; on the way I'll have a look at Chapligino; my oak-wood, d'you know? It's being felled." "Let's do that," I said. He ordered his horse to be saddled, put on a green coat with brass buttons shaped like a boar's head, a game-bag with a woolwork pattern, and a silver flask, shouldered a new French gun, took a self-satisfied turn in front of the looking-glass, and called to his dog Esperance, which had been given to him by a cousin, an old maid with an excellent heart but without a hair on her head. We set out. My neighbor took with him his constable Arkhip, a stout, thick-set peasant with a square face and the pronounced cheekbones of prehistoric man, also his newly-appointed agent, a youth of nineteen from the Baltic provinces, thin, fair, shortsighted, with sloping shoulders, by name Mr. Gottlieb von der Kock. My neighbor himself had only recently come into possession of his property. He had inherited it from an aunt, Mrs. State-Councillor Kardon-Kataeva, an extremely fat woman with a habit of groaning long and plaintively even when in bed. We reached the "brushwood." "Wait for me here in the clearing," said Ardalion Mikhailich (my neighbor) to his companions. The German bowed, dismounted, took a book from his pocket, probably a novel by Johanna Schopenhauer, and sat down beneath a bush; Arkhip halted in the sun and never stirred for a whole hour. We made a circle in the bushes without putting anything up. Ardalion informed me that he meant to go on into the wood. Somehow or other, that day, I had no confidence in our luck: I trailed after him. We went back to the clearing. The German marked his page, got up, put his book in his pocket, and, with some difficulty, mounted his sorry, dock-tailed hack, which whined and kicked at the slightest touch; Arkhip gave a start, pulled both reins at the same time, clattered his feet, and finally set his dazed, downtrodden little nag in motion. Off we went.

I had known Ardalion's wood since my childhood. In company with my French tutor, Monsieur Désiré Fleury, the best-hearted of men (who, incidentally, all but ruined my health by making me drink Leroy's mixture every night), I often used to go to Chapligino. The whole wood consisted of some two or three hundred huge oaks and ash-trees. Their majestic and mighty trunks stood out superbly in black against the translucent, golden green of the hazels and mountain ashes; higher up, they silhouetted themselves gracefully against the clear blue sky and threw out their spreading, knotty branches to make a tent; hawks, merlins, and kestrels came whistling past below the motionless tree-tops; spotted woodpeckers tapped sharply on the thick bark; the ringing song of the black thrush came suddenly through the thick foliage, following close on the staccato cry of the oriole; below, in the bushes, robins, siskins, and chiffchaffs chirruped and sang. Chaffinches hopped nimbly about the paths; a white hare stole along the edge of the wood, hopping cautiously, as if on crutches; a red-brown squirrel jumped now and then from tree to tree and sat still all of a sudden, with its tail raised above its head. In the grass beside the tall ant-hills, in the faint shade of the finely-carved bracken leaves, violets and lilies-of-the-valley blossomed, and mushrooms of all kinds—yellow and brown, oak-mushrooms and scarlet fly-agaric—grew there; on the turf, between the spreading bushes, was the bright red of the wild strawberry . . . And the shade there was inside the wood! In the sultriest heat, at noon, it was absolute night: stillness, perfume, freshness . . . The times I had spent at Chapligino had been happy, and consequently it was with a sad heart, I confess, that I went into this wood I had known so well. The disastrous snowless winter of 1840 had not spared my old friends,

the oaks and ashes; parched, stripped, just covered here and there with unhealthy verdure, they towered sadly up above the young trees, which had been planted instead but would never fill their place . . . *
Some of them, still overgrown with leafage at their base, raised dead shattered branches aloft, as if in protest or despair; on others, from foliage that was still fairly thick, though not so abundant or luxuriant as before, protruded stout, dried-up dead boughs; some had already lost all their bark; others had finally fallen right over and lay rotting on the ground like corpses. Who could have foreseen it—that at Chapligino there would be no shade to be found! Well, I thought, as I looked at the dying trees, I suppose it must be shameful for you and bitter? . . . I remembered the lines of Koltsov:

> *What is there left*
> *Of your lofty eloquence,*
> *Your proud strength,*
> *Your imperial brilliance?*
> *Where is it now,*
> *Your green majesty?* . . .

"How comes it, Ardalion," I began, "that these trees weren't felled the year after? Why, they won't fetch a tenth now of what they would have before."

He merely shrugged his shoulders. "Ask my aunt; the merchants came, brought the money, and pestered her to sell."

"Mein Gott! Mein Gott!" exclaimed von der Kock at every step. "Petty! Petty!"

"How d'you mean, petty?" remarked my neighbor with a smile.

"That's to say, vot a petty, vot a shame, that's vot I meant."

---

* In 1840, in spite of the severest frost, no snow fell until the very end of December; vegetation froze to death, and many fine oak-woods were ruined, in this pitiless winter. It is difficult to replace them: the productive power of the earth is visibly failing; on the plots of ground that have been "lustrated" (walked round with icons), instead of the noble trees that stood there before, birches and aspens are growing like weeds; we have not yet learned how to plant trees scientifically. —*Author.*

His compassion was especially aroused by the oaks that lay on
the ground—and he was right: any miller would have paid a good
price for them. Meanwhile the constable Arkhip preserved an imperturbable calm and showed no sign of grief. On the contrary, it
was even with a certain satisfaction that he jumped over them and
flicked them with his whip.

We were emerging on to the scene of the felling, when suddenly,
immediately after the crash of a falling tree, there was a cry and the
sound of voices, and a few minutes later a young peasant, pale and
shock-headed, came dashing out of the thicket towards us.

"What's the matter? Where are you off to?" Ardalion asked him.
He stopped at once.

"Oh, Ardalion Mikhailich, sir, something terrible!"

"What?"

"Maxim's been caught under a tree."

"How so? . . . D'you mean Maxim the contractor?"

"Yes, sir. We were felling an ash and he was standing watching. . . . He stood and stood, then off he went to the well to get
some water; you see, he was thirsty. Then suddenly the ash comes
toppling down just where he is. We shout to him, 'Run, run, run.'
He ought to have dodged to one side, but he went and ran straight
ahead . . . he must have been scared. The ash fairly hid him under
its top branches. Why it fell so soon, the Lord alone knows. Maybe
its heart was rotten."

"And it hit Maxim?"

"Yes, sir."

"Killed him?"

"No, sir, he's still alive—but then his legs and arms are crushed.
I was running to Seliverstich to get a doctor."

Ardalion ordered the constable to gallop to Seliverstich village,
and set off himself at a vigorous trot towards the clearing. . . . I followed him.

We found poor Maxim on the ground. Some half a dozen peasants were standing round him. We dismounted. There was scarcely
a groan from him; now and then he opened his eyes wide, looked
around as if in astonishment, and bit a bloodless lip. . . . His chin

trembled, his hair was plastered to his brow, his chest rose irregularly: he was dying. The gentle shade of a young lime-tree fell peacefully across his face.

We bent over him. He recognized Ardalion.

"Sir," he began indistinctly, "tell them . . . priest . . . to send . . . the Lord . . . punished me . . . my legs and arms, all broken . . . today . . . Sunday . . . and I . . . and I . . . you see . . . I didn't give the lads the day off."

He was silent. His breath came with difficulty. "My money . . . give it . . . my wife . . . when my debts are paid . . . Onisim knows what I owe . . . and who to . . ."

"We have sent for the doctor, Maxim," said my neighbor. "You may live yet."

He tried to open his eyes, and raised his eyebrows and eyelids with an effort.

"No, I'm dying. . . . Here . . . here it comes, here it is, here . . . Forgive me, lads, for anything . . ."

"God will forgive you, Maxim Andreich," said the peasants in gruff unison, and they took off their caps. "You forgive us."

All of a sudden he gave a desperate jerk of his head, and a mournful heave of his chest, then sank back again.

"But it isn't right for him to die here," exclaimed Ardalion. "Get the mat out of the cart, lads, and let's carry him to the infirmary."

Two men ran off to the cart.

"From Efim . . . at Sychovo . . ." whispered the dying man. "I bought a horse yesterday. . . . I paid a deposit . . . so the horse is mine . . . my wife to have it too. . . ."

They began to move him on to the mat . . . he shuddered all over, like a shot bird, then straightened himself out. . . .

"He's dead," murmured the peasants.

We mounted our horses in silence and rode away.

Poor Maxim's death plunged me in reflection. Strange how death takes the Russian peasant! His state of mind at his last hour cannot be called indifference or dull-wittedness; he dies as if he were going through a ceremony: coldly, and with simplicity.

Some years ago, on the land of another neighbor of mine, a

peasant was badly burnt in a drying-shed. (Indeed he might have been left there, if a passing townsman hadn't pulled him out, more dead than alive: he had plunged into a cask of water, then taken a run at the door and broken it in with the roof above it ablaze.) I visited the peasant in his cabin. Inside it was dark, stuffy. I asked where the patient was. "There he is, sir, on the stove-bench," answered a dejected-looking woman, in a singsong voice. I went across, and found the peasant lying covered with a sheepskin and breathing heavily. "Well, how do you feel?" The sick man fidgeted above the stove, tried to rise, all injured as he was and at the point of death. "Lie down, lie down . . . Well, how are you?" "Pretty bad," he said. "D'you feel pain?" Silence. "Is there anything you want?" Silence. "Shall I send you some tea, eh?" "I don't want it." I left him and sat down on a bench. I sat for a quarter of an hour, half an hour—and, in the cabin, the silence of the tomb. In a corner, at a table under the icons, a little girl of five was hiding and munching bread. Now and then her mother would scold her. In the passage there were comings and goings, knockings, voices: a brother's wife was chopping a cabbage. "Hey, Axinya!" said the patient at last. "What?" "Give me some kvass." Axinya gave him some kvass. More silence. I asked in a whisper if he had had communion. "Yes." Well, then, everything was in order: he was waiting for death and that was all there was to it. I could bear it no longer and left. . . .

Another time, I remember, I looked in at the village infirmary of Krasnogore to see my friend Kapiton, the medical orderly, who was a keen sportsman.

The infirmary consisted of what had been an outlying wing of the manor house; the lady herself had arranged it, that's to say, she had ordered that upon the door should be stuck up a blue board with the inscription in white letters "Infirmary of Krasnogore," and had herself given Kapiton a handsome album to record the names of his patients. On the first page of this album, one of the good lady's spongers and toadies had written the following lines:

> *Dans ces beaux lieux, où règne l'allégresse,*
> *Ce temple fut ouvert par la Beauté;*

De vos seigneurs admirez la tendresse,
Bons habitants de Krasnogorié!

and another gentleman had added below:

Et moi aussi j'aime la nature!
Jean Kobyliatnikoff.

The orderly had bought six beds at his own expense and, wishing himself luck, had launched out on his career of healing. Besides himself, the hospital staff consisted of two: Pavel the wood-carver, who was subject to fits of madness, and a peasant woman named Melikitrisa, who had a shrivelled arm and occupied the position of cook. Both of them prepared medicines and dried herbs and made infusions from them; they also calmed patients with the fever; the mad wood-carver had a surly appearance and was sparing of words; at night he sang a song about "Beauteous Venus," and approached every passer-by with the request that he should be allowed to marry a girl named Malanya, who had been dead for some time. The woman with the shrivelled arm used to beat him and make him take care of the turkeys. Well, one day I was sitting with Kapiton, the orderly. We had started talking about our last shoot, when suddenly a cart drove into the yard, harnessed to an unusually stout gray horse of the sort that only millers possess. In the cart sat a sturdy peasant in a new overcoat, with a pepper and salt beard. "Hey, Vasily Dmitrich," called Kapiton from the window, "welcome to you. . . . It's the miller from Lyubovshin," he whispered to me. With a groan, the peasant climbed down from the cart, came into the orderly's room, looked for the icon, and crossed himself. "Well, Vasily Dmitrich, what's the news? Why, you must be poorly: your face is off-color." "Yes, Kapiton Timofeich, I've got something wrong." "What's the matter?" "Here's the matter, Kapiton Timofeich. The other day I bought some grindstones in the town; well, I brought them home, and, as I was getting them out of the cart, I must have strained myself or something, there was a sort of 'plonk' in my innards as if something had torn . . .

And, ever since, I've been poorly all the time. To-day it's pretty bad." "H'm," said Kapiton, and took a pinch of snuff. "It must be rupture. Is it long since it took you that way?" "Ten days." "Ten?" The orderly drew in a long breath through his teeth and shook his head. "Let me feel you. . . . Well, Vasily Dmitrich," he said at last, "I'm sorry for you with all my heart, but you're in a bad way; you're ill, beyond a joke; you'd better stay here. I'll do my best for you, but I don't promise anything." "Is it as bad as that?" murmured the miller in astonishment. "Yes, Vasily Dmitrich, it's bad; if you'd come to me two days earlier, it would have been nothing at all, just a hand's turn; but now you've got inflammation, that's the trouble; before you've time to look, it'll have turned to gangrene." "But it can't be, Kapiton Timofeich!" "But I tell you it is." "But how can it be?" The orderly shrugged his shoulders. "And am I going to die from this sort of nonsense?" "That, I didn't say . . . but just you stay here." The peasant thought and thought, looked at the floor, then glanced at us, scratched the back of his head, and reached for his cap. "Where are you off to, Vasily Dmitrich?" "Where to? Why, home of course, if I'm as bad as that. I must put things in order, if that's how it is." "But you'll bring on the worst, Vasily Dmitrich, for goodness' sake; why, even as it is, I can't think how you got here. Stay." "No, Kapiton Timofeich, my friend, if I've got to die, I'll die at home; if I die here, God knows what will happen at home." "It's too early yet to say how it will go, Vasily Dmitrich. . . . Of course there's danger, great danger, and no denying it, but that's all the more reason for your staying." The peasant shook his head. "No, Kapiton Timofeich, I won't stay . . . just you prescribe me a little medicine." "Medicine alone won't help you." "I'm not staying, I tell you." "Well, do as you like, only don't blame me afterwards!"

The orderly tore a page from the album and, after writing out a prescription, gave certain further instructions. The peasant took the paper, gave Kapiton half a ruble, left the room, and took his place in the cart. "Well, good-bye, Kapiton Timofeich, don't hold it against me, and don't forget the orphans, if anything . . ." "Hey, Vasily, stay here!" The peasant simply jerked his head, flicked his horses with the reins and drove out of the yard. I went into the road and looked after him. The road was muddy and full of pot-holes; the miller was driving carefully, unhurriedly, guiding his horse with skill, exchanging greetings with passers-by. Three days later he was dead.

Yes, people die strangely in Russia. I can call many such cases to mind. I remember my old friend Avenir Sorokoümov, the student who never finished his studies—the best and noblest of men. I can see again his greenish, consumptive face, his thin blond hair, his gentle smile, his look of enthusiasm, his long limbs; I can hear his soft sweet voice. He lived with a landowner in Great Russia named Gur Krupyanikov, taught his children, Fofa and Zyozya, reading and writing in Russian, geography, and history, patiently bore the heavy jokes of Gur Krupyanikov himself and the coarse familiarities of the butler and the vulgar pranks of the naughty little boys; with a bitter smile, but without a murmur, he carried out the capricious demands of his bored lady; then the relief, the sheer bliss, when, after dinner, finished at last with all duties and occupations, he could sit down before the window and reflectively smoke a pipe, or dip avidly into some mutilated, greasy copy of a bulky journal, brought from town by the surveyor, another home-less wretch like himself! How he loved all kinds of poems and stories; how easily tears started in his eyes; how gaily he laughed; how sincerely he loved his fellows; how penetrated with noble sympathy for everything good and beautiful was that pure and youthful soul! The truth must out: no special brilliance was his; nature had endowed him with neither memory nor concentration; at the University he passed for one of the worst students; at lectures he slept, at examinations he preserved a solemn silence; but whose were the eyes that shone with joy, whose the breath that had a catch in it, at the success or triumph of a comrade? Avenir's. . . . Who believed blindly in the high calling of his friends? Who would extol them with pride and defend them with ferocity? Who knew no envy, no self-love? Who would sacrifice himself without a thought of his own interests? Who would eagerly take second place after people unworthy to undo the latchet of his shoes? . . . Always our good Avenir! I remember how brokenheartedly he took leave of his friends as he drove away on his "contract"; what evil forebodings beset him . . . And with reason: in the country he fared ill; in the country there was no one for him to listen to with reverence, no one to admire, no one to love. . . . The gentry, boors and cultivated ones alike, treated him as a tutor, some roughly, others with indifference. Indeed he was not an impressive figure; shy, blushing, sweating, stammering. . . . Even his health got no benefit from the country air; the poor fellow wasted away like a candle. True, his little room opened on to the garden; cherries, apple-trees, and limes scattered over his table, his ink-pot, his books, their light blossoms; on the wall hung a little blue silk cushion for his watch, given to him at the moment of parting by a kind and sensitive German governess with fair hair and blue eyes; now and then an old friend came out to see him from Moscow and delighted him with verses composed by others or even by himself; but the loneliness, the intolerable slavery of the tutor's condition, the impossibility of freeing himself from it, the endless autumns and winters, the persistent malady . . . Poor, poor Avenir!

I visited Sorokoümov not long before his death. He was already practically unable to walk. The landowner Gur Krupyanikov did not turn him out of his house, but stopped paying his wages, and Zyozya was given another tutor. Fofa had been sent off to the Corps of Cadets. Avenir was sitting by the window in an old armchair of Voltairean design. It was a wonderful day. The bright autumn sky was gay and blue above a dark-brown wall of bare lime trees, on which, here and there, the last bright-gold leaves stirred and fluttered. The frost-pierced earth was sweating and thawing in the sun; its slanting, ruddy rays fell lightly on the pale grass; a faint crackling could be heard in the air; workers' voices came loud and clear from the garden. Avenir wore an old Bokhara robe; a green neckerchief threw a corpse-like tinge over his terribly emaciated face. He was very glad to see me, held out his hand, talked, and coughed. I made him collect himself and sat down beside him . . . On Avenir's knees lay a notebook containing Koltsov's poems, carefully written out; he tapped it, with a smile. "There's a poet for you!" he murmured,

smothering a cough with an effort and beginning to recite in a
scarcely audible voice:

> *Is the falcon's*
> *Pinion bound?*
> *Or his journeying*
> *Hedged around?*

I stopped him: it was against doctor's orders for him to talk too
long. I knew how to please him. Sorokoúmov had never "kept up,"
as they say, with science, but he liked hearing, as he put it, "how
far our great minds have got." He would take a friend aside into a
corner and begin cross-examining him: he would listen, he would
be astonished, he would believe every word, and repeat it all after
his friend. German philosophy interested him especially. I began
talking to him about Hegel. (It is a story of days long since, as you
can see.) Avenir nodded his head approvingly, raised his eyebrows,
smiled, whispered: "I see, I see! . . . Oh, good, good!" I confess
that the childlike curiosity of this poor wretch, dying homeless and
abandoned, touched me to tears. I should observe that Avenir, unlike consumptives in general, had no sort of illusions about his illness . . . and yet he never sighed, showed no sign of distress, never
even alluded to his condition. . . .

After mustering his strength, he began to talk of Moscow, his
friends, Pushkin, the theater, Russian literature; he mentioned our
carouses, the heated discussions of our circle, and pronounced with
regret the names of two or three of our friends who had died.

"D'you remember Dasha?" he added at last. "There was a heart
of solid gold! and how she loved me! . . . What's become of her now?
I suppose the poor girl has faded and pined away?"

I had not the heart to disillusion the sick man—and indeed,
why should he know that his Dasha was now broader than she
was long, went around with merchants, with the brothers Kon-
drachkov, that she powdered and rouged herself and had become a
squeaking scold. And yet, I thought, looking at his exhausted face,
is it impossible to get him out of here? It may be that there is still

a chance of moving him . . . But Avenir didn't allow me to finish my suggestion.

"No, thank you, my friend," he said. "It's all the same to me where I die. I shan't see the winter . . . Why upset people to no purpose? I've got used to this house! It's true that the family here . . ."

"Nasty, eh?" I took him up.

"No, not nasty; just wooden. But I can't complain about them. There are neighbors: the landowner Kasatkin has a daughter, a cultivated, charming, delightful girl . . . not proud . . ."

Sorokoümov had another coughing fit.

"I shouldn't mind at all," he went on, when he had got his breath, "if only they allowed me to smoke my pipe . . . But I won't die without managing to smoke one first," he added with a cunning wink. "Praise be to God, I've lived my time, I've known some good people . . ."

"You might write to your family," I interrupted him.

"What for? Help—they won't give it; if I die—they'll find out. So there's nothing more to be said about it. No, tell me what you saw when you were abroad."

I began to tell him. He fairly drank my words in. Towards evening I left, and ten days later I got the following letter from Mr. Krupyanikov.

"I have the honor, my dear Sir, to advise you hereby that your friend, the student who lived in my house, Mr. Avenir Sorokoümov, passed away three days ago at 3 o'clock in the afternoon and that to-day he was buried at my expense in my parish church. He asked me to forward to you the enclosed books and notebooks. He left 22½ rubles, which, with his other effects, are being duly transmitted to his relatives. Your friend was fully conscious when he passed away and, I may also say, fully insensible, for he showed no signs of regret, even when my whole family said good-bye to him. My wife Kleopatra Alexandrovna sends you her regards. The death of your friend could not fail to have its effect on her nerves; for *my own part, I am, thank God, in good health, and have the honour to remain,*

Your most humble Servant,
   G. Krupyanikov."

Many more instances still come to mind, but I cannot relate them all. I will confine myself to one.

I was present at the death of an old lady, the wife of a landowner. The priest had begun to read the last rites over her, when suddenly he noticed that the sick woman was really expiring and hurriedly gave her the cross. The lady moved back in displeasure. "Why so quick, Father?" she said, with faltering tongue. "There's plenty of time . . ." She kissed the cross, put her hand under the pillow, and— drew her last breath. Under the pillow lay a silver ruble: she had wanted to pay the priest for her own last rites . . .

Yes, death takes the Russian strangely!

The Singers

THE SMALL VILLAGE OF KOLOTOVKA, WHICH ONCE BELONGED
to a lady known in the neighborhood as Fidget from her bold and
spirited ways (her real name is not recorded) but is now owned by
some German or other from Petersburg, lies on the slope of a bare
hill, cleft from top to bottom by a fearsome ravine, which, yawning
like an abyss, winds its hollow, eroded way along the very middle of
the village street, and, worse than any river (for a river could at least
be bridged), divides the unfortunate hamlet into two. A few lean
willows droop timidly along its sandy sides; at the bottom, which
is dry and copper-yellow, lie huge flagstones of shale. A cheerless
sight, there's no denying—but nevertheless the road to Kolotovka
is well-known to all the people of the neighborhood: they use it
frequently and as a matter of course.

Right at the top of the ravine, a few paces off the spot where it
begins as a narrow crevice, stands a small square cabin, on its own,
apart from the others. It is thatched with straw and has a chimney; a
single window, like a watchful eye, looks towards the ravine, and on
winter evenings, lit up from within, can be seen from afar through
the dull frost-haze and, for many a peasant on his way, shines out
like a guiding star. Over the door of the cabin is nailed a little blue
board; the cabin is a pot-house, and goes by the name of the "Snug
Nook." It is a pot-house where in all probability drinks are sold no
cheaper than the fixed price, but it is much better attended than
any other establishment of the same sort in the neighborhood. The
reason for this is the tapster, Nikolai Ivanich.

Nikolai Ivanich was once a lithe, curly-headed, ruddy peasant lad, but is now an extremely stout, already grizzled man, with a face deep in fat, eyes of a sly benevolence, and a greasy forehead criss-crossed with a web of wrinkles. He has lived at Kolotovka for more than twenty years. Nikolai is a man of sagacity and resource, as most tapsters are. Without any special amiability or talkativeness, he has the knack of attracting and holding customers, who somehow find it entertaining to sit in front of his counter, under the calm, hospitable, but watchful eye of their phlegmatic host. He has plenty of common sense; he is well acquainted with the ways of landowner, peasant, and townsman; in difficult situations he can give shrewd advice, but, like the cautious egoist that he is, he prefers to stay on the sideline and goes no further than a vague hint, uttered as if without the least purpose, to guide his clients—and then only his favorite clients—in the way of truth. He knows what he is talking about on every subject of importance or interest to the Russian male: horses and cattle, timber, bricks, crockery, textiles and leather, singing and dancing. When he has no custom, he is in the habit of sitting like a sack on the ground in front of the door of his cabin, his thin legs tucked up beneath him, swapping pleasantries with every passer-by. He has seen plenty in his time, has outlived more than a dozen of the lesser gentry who used to look in on him for a drop of "distilled," knows everything that happens for a hundred versts around, never lets on, never shows so much as in his look that he knows what even the most penetrating police officer fails to suspect. He simply keeps mum, chuckles, and busies himself with the glasses. The neighbors respect him deeply: His Excellency Mr. Shcherepetenko, the leading magnate of the district, bows to him affably every time he passes his abode. Nikolai Ivanich is a man of influence: he forced a well-known horse-thief to return a horse stolen from someone of his acquaintance; he made the peasants of a neighboring village listen to reason when they had refused to accept a new factor, and so on. Incidentally, it mustn't be supposed that he did this from love of fair play, from any zeal for his neighbors' interest; no, he is simply at pains to avert anything that might in any way disturb his own peace. Nikolai Ivanich is married and has children. His wife, a brisk, sharp-nosed, quick-eyed townswoman, has lately put on a good deal of weight, just like her husband. He relies on her absolutely, and the money is locked up in her charge. The noisily-drunk hold her in awe; she dislikes them; there is no profit from them, only a lot of noise; the silent and sullen ones are closer to her heart. Nikolai's children are still small. The first ones all died, but the survivors resemble their parents; it is a pleasure to look at these healthy children with their clever little faces.

It was an unbearably sultry July day, when I trudged slowly, accompanied by my dog, up the Kolotovka ravine in the direction of the "Snug Nook" pot-house. The sun was blazing away in the sky with a kind of fury; it was mercilessly, bakingly hot; the air was absolutely saturated with choking dust. Glossy rooks and crows, with gaping beaks, looked piteously at the passer-by, as if to beg his sympathy; only the sparrows were undistressed and, fluffing out their feathers, twittered and scuffled about the fences even more actively than usual, or flew up from the dusty road in a flock, or hovered in gray clouds over the green hemp-yards. I was tortured by thirst. There was no water at hand: at Kolotovka, as in many other steppe-villages, in the absence of springs and wells, the peasants drink a sort of liquid filth from a pond . . . But who would give the name of water to this repulsive draught? I had it in mind to ask Nikolai Ivanich for a glass of beer or kvass.

It has to be admitted that at no season of the year does Kolotovka present a cheering spectacle; but it arouses a particularly mournful emotion when the blazing sun of July rains its pitiless rays on the tumbledown brown roofs, the deep ravine, the parched, dusty common-land, on which some thin, long-legged chickens are roaming despondently, and the shack of gray aspenwood with holes for windows, a remnant of the former manor house, grown over with nettles, weeds, and wormwood, and the pond, covered with goose-feathers, black, molten-looking, fringed with half-dried mud, and the side-ways listing dam, near which, on the fine-ground, cinder-like earth, sheep, breathless and sneezing from the heat, crowd lugubriously together and with a dismal patience hang their heads as low as can be, as if waiting for the moment when the unbearable sultriness will finally pass. With exhausted steps I was at last nearing Nikolai Ivanich's place, exciting in children the usual amazement, expressed in intense and inane stares, and in dogs the usual indignation, voiced in such hoarse and savage barking that all their insides seemed to be torn loose, afterwards subsiding into a fit of coughing and choking, when suddenly, on the threshold of the pothouse, there appeared a tall man, capless, in a frieze overcoat held below the waist with a blue belt. He had the look of a house-serf; thick gray hair burst out untidily above his dry wrinkled face. He was calling somebody and making vigorous gestures with his arms, which were clearly swinging out much farther than he intended. It was evident that he had already had a drop.

"Come on, come *on*!" he stuttered, raising his thick eyebrows with an effort. "Come on, Blinker, come on! Why, man, you're simply crawling. It isn't right, man. They're waiting for you, and you're just crawling . . . Come on!"

"All right, all right," came a jarring voice, and, from behind the cabin to the right, a short, stout, lame fellow appeared. He wore quite a neat cloth coat, with only one sleeve on; a high, pointed hat, rammed straight down over his brows, gave his podgy, round face a sly, mocking look. His little yellow eyes fairly darted around; a contained, forced smile never left his thin lips, and his long sharp nose stuck jauntily out ahead like a rudder. "I'm coming, my friend," he went on, limping in the direction of the drinking establishment. "What are you calling me for? . . . Who's waiting for me?"

"What am I calling you for?" rejoined the man in the frieze coat, reproachfully. "You're a strange one, Blinker: you're called to the pot-house, and yet you ask: what for? There's all kind of good folk waiting for you: Yasha the Turk, and Wild Master, and the huckster from Zhizdra. Yasha and the huckster have made a bet: they've wagered a quart of beer to see which wins, that is, sings best . . . d'you see?"

"Yasha's going to sing?" said the man nicknamed Blinker, with animation. "You're not lying, Muddlehead?"

"I'm not," answered Muddlehead with dignity. "It's you that's the liar. Of course he's going to sing, if he's made a bet, you ladybird, you twister, you, Blinker!"

"Well, let's go, you ninny," rejoined Blinker.

"Well, kiss me at least, joy of my heart," stammered Muddle-head, flinging his arms out wide.

"You great milk-sop," replied Blinker, contemptuously elbowing him aside, and they both stooped and went in through the low doorway. The conversation I'd heard excited my keen curiosity. More than once rumors had reached me of Yasha the Turk, as being the best singer in the neighborhood, and now an opportunity had suddenly presented itself to hear him in competition with another master. I quickened my pace and entered the establishment.

Probably not many of my readers have had occasion to look inside a country pot-house—but we sportsmen, there's nowhere we don't go. The arrangement of these pot-houses is remarkably simple. They usually consist of a dark entrance-passage and a room divided in two by a partition, behind which none of the customers has the right to go. Cut in the partition, above a broad oak table, is a large longitudinal aperture. On this table or counter the drink is sold. Sealed flasks of different measures stand in a row on shelves immediately opposite the aperture. In the front part of the cabin, the part at the disposal of customers, are benches, two or three empty barrels, and a corner table. Country pot-houses are for the most part pretty dark and you hardly ever see on their log walls any of those brightly colored popular prints without which the ordinary peasant's cabin is seldom complete.

When I went into the "Snug Nook" pot-house a fairly numerous company was already assembled there.

Behind the counter, suitably enough, and filling almost the whole width of the aperture, stood Nikolai Ivanich. In a gay cotton shirt, with an indolent smile on his chubby cheeks, he was pouring out two glasses of spirits with his podgy white hand for the two friends, Blinker and Muddlehead, who had just come in; behind him, in the corner near the window, could be seen his sharp-eyed wife. In the middle of the room stood Yasha the Turk, a lean, well-built man of twenty-three, dressed in a long-skirted blue nankeen coat. He had the appearance of a dashing young mechanic and looked as if his health was nothing to boast about. His sunken cheeks, great, restless gray eyes, straight nose with its fine, mobile nostrils, his wide-domed forehead with the pale blond curls thrust back from it, his bold but handsome and expressive lips—his whole face revealed an impressionable, passionate nature. He was in great excitement, blinking, breathing irregularly, his hands trembling as if with the fever—and indeed he had a fever, that sudden trembling fever which is so familiar to all who speak or sing in public. Beside him stood a man of about forty, broad-shouldered, with broad cheek-bones, and a low forehead, narrow Tartar eyes, a short flat nose, a square chin, and black, shiny, bristle-like hair. The expression of his face, which was swarthy with a leaden undertone, and especially of his full lips, might almost have been called ferocious if it had not been so calmly reflective. He hardly stirred, just looked slowly around like an ox from below the yoke. He wore a sort of shabby frock-coat with smooth copper buttons; an old black silk handkerchief swathed his massive neck. He was nicknamed "Wild Master." Right in front of him, on the bench below the icons, sat Yasha's competitor, the huckster from Zhizdra: a short, sturdy man of about thirty, pock-marked and curly-headed, with a blunt, up-turned nose, lively brown eyes, and a sparse beard. He was looking briskly round, with his hands tucked up beneath him, carelessly swinging and stamping his feet, which were clad in dandified boots with trimmings. He wore a thin new overcoat of gray cloth with a velvet collar, against which a strip of scarlet shirt, buttoned up tightly round his throat, stood out sharply. At a table in the opposite corner, to the right of the door, sat a peasant in a threadbare, grayish coat with an enormous hole at the shoulder. The sunlight fell in a fine, yellowish stream through the dusty panes of the two small windows and seemed unable to dispel the normal darkness of the room: every object was sparsely and patchily illuminated. Nevertheless, it was almost cool in the room and the feeling of stuffiness and sultriness fell from my shoulders like a burden the moment I crossed the threshold.

My arrival, I could see, at first rather confused Nikolai Ivanich's guests; but, observing that he bowed to me as to an acquaintance, they set their minds at rest and paid me no more attention. I ordered some beer and sat down in the corner next to the peasant in the torn coat.

"Well, then," sang out Muddlehead all of a sudden, after drinking a glass at one gulp, and accompanying his exclamation with those strange gestures of the arms without which he evidently never uttered a word. "What are we waiting for? It's time to begin, eh, Yasha?"

"Time to begin," repeated Nikolai Ivanich with approbation.

"Let's begin, if you like," said the huckster coolly, with a self-confident smile. "I'm ready."

"So am I," pronounced Yasha excitedly.

"Well, begin, lads, begin," squeaked Blinker.

But notwithstanding this unanimously expressed wish, neither of them did begin; the huckster did not even rise from his bench—it was as if everyone was waiting for something to happen.

"Begin," said Wild Master sharply and with displeasure.

Yasha shivered. The huckster got up, tightened his belt, and cleared his throat.

"Who's to begin?" he asked, with a slight change of voice, addressing himself to Wild Master, who was still standing motionless in the middle of the room, his thick legs widely planted, his powerful arms thrust almost to the elbow into the pockets of his trousers.

"You, huckster, you," murmured Muddlehead; "you, lad."

Wild Master gave him a sidelong look. Muddlehead squeaked faintly, faltered, looked away at the ceiling, wriggled his shoulders, and fell silent.

"Draw for it," pronounced Wild Master with deliberation, "and set the quart out on the counter."

Nikolai stooped, groaned, fetched up a quart jug from the floor, and set it on the table.

Wild Master looked at Yasha and said: "Well!"

Yasha rummaged in his pockets, found a two-copeck piece, and marked it with his teeth. The huckster brought a new leather purse out from the skirt of his coat, slowly undid the strings, poured out a lot of small change into his hand, and chose a new two-copeck piece. Muddlehead held out his battered hat with its loose and crumpled peak: Yasha and the huckster threw their coins into it.

"You choose," said Wild Master to Blinker.

Blinker grinned with self-satisfaction, took the hat in both hands, and began to shake it up.

For a moment deep silence reigned; the coins chinked faintly against each other. I looked around attentively: every face expressed strained anticipation; even Wild Master had screwed up his eyes; even my neighbor, the peasant in the torn coat, had stuck out his head inquisitively. Blinker put his hand into the hat and drew out the huckster's coin: there was a general sigh. Yasha flushed, and the huckster passed his hand through his hair.

"I *said* it was you," exclaimed Muddlehead, "I said so."

"Now, now, don't get all of a flutter," observed Wild Master contemptuously. "Begin," he continued, nodding to the huckster.

"What shall I sing?" asked the huckster, with rising excitement.

"Whatever you like, of course," rejoined Nikolai Ivanich, slowly folding his arms on his chest. "We can't tell you what to choose. Sing what you like; only sing it well; and then we'll judge as our conscience tells us."

"That's right—as our conscience tells us," repeated Muddlehead, and he licked the rim of his empty glass.

"Just let me clear my throat," said the huckster, fingering the collar of his coat.

"Now, don't waste time—begin!" said Wild Master decisively, and he looked down.

The huckster thought for a moment, shook his head, and set off. Yasha stared at him with all his eyes. . . .

But before I proceed to describe the contest itself, it may be as well to say a few words about each of the personages in my story. The ways of some of them were already known to me when I met them in the "Snug Nook" pot-house; I found out about the rest subsequently.

To begin with Muddlehead. His real name was Evgraf Ivanov; but no one in the neighborhood ever called him anything but Muddlehead, and he used the nickname in speaking of himself, so well did it fit him. And indeed it could not have been better suited to his insignificant, perpetually-worried expression. He was an unmarried, drunken house-serf, whose master had long since despaired of him and who, having no duties and receiving not a farthing's wages, nevertheless found means of making merry every day at someone else's expense. He had many acquaintances who treated him to drinks and to tea, though they couldn't have said why, because, so far from being amusing in company, he fairly disgusted everyone with his witless chatter, his unbearable importunity, his feverish movements and his ceaseless unnatural laughter. He could neither sing nor dance; from birth he had never made a clever remark nor even a sensible one; he just muddled along and told any fib that came into his head—a regular Muddlehead! And, with it all, there wasn't a single drinking party for forty versts around at which his spindle-shanked figure failed to turn up among the guests, so used to him had people become, and so tolerant of his presence, as of an unavoidable mishap. True, they treated him contemptuously, but it was Wild Master alone who could put a curb on his crazy moods.

Blinker never left Muddlehead's side. He too was well-served by his nickname, although he didn't blink more than anyone else; but it is a plain truth that the Russians are past-masters at giving nicknames. In spite of my efforts to trace his past in every detail, I found—and so, probably, did many others—that there were dark passages in his career, places which, to use a bookish expression, were veiled in a thick mist of obscurity. I discovered only that he had once been coachman to an old, childless lady, had run away with the troika entrusted to his care, disappeared for a whole year, then, doubtless convinced by experience of the drawbacks and miseries of the vagrant's life, returned, now lame, thrown himself at his mistress's feet, and, having expiated his offence by several years of exemplary conduct, had gradually won his way back into her favor, had eventually earned her full confidence and been promoted to the post of clerk; that on the lady's death he had somehow or other acquired his freedom, registered as a burgess, begun leasing melon-gardens from the neighbors, grown rich, and now lived in clover. He was a man of experience, with his head well screwed on, neither bad nor good, but calculating, rather; a sly dog who understood people and knew how to make use of them. He was cautious and enterprising at the same time, like a fox; chattered like an old crone, never gave himself away, made everybody else speak their mind. What is more, he never posed as a simpleton, as some of the sly ones of his kind do; indeed, pretence could not have come easily to him. I have never seen more penetrating, shrewder eyes than his tiny, cunning "peepers."* They never simply looked, they were always searching and spying. Sometimes Blinker would spend whole weeks reflecting on some apparently simple enterprise, then suddenly resolve on a desperately daring course, and you would think he'd break his neck over it . . . you would look again—and it would have come off perfectly, smooth as a knife through butter. He was lucky, believed in his luck and in omens. In general, he was highly superstitious. He was not liked, because he was not in the least interested in others, but he was respected. His family consisted of one small son, whom he fairly adored, and who, brought up by such a father, would probably go far. "Little Blinker's the spit of his father," the old men were already saying of him in low voices, as they sat on the mounds of earth outside their cabins and gossiped on summer evenings; and they all understood what that meant, and didn't need to say more.

Of Yasha the Turk and the huckster there is not much to be said. Yasha, nicknamed the Turk, because he was indeed the offspring of a captured Turkish woman, was at heart an artist in all senses of the word, but by vocation a dipper in a merchant's paper-mill. As for the huckster, whose lot, I confess, remains unknown to me, he struck me as a smart, resourceful townsman. Of Wild Master, however, it is worth speaking in rather greater detail.

The first impression his appearance gave was one of rude, ponderous, irresistible force. He was clumsily built, "piled-on," as we say in our part of the country, but he fairly radiated irrepressible vitality, and, strangely enough, his bearish figure was not without a certain individual grace, which proceeded perhaps from a completely se-

---

* The people of Orel call eyes "peepers" in the same way as they call a mouth a "gobbler." —*Author.*

rene confidence in his own strength. It was difficult to determine at first glance to what condition of life this Hercules belonged. He resembled neither servant nor townsman, neither the impoverished scrivener living in retirement nor the ruined, horse-fancying, quarrel-picking member of the smaller landowning gentry. He was something absolutely special. No one knew whence he had descended on our district; it was said that he came of free-holding stock and had previously been in Government service somewhere or other, but nothing certain was known of this; and indeed there was no one to learn it from—certainly not from him himself: a more taciturn, surly fellow never existed. No one could say for sure, either, what he lived on; he plied no trade, visited no one, hardly knew anyone, and yet he had money; not much, it is true, but money, all the same. He conducted himself, not indeed with modesty—there was absolutely nothing modest about him—but quietly; he lived as if he noticed no one around him and definitely wanted nothing from anyone. Wild Master (such was his nickname; his real name was Perevlesov) enjoyed an enormous influence in the whole neighborhood; he was obeyed instantly and eagerly, although, so far from having any right to give anyone orders, he never made the slightest claim on the obedience of people with whom he came in contact. He spoke—and was obeyed: power always claims its due. He hardly drank, had no dealings with women, and was a passionate lover of singing. There was much that was puzzling about him; it was as if some immense forces were lying, sullenly inactive, within him, as if they knew that, once aroused, once let loose, they must destroy themselves and everything they touched; and I am sadly mistaken if some such explosion had not already occurred in the man's life, so that, taught by experience, and having just escaped destruction, he was now holding himself under an inexorable, iron control. What especially struck me about him was the mixture of a certain inborn, natural ferocity with an equally inborn nobility—a mixture such as I have met in no one else.

So the huckster stepped forward, half-closed his eyes, and began to sing in a very high falsetto. His voice was quite sweet and agreeable, though somewhat husky; he played with it, twirled it about like a toy, with constant downward trills and modulations and constant returns to the top notes, which he held and prolonged with a special effort; he stopped, then suddenly took up his previous tune again with a certain rollicking, arrogant boldness. His transitions were sometimes daring, sometimes rather comical. They would have given a connoisseur great pleasure; they would have shocked a German deeply. He was a Russian *tenore di grazia* or *ténor léger*. He sang a gay dance-tune, whose words, so far as I could catch them among the endless embellishments, extra harmonies, and exclamations, were as follows:

> *I'll plough a little ground, my lass,*
> *And sow it with scarlet flowers.*

He sang, and we all listened to him with close attention. He clearly felt that he had to do with experts, and so he fairly climbed out of his skin, as the saying goes. Indeed in our country we are connoisseurs of song, and it is not for nothing that the village of Sergievsk, on the Orel highway, is renowned throughout all Russia for its specially sweet and harmonious singing. The huckster sang on for quite a while, without arousing any marked sympathy in his hearers: he missed the support of a choir. At length, after one particularly successful transition, which made even Wild Master smile, Muddlehead could not contain himself and shouted out his satisfaction. Everybody jumped. Muddlehead and Blinker began taking up the tune, joining in and calling: "Smartly does it! . . . Strike it, rascal! . . . Strike it, hold it, you snake! Hold it, go on! Hotter still, you dog, you Herod's son!" and so on. Nikolai Ivanich, behind the counter, waved his head approvingly to right and left. At length Muddlehead began to stamp and scrape his feet and twitch his shoulder,—Yasha's eyes blazed like coals, he trembled all over like a leaf and smiled confusedly. Only Wild Master kept the same countenance and remained motionless as before; but his gaze, fixed on the huckster, softened a little, though his lips kept their contemptuous expression. Encouraged by the signs of general satisfaction, the huckster fairly whirled along and went off into such flourishes, such tongue-clickings and drummings, such wild throat-play, that at length, exhausted, pale, bathed in hot sweat, he threw himself back, let out a last dying note—and his wild outburst was answered in unison by the company. Muddlehead threw himself on his neck and began smothering him with his long bony hands; a flush came over Nikolai's greasy face, and he seemed to have grown younger; Yasha shouted like a madman, "Bravo, bravo!"—and even my neighbor, the peasant in the torn coat, could bear it no longer and, striking his fist on the table, exclaimed: "A-ha! good, devil take it—good!" and he spat to one side with determination.

"Well, lad, you've given us a treat!" cried Muddlehead, not letting the fainting huckster out of his embrace. "A treat, and that's the truth! You've won, lad, you've won! Congratulations—the quart is yours! Yasha can't touch you . . . Not by a long chalk, I tell you . . . Believe me!" And he again pressed the huckster to his bosom.

"Let him go: let him go, you leech . . ." said Blinker crossly. "Let him sit down on the bench here; he's tired, see . . . You're a fool, lad, a real fool! Why stick to him like a fly-paper?"

"Why, then, let him sit, and I'll drink his health," rejoined Muddlehead, going to the counter; "you're paying, lad," he added, turning to the huckster.

The huckster nodded, sat down on the bench, drew a towel out of his cap, and began to wipe his face. Muddlehead drank a glass in thirsty haste, groaned, and took on the sad, preoccupied look of the serious drinker.

"You sing well, lad, so you do," observed Nikolai Ivanich amiably. "Now it's your turn, Yasha: don't be nervous, mind. We'll see who's best, we will . . . But the huckster sings well, by God he does."

"Very well, so he does," observed Nikolai's wife, smiling at Yasha.

"So he does, too!" said my neighbor in a low voice.

"Eh, you Polesyan Thomas!"* sang out Muddlehead suddenly and, coming over to the peasant with the hole in the shoulder of his

---

* The inhabitants of Polesya have a name for incredulity and suspicion. —*Author.*

coat, pointed a finger at him, began to jump, and burst into a jarring laugh. "You Polesyan! What are you doing here? Come on! you
doubting Thomas!" he shouted through his laughter.

The poor peasant grew embarrassed and was just about to rise
and depart hurriedly, when all of a sudden came the metallic voice
of Wild Master:

"What's the unbearable animal up to now?" he said, grinding
his teeth.

"Nothing," muttered Muddlehead, "nothing . . . I just . . ."

"All right then, shut up!" rejoined Wild Master. "Yasha, begin!"

Yasha took his throat in his hand.

"Why, lad, there's something . . . why . . . H'm . . . I don't rightly
know . . ."

"Now, that'll do, don't be shy. Shame on you! . . . What's the
fuss? . . . Sing, as God tells you to."

And Wild Master looked down and waited.

Yasha said nothing, but glanced round and covered his face
with his hand. The whole company stared at him with all their
eyes, especially the huckster, whose face showed, through its usual
self-confidence and the triumph of his success, a faint, involuntary
anxiety. He leant against the wall, again tucked his hands in beneath him, but no longer swung his legs. When at last Yasha uncovered his face, it was as pale as a corpse's; his gleaming eyes hardly
showed through their lowered lashes. He breathed deeply and began to sing . . . His first note was faint and uneven, and came, it
seemed, not from his chest, but from somewhere far away, as if it
had chanced to fly into the room. This trembling, ringing note had a
strange effect on us all; we looked at one another, and Nikolai's wife
stood bolt upright. This first note was followed by another, firmer
and more prolonged, but still perceptibly trembling, like a string,
when, after the sudden pluck of a strong finger, it wavers with a
last, quickly-dying thrill: after the second came a third, and, gradually taking on warmth and breadth, the mournful song flowed on
its way. *The paths that lay across the field,*" he sang, and we all had
the feeling of something sweet and unearthly. Seldom, I confess,
have I heard such a voice: it was somewhat worn and had a sort of

cracked ring; at first it had even a certain suggestion of the mor-
bid; but it also held a deep, unsimulated passion, and youth, and
strength, and sweetness, and a deliciously detached note of melancholy. The truthful, fervent Russian soul rang and breathed in it and
fairly caught at your heart, caught straight at your Russian heart-
strings. The song developed, went flowing on. Yasha was clearly
overcome by ecstasy: his shyness had left him, he had surrendered
completely to his happiness; his voice trembled no longer—it quiv-
ered, but with the scarcely perceptible inner quivering of passion,
which pierces like an arrow into the hearer's soul. His voice grew
steadily in strength, firmness, and breadth. One evening, I remember, at low tide, on the flat sandy shore of the sea, which was roaring away menacingly and dully in the distance, I saw a great white
gull: it was sitting, motionless, its silky breast turned towards the
scarlet radiance of sunset, now and then slowly stretching its long
wings towards the familiar sea, towards the low, blood-red sun; I
remembered it as I listened to Yasha. He sang, completely oblivious
of his rival and of us all, but clearly sustained, as waves lift a strong
swimmer, by our silent passionate attention. He sang, and with every note there floated out something noble and immeasurably large,
like familiar steppe-country unfolding before you, stretching away
into the boundless distance. I could feel tears swelling up in my heart
and rising into my eyes; dull, muffled sobs suddenly fell on my
ears . . . I looked round—the tapster's wife was weeping as she leant
her breast against the window. Yasha threw her a quick glance and
his song flowed on still more sonorously and sweetly than before.
Nikolai Ivanich looked down, Blinker turned away; Muddlehead,
quite overcome by emotion, stood with his mouth stupidly gaping;
the little gray peasant was quietly whimpering in his corner and
shaking his head and muttering away bitterly to himself; down the
iron face of Wild Master, from under his deep overhanging brows,
slowly rolled a heavy tear; the huckster had raised a clenched fist to
his brow and never stirred. . . . I cannot imagine how this general
state of heartfelt rapture would have been dispelled if Yasha had
not suddenly ended on a high, extremely thin note—as if his voice
had broken. No one shouted, no one even stirred; everyone seemed

to be waiting in case he would sing on; but he opened his eyes, as if surprised at our silence, cast a questioning glance round at us all, and saw that victory was his. . . .

"Yasha," said Wild Master, putting a hand on his shoulder, and—said nothing more.

We all sat as though benumbed. The huckster got up quietly and went across to Yasha. "You . . . it's yours . . . you've won," he brought out at last with difficulty and dashed from the room. . . .

His swift decisive movement seemed to break the spell: everyone suddenly started talking loudly, joyfully. Muddlehead sprang up in the air and began to splutter and wave his arms like the sails of a windmill; Blinker stumbled over to Yasha and they began to kiss each other; Nikolai Ivanich stood up and solemnly announced that he would add another quart of beer on his own account; Wild Master laughed a good-natured laugh, such as I had certainly not expected to hear from him; the little gray peasant kept on repeating in his corner, wiping his eyes, cheeks, nose, and beard on both sleeves: "Good, by God, it's good, why, take me for a son of a bitch, it's good!" and Nikolai's wife, deeply flushed, stood up quickly and went away. Yasha enjoyed his victory like a child; his whole face was transfigured; in particular his eyes simply radiated happiness. He was dragged across to the counter; he summoned over to it the little gray peasant, who had burst into tears, he sent the host's boy after the huckster, whom, however, he failed to find, and the party began. "You'll sing to us again, you'll sing to us until evening," repeated Muddlehead, raising his arms aloft.

I looked once more at Yasha and went out. I did not want to stay—for fear of spoiling my impression. But the heat was still as unbearable as before. It was as if it hung right over the earth in a thick, heavy film; in the dark blue sky, little flashing lights seemed to be astir behind the fine, almost black dust. Everything was still; there was something hopeless, something oppressive about this deep stillness of enfeebled nature. I made my way to a hayloft and lay down on the newly-mown but already almost dried-up grass. For a while I could not drowse off; for a while Yasha's irresistible voice rang in my ears . . . but, at length, heat and exhaustion claimed their due, and I fell into a death-like sleep. When I awoke, it was dark all around; the litter of grass smelt strongly and there was a touch of dampness about it; between the thin rafters of the half-open roof, pale stars flickered faintly. I went out. The sunset glow had died away long ago, and had left behind only the faintest pallor on the horizon; in the air, so glowing-hot not long before, there was still a sense of heat underneath the freshness of night, and the lungs still thirsted for a breath of cold. There was no wind, no cloud; the sky stood round, clear, darkly translucent, quietly shimmering with countless hardly-visible stars. In the village, lights twinkled; from the brightly-lit pot-house near by came a discordant and confused hubbub, in the midst of which I thought I recognized Yasha's voice. At times there were bursts of wild laughter. I went across to the window and pressed my face against the pane. I saw a sad, though lively and animated scene: everyone was drunk—everyone, starting with Yasha. He was sitting, bare-chested, on a bench, singing in the huskiest voice some dance song of the streets, and lazily plucking and pinching the strings of a guitar. Clusters of wet hair hung above his livid face. In the middle of the pot-house, Muddlehead, coat-less and completely "unscrewed," was dancing and hopping away in front of the little peasant in the gray coat; the peasant, in turn, was laboriously stamping and scraping with his exhausted feet, smiling witlessly through his dishevelled beard, and occasionally waving a hand, as if to say: "Let it rip!" Nothing could have been more ludi-crous than his face; however high he lifted his brows, his heavy lids refused to stay up and drooped right down over his hardly visible, bleary eyes, which were nevertheless brimming with sweetness. He was in the endearing condition of the completely tipsy, when ev-ery passer-by who looks him in the face is absolutely bound to say: "A fine state, a fine state!" Blinker, red as a lobster, nostrils blown out wide, was laughing sardonically from a corner; only Nikolai Ivanich, as befits a good tapster, had kept his imperturbable sang-froid. Many new faces had collected in the room, but there was no sign of Wild Master.

I turned away and struck off quickly down the hill on which Kolotovka stands. A broad plain spreads out at the foot of this hill;

swamped as it was with the misty waves of evening haze, it seemed vaster than ever, and as if merged with the darkened sky. I was walking with great strides along the track beside the ravine, when suddenly, from far away on the plain, came a boy's ringing voice. "Antropka! Antropka-a-a! . . ." it called, in stubborn, tearful desperation, with a long dragging-out of the last syllable.

For a few moments it was silent, then began to call again. The voice carried clearly in the unmoving, lightly-sleeping air. Thirty times at least it had called Antropka's name, when suddenly, from the opposite end of the meadow, as if from a different world, came a scarcely audible reply:

"What-a-a-a-at?"

The boy's voice called at once, glad but indignant:

"Come here, you devil!"

"What fo-o-o-r?" answered the other, after a pause.

"Because father wants to be-ee-ee-eat you," called the first voice promptly.

The second voice made no further reply, and the boy again started calling "Antropka." I could still hear his cries, growing rarer and fainter, when it had become completely dark and I was passing the bend in the wood that surrounds my village, four versts away from Kolotovka.

"Antropka-a-a," I still seemed to hear in the air, which was full of the shadows of night.

Pyotr Petrovich Karataev

FIVE YEARS AGO, IN THE AUTUMN, ON THE ROAD FROM MOSCOW to Tula, I happened to spend the best part of a day sitting at the post station, as there were no horses for me. I was on my way back from shooting and had been unwise enough to have sent my troika on ahead. The postmaster, an old surly fellow, with his hair hanging down over his nose and little sleepy eyes, answered all my complaints and requests with an abrupt growl, slammed the door in a fury, as if by way of cursing his own duty—and, going out into the porch, scolded the drivers, who were slowly wandering about in the mud with heavy shaft-bows in their hands, or sitting on a bench yawning and scratching and paying no special attention to the wrathful exclamations of their chief. I had already managed to drink tea three times, had several times tried vainly to sleep, had read all the inscriptions on the windows and the walls: a terrible boredom oppressed me. With numb, hopeless despair, I was looking at the uplifted shafts of my travelling carriage, when suddenly I heard the jingling of bells, and a small cart harnessed to three exhausted horses came to a halt in front of the porch. The new arrival jumped from the cart and with a cry of "Horses—and be quick about it!" came into the room. While he listened, with the usual bewildered surprise, to the postmaster explaining that there was not a horse to be had, I contrived to scrutinize my new companion from head to foot with all the greedy curiosity of the bored. He looked about thirty. Smallpox had left its indelible traces on his dry, sallow face, which had a disagreeable coppery gleam to it; long bluish-black hair hung in ringlets over the back

of his collar and twisted itself up in front into rakish side-whiskers;
his puffy little eyes stared and stared. A few hairs sprouted from his
upper lip. He wore the clothes of a gentleman-rake and frequenter
of horse-fairs, namely, a gaily-colored, rather greasy Caucasian overcoat, a cravat of faded mauve silk, a waistcoat with copper buttons,
and gray trousers with enormous bell-bottoms, beneath which the
tips of his uncleaned boots were scarcely visible. He smelt strongly
of snuff and vodka; on his thick red fingers, practically hidden by
his coat sleeves, could be seen rings of silver and of Tula work. Such
creatures are to be met in Mother Russia, not by the dozen, but by
the hundred; their acquaintance, it must be confessed, affords no sort
of pleasure; yet in spite of the prejudice with which I looked at the
new arrival, I could not help remarking the carefree good-nature,
and the passion, expressed on his face.

"Why, this gentleman here has been waiting more than an hour,"
said the postmaster, indicating me.

More than an hour! The scoundrel was laughing at me.

"It may not matter so much to him," answered the new arrival.

"Well, that I couldn't say," said the postmaster sullenly.

"So you really can't do it? Positively no horses?"

"Nothing to be done. Not a single horse."

"Well, tell them to bring me a samovar. I'll wait, there's nothing
else for it."

The new arrival sat down on a bench, threw his cap on the table,
and passed his hand over his hair.

"Have you had tea?" he asked me.

"Yes."

"Won't you have some more, to keep me company?"

I consented. The fat, reddish samovar appeared for the fourth
time on the table. I got out a bottle of rum. I had not been wrong
in taking my interlocutor for one of the smaller landowning gentry.
His name was Pyotr Petrovich Karataev.

We fell into conversation. Not more than half an hour after his
arrival he had, with all the good nature and outspokenness in the
world, told me the story of his life.

"Now, I'm on my way to Moscow," he informed me, as he finished his fourth glass of tea. "There's nothing more I can do in the country."

"How so?"

"There just isn't. The land's been ruined by mismanagement, let's admit it. I've played havoc with the peasants; we've had some bad years: poor crops, and one thing and another, you know. . . . Yes, and anyway," he added, with a rueful sideways smile, "I'm a fine one for looking after land!"

"Why?"

"No," he broke in. "To be quite honest, you can't manage land the way I do. You see," he went on, screwing his head to one side and sucking away hard at his pipe, "you here, looking at me, might think that I'm . . . well, I must confess, I had a middling sort of education; we weren't well off. You'll forgive me, I'm an outspoken chap, and on the whole . . ."

He left the sentence unfinished and waved a hand. I began to assure him that he was mistaken, that I was very glad to meet him, and so forth, and then I remarked that the running of an estate didn't seem to me to call for any excessive degree of education.

"Agreed," he answered. "I quite agree with you. But you need a special sort of disposition. Some fellows play hell with it all, and no harm's done, but I . . . Tell me, sir, are you from 'Peter' or from Moscow?"

"From Petersburg."

He blew a long stream of smoke from his nostrils.

"I'm going to Moscow to join the Government service."

"Which branch d'you think of joining?"

"I don't know; it depends how things go there. I don't mind telling you, I'm scared of the Government service; you get landed with responsibilities at once. I've always lived in the country; I've grown used to it, you know . . . but it can't be helped . . . needs must! Oh, how I hate that 'needs must'!"

"But you'll be living in the capital."

"Yes . . . well, I don't know what's so good about that. I'll see, perhaps it *will* be good. But as for a home in the country, I don't think there's anything can be better than that."

"But can't you go on living there any longer?"

He sighed.

"No. It seems that it doesn't belong to me any more."

"What's happened, then?"

"There's a good man there, a neighbor . . . a bill of exchange . . ."

Poor Pyotr Petrovich passed a hand over his face, thought, and shook his head.

"Well, there it is! . . . And to tell the truth," he added after a slight pause, "I can't blame a soul—it's my own fault. I liked cutting a dash! . . . I still do, damn it!"

"You had a gay time of it at home?" I asked him.

"Sir," he answered with deliberation, looking me straight in the eyes, "I kept twelve couple of hounds, such hounds as you'll seldom see, I can tell you." He pronounced the word "seldom" in a sing-song tone. "They'd only to put up a hare or a deer—and they'd be off like snakes, regular snakes. And my horses were something to boast about, too. Now it's all past history, there's no point in telling lies. I used to go out shooting. I had a dog called Kontesska, a wonderful pointer, she had a sublime nose and never missed. I'd go up to a bog and say, seek! and if she wouldn't start seeking, then you could take a dozen dogs, but you'd be wasting your time, you wouldn't find a thing. But when she did start—why, she'd be ready to die on the spot! . . . And indoors she had such good manners. You'd give her a bit of bread in your left hand, and say, 'A Jew ate it,' and she wouldn't take it, but give it to her in your right hand, and say, 'A lady ate it'—she'd take it and eat it up at once. I had a puppy from her too, a capital puppy, I even wanted to take him to Moscow, but a friend of mine asked me for him and for my gun too. He said: 'In Moscow, my friend, you won't have time for this sort of thing; it's all quite different there.' I gave him the puppy, and the gun too; so, you see, I left everything behind."

"But even in Moscow you could get some shooting."

"No, what's the use? I couldn't control myself before, and now I've got to pay for it. I'd rather you told me, if you will, what it's like living in Moscow—expensive?"

"No, not too bad."

"Not too bad? . . . But, tell me, it's true that gypsies live in Moscow?"

"What gypsies?"

"The ones that go the rounds of the fairs?"

"Yes, in Moscow . . ."

"Well, that's good. I love the gypsies, damn it, so I do . . ." and Pyotr Petrovich's eyes sparkled with rakish merriment. But suddenly he began to fidget on his bench, then grew thoughtful, looked down, and held out to me his empty glass.

"Give me some of your rum," he said.

"But your tea is all finished."

"Never mind, I'll have it like that, without tea . . . Ugh!"

Karataev put his head in his hands and leant on the table. I looked at him in silence, anticipating those emotional exclamations, nay, those tears even, which come so easily to the man who has had a drop; but, when he raised his head, I confess I was struck by the expression of deep sorrow on his face.

"What's the matter?"

"Nothing. I'd remembered the old times. It's quite a story. . . . I'd tell you, only I don't want to bore you . . ."

"Please!"

"Yes," he continued with a sigh. "The things that happen . . . even in my case, for example. Why, if you like, I'll tell you about it. I don't know, though . . ."

"Tell me the story, my dear Pyotr Petrovich."

"Very well, although it's rather . . . Well, you see," he began, "but I really don't know . . ."

"Oh, that's quite enough, my dear Pyotr Petrovich."

"Very well then. This is roughly my story. I lived in the country . . . Suddenly a girl caught my fancy, oh, and what a girl she was . . . Beautiful, clever, and so good-hearted too! Her name was Matrona. She was a simple girl, that's to say a serf, you understand, just a serf-girl. And she was not mine, but someone else's—that was the whole devil of it. So I fell in love with her—quite a story you see—well, and so did she. So Matrona started to ask me to buy her from her mistress, and I'd had the same idea myself. . . . Her mistress was rich, a terrible old hag; she lived about fifteen versts away from me. Well, one fine day, as the expression is, I ordered my three-horse drozhky to be harnessed—my shaft-horse was a trotter, a regular rascal, he was called Lampurdos, too—I put on my best clothes and drove off to see Matrona's mistress. I arrived there; a big house with wings and a garden . . . Matrona was waiting for me at the turning, she seemed to want to talk to me, but she only kissed my hand and went away. So I went to the front hall and asked 'At home?' and a great tall footman says to me: 'Whom shall I announce?' I say: 'Announce, my friend, that the landowner Karataev has come to discuss business.' The footman went off, and I waited by myself and wondered what would happen. Supposing the beastly woman put a frightful price on her, in spite of being so rich. Suppose she asked five hundred rubles. Well, at last the footman comes back and says, 'This way, please.' I go after him into the drawing-room. In an armchair sits a little yellowish old woman and blinks her eyes and says, 'What can I do for you?' First of all, you know, I thought I ought to say that I was glad to make her acquaintance. 'You're mistaken, I'm not the lady of the house, I am a relation of hers. What can I do for you?' I told her on the spot that I had something to discuss with the lady of the house. 'Marya Ilyinichna is not receiving to-day: she is indisposed. . . . What can I do for you?' There was nothing for it, I thought to myself, but to explain my position to her. The old woman heard me out. 'Matrona? which Matrona?' 'Matrona Fyodorova, Kulik's daughter.'

"'Fyodor Kulik's daughter . . . and how do you know her?' 'Just by chance.' 'Is she aware of your intention?' 'Yes.' The old woman paused. 'Why, I'll give it her, the good-for-nothing hussy!' I confess I was surprised. 'Whatever for, for goodness' sake! . . . I'm ready to pay cash for her, if you'll kindly just name a sum.' The old sourpuss fairly began to hiss. 'That's a fine surprise you've planned: your money means such a lot to us! But I'll just show her. I'll give it her . . . I'll knock the nonsense out of her . . .' The old woman had a coughing-fit from sheer spite. 'Doesn't she like it here with us, or what? . . . Oh, she's a little devil, may the Lord forgive me my trespasses!' Here I confess that I exploded. 'What are you threatening the poor girl for, what is *she* to blame for?' The old woman crossed herself. 'Oh, Lord Jesus Christ! Can't I do what I like, even with my own serfs?'

"'But she's not yours!'

"'Well, that's Marya Ilyinichna's affair, it's nothing to do with you, sir; but I'll show that little Matrona whose serf she is.' I confess that I nearly went for the wretched hag, but I remembered Matrona and lowered my hands. I was so scared, I just can't tell you; I started begging the old woman to take whatever she liked. 'But what is she to you?' 'I like her, madam; put yourself in my situation . . . Allow me to kiss your hand.' And so I kissed the old villain's hand. 'Well,' muttered the old woman, 'I'll tell Marya Ilyinichna; it will be for her to decide; you come back in two days' time.' I drove home in great anxiety. I began to suspect that I had handled the affair clumsily, that I had been wrong to give my situation away, but I had spotted it too late. Two days later I went to see the lady. I was shown into the study. Masses of flowers, wonderful ornaments, and the lady herself, sitting in one of those funny armchairs, with her head thrown back on a pillow, and her relative, who had been there before, sitting there too, and also another lady with pale hair and a green dress and a crooked mouth—a companion, she must have been. The old lady bowed: 'Please be seated.' I sat down. She began asking me how old I was, where I had served, what my plans were, the whole thing very lofty and dignified. I answered her fully. The old lady took a handkerchief from the table and waved it and waved it towards herself. . . . 'I—' she said, 'I have learned from Katerina Karpovna of your intention. I have learned,' she said, 'but I have made it my rule,' she said, 'never to release my serfs for service elsewhere. It is not proper, it is not worthy of a well-ordered household: it is not in order. I have already taken the necessary steps,' she said. 'You have no further cause for concern.' 'How do you mean, please—concern? . . . But perhaps you need Matrona Fyodorova?' 'No,' she said, 'I don't need her.' 'Well, why ever don't you want to hand her over to me?' 'Because it doesn't suit me; it doesn't suit me, and that's the end of it. I have already told you that I have taken the necessary measures: she has been sent to my property in the steppes.' It hit me like a thunderclap. The old woman said a couple of words in French to the lady in green, who went out. 'And I,' she said, 'am a woman of strict principles, and my health is poor, I can't stand worry. You're still a young man: I'm an old woman and in a position to give you advice. Would it not be better for you to settle down, marry, look for a good *parti*; heiresses are scarce, but you ought to be able to find some poor girl of good character.' I looked at the old woman without understanding at all what she was driving at; I heard her speaking about marriage, but 'my property in the steppes' kept ringing in my ears. Marriage! . . . Damnation take it . . ."

Here the narrator suddenly stopped and looked at me.

"I say, you're not married?"

"No."

"Well, of course, you know how it is. I couldn't stand it any longer: 'For heaven's sake, madam, what nonsense is this, what has marriage got to do with it? I simply wish to learn from you whether you will hand over to me your girl Matrona or not.' The old woman groaned: 'Oh, he's upset me! Oh, tell him to go away! Oh! . . .' Her kinswoman darted up to her and started screaming at me and the old woman kept on groaning: 'What have I done to deserve this? Am I not mistress in my own house? Oh, oh!' I snatched up my hat and ran away like a madman.

"Perhaps," continued the narrator, "you will blame me for having formed such a strong attachment for a girl of low estate; indeed I have no intention of defending myself . . . It just happened like that! . . . Believe me, I had no peace, day or night . . . I was in torment! Why, I thought, I had ruined the poor girl! Then all of a sudden I would think of how she would be chasing geese, wearing a peasant's coat, and kept in disgrace by her mistress's orders, and how the overseer, a peasant in high boots, would be roaring loudly at her—and cold sweat would fairly roll off me. Well, I couldn't stand it; I found out what estate she had been sent to, saddled my horse, and rode over. It wasn't until nearly evening on the second day that I arrived. Evidently they had never expected me to make such a stroke, and no instructions had been given about me. I went straight to the overseer, as if I had been a neighbor; I went into his yard, and what did I see but Matrona, sitting on the porch with her head in her hands. She was just going to cry out, but I shook my finger at her and pointed towards the back yard and the fields. I went into the cabin; I had a chat with the overseer, spun him the devil of a yarn, waited for my moment, and went out to Matrona. Poor thing, she fairly hung on my neck. She had got pale and thin, my darling had. Then, you know, I told her: 'Never mind, Matrona, never mind, don't cry,' but the tears were simply streaming down my own cheeks. Then, at last, I grew ashamed. I said to her: 'Matrona, tears won't put things right, what we must do is this: we must take what they call decisive measures; you must run away with me, that's what we must do.' Matrona practically fainted. 'How can I! I'd be done for, they'd eat me right up!' 'You silly, who's going to find you?' 'They'll find me all right. Thank you, Pyotr Petrovich—I'll never forget your kindness, but you must leave me now; it's just the hand of fate.' 'Why, Matrona, and I took you for a girl of character.' And so she was, she had lots of character. She was gold, pure gold! 'Why on earth should I leave you here! Whatever happens, it can't be worse than this. Tell me: you've had a taste of the overseer's fists?' Matrona flared up and her lips began to tremble. 'But my family won't be given any peace, all on my account.' 'Well, what will they do to your family? . . . Send them away, will they?' 'Yes, they'll send my brother away, for sure.' 'And your father?' 'They won't send my father away, he's the only good tailor in the place.' 'Well, there you are, you see; and it won't mean the end of your brother.' I can tell you, I had a job to talk her around; she had the idea of arguing some more, about how I would have to answer for it. . . . 'But that isn't your affair,' I told her. . . . Anyway I just carried her off. . . . Not that time, but another time: it was at night, I came with a cart—and carried her off."

"You carried her off?"

"Yes . . . So she settled down at my place. I had a small house and not many servants. My people adored me, I'll make no bones about it; they wouldn't have given me away for anything in the world. I was in clover. Matrona had a good rest and got better; I grew fonder and fonder of her. . . . What a girl she was! Where had she got it all from? She could sing, dance, play the guitar . . . I didn't show her to the neighbors, they'd only have talked. But I had a friend, a bosom friend, Pantelei Gornostaev—you may know him? He simply worshipped her; he kissed her hand as if she had been a lady, really he did, and I can tell you, Gornostaev is not my sort: he's an educated man, he's read the whole of Pushkin; he would get talking to Matrona and me, and we'd be all ears. He taught her to write, amazing fellow! And then the clothes I gave her—better than the governor's wife's, absolutely they were; I had a coat made for her of raspberry-colored velvet with trimmings of fur . . . and how that coat suited her! It had been made by one of those Madams in Moscow, in the new style, with a tight waist. Oh, she was a marvellous girl, Matrona! She would start thinking and sit for hours on end, looking at the floor, not moving an eyebrow; and I would sit too, and look at her, and I just couldn't look at her enough, it was as if I'd never seen her in my life. She would smile, and my heart would give a sort of shiver, as if somebody was tickling it. Then suddenly she'd be in the mood to laugh and joke and dance, she'd embrace me so warmly, and hold me so tight, that my head would be in a whirl. From morning to night all I'd think about was how I could make her happy. And I tell you, I'd give her presents, just to see how pleased she'd be, the darling, how she'd go all red from joy, how she'd try my present on, how she'd come up to me in her new clothes and give me a kiss. I can't think how her father, Kulik, smelt the story out, but the old man came to have a look at us and fairly burst into tears. . . . Tears of joy, of course, what did you think? We gave him presents. As he was leaving, she gave him a five-ruble note, the darling—and he plumped down at her feet—it was so funny! We lived for five months in this way; and I wouldn't have minded living like that with her for ever. But I reckoned without my cursed bad luck."

He paused.

"What happened, then?" I asked sympathetically.

He waved his hand.

"It all ended devilish badly. I was the ruin of her, too. My little Matrona was mad keen on sledge rides, and used to drive herself; she'd put on her fur coat and her embroidered gloves, and simply

shout for joy. We always went for our drives in the evening, so
as not to meet anybody. Then there came one really glorious day:
frosty, clear, not a breath of wind. We set out. Matrona took the
reins. Suddenly I looked and saw where she was making for. Could
she really be making for Kukuevka, for her mistress's estate? Yes,
Kukuevka it was. I said to her: 'Are you crazy? Where are you going?' She gave me a look over her shoulder and grinned. 'Let's cut
a dash,' she said. Oho, I thought, let's . . . it's a good idea to drive
right past the mistress's house—don't you think? On we drove. My
trotter fairly swam along; as for the side-horses, I can tell you, they
absolutely whirled—already we could see the church at Kukuevka;
and then, creeping along the road, comes an old green winter-
carriage with a footman sticking up on the boot . . . It was the
mistress, so it was, driving towards us! I was getting scared, but
Matrona flicked the horses with the reins and darted straight at the
carriage! The coachman saw us flying towards him—tried to get
out of the way, turned too sharply and tipped the carriage up into a
snowdrift. The window broke—the lady screamed, 'Ai-ai-ai! ai-ai-
ai!'—the companion squeaked, 'Hold on! Hold on!' and we—God
give us legs to run with—got past. We galloped off, and I thought
to myself: it will be a bad business, I was wrong to let her drive to
Kukuevka. Well, what d'you expect? The old lady had recognized
Matrona and myself, and she started proceedings against me: 'A
runaway girl of mine is living at Mr. Karataev's,' she said; and she
produced something suitable in the way of a sweetener. The next
thing I knew, I got a visit from the district police-inspector; he was
an acquaintance of mine, Stepan Sergeich Kuzovkin, a good man,
or rather, not really a good man. Well, he arrives and says: 'It's like
this and like that, Pyotr Petrovich—what's this that you've been
up to? . . . It's a serious responsibility, the law is quite clear on the
point.' I say to him: 'Well, of course, we must have a chat about
that, but won't you have a bite after your journey?' He agreed to
have a bite, but he said: 'The law must take its course, Pyotr Petrovich, you can see for yourself that it must.' 'Yes, of course, the law,'
I said; 'of course . . . By the way, I believe you've got a black horse,
you wouldn't like to change it for my Lampurdos? . . . But there's

no such girl as Matrona Fyodorova here!' 'Well,' he said, 'Pyotr Petrovich, the girl's here, we don't live in Switzerland . . . but as for Lampurdos, I could certainly change my horse for him; or, if you liked, I could just take him.' 'Well, on that occasion, somehow or other, I got him out of the house. But the old lady made a worse fuss than ever: 'I shan't mind if it costs me ten thousand,' she said. You see, when she first saw me, she had suddenly taken it into her head to marry me off to her green companion—so I found out afterwards: that's why she took it all so much to heart. What ideas these ladies get! It must be the boredom, I suppose. Things went badly for me. I didn't spare money, and I kept Matrona hidden— but no! They harried me like a driven hare. I got into debt, my health failed, and, well, one night I was lying in bed thinking: Oh Lord, what am I suffering for? What am I going to do, if I can't stop loving her? . . . and I just can't, and that's all there is to it!—when suddenly Matrona came into my room. At that time I'd been hiding her in one of my farms, two versts away from the house. I had quite a shock. 'What? Have they been bothering you, even there?' 'No, Pyotr Petrovich,' she said. 'No one disturbs me at Bubnov; but this can't go on any longer. It tears my heart,' she said; 'I'm so sorry for you, my darling; I'll never, never forget your kindness, Pyotr Petrovich, but now I've come to say good-bye.' 'What d'you mean? Are you crazy? . . . What d'you mean, to say good-bye?' 'Just like that . . . I'm going to give myself up.' 'You're crazy, I'll lock you up in the attic . . . D'you want to be the death of me, d'you mean to kill me, or what?' But the girl said nothing, and looked at the floor. 'Well, go on, say something!' 'I don't want to cause you any more trouble, Pyotr Petrovich!' Well, go on, argue with her . . . 'But you see, you fool, you see, you crazy girl . . .'"

And Pyotr Petrovich began to sob bitterly.

"Well, what d'you think?" he continued, striking his fist on the table and trying to frown, with the tears still running down his burning cheeks: "The girl gave herself up—she went and gave herself up . . ."

"The horses are ready, sir," exclaimed the inspector solemnly, coming into the room.

We both stood up.

"And what became of Matrona?" I asked.

Karataev waved his hand.

A YEAR AFTER MY ENCOUNTER with Karataev I happened to go to Moscow. One day, before dinner, I dropped in to the coffee-house in Huntsman's Row—that singular Moscow coffee-house. In the billiard-room, through clouds of smoke, loomed crimson faces, moustaches, tufts of hair, old-fashioned Hungarian jackets, and coats of the latest cut. Thin old men in modest frock-coats were reading the Russian papers. Servants were flashing past briskly with trays, stepping softly over the green carpet. Merchants were drinking tea with agonized intensity. Suddenly, from inside the billiard-room, came a man—somewhat dishevelled and not altogether steady on his legs. He put his hands in his pockets, let his head fall forward, and looked heedlessly around.

"Hey, hey! Pyotr Petrovich . . . How are you?"

Pyotr Petrovich practically threw himself on my neck and with a slight stagger dragged me into the little private room.

"Here," he said, carefully seating me in an armchair, "here you'll be comfortable. Waiter, beer! No, I mean champagne! Well, I must say I never, never expected . . . Been here long? Staying long? Why, heaven must have sent you, so to speak, I mean . . ."

"Yes, d'you remember . . ."

"Of course I do, of course I do," he interrupted me hurriedly. "That old story . . . that old story . . ."

"Well, what are you doing here, my dear Pyotr Petrovich?"

"Just living, sir—as you may perhaps have observed. It's a good life here, they're a jolly lot. I've found peace here."

He sighed and raised his eyes to heaven.

"Are you in the Government service?"

"No, not yet, but I hope to fix up something soon. What's a job, anyway? . . . People, that's the main thing. The people I've got to know here! . . ."

The boy came in with a bottle of champagne on a black tray.

"Here's a good fellow, too . . . aren't you a good fellow, Vasily? Your health!"

The boy stood, shook his head respectfully, smiled, and went out.

"Yes, they're good people here," continued Pyotr. "They've got feelings, they've got souls. . . . Would you like me to introduce you? Such splendid chaps . . . They'll all be glad to know you. I'll tell them . . . Bobrov's dead, that's the pity of it."

"Who is Bobrov?"

"Sergei Bobrov. He was a splendid fellow; he took me under his wing when I was just an ignorant bumpkin from the steppes. Pantelei Gornostaev's dead too. Everybody's dead!"

"Have you been in Moscow all the time? Haven't you been away to the country?"

"Country . . . my place in the country has been sold."

"Sold?"

"By auction. . . . It's a shame you didn't buy it!"

"What are you going to live on, Pyotr Petrovich?"

"With God's help, I won't die of hunger! I may not have money, but I'll have my friends. What's money anyway? Dirt! Gold is just dirt!"

He screwed his eyes up, rummaged with his hand in his pocket, and offered me in his palm two pieces of fifteen copecks and one of ten.

"What is it? Just dirt!" The money went flying to the floor. "But, tell me, have you read Polezhaev?"

"Yes."

"Have you seen Mochalov in *Hamlet*?"

"No, I haven't."

"You haven't, you haven't . . ." And Karataev's face went pale, his eyes began roaming restlessly; he turned away; faint spasms passed across his lips. "Oh, Mochalov, Mochalov! To die, to sleep," he said dully.

> No more; and by a sleep to say we end
> The heart-ache, and the thousand natural shocks

That flesh is heir to, 'tis a consummation
Devoutly to be wished. To die, to sleep! . . .

"To sleep, to sleep!" he whispered several times.
"Tell me," I began; but he continued fervently:

For who would bear the whips and scorns of time,
The oppressor's wrong, the proud man's contumely,
The pangs of despised love, the law's delays,
The insolence of office, and the spurns
That patient merit of the unworthy takes,
When he himself might his quietus make
With a bare bodkin . . . Nymph, in thy orisons
Be all my sins remembered.

He dropped his head on the table. He began to stammer and
drivel.

"A little month," he pronounced with renewed strength:

A little month, or ere those shoes were old
With which she followed my poor father's body,
Like Niobe, all tears:—why she, even she—
O God! a beast that wants discourse of reason
Would have mourn'd longer . . .

He lifted a glass of champagne to his lips but, without drinking,
continued:

For Hecuba!
What's Hecuba to him, or he to Hecuba,
That he should weep for her? . . .
Yet I . . . a dull and muddy-mettled rascal . . .
Am I a coward?
Who calls me villain? . . . gives me the lie in the throat?
'Swounds, I should take it: for it cannot be.

But I am pigeon-liver'd and lack gall
To make oppression bitter . . .

Karataev dropped the glass and held his head in his hands. I had an idea that I understood him.

"Well, anyway," he said at last. "When sorrow sleeps, wake it not. . . . Isn't that right?"

He laughed. "Your health!"

"Are you staying on in Moscow?" I asked him.

"I shall die in Moscow."

"Karataev!" came a voice from the next room. "Karataev, where are you? Come here, there's a good fellow!"

"They're calling me," he said, rising heavily from his chair.

"Good-bye, come and see me if you can. I live at ——"

But on the following day unforeseen circumstances obliged me to leave Moscow and I never saw Pyotr Petrovich Karataev again.

The Rendezvous

I WAS SITTING IN A BIRCH-WOOD ONE AUTUMN, ABOUT THE middle of September. Ever since morning a fine drizzle had been falling, giving way now and again to warm sunshine: it was fluky weather. One moment the sky would be all overcast with puffy white clouds, at another it would suddenly clear in places for a moment, and, through the rift, the azure would appear, clear and smiling, like the glance of a brilliant eye. I sat and looked about me and listened. The leaves were whispering faintly over my head: you could have told the time of year from their whisper alone. It was not the gay, laughing shiver of spring, nor the soft murmur, the long discourse of summer, nor the cold, frightened rustling of late autumn, but a scarcely perceptible, drowsy converse. A little breeze was just stirring among the treetops. The interior of the wood, drenched with rain, kept changing its appearance as the sun shone out or went in behind the clouds: sometimes it was all ablaze, as if everything there was smiling: the slender boles of the scattered birches suddenly took on the fresh brilliance of white silk, the tiny leaves on the ground gleamed and blazed with purple and gold, and the handsome stems of the tall, curly bracken, already tinged with their autumn hue, the hue of overripe grapes, stood out luminously before me in an infinite, criss-crossed maze; then suddenly the whole scene took on a faint shade of blue: in an instant, the bright colors went out, the birches stood blankly white as new-fallen snow, not yet touched by the cold light of the winter sun; and furtively, slyly, the finest of drizzles began to spray and whisper through the wood. The leaves of the birches were almost all of them still green, though of a marked pallor; only here and there stood a single young one, quite red or quite gold, and it was a sight to see how brightly it flared up when the sun's rays suddenly found their way to it, slipping and dappling through the thick net of fine branches, all newly washed in sparkling rain. There was not a sound from the birds: they were all snuggled down and keeping quiet; just occasionally the laughing voice of the tit-mouse rang out like a tiny steel bell. Before coming to a halt in this birch-wood, my dog and I had passed through a tall spinney of poplars. I confess that I am not overfond of this tree—the poplar—with its pale lilac-colored trunk and the gray-green, metallic foliage which it lifts up as high as it can and throws out in a trembling fan into the air; I dislike the perpetual shaking of its untidy round leaves, fixed so awkwardly on their long stems. The poplar is good only on certain summer evenings when, standing out sharply from amidst the low brushwood, it faces straight into the glowing rays of the setting sun, and blazes and shines, suffused from root to summit with an even, yellowish purple—or on a clear windy day, when the whole tree ripples and murmurs under the blue sky, and every leaf is as if seized with a longing to break loose and fly off far away into the distance. But for the most part I am no lover of this tree, and so I didn't pause for rest in the poplar-spinney, but went on to the birch-wood, curled myself up under a tree whose branches began close to the ground and so could give me shelter from the rain, and, after admiring the scene around me, fell into the unbroken and tranquil sleep which is known only to the hunter.

I cannot say for how long I slept, but, when I opened my eyes, the whole inside of the wood was filled with sunlight, and in all directions, through joyfully murmuring foliage, the sky appeared, bright blue and sparkling; the clouds had vanished, chased by a newly-risen breeze; the weather had cleared, and you could feel in the air that special dry freshness which, filling the heart with a sense of well-being, nearly always presages a calm bright evening after a day of rain. I was preparing to get up and try my luck again, when suddenly my eyes came to rest on a motionless human figure. I peered at it: it was a young peasant-girl. She was sitting twenty yards away from me, her head sunk in reflection, and both hands dropped on her knees; in one hand, which was half-open, a thick bunch of wild flowers lay, and every time she breathed it slipped quietly farther down on to her check skirt. A clean white blouse, buttoned at the front and wrists, lay in short, soft folds around her body; two rows of thick yellow beads fell from her neck on to her breast. She was quite pretty. Dense fair hair, of a fine ash color, emerged in two carefully-brushed half-circles from beneath a narrow head-band, worn right down on her forehead, which was white as ivory; the rest of her face was faintly sunburnt, with that golden tan which comes only to a fine skin. I couldn't see her eyes—she did not raise them; but I saw clearly her fine, arched brows, her long eyelashes: they were wet, and, on one of her cheeks, the sun caught the drying streak of a tear that had stopped just at the side of her palish lips. It was a charming head; even a somewhat thick round nose didn't spoil it. I liked especially the expression of her face. It was so simple and gentle, so sad, so full of a childlike bewilderment in the presence of a private sorrow. Evidently she was waiting for someone; there was a faint crackling in the wood; she lifted her head at once and looked around; in the translucent shadow I could see the swift flash of her eyes, large, bright, and timid, like a doe's. For a few moments she listened, without moving her wide-open eyes from the place whence the faint sound had come, sighed, quietly turned her head, bent down even lower and began slowly to arrange her flowers. Her eyelids reddened, her lips trembled with grief, and a fresh tear rolled out from beneath her thick lashes, halting and sparkling brilliantly on her cheek. Quite a while passed like this. The poor girl never stirred—only now and then a cheerless gesture of her hands—and listened and listened . . . Again there was a noise in the wood—she started. The noise continued, grew clearer, approached, and at last swift decisive steps could be heard. She sat up and seemed to be afraid; her attentive gaze wavered, kindled with anticipation. Soon a man's figure appeared through the undergrowth. She stared, blushed suddenly, burst into a joyous, blissful smile, made as if to get up, and at once sank back again, turned pale, became embarrassed, and only raised her trembling,

almost imploring look to the new arrival when he had already come
to a halt beside her.

I looked at him curiously from my hiding-place. I confess that
the impression he made on me was disagreeable. By all appearances he must have been the spoiled valet of a rich young master.
His clothes displayed a pretension to good taste and a dandyish
negligence; he wore a short, bronze-colored overcoat, probably off
his master's shoulders, buttoned right up, a pink cravat with lilac
ends, and a black gold-laced velvet cap rammed right down on his
forehead. The rounded collar of his white shirt pushed up mercilessly against his ears and cut into his cheeks, and starched cuffs
covered his whole hand down to his curving red fingers, which
were adorned with silver and gold rings with forget-me-nots in tur-
quoise. His face, ruddy, fresh, cheeky, was one of those which, so
far as my observation goes, exasperate men and, unfortunately, very
often appeal to women. He was clearly trying to give his coarse features an expression of contempt and boredom; he kept narrowing
his milky-gray eyes, which were anyway tiny enough, making wry
faces, dropping the corners of his lips, yawning constrainedly and
with a careless, but not quite easy nonchalance, adjusting his reddish, nattily-brushed temples, or fingering the yellow hairs which
bristled from his thick upper lip—in a word, he was intolerably affected. His affectation began from the moment he caught sight of
the young peasant-girl waiting for him; he came up to her slowly,
with a lounging gait, halted, worked his shoulders, plunged both
hands into the pockets of his overcoat, and, hardly bestowing on
the poor girl so much as a cursory, indifferent glance, sank down
on the grass.

"Why," he began, still looking far away into the distance, fidgeting his leg and yawning, "been here long?"

The girl could not answer him immediately.

"Yes, Viktor Alexandrich," she said at last, in a hardly audible
voice.

"Oh!" He took off his cap, passed his hand majestically over his
thick, tightly-curled hair, which began practically at his eyebrows,
and, looking round with dignity, scrupulously covered his precious

head again. "I nearly forgot altogether. Besides, there was the rain, you see!" He yawned again. "Lots of work: you can't keep your eye on everything, with him scolding you into the bargain. We leave to-morrow . . ."

"To-morrow?" the girl brought out, turning a frightened gaze upon him.

"To-morrow . . . There, there, there, for goodness' sake!" he interjected hurriedly and with irritation, seeing that she had started to tremble all over and had quietly dropped her head. "For goodness' sake, Akulina, don't cry. You know I can't bear it." And he wrinkled his snub nose. "Or else I'll go away at once. It's too stupid—grizzling!"

"No, no, I won't," said Akulina hurriedly, swallowing her tears with an effort. "So you're leaving to-morrow?" she added after a short silence. "When will God grant us to see each other again, Viktor Alexandrich?"

"We'll see each other again all right. If not next year—then later. I think the master wants to go to Petersburg and get a Government job," he went on, pronouncing the words negligently and slightly through his nose, "but it's possible that we shall go abroad."

"You'll forget me, Viktor Alexandrich," said Akulina sorrowfully.

"No, why should I? I won't forget you: but just you be sensible; don't do silly things, do what your father tells you . . . I won't forget you—no-o." And he stretched calmly and yawned again.

"Don't forget me, Viktor Alexandrich," she went on, in an imploring voice. "I do love you so much, there's nothing I wouldn't do for you . . . You tell me to obey my father . . . But how can I obey him? . . ."

"Well?" He pronounced the word as if from his stomach, lying on his back, with his hands folded beneath his head.

"But how can I, Viktor Alexandrich—you know very well . . ." She paused. Viktor played with his steel watch-chain.

"You're no fool, Akulina," he began at length, "so you mustn't talk nonsense. I've got your interests at heart, d'you see? Of course, you're no fool, you're not just an ordinary peasant-girl, as it were;

your mother wasn't always a peasant, either. All the same, you've got no education—so you ought to do as you're told."

"But I'm scared, Viktor Alexandrich."

"Pooh, what nonsense, my dear; what is there to be scared about? What have you got there?" he added, moving closer to her. "Flowers?"

"Yes," answered Akulina sadly. "This I picked from a wild costmary," she went on, with somewhat more animation, "it's good for calves. This one's marigold—good against the scrofula. Then look at this wonderful flower; such a wonderful flower as I've never seen in all my days. These are forget-me-nots, and this one's called mother's darling. And these are for you," she added, taking out, from below the yellow costmary, a small bunch of blue cornflowers bound with a slender grass. "Would you like them?"

Viktor lazily stretched out a hand, took the flowers, smelt them indifferently, and began to turn them over between his fingers, looking up meanwhile, meditative and aloof. Akulina gazed at him. . . . In her sad glance there was so much tender devotion, reverent submissiveness, and love. She was afraid of him, she didn't dare cry, she was saying good-bye to him, admiring him for the last time: while he lay, sprawling like a sultan, and suffered her adoration with magnanimous patience and condescension. I confess that I looked indignantly at his red face, in which, through the pretence of contemptuous indifference, a contented, surfeited egoism peeped out. Akulina was so lovely at that moment: her whole soul bared itself trustfully, passionately, to him, and strove in all humility to approach him, while he . . . he dropped the cornflowers in the grass, brought out from the side pocket of his coat a little round glass in a bronze frame, and proceeded to squeeze it into his eye; but, try as he might to hold it in, with screwed-up brow, raised cheek, even with his nose—the glass kept falling out and dropping into his hand.

"What's that?" asked Akulina at length, in astonishment.

"A lorgnette," he answered, with dignity.

"What for?"

"To see better with."

"Let me look."

Viktor scowled, but gave her the glass.

"Look out, don't break it."

"Don't worry, I won't break it." She put it shyly up to her eye. "I can't see anything," she observed innocently.

"But your eye—you must screw up your eye," he rejoined in the voice of a dissatisfied instructor. She screwed up the eye in front of which she was holding the glass. "Not that one, not that one, stupid! The other one!" exclaimed Viktor and, without allowing her to correct her mistake, took the lorgnette away from her.

Akulina flushed, laughed faintly, and turned away.

"It's not meant for the likes of us, I can see," she said.

"It certainly isn't!"

The poor girl was silent and sighed deeply.

"Oh, Viktor Alexandrich, it'll be so hard for us, without you," she said suddenly.

Viktor wiped the lorgnette with his coat-tail and put it back in his pocket.

"Yes, yes," he said at length; "it'll be hard for you at first, certainly." He patted her condescendingly on the shoulder; she gently took his hand from her shoulder and shyly kissed it. "Well, yes, you're certainly a good girl," he went on, smiling complacently; "but there's nothing for it, is there now? The master and I can't stay here; it'll soon be winter now, and winter in the country—you know it yourself—is sheer misery. While, in Petersburg! There are such marvellous sights there, such as you could never imagine, you stupid, not even in a dream. The houses, the streets, the society, the education—simply amazing! . . ." Akulina listened to him with consuming attention, her lips slightly parted, like a child's. "But anyway," he added, turning over on the ground, "what's the good of my telling you all this? It's something that you can never understand."

"Why not, Viktor Alexandrich? I've understood; I've understood it all."

"There you go!"

Akulina lowered her head.

"There was a time once when you didn't talk to me like this, Viktor Alexandrich," she said, without looking up.

"Once? . . . once! There you are! . . . Once!" he observed, with a hint of indignation.

They were both silent.

"Well, it's time I was going," said Viktor, who had already propped himself up on his elbow. . . .

"Wait a little longer," said Akulina imploringly.

"What for? . . . I've already said good-bye to you."

"Wait," repeated Akulina.

Viktor lay back again and started to whistle. Akulina still kept her eyes fixed on him. I could see that she was growing more and more agitated: her lips twitched, her pale cheeks were faintly flushed.

"Viktor Alexandrich," she began, at length, chokingly. "It's wrong of you . . . it's wrong, before God, it is."

"What's wrong?" he rejoined, scowling, and he lifted himself slightly and turned his head towards her.

"It's wrong, Viktor Alexandrich. You might at least have had a kind word for me when you're saying good-bye; you might have had a word for me, poor little orphan that I am . . ."

"What can I say to you?"

"I don't know; it's you who should know, Viktor Alexandrich. Here you are, leaving, and not so much as a word. . . . What have I done to deserve it?"

"What a funny girl you are! What else can I do?"

"Only a word . . ."

"Always the same thing," he said crossly, and got up.

"Don't be angry, Viktor Alexandrich," she added hastily, hardly holding in her tears.

"I'm not angry, you're just such a fool . . . What d'you want? I can't marry you—can I now? So what else d'you want? What is it?" He looked blank, as if waiting for an answer, and spread out his fingers.

"Nothing . . . I want nothing," she answered, stammering, and only just daring to stretch her trembling hands out towards him: "Just a word, to say good-bye . . ."

And her tears started streaming down.

"There it is, she's started to cry," said Viktor coldly, tilting his cap forward over his eyes.

"I want nothing," she went on, gulping and covering her face with both hands; "but what will it be like for me at home now, what'll it be like? What will become of me, poor wretch that I am? They'll marry me off to someone I don't love . . . poor, wretched me."

"Sing away, sing away," muttered Viktor in a low voice, shifting his position.

"He might have said a word, just one even . . . 'Akulina,' he might have said, 'I . . .'"

Sudden heart-rending sobs prevented her from finishing—she buried her face in the grass and burst into bitter, bitter tears . . . Her whole body shook spasmodically, she raised her head . . . Her long pent-up grief had at last found a way out. Viktor stood over her, stood, shrugged his shoulders, turned, and strode away.

A few moments passed . . . She grew quiet, lifted her head, jumped up, looked around, and threw up her arms: she made as if to run after him, but her legs failed her, and she fell on her knees . . . I could stand it no longer and rushed towards her—but the moment she saw me, goodness knows where she got the strength from, she rose with a faint cry and vanished behind the trees, leaving the flowers scattered on the ground.

I stopped, picked up the bunch of cornflowers and walked out of the wood into the field. The sun stood low in the pale, clear sky, and its rays seemed to have faded and grown cold: they had no radiance; it was an even, almost watery light they distilled. There was only half an hour to nightfall, but the sunset had hardly begun to glow. A gusty wind blew headlong towards me over the parched yellow stubble; tiny, shrivelled leaves, whirling swiftly up before it, flew past across the road, along the edge of the wood; the side of it that abutted like a wall on the field was all shivering and sparkling with a fine glitter that had clarity but no brilliance; on the reddish grass, on blades and straws, everywhere, in glittering festoons, lay countless autumn spiders' webs. I stopped . . . sadness overcame me; behind the crisp yet cheerless smile of languishing nature, I thought I sensed the gloom and dread of approaching winter. High above me, cutting the air with sharp, heavy wing-strokes, flew a cautious raven: he looked at me with a sideways turn of his head, shot upwards and disappeared, croaking abruptly, behind the wood; a big flock of pigeons, flying gaily from the threshing-floor, suddenly formed up into a pillar and settled swiftly on the field—sure sign of autumn! On the other side of the bare hill, someone was driving by in a loud-rattling, empty cart.

I returned home; but it was some time before poor Akulina's image went out of my head, and I still have her cornflowers, faded long since.

Prince Hamlet of Shchigrovo

ON ONE OF MY TRAVELS I RECEIVED AN INVITATION TO DINE with a rich landowner and sportsman named Alexander Mikhailich G——. His village lay about five versts away from a small one where I was staying at the time. I put on a tailcoat, without which I advise nobody to travel, even on a shooting trip, and set out for Alexander Mikhailich's. Dinner was at six o'clock. I arrived at five and found a large number of gentlemen already there in uniform, civilian dress, and other less distinctive attire. My host received me amiably but then ran away at once to the pantry. He was expecting a great Personage and was a prey to a certain agitation, which suited oddly with his wealth and independent situation in the world.

Alexander Mikhailich had never married and disliked women; his parties were of the bachelor type. He lived in great style, had improved and decorated his ancestral halls with magnificence, ordered about 15,000 rubles' worth of wine from Moscow every year, and in general stood in the highest esteem. He had been in retirement for some considerable time and was not interested in acquiring distinctions. What was it then that impelled him to force his invitation upon this Personage and to spend the day of the great dinner, from dawn onwards, in trepidation? That must remain shrouded in deepest mystery, as a pettifogging lawyer of my acquaintance used to say when asked whether he accepted bribes offered him by voluntary contributors.

After parting from my host, I began to stroll through the rooms.

Almost all the guests were complete strangers to me; a score or so were already sitting around the card-tables. Among these amateurs of Preference were two military gentlemen with noble but somewhat worn features, a number of civilian characters with high, tight cravats and those pendulous dyed whiskers which are found only on men of determination but also of the best intentions (these well-intentioned ones picked up their cards with dignity and threw sidelong glances at the passersby without turning their heads); five or six district functionaries with pot-bellies, chubby, sweating hands, and modest, stuffed demeanors (these gentlemen spoke in soft voices, smiled timidly in all directions, held their cards right up against their shirt-fronts, and, when trumping, did not thump the table, but allowed their card to fall with a wavering motion on the green cloth, and collected the trick to the accompaniment of a faint, a very polite and respectful scraping sound). Other gentlemen were sitting on sofas, standing in groups in doorways and beside windows; one landowner, no longer young, but of feminine appearance, was standing in a corner, wincing, blushing, and awkwardly twisting his watch-fob on his stomach, although nobody was paying him any attention; some gentlemen in tail-coats of rounded cut and check trousers, from the hand of the Moscow tailor and master craftsman Firs Klyukhin, were conversing with remarkable briskness and abandon, freely turning the bare and fleshy napes of their necks this way and that; a blond, short-sighted young man of about twenty, in black from head to foot, was smiling sardonically despite his obvious shyness. . . .

I was beginning to get rather bored, when all of a sudden I was joined by one Voinitzin, a student who had never finished his studies and was living in the house of Alexander Mikhailich as . . . it is hard to say exactly what. He was a capital shot and knew how to train a dog. I had known him in Moscow. He was one of those young fellows who at every examination "get lockjaw," that is, never answer a word when questioned by the indignant professors. Such gentlemen, from their elegance of style, were also known as "whisker-fanciers." (It is a story of days long passed, as you may have been pleased to observe.) This is what would happen: they would call out, for instance,

Voinitzin—Voinitzin, who up till then had been sitting motionless and upright on his bench, bathed from head to foot in warm sweat, and looking slowly but blankly around, would rise hurriedly, button up his tunic, and make his way sideways to the examiners' table. "Please to take a ticket," the professor would say to him agreeably. Voinitzin would stretch out a hand and touch the piles of tickets with trembling fingers. "Kindly do not choose," would say the jarring voice of some strange but irritable old gentleman, a professor from another faculty who had taken a strong dislike to the unhappy whisker-fancier. Voinitzin would submit to his fate, take a ticket, show the number, and go and sit in the window while his predecessor answered his question. In the window Voinitzin would never take his eyes off the ticket, except just to look round slowly as before, but without the slightest movement of any other part of his body. Then they would finish with his predecessor and would be saying to him, "Very well, you can go," or perhaps, "Good, very good," according to his abilities. Now they are calling Voinitzin—Voinitzin stands up, and walks across to the table with a firm tread. "Read the ticket," they tell him. Voinitzin takes the ticket in both hands, lifts it right up to his nose, slowly reads it, slowly lowers his hand. "Well, your answer, please," pronounces the same professor lazily, folding his arms across his chest. A silence of the grave ensues. "Well?" Voinitzin says nothing. The old visiting professor begins to twitch. "Well, say something!" My friend Voinitzin preserves a frozen silence. The close-cropped back of his head sticks up, steep and motionless, under the curious gaze of all his comrades. The eyes of the old visiting professor are ready to pop out of his head: he loathes Voinitzin for good and all. "It's strange, though," observes another examiner. "Why stand there as if you were dumb? You don't know, I suppose? Well say so, then." "Let me take another ticket," the poor wretch brings out dully. The professors exchange glances. "Very well," answers the head examiner, with a movement of his hand. Again Voinitzin takes a ticket, again he goes over to the window, again he returns to the table, and is again smitten with the same silence. The old visiting gentleman is quite ready to eat him up alive. Finally they dismiss him and give him nought.

You may think that now at last he will go away? What else could he do? No, he returns to his place, sits motionless until the end of the examination, and, as he leaves, exclaims: "Phew! *What* a question!" And he walks about Moscow for a whole day, now and then putting his hands to his head and railing bitterly against his ill-starred fate. Needless to say he doesn't touch a book, and the next morning the same story happens all over again.

This was the Voinitzin who joined me. We talked about Moscow, about shooting.

"Wouldn't you like me," he whispered to me suddenly, "to introduce you to our leading local wit?"

"Yes, it would be a pleasure."

Voinitzin led me up to a short man with a tall tuft of hair and side-whiskers, a brown tail-coat, and a gay cravat. His mobile, bilious-colored features certainly radiated wit and malice. A passing, mordant smile kept twisting his lips; his black, narrowed eyes looked insolently out from beneath straggling lashes. Beside him stood a broad, soft, sugary gentleman—a real Sakhar Medovich*— and one-eyed as well. He was laughing at the little fellow's sallies in advance and fairly melting with delight. Voinitzin introduced me to the wit, whose name was Pyotr Petrovich Lupikhin. We made each other's acquaintance and exchanged the opening civilities.

"But let me introduce my best friend," began Lupikhin suddenly, in a sharp voice, seizing the sugary gentleman by the arm. "Don't resist, Kiril Selifanich," he added. "We're not going to eat you. Yes," he continued, while the embarrassed Kiril bowed as awkwardly as if his stomach was falling off, "let me introduce this remarkable gentleman. He enjoyed excellent health until the age of fifty, then suddenly had the idea of treating his eyes, as a result of which he lost one of them. Since then he has been treating his peasants—with the same fortunate results. And they of course are more devoted to him than ever."

"There he goes," murmured Kiril Selifanich, and burst out laughing.

---

* Sakhar Medovich—"Sugar son of Honey." —*Translators*.

"Carry on, my friend, just carry on," repeated Lupikhin. "I'm awfully afraid you may be appointed a justice—you certainly will be, just you see. Well, of course, all the thinking will be done for you by the jurymen; but, even so, one's got to be able to express a thought, even when it *is* someone else's. Suppose the Governor calls—and asks why the judge is stammering; well, suppose they say, 'It's a case of paralysis.' 'Well, bleed him, then,' the Governor will say. But in your position it is unseemly, you're bound to agree."

The sweet-looking gentleman was simply rocking.

"Just look at him laughing," Lupikhin continued, with a vindictive glance at the quivering belly of Kiril Selifanich. "And why shouldn't he," he added, turning to me; "he's well-fed, healthy, no children, peasants unmortgaged—under treatment from him, what's more—and a wife who's half-cracked." Kiril turned slightly away as though he hadn't quite heard, and went on guffawing away as before. "I'm laughing too, although *my* wife ran away with a surveyor." He showed his teeth. "Didn't you know? Of course, of course. She just went and ran off and left me a letter saying: 'Dear Pyotr Petrovich, Forgive me; carried away by passion, I am departing with the friend of my heart.' And the surveyor only got her by not cutting his nails and wearing tight-fitting trousers. You're surprised? There's an outspoken fellow, you're thinking. Good heavens, yes! We steppe-folk always tell God's own truth. But let's go away over here. . . . Why should we stand beside this judge-to-be?"

He took my arm and we went over to a window.

"I pass hereabouts as a wit," he told me in the course of conversation, "but don't you believe it, I'm just an ill-natured fellow roaring aloud; that's why I'm so free and easy about it. And why should I stand on ceremony, if it comes to that? I don't care a farthing for anyone's opinion; I've no axe to grind; I'm an ill-natured fellow—and what of it? At least an ill-natured fellow stands in no need of wit. But you'll never believe how refreshing it is . . . Well, for instance, take our host! What makes him run, I ask you—and keep on glancing at the time, smiling, sweating, looking important, and starving us to death? What is there so wonderful about a Personage? Look, he's started running again—tripped up, too, just look."

And Lupikhin laughed wheezily.

"The only pity of it is, there are no ladies," he continued with a deep sigh. "It's a bachelor dinner—but it's the other sort that does good to fellows like us. Look, look," he exclaimed suddenly, "here comes Prince Kozelsky—that tall man there, with a beard and yellow gloves. You can see at once that he's lived abroad . . . he always arrives late like this. I can tell you, he's stupid enough for a pair of merchant's horses; but you may have noticed how condescendingly he talks to the rest of us, how magnanimously he deigns to smile at the civilities of our famished mothers and daughters! . . . And at times he tries to be witty, too, though he only comes here on visits— and how witty! It's exactly like sawing with a blunt knife at a piece of twine. He can't stand me . . . I shall go and say how do you do to him."

And Lupikhin ran off to meet the prince.

"Here comes my special enemy," he said, suddenly returning to me: "you see that fat fellow, with a brown face and a bristly head— the one who's squeezing his cap, and creeping along the wall, and looking out in all directions like a wolf? I sold him, for four hundred rubles, a horse that was worth a thousand, and that dumb animal now has every right to despise me; and yet he's so bereft of all power of thought, especially in the morning, until he's had his tea, or immediately after dinner, that you could say to him 'Good day' and he'll answer 'What for?' And here comes the Excellency," continued Lupikhin: "the retired, ruined Excellency. He's got a sugar-beet daughter and a scrofulous factory . . . I'm sorry, I got it wrong . . . well, anyway, you understand. Oh! The architect's turned up, too! He's a German, but he's got whiskers and doesn't know his job. Very unusual! . . . But indeed, what's the use of his knowing his job? All he needs do is take bribes, and run up more columns and pillars for the pillars of our nobility!"

Lupikhin chuckled again . . . But suddenly a tremulous excitement spread through the whole house. The great Personage had arrived. Our host fairly rushed into the hall. After him pressed a few faithful domestics and some assiduous guests. The roar of talk turned to a soft, pleasant buzz, like the springtime humming of bees in their native hives. Only that irrepressible wasp, Lupikhin, and that magnificent drone, Kozelsky, failed to lower their voices . . . And now, at last, the queen bee, the great Personage, came in. Hearts went out to meet him, seated bodies arose; even the gentleman who had bought Lupikhin's horse cheap, even he pressed his chin into his breast. The Personage kept his dignity admirably; with a backward movement of his head, as if bowing, he pronounced a few words of approbation, each one of which began with the letter "a" pronounced drawlingly through the nose; he looked at Prince Kozelsky's beard as angrily as if he wanted to eat him, and gave the ruined Excellency with the factory and the daughter the index finger of his left hand. After a few minutes, during which the Personage managed to observe twice that he was very glad not to be late for dinner, the whole company made its way to the dining-room, the bigwigs leading.

Need I tell the reader how the great Personage was given the place of honor between the Excellency and the Marshal of Nobility of the Province, a man with a frank, dignified expression, completely in keeping with his starched shirt-front, immense waistcoat, and round snuff-box full of French snuff; how the host fussed, ran about, worried, pressed his guests to fall to, smiled at the great Personage's back as he passed, and, standing in a corner like a schoolboy, hurriedly gulped down a plate of soup or a morsel of beef; how the butler handed round a fish a yard long with a bouquet in its mouth; how liveried, severe-looking footmen gloomily plied each gentleman, now with Malaga, now with dry Madeira; how almost all the gentlemen, especially those of a certain age, as if in reluctant obedience to a sense of duty, drank down glass after glass, and how at last the champagne bottles popped and the toasts began coming out: this is probably all too familiar to the reader. But I was especially struck with a story told by the great Personage himself in the midst of a general, joyful silence. Someone, acquainted with modern literature, I think it was the ruined Excellency, had referred to the influence of women in general and in particular their influence on young men. "Yes, yes," rejoined the Personage. "That's true; young men must be kept under strict obedience to orders, or else

they go off their heads at the sight of a skirt." A smile of childish
hilarity darted over the faces of all the guests; one gentleman even
had a look of gratitude in his eye. "Because young men are fools."
Probably to sound important, the great Personage now and then
altered the normal accentuation of his syllables. "Take my own son
Ivan," he continued; "the fool's only just twenty, and suddenly he
says to me: 'Please, father, I want to get married!' I tell him he's
a fool, he must see some service first . . . Well, there were tears of
despair . . . But I made him. . . ." These last words the Personage
pronounced with his stomach rather than with his lips; he paused,
and looked majestically at his neighbor, the Excellency, meanwhile
raising his brows far higher than one could have thought possible.
His Excellency leaned his head amiably to one side and blinked with
extraordinary speed, while still gazing at the Personage. "So now,"
began the Personage again, "he writes to me saying, 'Thank you, father, for teaching me such a good lesson.' . . . That's how one ought
to treat them." All the guests, needless to say, were in full agreement
with the narrator, and seemed to gain in animation from the pleasure
and instruction they had received. . . . After dinner the whole company rose and moved to the drawing-room with a noise that was loud,
but all the same correct, and seemingly designed expressly for this
particular occasion. . . . They sat down to cards.

Somehow or other I got through the evening and, after telling my coachman to harness my carriage at five o'clock the next
morning, I retired to sleep. But I was fated that day to make a most
remarkable new acquaintance.

Owing to the number of guests who had turned up, no one was
able to sleep alone. In the small, greenish, dampish room to which
Alexander Mikhailich's butler conducted me, I found another guest,
already fully undressed. At the sight of me he darted nimbly under
the blanket, covered himself with it right up to his nose, fidgeted
a bit on the yielding feather-bed, and lay still, looking sharply out
from below the round brim of a paper night-cap. I went over to the
other bed (there were only two of them in the room), undressed,
and lay down between the damp sheets. My neighbor turned over in
bed . . . I wished him good night.

Half an hour went by. Try as I might, I could not get to sleep. . . .
One vague, useless thought after another went past in endless file,
with the stubborn monotony of buckets on a dredging machine.

"Can't you sleep?" said my neighbor.

"I can't, as you see," I answered. "Nor you either?"

"I never feel sleepy."

"How so?"

"It's like this. I fall asleep without knowing how; I lie and lie,
and then I go to sleep."

"Then why d'you go to bed before you feel sleepy?"

"What else d'you expect me to do?"

I didn't answer my neighbor's question.

"I'm surprised," he went on, after a slight pause, "that there are
no fleas here. Wherever d'you think they've got to?"

"You speak as if you missed them," I remarked.

"No, I don't miss them, but I like due sequence in all things."

I say, I thought to myself, what words he uses! My neighbor was
silent again.

"Would you like to have a bet with me?" he said suddenly, in a
rather loud voice.

"About what?"

My neighbor was beginning to entertain me.

"H'm, about what? I'll tell you about what. I'll bet that you take
me for a fool."

"For goodness' sake," I murmured in amazement.

"For a boor, a wild man from the steppes . . . Admit it . . ."

"I haven't the pleasure of knowing you," I rejoined. . . . "How you
can have concluded . . ."

"How! Why, by the very sound of your voice: you answer me so
casually. . . . But I'm not at all what you think . . ."

"If you please . . ."

"No, if *you* please. In the first place, I speak French no worse
than you, and German even better than you; secondly, I have lived
abroad for three years; in Berlin alone I spent eight months. I have
made a thorough study of Hegel, my dear sir, and I know Goethe
by heart; and into the bargain I was for a long time in love with

the daughter of a German professor, and got married, at home, to a consumptive young lady, a bald but very remarkable person. So I'm a bird of the same feather as yourself; I'm no bumpkin from the steppes, as you suppose. . . . I too am a prey to reflection, and there's nothing spontaneous about me at all."

I raised my head and gazed at the strange fellow with redoubled attention. In the dim glow of the night-light I could hardly make out his features.

"You see, now you're looking at me," he continued, straightening his night-cap, "and you're probably wondering how it was that you never noticed me this evening. I'll tell you why not; because I never raise my voice; because I hide behind other people, stand behind doors, speak to nobody; because a butler with a tray, going past me, raises his elbow beforehand to the level of my chest. And why docs all this happen? For two reasons: first, I'm poor, and secondly . . . I've resigned myself . . . Tell me the truth, you *didn't* notice me."

"I certainly had not the pleasure . . ."

"There you are, there you are," he interrupted me. "I knew it." He lifted himself slightly and folded his arms; the long shadow of his night-cap twisted its way from the wall up to the ceiling.

"But admit it," he added, with a sudden sidelong look at me. "I must strike you as a very odd fellow, as what they call an original, or perhaps, if you like, something even worse: perhaps you think that I'm just pretending to be odd?"

"I must repeat to you again, that I don't know you . . ."

He looked down for a moment.

"Why I've so unexpectedly got into conversation with a complete stranger like yourself—the Lord alone knows!" He sighed. "Not because of any affinity between our souls! You and I are both decent people, that's to say, egoists: you haven't the slightest concern with me, nor I with you; isn't that so? But we can neither of us get to sleep . . . so why not talk? I'm in good form, too, which seldom happens to me. I'm shy, you see, not shy in the sense of being an insignificant wretch of a provincial, but in the sense of being a man of intense self-esteem. But sometimes, under the influence of favorable circumstances, of events which I'm not in a position to determine or foresee, my shyness vanishes completely, as now for instance. Now you could put me face to face with the Dalai Llama—and I would just ask him for a pinch of snuff. But perhaps you want to go to sleep?"

"On the contrary," I rejoined hurriedly, "I'm enjoying our conversation very much."

"That is, I am amusing you, you mean . . . So much the better . . . And so, I must inform you, I'm described hereabouts as an original, described, that is, by those who happen, in the midst of other trifles, to mention my name: 'For no one feels greatly concerned with my estate.' They want to hurt me . . . Oh, my God, if they only knew . . . Why, in fact, I'm dying just because there's absolutely nothing original about me, nothing but such pranks as, for example, my present conversation with you; pranks that are not worth a brass farthing. It's the cheapest and basest form of originality."

He turned his face towards me and threw up his hands.

"My dear sir," he exclaimed, "my opinion is that only originals are fit to live on earth: only they have the right to live. *Mon verre n'est pas grand, mais je bois dans mon verre*, as someone said. You see," he added in a low voice, "how pure my French pronunciation is. What does it matter to me that someone has a high, capacious brow, understands everything, knows a lot, keeps up with the times—if he's got absolutely nothing individual and peculiar to himself? If there's one more storage-place for platitudes in the world—who gets any satisfaction out of that? No, be as stupid as you like, but in your own way! Have your own smell, your individual smell, that's the answer! And don't think that I expect a great deal from this smell . . . Quite the contrary! There are any number of such originals; look where you will, you'll see one; every man alive is an original, and yet I don't happen to be one of them!

"But all the same," he continued after a pause, "in my young days, what expectations I aroused! What a high opinion I cherished of myself, before I left to go abroad, and immediately after my return! Well, abroad I kept my ears pricked, I went my own way, as befits those of us who know a thing or two, but finally realize that they don't even know as far as the letter 'A'.

"Original, original!" he repeated, reproachfully shaking his head. "They call me an original . . . but in practice it seems that in the whole world there's no man less original than your very humble servant. I must have been born imitating someone else . . . My God! I even live in imitation of various favorite authors of mine. I live by the sweat of my brow. I studied, fell in love, eventually got married, all as it were against my own will, but carrying out a duty or a lesson—goodness knows what!"

He tore his night-cap from his head and threw it down on the bed.

"Would you like me to tell you about my life?" he asked me abruptly. "Or rather certain features of my life?"

"Please do."

"Or no; I'd do better to tell you how I got married. You see, marriage is the principal thing, the touchstone of the whole man; it reflects like a mirror. . . . No, that comparison is too hackneyed. . . . Forgive me, I must take a pinch of snuff."

He took out a snuff-box from under his pillow, opened it, and began speaking again, waving the open snuff-box.

"Now, my dear sir, put yourself in my shoes. Just tell me, I ask you, what good could I have derived from Hegel's *Encyclopædia*? Just tell me, what is there in common between this *Encyclopædia* and life in Russia? How can one be expected to apply it to our existence, not the *Encyclopædia* only, but German philosophy in general, or rather German science?"

He started up in bed and began muttering under his breath, his teeth fiercely clenched.

"So that's how it is, is it? . . . Then why did you go trailing off abroad, why didn't you stay at home and study the life of your environment on the spot? You would have learned to know its needs and its future, and you would also have seen more clearly what your own calling was to be . . . But, for goodness' sake," he went on, with another change of tone, as if in timid self-justification, "how can the likes of us be expected to learn what no genius has yet written in any book! I should have been delighted to take lessons from the Russian way of life—but it keeps mum, the old dear, 'Just take me as I am,' it says; but I can't manage that; I need the upshot of it, the conclusion. . . . 'Conclusion!' it says. 'Here's the conclusion for you: listen to our learned Muscovites—aren't they "nightingales"?' Yes, there's the trouble, that they sing like nightingales from Kursk and don't talk as the people do . . . So I thought to myself: after all, science is the same everywhere and truth's the same too—and so I went off with God's blessing and landed in a strange country, among the heretics . . . What can you expect? I was carried away by youth and pride. I didn't want to run to fat before my time, although it's supposed to be quite healthy to do so. And anyway, if Nature gave you no flesh, how can you expect your body to run to fat?

"However," he added, after reflecting a while, "I think I promised to tell you how I came to get married. So listen. First of all, I must tell you that my wife is no longer in the world of the living; secondly . . . but, secondly, I see that I will have to tell you the story of my youth, otherwise you won't understand anything about it . . . But don't you want to go to sleep?"

"No, I don't."

"Splendid! Listen . . . There is Mr. Kantagryukhin in the next room, snoring away—so commonly! I was born of poor parents—I say parents, because tradition has it that as well as a mother I had a father! I don't remember him; they say he was not too clever, had a big nose, freckles, and red hair and took snuff up one nostril; his picture hung in my mother's bedroom, in a red tunic with a black collar up to his ears, as ugly as can be. I used to be taken past him to be whipped and on such occasions my mother used to always point to him and say: '*He* would *really* give it to you.' You can imagine how that encouraged me. I had no brothers or sisters; or rather, to be quite accurate, I had a poor devil of a little brother with the English disease* at the back of his neck, but somehow or other he died very quickly . . . And what business had the English disease to come all the way to the Government of Kursk and the District of Shchigrovo,

---

* Rickets. —*Translators.*

you might ask? But that's by the way. My mother took my education in hand with all the impetuous earnestness of the steppe-land-owner's lady: she took it in hand from the red-letter day of my birth until the advent of my sixteenth year. . . . You follow the thread of my discourse?"

"Of course I do, please go on."

"Very well. On the advent of my sixteenth year, my mother, without an instant's delay, went and dismissed my French tutor, who was a German called Philippovich, from the Ukrainian Greeks. She took me to Moscow, entered me at the University, and yielded up her soul to the Almighty, leaving me in the charge of my uncle, Koltun-Babur, the lawyer, a bird whose fame had spread even outside the district of Shchigrovo. My uncle Koltun-Babur, the lawyer, fleeced me good and proper . . . But that again is by the way. When I entered the University—I must give my mother all credit for it—I was pretty well prepared; but, even then, a lack of originality could be detected in me. My childhood had been in no way different from the childhood of quantities of other young gentlemen. I grew up in the same stupid, sluggish way, as if underneath a feather-bed. I began repeating verses by heart at the same early age, and languishing under the pretext of a dreamy predilection . . . for what?—Oh, for the beautiful of course . . . and so on. At the University I didn't strike out a new course; I immediately got into a set. Times were different then . . . but perhaps you don't know what these sets are? I remember Schiller said somewhere:

> *Gefährlich ist's den Leu zu wecken*
> *Und schrecklich ist des Tigers Zahn,*
> *Doch das schrecklichste der Schrecken*
> *Das ist der Mensch in seinem Wahn!*

"I assure you he didn't mean to say that: he meant to say: '*Das ist ein* "set" *in der Stadt Moskau.*'"

"What do you see that's so awful about a set?" I asked.

My neighbor seized hold of his night-cap and pushed it forward over his nose.

"What do I see that's so awful?" he exclaimed. "I'll tell you: a set is the destruction of all individual development; a set is a hideous substitute for society, for women, for life; a set . . . Oh, just wait; I'll tell you what a set is like! It's a lazy, sluggish way of living together, and as such has significance and an appearance of reason; it replaces conversation by argument, induces a habit of fruitless chatter, distracts you from solitary and useful work, gives you a literary itch, and finally deprives you of all freshness and integrity of soul. A set is just triviality and boredom masquerading as brotherliness and friendship, a combination of misunderstandings and pretensions under the guise of frankness and sympathy. In a set, thanks to the right all your friends have, at every hour and every minute, to put their unwashed fingers right into your heart, no one has any clean, untouched place left in his soul; in a set every empty rhetorician, every conceited genius, every premature old man, is received with reverence, every talentless versifier with esoteric ideas is carried shoulder-high; in a set, young lads of seventeen talk slyly and sagely of women and love, but with women they are silent or else they talk the language of books to them—and what they talk about! A set is the forcing-house for a subtilized eloquence; in a set, everyone watches his neighbour as sharply as so many police officials . . . Oh, a set! It's not a set at all: it's a vicious circle which has been the undoing of more than one decent man."

"No, that's exaggerated, if I may say so," I interrupted him.

My neighbor looked at me in silence.

"It may be, the Lord knows, it may be. You see, people like myself have only one pleasure left—exaggeration. Anyway, that's how I spent four years in Moscow. I cannot describe to you, my dear sir, how quickly, how terribly quickly, that time passed; besides, it saddens and mortifies me to remember. You would get up in the morning and it would be like going down-hill on a sledge . . . You look, and you're already at the end of the run; already it's evening, and a sleepy servant is helping you on with your frock-coat—you dress and wander around to see a friend, you smoke a pipe, you drink weak tea by the glassful and talk about German philosophy, love, the eternal sunshine of the spirit, and other abstruse topics. But even there I

met original, individual people: with some people, force themselves
as they might, struggle as they might to accustom themselves to the
yoke, nature nevertheless prevailed. I alone was unlucky enough to
let myself be molded like soft wax, and my wretched nature put up
not the slightest resistance! Meanwhile I had reached the age of
twenty-one. I became master of my inheritance, or, more accurately,
of that part of my inheritance which my guardian had thought fit
to let me have. I gave full powers for the administration of all my
estates to a freed serf in my employment named Vasily Kudryashov
and went abroad, to Berlin. I lived abroad, as I have already had
the pleasure of telling you, for three years. And what of it? Even
there, even abroad, I remained the same unoriginal creature. First
of all, I need not tell you that I did not learn the slightest thing
about Europe or the European way of life; I listened to German
professors and read German books, on their native soil . . . That
was the only difference. I lived a solitary, monastic sort of life. I
made the acquaintance of retired Russian lieutenants, stricken, as
I was, with a thirst for knowledge, and incidentally very slow in
the uptake and with no gift of self-expression; I hobnobbed with
dull-witted families from Penza and other corn-growing provinces;
I crawled round the coffee-houses, read the papers, went to the theater in the evening. I had but a slight acquaintance with the natives,
talked to them with a sense of strain, and entertained none of them
except two or three importunate youths of Jewish origin who constantly came running to me and borrowed money from me—since
der Russe is a gullible creature. A strange trick of fate eventually
brought me to the house of one of my professors. This is how it was:
I asked to see him to enter my name for a course, and he suddenly
went and asked me to his house one evening. This professor had
two daughters, about twenty-seven, strapping girls, good luck to
them—magnificent noses, ringlet-curls, pale blue eyes, red hands
with white nails. One was called Linchen, the other Minchen. I
began to go often to the professor's house. I must explain that this
professor was, not exactly stupid, but a bit cracked; when he was
lecturing, he spoke quite consecutively; but at home he lisped and
kept his spectacles up on his forehead; incidentally he was an ex-

tremely learned man . . . And what next? Suddenly I thought I was in love with Linchen—and I thought so for a whole six months. It's true that I spoke to her little—I just looked at her, rather; but I used to read aloud to her various touching compositions, and squeeze her hands furtively, and in the evening I used to dream beside her, staring at the moon, or else simply looking up. Besides, she made such excellent coffee! . . . What else could I want, I thought. One thing confused me: even in the so-called moments of indescribable bliss, somehow or other I felt queer in the pit of my stomach, and a depressing, cold shudder ran over my belly. Eventually I could bear my happiness no longer and ran away. After this I spent two more whole years abroad: I was in Italy. In Rome I stood in front of the Transfiguration, in Florence, in front of the Venus; I would suddenly plunge into an extravagant rapture, as if a violent fit had come over me; in the evenings I wrote verses, began a diary; in a word, there too I behaved the same as everybody else. Meanwhile, how easy it would have been to be original. For instance, I don't understand the first thing about painting and sculpture. . . . Why not say so aloud? . . . No, quite impossible! Off I went to take a Cicerone and run around looking at frescoes. . . ."

He lowered his gaze again, and again took off his night-cap.

"So, at last, I returned to my native land," he continued in a tired voice. "I came to Moscow. In Moscow I underwent a surprising change. Abroad I had been rather silent, but there I suddenly began to talk with unexpected briskness and at the same time I put on goodness knows what airs. There were amiable people who thought I was practically a genius; ladies listened sympathetically to my spoutings, but I did not manage to stay at the height of my glory. One fine morning a story about me began to circulate (I don't know who brought it to the light of day: it must have been one of those old maids of the male sex who swarm in Moscow), but it started, and began putting out shoots and tendrils, like a strawberry plant. I got entangled, tried to jump clear, to burst the clinging threads—I couldn't do it . . . I went away. Even in that, I showed my absurdity. I had only to wait quietly for the end of the trouble, like waiting for the end of a nettle-rash, and the same amiable people would

again have opened their doors to me, the same ladies would again
have smiled at my remarks. But that's the whole trouble: I'm not an
original man. It was conscience, I beg you to remark, which suddenly awoke in me: I felt somehow ashamed of chattering, chattering without pause, chattering away—yesterday in Arbat, to-day
in Truba, to-morrow in Sivtsev Vrazhok, and always on the same
themes . . . But if they asked for it? Look at the real champions in
this line of business: they find no difficulty about it; on the contrary,
it's exactly what they need; some of them will work away with their
tongues for twenty years, and all the time in the same direction. . . .
What self-confidence and conceit can do to you! I had it too, conceit, and even now it's not completely dead. But the trouble is, I'll
say it again, that I'm not an original man, I have got caught between
two stools: nature should either have vouchsafed me much more
conceit, or should have given me none at all. But I had a really hard
time in my early days; on top of it, my journey abroad had finally ruined my fortune, and I didn't want to marry some merchant's widow
with a young body, but already flabby as a jelly—so I went home
to the country. I think," added my neighbor, with another sidelong
look at me, "that I can pass over in silence the first impressions of
country life, allusions to the beauty of nature, the quiet charm of
solitude and so on!"

"You can indeed," I rejoined.

"The more so," continued the narrator, "that it is all nonsense,
at least so far as I am concerned. In the country I was as bored as a
locked-up puppy. Although I must admit that on the way home—it
was spring—when for the first time I drove past the familiar birch-
wood, my head began to spin and my heart to beat with a vague,
sweet feeling of anticipation. But those vague feelings of anticipation, as you know, are never realized; on the contrary, other things
are realized instead which you don't at all expect, like cattle dis-
eases, arrears of rent, sales by public auction and so on and so forth.
Existing from hand to mouth, from one day to another, with the
help of my bailiff Yakov, who had superseded my previous agent,
and who in the course of time proved to be just as much of a swin-
dler, if not more, and on top of that poisoned my existence with the

smell of his tarred boots, I remembered one day about a family I knew in the neighborhood, consisting of a retired colonel's widow and two daughters, ordered my drozhky to be harnessed and drove over to see them. For me that day must remain for ever memorable: six months later I married the colonel's widow's second daughter!"

The narrator lowered his head and raised his hands to heaven.

"And incidentally," he added with some warmth, "I wouldn't wish you to have a bad opinion of the dead lady. Heaven forbid! She was the noblest, best-hearted of creatures, a creature full of affection and of infinite capacity for self-sacrifice, though, it must be admitted, between ourselves, that if I had not had the misfortune to lose her, I would probably have been in no position to converse with you to-day, because in my shed the beam is still extant from which on more than one occasion I planned to hang myself! . . .

"There are certain pears," he began again, after a short pause, "which need to lie for some time underground in a cellar, in order to find their true flavor; my late wife was evidently another of Nature's works with the same quality. It is only now that I do her full justice. It is only now, for instance, that the memory of certain evenings which I spent with her before our marriage has ceased to awake the slightest bitterness in me, but on the contrary moves me almost to tears. They were people of no fortune; their house, which was very old, wooden but comfortable, stood on a hill between a garden that had run riot and an overgrown courtyard. At the foot of the hill a river flowed by, hardly visible through thick foliage. A big terrace led from the house to the garden, and in front of the terrace lay an oblong bed which was a mass of roses; at each end of the bed grew two acacias, which the late master had trained to the shape of a screw while they were still young. A little farther on, in the very heart of a raspberry thicket which had been let go and had run wild, stood a summer-house, elaborately painted inside, but so old and decrepit outside that it gave one an eerie feeling to look at it. From the terrace a glass door led into the drawing-room; and in the drawing-room this is what met the curious eye of the spectator: tiled stoves in the corners, on the right a broken-down piano, littered with manuscript music, a sofa covered in a faded blue stuff

with a whitish design, a round table, two cabinets with nicknacks
in porcelain and beads from the time of Catherine the Great, on the
wall the well-known portrait of the blonde girl with the little dove
in her bosom and the upturned eyes, on the table a vase of fresh
roses. You see how exactly I describe it. In that drawing-room, on
that terrace, was played out the whole tragi-comedy of my love. My
neighbor was an ill-natured woman with a permanent ill-natured
wheeze in her throat, a nagging cantankerous creature; one of her
daughters, Vera, was in no way different from the ordinary run of
young country ladies; the other, Sofya—with Sofya I fell in love.
The two sisters had another room, a bedroom, which they shared,
with two pure little wooden beds, little yellowish albums, mignonette, and portraits of their friends, rather badly done in pencil (out-
standing among them was a gentleman with an unusually energetic
expression and an even more energetic signature, who in his youth
had aroused unlimited expectations, but who ended, as we all do,
nowhere at all); busts of Goethe and Schiller, German books, withered wreaths and other objects kept for memory's sake. Into this
room I went but rarely and reluctantly; I found something stifling
about it. Besides, it is an extraordinary thing, but I liked Sofya best
when I was sitting with my back to her, or perhaps even when I was
thinking or rather dreaming about her, especially in the evening,
on the terrace. Then I would look at the sunset, at the trees, at the
slender green leaves, already growing dark, but still sharply defined
against the rosy sky; Sofya would be sitting in the drawing-room
at the piano, constantly playing over some favorite, passionately
brooding phrase of Beethoven's; the ill-natured old woman would
be snoring peacefully as she sat on the sofa; in the dining-room,
in a flood of warm light, Vera would be bustling about preparing
tea; the samovar would be whistling fancifully, as if it was pleased
about something; there would be the cheerful crackle of breaking
pretzels, the musical chime of spoons on cups; the canary, which
had trilled away unmercifully all day, had suddenly fallen silent,
with only an occasional chirrup, as if asking about something; a
small, transparent cloud went by and a few raindrops fell . . . And
I sat, and sat, and listened, and listened, and looked, and my heart

expanded, and I thought again that I must be in love. So, under the influence of such an evening, I asked the old woman one day for her daughter's hand, and two months later I got married. I thought I was in love with her. . . . Even now, though it's high time I did, I still don't know whether I was in love with Sofya. She was a good-natured, intelligent, silent creature, with a warm heart, but, goodness knows why, whether it was from having lived so long in the country, or from some other cause, she had at the bottom of her soul (if the soul has such a thing as a bottom) a secret wound, or, to put it better, a running sore, which nothing could heal, and neither she nor I could even put a name to it. Of course, I didn't guess the existence of this wound until after our marriage. Worry myself about it as I might, nothing helped. When I was a child, I had a pet siskin, which a cat had once caught in its claws; though he had been saved and healed, my poor siskin never recovered; he pouted, he languished, he stopped singing. . . . The end of the story was that one night a rat found its way into his open cage and bit his beak off, as a result of which he finally made up his mind to die. I don't know what cat had held my wife between its paws, but anyway she too pouted and languished like my poor siskin. Sometimes she plainly wanted to shake it off, to leap for joy in the fresh air, in the sunshine, in complete freedom; she would try to—and then roll herself up into a ball again. And yet she loved me; how many times did she assure me that she had nothing more to wish for—and then, devil take it, her eyes would go all dull. I wondered if there wasn't some story in her past life. I made inquiries; I could find nothing. Well, now, you can form your own opinion: an original man would have shrugged his shoulders, perhaps heaved a couple of sighs, and then set about leading his own life; but I, like the unoriginal creature I am, began casting an eye up at the beams. My wife had so far succumbed to the habits of an old maid—Beethoven, walks at night, mignonette, correspondence with friends, albums—that she was quite unable to accustom herself to any new way of life, particularly to that of mistress of a house; and you must admit it was ridiculous for a married woman to languish under a nameless regret and sing, of an evening: 'Awake her not at dawn.'

"Well, we enjoyed this sort of bliss for three years; in the fourth year Sofya died, of her first child, and—a strange thing—I had had a kind of premonition beforehand that she would not be able to present me with a daughter or a son, or the earth with a new inhabitant. I remember her funeral. It was in the spring. We have a little old parish church, with a blackened iconostasis, bare walls, and a dilapidated tiled floor; in the choir, on either side, there is a huge old icon. They carried in the coffin, put it down right in the middle, in front of the main doors of the iconostasis, covered it with a faded cloth, and set three candlesticks round it. The service started. A little doddering clerk, with a little pigtail behind, and a green belt below his waist, was mumbling lugubriously in front of the lectern; the priest, who was old too, with a good-natured, short-sighted face, in a purple vestment with a yellow pattern, was conducting the service and acting as deacon as well. Across the open windows the fresh young leaves of the weeping birch-trees murmured and stirred; from outside came the smell of grass; the red flame of the wax candles paled in the gay light of the spring day; the twittering of the sparrows filled the whole church, and now and then, from under the dome, came a cheerful exclamation from a swallow which had flown in. In the golden dust of the sunlight, the fair heads of a few peasants, zealously praying for the dead lady, rose and fell busily; in a fine, bluish wisp, smoke rose from the mouth of the censer. I looked on the dead face of my wife . . . God! Even death, death itself, had not freed her, had not healed her wound: the same ailing, frightened, dull expression—as if she was ill at ease even in her coffin. . . . I felt the ache of the blood stirring within me. She had been such a good creature, but she had done well for herself to die!"

The narrator's cheeks were flushed and his eyes were dimmed.

"Finally," he began again, "when I had got over the deep depression which seized me after the death of my wife, I thought I would set my hand to the plough, as the saying goes. I took up official duties in the provincial capital, but in the big rooms of the government building my head would begin to ache and my eyes to do their job badly; there were other reasons as well . . . and I retired from my appointment. I wanted to visit Moscow, but, first of all, I hadn't enough money, and secondly, I've already told you of my mood of resignation. It had come over me suddenly, and yet not so suddenly after all. In spirit I had resigned myself long ago, but my head still refused to be bowed. I attributed the placid state of my emotions and thoughts to the influence of country life, to my unhappiness. . . . On the other hand, I had long since observed that almost all my neighbors, young or old, who had at first been stunned by my erudition, my travels abroad, and the other advantages of my education, had not only managed to get completely accustomed to me, but had even begun to treat me in an offhand manner, didn't wait for the end of my stories, and, when they talked to me, no longer used polite forms of speech. I have also forgotten to tell you that, during the first year after my marriage, out of boredom, I had tried to go in for literature, and had even sent in a contribution to a paper—a story, if I am not mistaken—but some little time later I received from the editor a polite letter saying, amongst other things, that though he could not deny me intelligence, he had to deny me talent, and that in literature only talent was required. On top of that, the news got around to me that a visitor from Moscow, incidentally a very good-natured young fellow, had made a passing reference to me at a party of the Governor's as being someone who was finished and played out. But my half-deliberate blindness continued. You see, I didn't want to give myself a smack in the face: but at last, one fine morning, my eyes were opened. This is how it happened. The police inspector had called on me with the object of drawing my attention to a broken-down bridge on my estate, which I was unable to repair for lack of funds. After chasing down a glass of vodka with a piece of smoked sturgeon, this affable guardian of the public peace reproached me in a fatherly way for my lack of circumspection, but put himself in my position and advised me just to tell my peasants to put on more manure, lit a pipe, and began talking about the elections which were shortly to take place. The high estate of Marshal of Nobility of the Province was at that time coveted by one Orbassanov, an empty wind-bag, and a taker of bribes into the bargain. Besides, he had neither wealth nor fame to distinguish him. I spoke my mind on this score with some degree of superiority: I must admit that I looked down on Mr. Orbassanov from somewhere far above. The inspector glanced at me, clapped my shoulder in a friendly way, and said good-naturedly: 'Hey, Vasily Vasilyich, it's not for the likes of you and me to judge such folk—who are we to do so? . . . The cricket must know his own hearth.' 'But, for goodness' sake,' I rejoined indignantly, 'what is the difference between me and Mr. Orbassanov?' The inspector took his pipe out of his mouth, opened his eyes wide—and fairly spluttered with laughter. 'You are a one,' he brought out at length, through tears. 'That's a good one . . . eh?' and from then on until he took his departure he kept making fun of me, giving me an occasional dig in the ribs with his elbow and addressing me in the second person singular. Finally he left. It was the last drop needed; the cup brimmed over. I paced several times up and down the room, halted in front of the looking-glass, gazed and gazed at my embarrassed countenance, slowly put out my tongue, and shook my head in bitter mockery. The veil had fallen from my eyes; I could see clearly, more clearly than my own face in the looking-glass, what an empty, insignificant, useless, unoriginal fellow I was!"

The narrator paused.

"In one of Voltaire's tragedies," he went on sadly, "there is a gentleman who rejoices in having reached the extreme limit of misfortune. Although there is nothing tragic about my fate, I must confess that I have experienced something of the same sort. I have known the poisonous delights of cold despair; I have learned how sweet it is to spend a whole morning lying motionless in bed and cursing the day and hour of my birth;—I could not resign myself straight away. And I had some reason, you know: my straitened circumstances chained me to my detested country home; agriculture, state service, literature, nothing had suited me. I shunned my neighbors; books had become repugnant to me. Your insipidly plump, morbidly sensitive young ladies, who shake their curls and feverishly repeat the word 'freedom,' found me uninteresting, since I had stopped chattering and waxing enthusiastic. A life of complete seclusion was beyond my abilities and my powers. I began . . . what d'you suppose? I began dragging myself round to visit my neighbors. As if drunk with self-contempt, I deliberately submitted to every trivial humiliation. I was left out when the dishes came around, greeted coldly and haughtily, finally not even noticed; I was not even allowed to join in a general conversation, and I would purposely sit in a corner agreeing with some perfectly stupid chatterbox who in the old days, in Moscow, would have been enraptured to lick the dust off my feet or the hem of my coat. I didn't even allow myself to believe that I was enjoying the bitter-sweets of irony. . . . What's the good of irony in solitude! So that, sir, is how I continued for several years on end, and how I am still continuing to-day . . ."

"But I've never heard of such a thing," grumbled the sleepy voice of Mr. Kantagryukhin from the next room. "Who's the fool there who's taken it into his head to talk all night?"

The narrator darted swiftly under his blanket and, looking timidly forth, shook his finger at me.

"Sh . . . sh . . ." he whispered and, as if with an apologetic bow in the direction of Kantagryukhin's voice, he said respectfully: "Yes, very good, very good, I'm sorry, sir . . . He's got every right to sleep, he ought to sleep," he went on again in a whisper; "he must get new strength, well, even if only to be able to eat to-morrow with the same satisfaction. We have no right to disturb him. Anyway, I think I have told you all I want; probably you too would like to sleep. I wish you good night."

The narrator turned away with feverish haste and buried his head in his pillows.

"At least let me know," I asked, "with whom I have had the pleasure . . ."

He lifted his head briskly.

"No, for heaven's sake," he interrupted me, "don't ask me or anyone else my name. Let me remain for you an unknown creature, the ill-starred Vasily Vasilyich. Besides, an unoriginal fellow like myself doesn't even deserve a name of his own. . . . But if you positively wish to call me something, then call me . . . call me the

Hamlet of Shchigrovo district. There are numbers of such Hamlets in every district, but it may be that you have not come across the others. Therewith, I wish you farewell."

He buried himself again in his quilt, and next morning when they came to call me he was no longer in the room. He had gone away before daybreak.

Chertopkhanov and Nedopyuskin

One hot summer's day I was returning in the cart from shooting; Ermolai sat dozing and nodding beside me. The dogs twitched as they lay at our feet in a dead sleep. Now and again the coachman flicked the gad-flies off the horses with his whip. A faint cloud of white dust floated after the cart. We drove into the brushwood. The road grew worse and our wheels began catching on roots. Ermolai started up, looked around . . . "Hey!" he said. "There ought to be blackcock here. Let's get out." We halted and went into the undergrowth. My dog put up a covey. I fired, and was beginning to reload my gun, when suddenly, from behind me, I heard a loud crackling and, parting the bushes with his hands, a man on horse-back came riding up to me. "But kindly inform me," he began in a haughty voice, "by what right you are shooting here, my dear sir?" The stranger spoke extremely quickly, jerkily, and through his nose. I looked him in the face: never in all my life have I seen anything like him. Imagine, dear reader, a small, fair-haired man with a little red turned-up nose and interminable ginger side-whiskers. A pointed Persian cap with a top made of raspberry-colored cloth covered his forehead right down to the eyebrows. He wore a shabby yellow coat with black cartridge-pleats at the chest and faded silver braid at all the seams; from his shoulders hung a horn, out of his belt stuck a dagger. His scraggy, hook-nosed, sorrel horse fidgeted under him like one possessed; two thin crooked-legged borzoi dogs kept circling close beneath it. The stranger's face, his look, his voice, all his movements, his whole being, breathed a crazy bravado and a limitless, unheard-of arrogance; his pale-blue, glassy eyes rolled and squinted like a drunkard's; he threw his head back, puffed out his cheeks, whinnied, and twitched all over, as though from a surfeit of dignity—a regular turkey-cock of a man. He repeated his question.

"I didn't know it was forbidden to shoot here," I answered.

"My dear sir," he went on, "you are on my land."

"Very well, I'll go away."

"But kindly inform me," he rejoined, "have I the honor to address a nobleman?"

I told him my name.

"In that case, please go on shooting. I am a nobleman myself, and very glad to oblige one of my peers . . . My name is Pan-telei Chertopkhanov!"

He leaned forward, whooped, and gave the horse its head; the horse started, reared up, bucked to one side, and trod on the paw of one of the dogs. The dog gave a piercing yelp. Chertopkhanov boiled, hissed, punched the horse on the head between the ears, jumped down quicker than lightning, looked at the dog's paw, spat on the wound, gave the dog a push in the side with his foot to stop it whining; took hold of the horse's withers and put his foot in the stirrup. The horse threw up his head, lifted his tail, and bucked sideways into the bushes; Chertopkhanov went after him hopping on one leg, managed at last to scramble into the saddle, whirled his whip like a raving madman, blew his horn, and galloped off. I had not had time to recover my senses after Chertopkhanov's unexpected apparition, when suddenly, almost noiselessly, there rolled out of the bushes, on a smallish, blackish horse, a fat little man of about forty. He stopped, took off his green leather cap, and asked me in a faint soft voice if I hadn't seen a man on a sorrel horse. I answered that I had.

"Which way would he have gone?" he continued, in the same voice, and without replacing his cap.

"That way."

"Thank you very much indeed, sir."

He smacked his lips, swung his legs against his horse's sides, and jogged away—trit-trot, trit-trot—in the direction indicated. I looked after him until his horned cap disappeared behind the branches. This new stranger in no way resembled his predecessor in appearance. His face, which was chubby and round as a ball, wore an expression of embarrassment, good nature, and timid resignation; his nose, which was also chubby and round and mottled with blue veins, indicated the good liver. There was not a single hair left on the front of his head, but at the back there were some sparse blond tufts sticking up; his little eyes, which were like slits made with a reed, twinkled amiability; there was a pleasant smile on his red, puffy lips. He wore a coat with a stand-up collar and copper buttons, very worn, but clean; his little cloth breeches were rucked up high; a pair of fat little calves showed above the yellow turnovers of his boots.

"Who is that?" I asked Ermolai.

"That? Tikhon Ivanich Nedopyuskin. He lives at Chertopkhanov's."

"What, is he badly off?"

"Not well off; and Chertopkhanov has not got a brass farthing either."

"Then why has he gone to live with him?"

"Well, you see, they became friends, they're always together . . . thick as the horse and his hoof, or the crab and his shell, as the saying goes."

We walked out of the brushwood; suddenly two beagles gave tongue near at hand, and a big white hare came darting through the oats, which were already standing fairly high. Close on his heels there burst from the trees a pack of beagles and borzois, and close on their heels Chertopkhanov himself came flying out. There were no shouts from him, no cries of "go on" or "seek": he was puffing and choking; from his half-open mouth burst now and again an abrupt inarticulate sound; he flashed past, eyes bursting out of his head, flogging his unlucky horse furiously with his whip. The borzois were gaining ground, when the hare crouched down, doubled sharply back, and bolted past Ermolai into the bushes. The borzois streamed past. "Go *on*, go *on!*" the fainting huntsman whispered laboriously, as if tongue-tied. "Good boy, you take care of him!" Ermolai fired . . . The wounded hare spun round like a top on the smooth, dry grass, sprang up into the air, and screamed between the teeth of a hound that was worrying him furiously. The pack had swooped on him at once.

Chertopkhanov threw himself from his horse like a whirlwind, snatched out his dagger, ran straddle-legged over to the pack, tore the mangled hare away from them with furious oaths, and, with his whole face distorted, plunged his dagger into its throat right up to the hilt . . . plunged it in, and began to roar with laughter. Tikhon Ivanich appeared at the edge of the wood. "Ho, ho, ho, ho, ho!" bawled Chertopkhanov for the second time. "Ho, ho, ho, ho, ho," repeated his companion calmly.

"But it isn't right to hunt in the middle of summer," I observed, drawing Chertopkhanov's attention to the trampled oats.

"It's my land," answered Chertopkhanov, hardly breathing. He disembowelled the hare, quartered it, and distributed its paws among the dogs.

"I must pay for your shot, my friend, according to the rules of the chase," he said, addressing Ermolai. "And as for you, my dear sir," he added in the same abrupt, sharp voice, "thank you."

He mounted his horse.

"Kindly tell me . . . I have forgotten your name."

I told him again.

"Very glad to make your acquaintance. If opportunity offers, I hope you'll pay me a visit . . . But where's that fellow Fomka?" he went on, with feeling. "They got the hare without him."

"His horse fell," answered Tikhon with a smile.

"Fell? Orbassan fell? Where . . . where is he?"

"Over there, behind the wood."

Chertopkhanov struck his horse's head with the whip and galloped off helter-skelter. Tikhon bowed to me twice—once for himself, and once for his friend, and again went off at a jog-trot into the bushes.

These two gentlemen stirred my curiosity strangely . . . What was it that could hold two such different creatures together in the bonds of inseparable friendship? I began to make inquiries, and this is what I learned.

Throughout the district Pantelei Eremeich Chertopkhanov had

the reputation of a dangerous, crazy, proud fellow, and a first-class picker of quarrels. He had served for a very short time in the army and had resigned as a result of "unpleasantnesses" with the rank that has given rise to the saying that a hen is no bird.* He came of an old family which had once been wealthy. His ancestors had lived sumptuously, after the manner of the steppes; that is to say, they received all and sundry, fed them to surfeit, allowed visiting coachmen a quarter of oats for each troika, kept musicians, singers, buffoons, and hounds, treated their people to wine and home-brewed beer on feast-days, drove away in the winter to Moscow in heavy travelling-coaches drawn by their own horses, and now and then sat for months on end without a farthing and lived on home-grown poultry. The family fortune was already dissipated when Pantelei's father succeeded to it; he in his turn enjoyed life heartily, and, when he died, left to his sole heir, Pantelei, the mortgaged village of Bessonovo, with thirty-five serfs and seventy-six women, and thirty-nine acres and one rood of poor land in the wilderness of Kolobrodova, on which, incidentally, there were no serfs entered in the title-deeds of the deceased. The deceased, it must be agreed, had ruined himself in the most remarkable way: "Cost Accounting" had been his undoing. According to his principles, a gentleman ought not to depend on merchants, townsmen, and other such "pilferers," as he termed them; he imported into his estate every possible trade and skill. "It looks better and costs less," he said. "Cost Accounting!" This disastrous idea stuck with him to the end of his life; and this it was that ruined him. But he had a good run for his money! There was no whim that he denied himself. Among other inspirations, he rigged up one day, following his own calculations, such a huge family coach, that, notwithstanding the combined efforts of peasants' horses, rounded up from the whole village, and of their owners, it came to grief and disintegrated on the first slope. Eremei Lukich (such was the name of Pantelei's father) gave orders for a monument to be erected on the slope, but otherwise was not in

---

* The lowest rank. "A hen is no bird, a woman no human being, an ensign no officer." —*Translators.*

the least put out. He also had the idea of building a church, on his own, of course, and without the help of an architect. He burnt up a whole forest in baking the bricks, he laid the foundations—and they were immense: fit for a cathedral in a provincial capital! He built the walls, and started putting on the dome: the dome collapsed. He started again, again the dome fell in; he did it a third time, a third time the dome crashed. Eremei Lukich took thought: there must be something a bit wrong . . . he pondered . . . there must be an evil spell on it . . . so suddenly he gave orders that all the old women in the village were to be whipped. And whipped they were—but all the same the dome never went up. He started rebuilding his peasants' huts on a new plan, all based on Cost Accounting; he grouped every three back-yards together in a triangle, and in the middle he put up a pole, with a painted box full of starlings, and a flag. Every day he would have a new brain-wave: now it would be making soup out of dock-leaves, now it would be clipping horses' tails to make caps for the house servants, now it would be plans to substitute nettles for flax or to feed pigs on mushrooms. His brain-waves were not only financial, either; he also worried his head about the welfare of his servants. One day he read in the *Moscow News* an article by a land-owner from Kharkov, a certain Mr. Khryakà-Khrupyorski, about the importance of morality in the peasants' life, and the very next day he gave orders that all his peasants were forthwith to learn the landowners' article by heart—this is how it began: "Attained at last, thanks to the redoubled exertions of a humane administration, the exalted goal dear to every true scion of the fatherland," and so on. The peasants learned the article; their master asked them if they understood what it said, and the agent answered that of course they understood! About the same time he ordered that numbers should be given to all his serfs, in the interests of orderliness and Cost Accounting, and that each one should have his number sewn on his collar. On meeting the master, each one of them would cry: "Here comes such and such a number!" And the master would answer affably: "Carry on, bless your heart."

Nevertheless, in spite of his orderliness and Cost Accounting, Eremei Lukich fell on very hard times: he began by mortgaging his

villages, then he went on to sell them; finally the cradle of his ancestors, the village with the unfinished church, was sold by the public
exchequer, luckily not in Eremei's lifetime—he could never have
withstood the blow—but two weeks after his decease. He managed
to die in his own house, in his own bed, surrounded by his own
servants and under the care of his own doctor; but all that was left
to poor Pantelei was Bessonovo.

When he heard of his father's illness, Pantelei was already on
military service, right in the thick of the "unpleasantness" referred
to above. He had just turned nineteen. Since childhood he had
never left home, and, under the guidance of his mother, a very kind-
hearted but absolutely dull-witted lady named Vasilisa Vasilyevna,
he had grown up into a thoroughly spoiled young gentleman. It was
she alone who saw to his education; Eremei Lukich, plunged in his
economic calculations, had no time for that. It is true that one day
he personally gave his son a beating with a whip for saying "artsy,"
instead of "rtsy," but that was a day when Eremei Lukich was suffering from a deep and secret wound: his best dog had run into a tree
and killed itself. Anyhow Vasilisa Vasilyevna's exertions in regard
to Pantyusha's education were confined to a single painful effort:
by the sweat of her brow she managed to give him a tutor, in the
shape of a retired Alsatian soldier, one Bierkopf, and to the day of
her death she trembled like a leaf before him: if he leaves, she would
think—I'm done for! which way shall I turn? wherever shall I find
another tutor? Even Bierkopf had only been enticed away from a
neighbour with the greatest difficulty! And he, like a man of sagacity, at once exploited his monopoly: he drank himself silly and slept
from morning to night. On the conclusion of his "course of studies"
Pantelei went into the army. Vasilisa Vasilyevna was already dead.
She passed away six months before this important event—from
shock: in a dream she had seen a man in white riding a bear and,
written on his chest, "Antichrist." Eremei Lukich soon followed his
spouse.

At the first news of his illness, Pantelei galloped off home
helter-skelter, but was too late to find his parent alive. What was
the astonishment of the dutiful son when he found himself quite

unexpectedly transformed from the heir to a fortune into a beggar? There are few who can withstand such a violent change of fortune: Pantelei grew savage and embittered. From a man of honor, sobriety, and good nature (though also a flighty and quick-tempered one) he changed into an arrogant picker of quarrels, broke off relations with his neighbors—he was ashamed to meet the rich ones and despised the poor ones—and treated everyone with unheard-of impertinence, including even the powers that be, as much as to say: "I am a member of the old nobility." Once he practically shot a police inspector who came into his room without taking his cap off. Of course the powers that be, on their side, did not forgive him, and reminded him of their existence on occasion; but all the same they were afraid of him because he was such a terrible hot-head and after the second word would be ready to fight you with knives. At the slightest rejoinder Chertopkhanov's eyes would begin to rove, his voice would crack. . . . "Why, why—why," he would mutter, "damn my eyes!" . . . and he would be ready to run up the walls! Yet with all that he was an honest man and never mixed up in any intrigue. Of course no one ever went to see him . . . And yet he was good-hearted, even great-hearted, in his own way: he could not stand the sight of others' suffering, of injustice or oppression; he was a tower of strength to his peasants. "What?" he would say, furiously beating his own head. "Interfering with my people, *mine*? As if I was not Chertopkhanov!!! . . ."

Unlike Pantelei, Tikhon Ivanich Nedopyuskin could not boast of his origins. His father came of freeholder stock and only acquired noble rank after forty years of state service. Mr. Nedopyuskin the father belonged to that class of people whom misfortune dogs with unflagging, inexorable cruelty, with a cruelty like a personal hatred. Throughout his sixty years, from the day of his birth to the day of his death, the poor wretch had wrestled with all the constraints, ailments, and miseries which are the lot of small folk; he struggled like a fish on ice, never ate enough, never slept enough, bowed, fussed, brooded, and languished, trembled over every copeck, suffered quite unfairly in his official career, and died at last, in a garret or a cellar, without having managed to earn himself or his children their daily bread. Destiny had harried him like a hunted hare. He was a good, honest man, but took bribes—"according to rank"—from a ten-copeck piece up to two silver rubles inclusive. He had a thin, consumptive wife; there were children too; luckily they all died young, except for Tikhon and one daughter, Mitrodora, nicknamed the "merchant's glory," who after many sad and laughable adventures married a retired attorney. Mr. Nedopyuskin the father, while still alive, had managed to find Tikhon a place as a minor official in a chancery, but as soon as his father died Tikhon retired. The perpetual anxieties, the anguished struggles with cold and hunger, his mother's brooding depression, the worrying and despair of his father, the bullying rudeness of landlords and shopkeepers, all this daily, continual suffering had engendered an indescribable shyness in Tikhon: the mere sight of his chief made him tremble and swoon like a bird in a snare. He gave up the service. An indifferent and perhaps mocking Nature endows people with different capacities and inclinations, without any regard to their means and position in society; with the care and love which are peculiar to her, she had molded Tikhon, the son of a poor official, into a sensitive, soft, susceptible creature—a creature excessively intent on enjoyment, gifted with an extraordinarily fine sense of smell and taste. . . . She molded him, carefully put the finishing touches, and—left her product to grow up on sour cabbage and rotten fish. And so this product grew up, and began, as it is called, to "live." The fun started. Destiny, which had tormented Nedopyuskin the father unceasingly, now started on the son: she had clearly acquired a taste for it. But with Tikhon she used a different method: instead of tormenting him, she played with him. She never brought him to despair, never forced him to feel the shameful pangs of hunger, but tossed him about, from one end of Russia to another, from Veliky-Ustyug to Tsarevo-Kokshaisk, from one humiliating and ridiculous employment to another. First she would appoint him "major-domo" to an ill-tempered, bilious lady-bountiful, then she would place him as hanger-on to a rich skinflint of a merchant, then she would make him principal private secretary to a pop-eyed Muscovite prince with his hair cut in the English fashion, then

she would promote him to be half-butler, half-buffoon to a steppe
landowner, a keeper of hounds and picker of quarrels. . . . In a
word, destiny made poor Tikhon drink, drop by drop and to the
last dregs, the bitter, poisonous draught of the underdog's life. He
knew what it was to serve the oppressive caprice, the sleepy, ill-
natured boredom, of idle masters. How often, alone in his room,
released at last with God's blessing by a pack of guests who had had
their fill of amusement, fairly bursting with shame, and with cold
tears of despair in his eyes, did he swear to run away secretly the
next day, to try his luck in the town, to find himself if it were only a
job as clerk, or just to die once and for all from hunger in the street.
But, first, God had not given him the strength; secondly, his timidity was too much for him; and thirdly and lastly, how was he going
to find himself a job, whom was he going to ask? "They'll never give
me one," the poor wretch would murmur, dozing miserably on his
bed, "they'll never give me one!" And the following day he would
return to his tread-mill. The situation was all the more painful in
that the same considerate Nature had not bothered to endow him
with the smallest share of those qualities and talents without which
the buffoon's profession is all but impossible. For instance, he could
neither dance until he fell down, wearing a bearskin inside out, nor
crack jokes and exchange pleasantries in the midst of a throng of
excited whippers-in; if driven out stark naked into twenty degrees
of frost, he sometimes caught cold; his stomach could not digest
wine mixed with ink and other filth, nor fly-agaric and toad-stool
minced in vinegar. Lord knows what would have become of Tikhon if the last of his benefactors, a newly-rich tax-farmer, had not
had the idea, by way of a joke, of adding to his will: "To Zyozyo
(or Tikhon) Nedopyuskin, I bequeathe, for himself and his descendants in perpetuity, the village of Besselendeyevka, acquired by
me, with all the dependencies thereto appertaining." A few days
later, over his sterlet soup, the benefactor died of a stroke. There
was a great to-do; the law arrived unexpectedly and put seals on
the property in due form. The relations assembled; they opened
the will; they read it, they called for Nedopyuskin. Nedopyuskin

appeared. The majority of those present knew what had been Tikhon's functions in his benefactor's household. He was met by deafening shouts and jocular congratulations. "Here he is, the new
landowner!" shouted the other heirs. "Here he is," repeated one of
them, a well-known joker and wit, "yes, here he is, definitely . . .
in actual fact . . . the . . . what d'you call it . . . the heir . . ." and
everyone fairly exploded with laughter. For a while Nedopyuskin
could not believe his good fortune. They showed him the will—he
blushed, screwed up his eyes, and began throwing out his hands,
and sobbing, and weeping buckets. The laughter of those present
turned into a single sustained roar. The village of Besselendeyevka
consisted of only twenty-two peasants; nobody minded much about
it, so why not take the opportunity for a good laugh? Only one of
the heirs, an official from Petersburg, a striking-looking man with
a Greek nose and a noble expression, Rostislav Adamich Stoppel,
was unable to restrain himself, and sidled up to Nedopyuskin and
looked at him contemptuously over his shoulder. "As far as I can
observe, my dear sir," he began in a tone of contemptuous indifference, "you were employed by the respected Fyodor Fyodorich in
the capacity of a kind of house-jester?" The official from Petersburg
expressed himself in language that was unbeatably clear, crisp, and
precise. In his distraction and excitement, Nedopyuskin did not
take in the words of the gentleman, who was a stranger to him, but
all the others immediately stopped talking: the wit smiled condescendingly. Mr. Stoppel rubbed his hands and repeated his question. Nedopyuskin looked up in amazement and opened his mouth.
Rostislav Adamich narrowed his eyes offensively.

"Congratulations, my dear sir, congratulations," he went on; "it's
true that not everyone would be prepared to earn his daily bread in
such a fashion, but *de gustibus non est disputandum*, that is to say, we
all have our own tastes . . . Haven't we?"

Someone in the back rows gave a short, discreet whoop of astonishment and delight.

"Tell me," went on Mr. Stoppel, much encouraged by the smiles
of the whole company, "to what talent in particular do you owe your

good fortune? No, don't be shy, tell us; all of us here are, as it were, *en famille*. Isn't that so, gentlemen, that we are *en famille* here?"

The gentleman to whom Rostislav Adamich happened to address this question unfortunately knew no French, and therefore confined himself to a single faint grunt of approbation. But another beneficiary, a young man with yellowish blotches on his forehead, asserted hastily: "*Voui, voui*, of course."

"Perhaps," began Mr. Stoppel again, "you can walk on your hands, with your legs in the air, as it were?"

Nedopyuskin looked round unhappily—every face wore a malicious grin, every eye was wet with mirth.

"Or, perhaps, you can crow like a cock?"

There was a burst of laughter all round which died away at once, stifled by anticipation.

"Or, perhaps, on your nose, you . . ."

"Stop!" A sharp and ringing voice suddenly broke in. "You ought to be ashamed to tease the poor fellow like that!"

Everyone looked round. In the doorway stood Chertopkhanov. As a third cousin of the deceased tax-farmer, he too had received a letter of invitation to the family gathering. While the will was being read he had, as usual, kept proudly at a distance from the others.

"Stop," he repeated, arrogantly throwing back his head.

Mr. Stoppel turned round quickly and, seeing a badly-dressed, insignificant-looking man, asked his neighbor under his breath (for caution never harmed anyone): "Who's that?"

"Chertopkhanov—a smallish bird," replied the neighbor in his ear.

Rostislav Adamich assumed an expression of contempt: "And who are you to give orders?" he said, through his nose, with his eyes screwed up. "What sort of bird are you?"

Chertopkhanov blew up like powder from a spark. Rage hampered his breathing.

"Dz-dz-dz-dz," he hissed, as if he was being throttled, then suddenly thundered out: "Who am I? Who am I? I am Pantelei Chertopkhanov, a man of the oldest nobility, my great-great-great-great-grandfather served the Tsar, and who are you?"

Rostislav Adamich turned pale and took a step back. He had not expected such a repulse.

"A bird, *me, me*, a bird . . . Oh, oh, oh!"

Chertopkhanov rushed forward; Stoppel jumped away in great agitation, and the guests dashed in to meet the indignant landowner.

"Shoot it out, shoot it out at once, across a handkerchief!" cried Pantelei in a frenzy. "Or apologize to me and to him too . . ."

"Apologize, apologize," whispered the anxious beneficiaries surrounding Stoppel. "You see what he is; a madman—and a homicidal one, too."

"Forgive me, forgive me, I didn't know," began Stoppel in a faltering voice. "I didn't know."

"Apologize to him, too!" shouted Pantelei indefatigably.

"*You* forgive me, too," added Rostislav Adamich, addressing Nedopyuskin, who himself was trembling as if in a fever.

Chertopkhanov calmed down, went over to Tikhon, took his arm, looked arrogantly around, and, not meeting a single glance, solemnly, in the midst of a deep silence, walked from the room accompanied by the new owner of the Besselendeyevka property.

From that day on they were inseparable. (The village of Besselendeyevka was only eight versts away from Bessonovo.) Nedopyuskin's unbounded gratitude soon changed to an obsequious devotion. Weak, soft, and not entirely straight, Tikhon humbled himself to the dust before the fearless, reproachless Pantelei. It's tremendous! he thought to himself from time to time: he talks to the Governor, looks him straight in the eye . . . why, you would think he was Christ himself!

He admired him to stupefaction, until his faculties became confused; he thought of him as a man of extraordinary intelligence and learning. And indeed, poor as Chertopkhanov's education was, nevertheless compared with Tikhon's it could be termed brilliant. It is true that Chertopkhanov read little in Russian and understood badly in French, so badly that one day, when a Swiss tutor asked him: "*Vous parlez français, monsieur?*" he answered: "*Je ne* understand," and after a moment's thought added, "*pas*"; but all the same, he knew that there had once been a very clever writer called Voltaire and that

Frederick the Great, King of Prussia, had had a distinguished military career. Among Russian writers he admired Derzhavin, loved Marlinsky, and called his best hound Ammalat Bey . . .

A few days after my first encounter with the two friends, I went over to Bessonovo to call on Pantelei. His little house could be seen from afar; it stood in a bare patch half a verst away from the village, conspicuous as a hawk above a ploughed field. Chertopkhanov's whole establishment consisted of four old wooden structures of various sizes, namely, the house, the stable, the barn, and the bath-house. Each of these structures sat by itself, apart from the others; there was no fence around, no gate to be seen. My coachman stopped in perplexity beside a crumbling, choked-up well. By the barn some thin, dishevelled borzoi puppies were worrying a dead horse, probably Orbassan; one of them lifted a blood-stained muzzle, gave a hasty bark, and again set about gnawing the exposed ribs. Beside the horse stood a lad of about seventeen, with a plump, sallow face, Cossack's dress, and bare feet; he looked solemnly at the dogs entrusted to his care, and now and then gave the greediest of them a flick of his whip.

"Is the master at home?" I asked.

"The Lord knows!" answered the lad. "Knock on the door."

I jumped down from the drozhky and went up to the porch of the house.

Mr. Chertopkhanov's residence had a very sorry look: the woodwork was blackened and bellying out in front, the chimney had slipped, the corners had been propped up but even so were out of true, and little windows of a dim, dove-gray color looked out with an indescribably sour expression from beneath the shaggy roof that was jammed down above them: they looked like the eyes of some old prostitute. I knocked; no one answered. But, behind the door, I heard words sharply spoken: "A, B, V; well, go on, you fool," said a husky voice. "A, B, V, G . . . no! G, D, E! E! E for Eat! Go on, you fool!"

I knocked again.

The same voice shouted: "Come in—who is it?"

I went into a little, empty front hall, and through an open door

I caught sight of Chertopkhanov himself. He was sitting in a chair, in a greasy Bokhara robe, wide trousers, and a red skull-cap; with one hand he was squeezing the muzzle of a young poodle, and with the other he was holding a piece of bread right in front of his nose.

"Ah!" he said with dignity, not stirring from his place. "Very glad to see you. Kindly be seated. I am having trouble with Venzor here . . . Tikhon," he added, raising his voice, "come here, will you. We have a visitor."

"Coming, coming," answered Tikhon from the next room. "Masha, give me my cravat."

Chertopkhanov addressed himself again to Venzor and put the piece of bread on his nose. I looked around. The room had no furniture except a warped folding-table on thirteen uneven legs, and four sagging straw-chairs; the walls, which ages ago had been painted white with blue star-shaped spots, were peeling in many places; between the windows hung a dim, battered little looking-glass in a massive frame of imitation mahogany. Guns and chibouks stood in the corners; spiders' webs hung, dense and black, from the ceiling.

"A, B, V, G, D," said Chertopkhanov slowly, then all of a sudden he exclaimed furiously: "E! E! E! for Eat! . . . what a stupid creature . . . E for Eat!"

But the unlucky poodle only shivered and could not make up his mind to open his mouth; he went on sitting, with his tail pressed miserably down, his mouth screwed up, humbly blinking and narrowing his eyes, as if to say: "Of course, you're the master."

"Well, eat it, go on! Take it!" repeated the indefatigable landowner.

"You've frightened him," I observed.

"Well, get away with you, then!" He gave him a push with his foot. The poor wretch got up, quietly dropped the bread off his nose and went, as it were on tiptoe, into the front hall, deeply offended. And with reason: a stranger had come to the house for the first time, and this was how they treated him.

The door leading from the next room squeaked discreetly and Mr. Nedopyuskin came in, bowing amiably and smiling.

I got up and bowed.

"Don't move, don't move," he murmured.

We sat down. Chertopkhanov went out into the next room.

"Have you been long in our part of the world?" began Nedopyuskin in a soft voice, after coughing carefully into his hand and holding his fingers in front of his lips for good manners' sake.

"Nearly two months."

"Quite so."

Silence descended.

"Delightful weather now," continued Nedopyuskin, and he looked gratefully at me, as though the weather depended on me. "We ought to have a fine crop."

I nodded my head in sign of agreement. There was a silence.

"Yesterday Pantelei Eremeich caught two hares," began Nedopyuskin, not without effort, with an obvious wish to enliven the conversation. "Yes, sir, very big hares, sir."

"Has Mr. Chertopkhanov got good hounds?"

"They're remarkable, sir!" rejoined Nedopyuskin with gusto. "I dare say they are the best in the province." He drew closer to me. "Why, Pantelei Eremeich is a wonderful fellow! Anything he wants, any idea he has—you look, and it's all prepared, the whole thing fairly on the boil. I tell you, Pantelei Eremeich . . ."

Chertopkhanov came into the room. Nedopyuskin chuckled, fell silent, and indicated him to me with his eyes, as much as to say: Just see for yourself. We started to talk about hunting.

"Would you like me to show you my leash of hounds?" Chertopkhanov asked me and, without waiting for an answer, he called: "Karp!" A sturdy lad came in, wearing a green nankeen coat with a blue collar and livery buttons.

"Tell Fomka," said Chertopkhanov abruptly, "to bring around Ammalat and Saiga, and tidily, too, understand?"

Karp smiled with his whole mouth, uttered an indeterminate sound, and went out. Fomka appeared, neat-headed, tightly buttoned, wearing shoes, and accompanied by his hounds. For politeness' sake I admired these stupid animals (all borzois are extraordinarily stupid). Chertopkhanov spat right into Ammalat's nostrils, which appeared to give the hound not the slightest satisfaction. Nedopyuskin stroked Ammalat on the hind-quarters. We resumed our conversation. By degrees Chertopkhanov softened up completely, and stopped crowing and snorting; the expression on his face changed. He looked at me and Nedopyuskin . . .

"Hey!" he exclaimed suddenly. "Why should she sit there all by herself? Masha! I say, Masha! Come here." Someone moved in the next room, but there was no answer.

"Ma-a-sha," repeated Chertopkhanov pleadingly. "Come here. Never mind, you needn't be afraid."

The door opened quietly and I saw a woman of about twenty, tall and well-built, with a dark, gypsy face and yellowish-brown eyes and pitch-black locks; her big white teeth fairly glittered between full, red lips. She wore a white dress; a blue shawl, fastened at the throat with a gold pin, half hid her slender thoroughbred arms. She took two steps forward, with the embarrassed clumsiness of a wild thing, then halted and looked down.

"Well, let me introduce you," said Pantelei. "Wife or no wife, let her pass for one."

Masha blushed slightly and smiled from embarrassment. I gave her a specially deep bow. I liked her very much. Her fine aquiline nose, with its arched, transparent-looking nostrils, the bold, high sweep of her eyebrows, her pale, slightly sunken cheeks—all her features spoke of self-willed passion and reckless daring. From her braided hair down to her sturdy neck ran two lines of tiny gleaming hairs—the sign of blood and vigor.

She went to the window and sat down. I had no wish to add to her confusion, and began talking to Chertopkhanov. Masha turned her head slightly and began to study me with a sidelong, furtive, wild, swift gaze. Her glance flashed like a viper's fang. Nedopyuskin sat down beside her and whispered something in her ear. She smiled again. When she smiled, she slightly wrinkled her nose and raised her upper lip, which gave her face an expression which was half-cat, half-lioness.

Oh, you're an elusive one, I thought, shooting a furtive glance in my turn at her willowy waist, her deep breast, and angular, nimble movements.

"Well, Masha," asked Chertopkhanov, "we ought to offer something to our guest, eh?"

"We have got some jam," she answered.

"Well, bring it here, and some vodka, too, and listen, Masha," he called after her, "bring your guitar as well."

"Why the guitar? I'm not going to sing."

"Why not?"

"I don't want to."

"Oh, nonsense, you'll want to, if . . ."

"If what?" asked Masha with a swift wrinkling of the brows.

"If you're asked to," Chertopkhanov concluded with a certain embarrassment.

"Oh!"

She went out, soon returned with the jam and vodka, and sat down again in the window. A little furrow had already appeared on her forehead. . . . Her brows kept darting up and down like a wasp's whiskers. . . . Have you ever noticed, reader, what a wicked face a wasp has? Well, I thought, there's going to be a storm. The conversation was not going well. Nedopyuskin had dried up completely and wore a constrained smile; Chertopkhanov puffed and flushed and his eyes were starting out: I began making as if to leave. . . . Suddenly Masha rose, and in a flash opened the window, leaned her head out, and gave a hearty shout of "Axinya!" after a passing peasant-woman. The woman started, began to turn round, slipped, and fell down heavily on the ground. Masha threw herself back with a ringing laugh; Chertopkhanov chuckled, too, and Nedopyuskin squeaked with delight. We all came to life. The storm had broken with nothing but lightning . . . the air had cleared.

Half an hour later no one would have recognized us: we were talking and laughing away like children. Masha was in higher spirits than anyone. Chertopkhanov fairly devoured her with his eyes. Her face had gone paler, her nostrils had expanded, her glance blazed up and dimmed again all at the same time. The wild creature was well away. Nedopyuskin stumbled after her on his fat little legs, like a drake following a duck. Even Venzor crept out from under the bench in the hall, stood in the doorway, looked at us, and suddenly started jumping up and barking. Masha fluttered out into the next room, brought her guitar, threw the shawl off her shoulders, sat quickly down, lifted her head, and struck up a gypsy song. Her voice rang and thrilled like a cracked glass bell, blazed out, faded away . . . It gave one a pleasant creepy feeling inside. "*Ay, burn and speak!* . . ." Chertopkhanov embarked on a dance. Nedopyuskin stamped and jumped and took little mincing steps. Masha was all a-quiver, like birch-bark on a fire: her slender fingers ran gaily over the guitar, her brown throat rose slowly under her double necklace of amber. One moment she would suddenly be silent, sink into a doze, pluck the strings with seeming reluctance, and Chertopkhanov would halt with only his shoulder twitching and shuffle from one foot to the other where he stood, and Nedopyuskin would shake his head like a porcelain Chinaman; then she would be off again in a frenzy, straighten her back, throw out her breast, and Chertopkhanov would be squatting on the ground again, jumping up to the ceiling, spinning like a top, and shouting "Bravo! . . ."

"Bravo, bravo, bravo!" Nedopyuskin gabbled after him.

It was late in the evening when I left Bessonovo. . . . As for Masha's own story, I shall tell it to my forbearing readers some other time.

The End of Chertopkhanov

I

Two years after my visit, Pantelei's disasters began—"disasters" is the only word. Disappointments, failures, misfortunes had pursued him even before then; but he paid them no attention and "reigned" as before. The first disaster which struck him was the most painful one of all: Masha left him.

What induced her to forsake his roof, to which she had seemed so well-accustomed, it would be hard to say. Until his dying day, Chertopkhanov remained convinced that the blame for Masha's treachery lay with a certain young neighbor, a retired captain of Lancers by the name of Yaff, who, in Pantelei's words, got his way just by perpetually twisting his whiskers, thickly oiling his hair, and sniffing significantly; but it may be supposed that it was rather the effect of the wandering gypsy blood which flowed in Masha's veins. Anyway, however that may be, one fine summer evening Masha tied a few rags together into a small bundle and walked out of Chertopkhanov's house.

For three days previous to this she had been sitting in a corner writhing and pressing up against the wall like a wounded vixen. If only she had said a word to somebody—but no, she just rolled her eyes the whole time, looked thoughtful, twitched her eyebrows, bared her teeth slightly, and fidgeted with her hands, as if to wrap herself up. The same sort of mood had come over her before, but had never lasted long; Chertopkhanov knew this, and consequently was not disturbed himself and didn't disturb her either.

But when returning from the kennels, where, in the words of his whipper-in, the last two hounds had "gone stiff," he met a maid who announced to him in a trembling voice that Marya Akinfyevna sent her compliments and said that she wished him all the best, but would never return to his house again, Chertopkhanov, after turning round twice where he stood and giving vent to a husky roar, at once dashed after the fugitive—snatching up his pistol on the way.

He found her about two versts from his house, beside a birchwood, on the high road leading to the nearest town. The sun stood low over the horizon and everything round suddenly turned scarlet: trees, grass, and earth.

"To Yaff, to Yaff!" groaned Chertopkhanov as soon as he caught sight of Masha. "To Yaff," he repeated, running up to her and almost tripping with every step.

Masha halted and turned to face him. She stood with her back to the light—and looked quite black, as if carved in ebony. Only the whites of her eyes showed up as little silver almonds, but her eyes themselves—the pupils—were darker than ever.

She threw her bundle aside and folded her arms.

"You're on the way to Yaff's, you hussy!" repeated Chertopkhanov, and tried to seize her by the shoulder, but met her gaze, faltered, and fidgeted where he stood.

"I'm not going to Mr. Yaff's, Pantelei Eremeich," answered Masha calmly and evenly. "I just can't live with you any more."

"Why can't you? What for? Have I done anything to offend you?"

Masha shook her head. "You've done nothing to offend me, Pantelei Eremeich. I have just got bored living with you. . . . Thanks for times past, but I can't stay on—no!"

Chertopkhanov was dumbfounded; he even slapped his thighs and jumped up into the air.

"How can that be? You've lived, and lived, and known nothing but pleasure and peace—and suddenly: you're bored! So you tell yourself, I'll chuck him! You go and throw a handkerchief over your head and set off. You've been treated with every respect, the same as a lady."

"Not that I wanted it at all," interrupted Masha.

"You didn't want it? Turned from a wandering gypsy into a lady—you didn't want it? What d'you mean, you child of Ham? D'you expect me to believe that? There's treachery behind this, treachery."

He had begun to hiss with rage again.

"There's no thought of treachery in my mind and never has been," said Masha in her clear, sing-song voice. "I've already told you: I got bored."

"Masha," exclaimed Chertopkhanov, and punched himself in the chest. "Stop, that's enough, you've made me suffer quite enough. Good heavens! Just think what Tisha will say; you might have thought about him!"

"Please give my respects to Tikhon Ivanich and tell him . . ."

Chertopkhanov waved his arms.

"Oh, no, you're wrong—you won't get away! Your Yaff can go on waiting for you."

"Mr. Yaff——" began Masha.

"Mr. Yaff, indeed," imitated Chertopkhanov. "He's a twister and a rogue, if ever there was one—and a face like a monkey, too!"

For a whole half-hour Chertopkhanov argued with Masha. Now he would go close up to her, now he would dart away, now he would lift his arm at her, now he would bow to her from the waist and weep and curse.

"I can't," asserted Masha. "I'm so sad there . . . so bored and miserable."

Her face had gradually assumed such an indifferent, almost sleepy expression that Chertopkhanov asked her if she had not taken a nip of thorn-apple spirit.

"Bored," she said for the tenth time.

"And supposing I were to kill you?" he cried all of a sudden, and pulled the pistol out of his pocket.

Masha smiled; her face became animated. "Why, kill away, Pantelei Eremeich: I'm at your mercy; but one thing I won't do, and that's come back."

"You won't come back!" Chertopkhanov pulled back the cock.

"No, my dear . . . Never in my life, and I mean it."

Chertopkhanov suddenly thrust the pistol into her hand and sat down on the grass.

"Well, then, *you* kill me! I don't want to live without you. If you're tired of me—then I'm tired of everything else."

Masha bent down, picked up her bundle, put the pistol down in the grass with the muzzle away from Chertopkhanov, and went up to him.

"Why, my dear, what's all the fuss about? Don't you know us gypsy girls? It's our way, it's how we are. Once the longing to be off comes over us, and calls our hearts away to somewhere else far off, how can we stay where we are? Remember your Masha—you won't find another friend like her—and I, too, I won't forget you, my falcon; but our life together is over!"

"I loved you, Masha," mumbled Chertopkhanov into his fingers, with which he was clutching his face.

"And I loved you, Pantelei Eremeich, my friend."

"I loved you, I still love you to distraction—and when I think now that here you are, for nothing at all, without rhyme or reason, chucking me, and starting to wander about the world—well, it strikes me that if I wasn't a poor wretch of a beggar you wouldn't leave me."

At these words Masha simply chuckled.

"And you used to tell me I had no thought for silver," she said, and with a sweep of her arm she hit Chertopkhanov on the shoulder.

He jumped to his feet.

"Well, at any rate take some money from me—otherwise how will you manage, without a farthing? But, best of all: kill me! I tell you plainly, kill me once and for all!"

Masha again shook her head. "Kill you? What do they send people to Siberia for, my dear?"

Chertopkhanov shuddered. "So it's just because of this, for fear of punishment that you . . ."

He collapsed again on the grass. Masha stood over him in silence. "I'm sorry for you, Pantelei Eremeich," she said with a sigh; "you're a good man . . . but there's nothing for it. Goodbye!"

She turned away and took two steps. Darkness had fallen and the shadows of night were welling up on every side. Chertopkhanov got up nimbly and seized Masha from behind by both elbows.

"So you're off, you snake? To Yaff's!"

"Good-bye!" repeated Masha sharply and with emphasis, and she broke loose and went on her way.

Chertopkhanov looked after her, ran over to the spot where the pistol lay, picked it up, aimed, fired . . . but, before pressing the trigger, he raised his hand: the bullet hummed over Masha's head. She looked at him over her shoulder as she went, and continued on her way with a waddling motion, as if to mock him.

He covered his face—and set off at a run . . .

But he had not run as much as fifty paces, when suddenly he stopped as if rooted to the spot. A familiar, a too familiar voice floated to his ears. Masha was singing. *"Days of youth so charming,"* she sang; and every note was magnified in the evening air, in a plaintive, sultry way. Chertopkhanov listened with his head on one side. The voice went farther and farther into the distance; now it faded, now it came floating back again, hardly perceptible, but still burning . . .

She's doing it to spite me, thought Chertopkhanov; but the same moment he groaned: "Oh, no! She's saying good-bye to me for ever"—and he burst into floods of tears.

The following day he turned up at the residence of Mr. Yaff, who, like a true man of the world, disliked country solitude, and had settled in the nearest town, "nearer to the ladies," as he expressed it. Chertopkhanov did not find Yaff at home: the footman said that he had left the day before for Moscow.

"That's it!" exclaimed Chertopkhanov furiously. "They had a plot; she's run off with him . . . but just wait!"

He forced his way into the young captain's study, despite the opposition of the footman. In the study, over the sofa, hung an oil portrait of the master in Lancer uniform. "So that's where you are, you monkey without a tail!" thundered Chertopkhanov, jumping on to the sofa—and he struck his fist against the stretched canvas and burst a great hole in it.

"Tell your good-for-nothing master," he said to the footman, "that, failing his own odious face, Mr. Chertopkhanov, gentleman, has disfigured the painted version of it; and that if he desires satisfaction from me, he knows where to find Mr. Chertopkhanov, gentleman! Otherwise I'll find him myself! I'll find the dirty monkey if I have to go to the bottom of the sea!"

With these words, Chertopkhanov jumped off the sofa and solemnly took his departure.

But Captain Yaff demanded no satisfaction from him—he never even met him—and Chertopkhanov didn't think it worth searching for his enemy, so nothing happened between them. Soon afterwards Masha herself vanished without trace. Chertopkhanov started drinking; but in time he "came round again."

Here, however, his second disaster overtook him.

II

That is to say, his bosom friend Tikhon Ivanich Nedopyuskin died. Some two years before his death, his health had started to fail; he began suffering from asthma, kept dropping off to sleep and, on waking up, couldn't at once recover his senses. The local doctor asserted that these attacks of his were "little strokes." During the three days preceding Masha's departure, the three days in which she got "bored," Nedopyuskin had been lying at home at Besselendeyevka: he had caught a bad chill. The effect on him of Masha's action was all the more unexpected: it was almost more profound than on Chertopkhanov himself. In keeping with his gentle, timid disposition, he showed nothing except the tenderest sympathy with his friend and a certain painful incomprehension, but something had burst and sagged inside him. "She has stolen my soul away," he whispered to himself, as he sat on his favorite oilskin sofa and twined his fingers round each other.

Even when Chertopkhanov recovered, Nedopyuskin didn't—and went on feeling that he was "empty inside." "Just here," he would say, pointing at the middle of his chest, above the stomach.

In this way he dragged on until winter. At the first frosts, his asthma got better, but, against this, he had what was no longer a little stroke, but a real proper one. He did not lose consciousness at once; he could still recognize Chertopkhanov, and even, in answer to the despairing exclamation of his friend: "How is this, Tisha, that you're leaving me, without my permission, just as bad as Masha?" he stammered: "But, Pa . . . lei E . . . E . . . ich, I've al . . . ays o . . . eyed you." Yet this did not prevent him from dying the same day, without waiting for the local doctor, who, at the sight of his cold corpse, had nothing left to do but sadly admit the transitoriness of earthly things and ask for "a drop of vodka with a piece of smoked sturgeon." Tikhon Ivanich left his property, as was only to be expected, to his revered benefactor and magnanimous protector, Pantelei Eremeich Chertopkhanov. But his revered benefactor did not derive much advantage from this, since it was quickly sold by auction—chiefly to cover the expenses of his funerary monument, a statue which Chertopkhanov (his father's strain coming out in him!) had the idea of erecting over his friend's ashes. This statue, which was supposed to represent an angel in prayer, he had ordered from Moscow, but the contractor who had been recommended to him, calculating that but few experts on sculpture are to be met in the provinces, sent him, instead of an angel, a goddess Flora which had for many years adorned one of those neglected parks in the neighborhood of Moscow which date back to the time of Catherine the Great—this statue, which incidentally was very elegant, in the rococo manner, with chubby hands, fluffy curls, a garland of roses hung round its bare breast, and a curved waist, having come into the contractor's possession free of charge. So over Tikhon's grave there stands to this day a mythological goddess, with one foot graciously raised, gazing with a truly Pompadour-like grimace at the calves and sheep which wander around it—those unfailing visitors of our village graveyards.

III

After the loss of his faithful friend, Chertopkhanov began drinking again, this time much more seriously. His affairs went straight downhill. There was nothing to shoot, the last money was spent, the last servants departed. Pantelei Eremeich was left completely alone; there was no one to speak a word to, no one to confide in. Only his pride remained undiminished. Indeed, the worse his affairs became, the more arrogant and overbearing and inaccessible he grew. Finally he went completely wild. One consolation, one joy remained to him: a remarkable saddle-horse, a gray, bred by the Don, named by him Malek Adel, an extraordinary animal indeed.

He had acquired this horse in the following manner.

Riding one day through a neighboring village, Chertopkhanov heard a babble of peasant voices and the roar of a crowd from the direction of the pot-house. In the middle of this crowd, at one particular spot, sturdy hands were steadily rising and falling.

"What's going on here?" he asked, in the tone of command which was peculiar to him, addressing an old peasant-woman who was standing in the doorway of her cabin.

Leaning against the lintel, as if in a dream, the old woman was looking towards the pot-house. A small white-headed boy in a cotton shirt, with a little crucifix of cypress-wood on his bare chest, was sitting, with spread-out legs and clenched fists, between her bast-shoes; close by a chick was picking at a crust of rye bread which had gone as hard as wood.

"The Lord knows, sir," answered the old woman, and, leaning forward, she put her dark wrinkled hand on the boy's head. "I heard that our lads are beating a Jew."

"A Jew? What Jew?"

"The Lord knows, sir. A Jew of sorts turned up here, and as for where he came from—who can tell? Vasya, sir, come to mother: tch-tch, you rascal." She drove off the chick, and Vasya grasped her skirts.

"So now they're beating him, sir."

"Why? What for?"

"I don't know, sir. It must be for something he has done. Anyway, what should they do but beat him? Wasn't it he that crucified Christ!"

Chertopkhanov gave a whoop, put his horse into a gallop with a blow of the whip, rode straight at the crowd—and, tearing his way into it, began indiscriminately whacking the peasants to right and left with the said whip, saying in a staccato voice: "Taking . . . the law . . . into . . . your own hands! Punishment is for the law to give—not for pri . . . vate per . . . sons! The law! The law!! The LAW!!"

Inside of two minutes the whole mob had retreated in various directions—and on the ground, in front of the door of the pothouse, appeared a small, thinnish, darkish creature, wearing a nankeen coat, tousled and tattered . . . A pale face, eyes rolled up, mouth open . . . What was it? A terror-stricken faint, or death itself?

"Why have you killed the Jew?" exclaimed Chertopkhanov in a voice of thunder, with a threatening wave of the whip.

There was a faint buzz from the crowd in answer. One peasant was holding his shoulder, a second his side, a third his nose.

"He's asking for a fight!" came a voice from the back rows.

"With his whip! Anyone could do that!" said a second voice.

"Why have you killed the Jew? I'm asking you, you pack of Tartars!" repeated Chertopkhanov.

But the creature who had been lying on the ground now jumped nimbly to his feet and, running up behind Chertopkhanov, took hold convulsively of the edge of his saddle.

There was a general roar of laughter from the crowd.

"He's got nine lives!" came a voice, again from the back rows. "Just like a cat!"

"Your worship, protect me, save me!" lisped the unhappy Jew meanwhile, pressing his whole chest against Chertopkhanov's leg, "or they'll kill me, so they will, your worship!"

"Why did they do it to you?" asked Chertopkhanov.

"I swear I don't know! You see, their cattle began to die . . . so they suspected . . . and I . . ."

"Well! We'll go into that later!" interrupted Chertopkhanov. "But now you hang on to my saddle and follow me. And as for you!"

he added, turning to the crowd. "Do you know me? I am Pantelei Chertopkhanov, landowner, I live in the village of Bessonovo—and, well, I mean, you can put in a complaint against me whenever you like, and against the Jew, too!"

"Why should we complain?" said a staid, gray-bearded peasant, a regular ancient patriarch, bowing low. (Incidentally he had pommelled the Jew as soundly as the best of them.) "We know your kind heart well, Pantelei Eremeich, sir; we're very grateful to your good self for giving us a lesson!"

"Why should we complain?" repeated the others. "But as for that infidel, we'll get our way with him! He won't escape us! We'll run him down like a hare in a field . . ."

Chertopkhanov fidgeted his brows, snorted, and set off at a walk to his own village, accompanied by the Jew whom he had delivered from his persecutors in exactly the same way as he had once delivered Tikhon Nedopyuskin.

IV

A few days later, Chertopkhanov's only surviving boy-servant announced to him that a man on horseback had arrived and wished to speak to him. Chertopkhanov went out into the porch and saw his acquaintance, the Jew, mounted on a magnificent Don horse, which was standing proud and immobile in the middle of the yard. The Jew wore no cap: he was holding it under his arm, his feet were not in the stirrups, but resting against the stirrup-leathers, and his tattered coat-tails hung down on both sides of the saddle. Seeing Chertopkhanov, he smacked his lips, twitched his elbows, and swung his legs. But Chertopkhanov, far from acknowledging his greeting, grew furious and suddenly exploded. A dirty Jew, daring to sit on such a splendid horse . . . it was quite shocking!

"Hey, you black devil!" he shouted. "Get off at once, if you don't want to be pulled off into the mud!"

The Jew at once obeyed, fell out of the saddle like a sack, and, holding the reins in one hand, smiling and bowing, came towards Chertopkhanov.

"What d'you want?" asked Pantelei Eremeich with dignity.

"Your honor, can you see what sort of horse it is?" said the Jew, without ceasing to bow.

"Well . . . yes . . . he's a good horse. Where did you get him? Stole him, I suppose?"

"Whatever next, your honor! I'm an honest Jew. I didn't steal him, I got him specially for your honor! I tried and tried! and here he is. On the whole of the Don you won't find another horse like him.—Look, your honor, there's a horse for you! Just come over here!—Go on . . . go on . . . turn around, stand sideways on!—We'll just take the saddle off. Do you see what sort of horse he is, your worship?"

"He's a good horse," repeated Chertopkhanov with feigned indifference, though his heart was fairly hammering away in his breast. He was a passionate fancier of horse-flesh and knew what was what.

"Just stroke him, your worship! Stroke his neck, hee-hee-hee, like this."

As if against his will, Chertopkhanov put his hand on the horse's neck, patted it twice, then drew his fingers from the withers along the back, and, when he came to the well-known spot above the kidneys, pressed the spot gently like a connoisseur. The horse arched his back, and, giving Chertopkhanov a sidelong look with his insolent black eye, snorted and fidgeted his four legs.

The Jew laughed and gently clapped his hands.

"He knows his master, your worship, so he does."

"Don't talk nonsense," Chertopkhanov interrupted angrily. "I have not the means to buy horses from you, and as for accepting a present, I've never accepted a present from the Lord God himself, let alone from a Jew!"

"And how should I dare to give you a present, for mercy's sake!" exclaimed the Jew. "Buy him, your worship . . . and as for the money—I'll wait for it."

Chertopkhanov reflected.

"What will you take for him?" he said at length, through his teeth.

The Jew shrugged his shoulders.

"What I paid for him myself. Two hundred rubles."

The horse was worth twice—perhaps even three times—that sum. Chertopkhanov turned away to one side and yawned nervously.

"But when . . . for the money?" he asked, scowling unnaturally and not looking at the Jew.

"When it suits your honor."

Chertopkhanov threw his head back, but without raising his eyes.

"That's nonsense. Talk sense, you spawn of Herod!—D'you want to put me under an obligation to you, or what?"

"Well, let's say," replied the Jew hurriedly, "in six months' time . . . Agreed?"

Chertopkhanov answered nothing.

The Jew made an effort to look him in the eye. "Agreed? Shall I put him in the stable?"

"I don't want the saddle," pronounced Chertopkhanov abruptly. "Take the saddle—d'you hear?"

"Of course, of course, certainly, certainly," murmured the delighted Jew, and he humped the saddle on his shoulder.

"And the money," Chertopkhanov went on, "in six months' time. And not two hundred, but two hundred and fifty. Silence. Two hundred and fifty, I tell you! To my account."

Chertopkhanov could still not make up his mind to raise his eyes. Never had his pride suffered so severely. It's an obvious present, he was thinking. The wretched fellow's brought it by way of gratitude! He could have embraced the Jew, he could have struck him . . .

"Your honor," began the Jew, who had grown bolder, and put on a smirk, "we ought to hand him over in the Russian way, from coat-tail to coat-tail . . ."

"Whatever next? A Jew . . . in the Russian way!—Hey! Who's there? Take the horse and put him in the stable. And give him some oats. I'll come along myself in a moment and have a look. And listen: his name is Malek Adel!"

Chertopkhanov was about to go up to the porch, but he turned sharply on his heels, ran up to the Jew, and squeezed his hand hard. The Jew bowed and was already offering his lips, but Chertopkhanov recoiled with a bound and, saying in a low voice, "Don't tell a soul!", vanished behind the door.

V

From that day forward, the main business, the main preoccupation and delight in Chertopkhanov's life, was Malek Adel. He loved him even more than Masha, grew more attached to him even than to Nedopyuskin. And what a horse he was! All fire and gunpowder—and yet with the gravity of a Boyar! Untirable, a stayer, ready to go anywhere, mild as a lamb; costing nothing to feed: if he couldn't get anything else, he would eat the ground under his feet.

He walks, and it's as if he's carrying you in his arms; he trots, and it's as if he is rocking you in a cradle; but when he gallops, not even the wind can catch him! He never loses his breath—his windpipe's too sound for that. His hooves are of steel; as for stumbling—there's never been the slightest question of it! Jumping a ditch or a fence means nothing to him; and what a brain he's got! You call him, and he'll come running up, head thrown back; you tell him to stop, and you leave him—he won't stir; as soon as you start coming back he'll whinny faintly: "Here I am." He fears nothing: in the darkest night or a snow-storm he'll find the way; and he'll never let a stranger take hold of him, he would tear him with his teeth! And woe betide any dog that bothers him: he'll get a forehoof to his skull at once—ponk! and the dog will have had its day. He's a horse with ambitions: you can wave the whip over him, just for show—but God help you if you touch him! Anyway, why make a long story of it: he's not a horse, he's a treasure!

If Chertopkhanov had sat down to describe his Malek Adel—heaven knows where he would have found the words to do so! And how he curried him and cosseted him! Malek Adel's coat was shot with silver—and not old silver, either, but new silver with a dull polish on it; if you stroked him with the flat of your hand, it was absolute velvet! Saddle, saddle-cloth, bridle—every bit of harness was so well-fitted, well-kept, well-scrubbed—you could just take a pencil and draw! It was Chertopkhanov himself—who else?—who

with his own hand plaited his darling's forelock, washed his mane
and tail in beer, and more than once anointed his hooves with oil.

He would mount Malek Adel and ride out, not exactly to visit
his neighbors—he had no more connection with them than before—
but over their land, and past their seats . . . as if to say: Admire, you
fools, from afar! Then he'd hear of hunting in progress somewhere—
some rich landowner visiting his outlying properties—and at once
he'd be off there, and prance about in the distance, on the horizon,
amazing all beholders with the beauty and speed of his horse, but
letting no one come near him. On one occasion a huntsman set off
after him, with all his suite in attendance, saw that Chertopkhanov
was walking away from him, and started shouting after him with all
his might, while at full gallop: "Hey, you, listen! Take what you like
for your horse! I won't grudge you a thousand! I'll give my wife and
children for him! Take my last penny!"

Chertopkhanov suddenly halted Malek Adel. The huntsman
dashed up to him. "Tell me, sir," he shouted, "what d'you want? My
own father?"

"If you were the Tsar," said Chertopkhanov deliberately (and in
all his born days he had never heard of Shakespeare), "you could
give me your whole kingdom for my horse, and even so I wouldn't
take it!" He spoke, he laughed, he made Malek Adel rear up, he
spun him round in mid-air, standing on nothing but his hind legs,
like a top—and gallop! He fairly streaked off across the stubble.
And the huntsman (who, so the story goes, was a prince, a man of
enormous wealth) threw his cap on the ground—and buried his face
in it. He lay like that for a good half-hour.

It was only natural that Chertopkhanov should treasure his
horse. Was it not through him that further proof had been given
of his own undoubted and final superiority over all his neighbors?

VI

Meanwhile time passed, the date of payment was approaching—
and, so far from having two hundred and fifty rubles, Chertopkhanov had not so much as fifty. What could he do, where could he

turn for help? Well, he resolved at last, if the Jew wouldn't relent and agree to go on waiting, he'd give him his house and land. "I'll mount the horse," he said to himself, "and ride off wherever the spirit moves me. I'll die of hunger rather than sell Malek Adel!" He was greatly disturbed, and was even reduced to reflection; but here, for the first and last time, fate took pity on him and smiled. A distant aunt, whose very name was unknown to Chertopkhanov, left him in her will a sum which in his eyes was enormous, a whole two thousand rubles! And he received this money in the very nick of time, the day before the Jew's arrival. Chertopkhanov was almost out of his mind with joy. But the thought of vodka never even entered his head: from the day that Malek Adel had come to him, not so much as a drop had passed his lips. He ran to the stable and kissed his friend on both sides of the muzzle, above the nostrils, on the spot where a horse's skin is so delicate. "No more parting for us now!" he exclaimed, slapping Malek Adel on the neck, below his combed-out mane. Returning to the house, he counted out two hundred and fifty rubles and sealed them up in a packet. Then, lying on his back and smoking his pipe, he dreamt of how he would dispose of the rest of the money—and in particular what hounds he would get: the proper Kostroma strain, and they must have red markings, too! He also spoke to Perfishka, promised him a new coat with yellow galloons at all the seams—and went to sleep in a most peaceful frame of mind.

He had a bad dream: he dreamed he was out hunting, mounted, however, not on Malek Adel, but on some strange animal like a camel. There came running to meet him a fox which was absolutely white like snow. He wanted to wave his whip, to set the hounds on the fox—but instead of a whip he found a wisp of straw in his hand and the fox ran just in front of him and put its tongue out at him. He jumped down from his camel, stumbled, fell . . . and fell straight into the arms of a gendarme, who was summoning him before the Governor-General, and whom he recognized as Yaff . . .

Chertopkhanov woke up. It was dark in the room; just after the second cockcrow . . .

From somewhere far, far away in the distance a horse neighed.

Chertopkhanov lifted his head. Once more came the faint, faint neighing.

That's Malek Adel's neigh! he thought. It's his neigh! But why so far away? My goodness . . . It can't be . . .

Chertopkhanov suddenly went cold all over, sprang from his bed in the twinkling of an eye, felt for his shoes and clothes, dressed, and, seizing the stable key from under the pillow, dashed out into the yard.

VII

The stable lay at the far end of the yard; one of its walls backed on to the fields. Chertopkhanov did not get the key into the lock at once—his hands were trembling—nor could he turn the key at once . . . He stood motionless, holding his breath: if only something would move behind the door! "Maleshka, Malek!" he called in a low voice: but silence! Without meaning to, Chertopkhanov pulled the key: the door squeaked and opened . . . So it wasn't locked. He strode across the threshold, and again called his horse, this time by its full name: "Malek Adel!" But there was no answer from his faithful friend, only the rustling of a mouse in the straw. Then Chertopkhanov rushed to the stall—one of three in the stable—in which Malek Adel was kept. He found his way straight to it although the darkness was dense enough to knock your eye out! Empty! Chertopkhanov's head began to reel; a bell seemed to be droning inside his skull. He wanted to say something—but could only wheeze; and, with hands groping, up, and down, and sideways, panting, with faltering knees, he made his way from one stall to another . . . In the third stall, which was piled almost to the top with hay, he ran into one wall, then into the other: he fell head over heels, got up, and suddenly ran out helter-skelter through the half-open door into the yard . . .

"He's been stolen! Perfishka! Perfishka! He's been stolen!" he roared at the top of his voice.

The boy Perfishka, in nothing but his shirt, flew out like a whirlwind from the garret where he slept.

The two of them, the master and his only servant, collided like drunken men in the middle of the yard; as if possessed, they circled round each other. The master could not explain what was the matter; the servant could not understand what he was called on to do. "Oh dear, oh dear," muttered Chertopkhanov. "Oh dear, oh dear," repeated the boy after him. "A lantern, come on, light a lantern, lights, lights!" Chertopkhanov brought out at length, in a fainting voice. Perfishka ran into the house. But it was no easy matter to light a lantern or to get a light. At that time wax matches were a rarity in Russia: the last fires in the kitchen had long been out, tinder and flint took time to find and worked badly. Grinding his teeth, Chertopkhanov snatched them from the hands of the dumbfounded Perfishka to strike a light himself, sparks flew in plenty, curses and even groans in greater plenty still—but the wick either wouldn't catch, or went out, notwithstanding the combined efforts of four concentrated cheeks and lips! At last, after a full five minutes, the greasy candle-end at the bottom of the broken lantern began to glimmer, and Chertopkhanov, accompanied by Perfishka, rushed into the stable, lifted the lantern above his head and looked round . . .

It was absolutely empty!

He darted out into the yard, ran round in all directions—no horse to be found! The fence which had surrounded Pantelei's seat had long ago become dilapidated and at many places had listed over and touched the ground. . . . Opposite the stable it was completely down to the width of a whole yard. Perfishka showed Chertopkhanov this spot.

"Master, just look here: it wasn't like this to-day. And here are the stakes, too, sticking out of the ground—someone must have pulled them up."

Chertopkhanov ran over with the lantern, and moved it close to the ground . . .

"Hooves, hooves, horse's shoe-marks, fresh marks!" he muttered quickly. "Here's where they took him over, here, here!"

In a flash he had jumped over the fence and, shouting, "Malek Adel, Malek Adel," was running straight out into the field.

Perfishka was left standing dumbfounded beside the fence. The circle of light from the lantern soon vanished from his sight, swallowed up in the dense gloom of the starless, moonless night.

Ever fainter and fainter sounded the despairing cries of Chertopkhanov.

VIII

The day was already dawning when he returned home. He looked like nothing human, his clothes were all covered in mud, his face had taken on a wild, terrifying look, his eyes had a dull, morose stare. He chased Perfishka away in a husky whisper and locked himself in his room. He could hardly stand from exhaustion, but, instead of lying down on his bed, he sat on a chair by the door and put his head in his hands.

"Stolen! Stolen!"

But how had the thief been clever enough to steal Malek Adel by night out of a locked stable? Malek Adel, who even by day would let no stranger approach him—to steal him without a knock, without a sound? And how was it to be explained that not one of the dogs had barked? True, there were only two of them, two young puppies, and they had dug themselves into the ground from cold and hunger; but all the same!

What am I going to do now without Malek Adel? thought Chertopkhanov. I've lost my last friend. It's time for me to die. Buy another horse, since I've got the money? But where shall I find another horse like him?

"Pantelei Eremeich! Pantelei Eremeich!" came a timid cry from behind the door.

Chertopkhanov jumped to his feet.

"Who's there?" he shouted in an unnatural voice.

"It's me, your boy Perfishka."

"Who d'you want? Has he been found? Has he come home?"

"No, no, sir; but the Jew-man, who sold him . . ."

"Well?"

"He's come."

"Ho, ho, ho." Chertopkhanov roared with laughter—and at once flung the door open. "Bring him here, come on! Bring him here!"

On the sudden appearance of the tousled, wild-looking figure of his benefactor, the Jew, standing behind Perfishka, tried to slink off, but Chertopkhanov took two bounds forward, caught him, and like a tiger fastened on to him by the throat.

"Ah, come for your money! money!" he wheezed, as if he were being strangled himself, instead of strangling the other. "Stole him by night, and come by day for your money? Eh?"

"Mercy, your ho . . . nor," the Jew was groaning.

"Tell me, where's my horse? What have you done with him? Who've you sold him to? Tell me, go on, tell me!"

The Jew could no longer even groan; his face had gone blue and had actually lost its expression of terror. His arms hung limply; his whole body, in response to Chertopkhanov's furious shaking, was swaying backwards and forwards like a reed.

"I'll pay you your money. I'll pay you in full, to the last copeck," shouted Chertopkhanov. "But I'll wring your neck like a miserable chicken, if you don't tell me at once . . ."

"But you *have* wrung his neck, master," observed the boy Perfishka humbly.

It was only then that Chertopkhanov came to his senses.

He let go of the Jew's neck; the Jew fairly thumped down on the ground. Chertopkhanov picked him up, sat him on a bench, poured a glass of vodka down his throat, and brought him round. And, having done so, began to talk to him.

It appeared that the Jew had not had the faintest inkling of Malek Adel's theft. Indeed, what motive could he have had for stealing the horse which he himself had found for "his deeply respected Pantelei Eremeich"?

Then Chertopkhanov led him to the stable. Together they inspected the stalls, the mangers, the lock on the door; they rummaged through the hay and the straw, and then walked round the back-yard; Chertopkhanov showed the Jew the hoof-marks by the fence and suddenly smacked his thighs.

"Wait," he exclaimed. "Where did you buy the horse?"

"In the district of Little Arkhangel, at Verkhosensk fair," answered the Jew.

"Who from?"

"A Cossack."

"Wait! This Cossack, was he young or old?"

"Middle-aged, a steady sort of fellow."

"But what was he like? What did he look like? A complete rogue, I suppose?"

"Certainly a rogue, your honor!"

"Well, what did he tell you, this rogue-fellow—had he owned the horse for long?"

"Yes, so I seem to remember, for some time."

"Well, then, he's the only one that could have stolen the horse! Listen, you, listen here, and tell me what you think . . . what's your name?"

The Jew started and his little black eyes shot a look at Chertopkhanov.

"What is *my* name?"

"Yes: what do they call you?"

"Moshel Leiba."

"Well, tell me what you think, Leiba, my friend—you're a clever chap. Would Malek Adel have let anyone take him, except his old master? Why, he saddled him, and bridled him, and took the blanket off him—there it is lying on the hay! . . . He simply behaved as if he was at home. Why, if it had been anyone else, who hadn't been his master, Malek Adel would have crushed him under his hooves. He would have made such a din he would have roused the whole village! Do you agree with me?"

"Certainly, of course, your honor."

"Well, then, it means we must first of all find that Cossack!"

"But how can we find him, your honor? I only saw him just once—I've no idea where he can be now, or what his name is. Ai, vai, vai!" added the Jew, shaking his side-curls sadly.

"Leiba!" shouted Chertopkhanov suddenly, "Leiba, look at me!

I'm out of my own mind, I'm not myself! . . . I'll do myself a mischief, unless you help me!"

"But how can I . . ."

"Let's go together—and start looking for the thief."

"But where shall we go?"

"Round the fairs, the highways and by-ways, round the horse-thieves, round towns, villages, and farms—everywhere, everywhere! And don't worry about money: I've had a legacy! I'll spend my last copeck—but I'll find my friend! And that Cossack won't escape us either, the villain—where he is, we'll be there too! If he's under the ground, so will we be. If he's gone to the devil, we'll go to Satan himself!"

"Oh, why to Satan?" observed the Jew, "we can manage without him."

"Leiba!" repeated Chertopkhanov, "Leiba, although you're a Jew and a heathen, you've got a better heart than many a Christian! Take pity on me! It's no good my going alone; I shan't be able to handle this by myself. I'm too quick-tempered—but *you* have got a head on your shoulders, a head of gold! Your tribe are all the same; get anything you want, without book-learning! You may be doubtful about my money. Come to my room—I'll show you the money too. Take it, take the cross from my neck—only give me back Malek Adel, give him back to me!"

Chertopkhanov was trembling as if from fear: a stream of sweat poured down his face and, mingling with his tears, lost itself in his whiskers. He pressed Leiba's hands, he implored him, he almost kissed him. He began to rave. The Jew tried to raise objections, to assert that it was quite impossible for him to absent himself, that he had business . . . but to no avail! Chertopkhanov would not listen to a word. There was nothing for it; the unhappy Leiba agreed.

The following day Chertopkhanov and Leiba drove away from Bessonovo in a peasant cart. The Jew looked somewhat confused, held on to the rail with one hand, his whole flabby body bouncing about on its shaky perch; he held his other hand pressed to his bosom, where he kept a packet of banknotes wrapped up in newspaper. Chertopkhanov sat like an idol, motionless, except for his roving eyes and deep-chested breathing. There was a dagger stuck in his belt.

"Well, my wicked rival, look out for yourself now," he muttered as they drove out on to the high road.

He had left his house in the care of the boy Perfishka and of the deaf old peasant-woman who cooked for him and whom he had taken in out of the kindness of his heart.

"I shall come back to you on Malek Adel," he called to them by way of farewell, "or not at all!"

"We ought to get married, eh?" laughed Perfishka, digging his elbow into the cook's ribs. "Why not?—we shall never see the master back, and you'll die of boredom otherwise!"

IX

A year passed, a whole year. There was not a whisper of news about Pantelei Eremeich. The cook died; even Perfishka was preparing to abandon the house and set off for the town, whither he was beckoned by a cousin, apprenticed to a barber—when suddenly it was rumored abroad that the master was returning. The parish deacon had received a letter from Pantelei Eremeich himself, announcing his intended arrival at Bessonovo, and asking him to warn the servants so that they could make suitable arrangements for his reception. Perfishka understood these words to mean that he must wipe away some of the dust—though he had no great faith in the accuracy of the news; he had, however, to admit that the deacon had spoken the truth, when a few days later Pantelei Eremeich himself, in person, appeared in the courtyard of his house, mounted on Malek Adel.

Perfishka dashed to his master and, taking hold of the stirrup, made as if to help him to dismount; but his master jumped down unaided, and, throwing a triumphant glance around, loudly exclaimed: "I said that I would find Malek Adel—and find him I did, to the mortification of my enemies and of destiny itself." Perfishka went and kissed his hand, but Chertopkhanov took no notice of his servant's attentions. Leading Malek Adel after him by the bridle, he strode off to the stable. Perfishka looked closely at his master—and had a shock. He thought: Oh, how thin and old he has got within the year—and how grim and stern his face has grown! You would suppose that Pantelei ought to have been glad he had found his own; and so he was, certainly . . . but all the same Perfishka had a shock: in fact he felt quite creepy. Chertopkhanov put the horse in his old stall, patted him gently on the quarters, and said: "Well, there you are, home again. Just look! . . ." The same day he engaged a reliable watchman—a peasant who had no taxes to pay—installed himself again in his rooms, and resumed his former life . . .

Not quite his former life, however . . . But of this later.

The day after his return, Pantelei sent for Perfishka and, for want of anyone else to talk to, began to tell him, without of course losing the sense of his own dignity, and in a gruff bass voice, how he had managed to find Malek Adel. As he spoke, Chertopkhanov sat facing the window, smoking a long chibouk; Perfishka stood in the doorway, hands clasped behind his back and, looking respectfully at the back of his master's head, heard how, after many vain attempts and excursions, Pantelei at length arrived at Romyon fair, by this time alone, since Leiba the Jew, from weakness of character, had not lasted out and had run away from him; how, on the fifth day, when getting ready to depart, he had taken a last turn along the rows of carts and suddenly, between three other horses tied to a post, he had seen—Malek Adel! How he recognized him at once—and how Malek Adel had recognized him too and started neighing and straining and tearing the ground with his hoof. "And he wasn't with the Cossack," continued Chertopkhanov, still without turning his head and in the same bass voice, "but with a gypsy horse-coper; naturally I at once took hold of my horse and tried to get him back by force; but the beastly gypsy started howling as if he'd been scalded, all over the square, began swearing that he had bought the horse from another gypsy and wanted to produce witnesses . . . I spat and paid him his money: may the devil fly with him! The great thing for me was that I had found my friend and set my soul at rest. Then, in the district of Karachevo, I ran into a Cossack who fitted the Jew's description—I took him for the thief and bashed his face in; but the Cossack turned out to be the son of a priest instead, and he took the skin off my back by way of damages—one hundred and twenty rubles. Well, money can always be made—but the main thing is that I've got Malek Adel back. I'm happy now and I shall be able to enjoy peace and quiet. But for you, Porfiry, I have only one instruction: as soon as you see a Cossack about—which heaven forfend—that very second, without saying a word, run and bring me a gun, and I shall know all right what to do next!"

This was how Pantelei spoke to Perfishka; these were the words he spoke; but his heart was far from being as calm as he declared.

Alas! at the bottom of his heart he was not wholly convinced that the horse he had brought back was really Malek Adel at all!

X

This was the beginning of a difficult time for Pantelei Eremeich. Peace and quiet was precisely what he enjoyed least of all. True, he had his good days, when the doubt which had dawned on him seemed to be nonsensical; he chased the absurd idea away like an importunate fly, he even laughed at himself; but he also had his bad days, when the nagging idea began again to gnaw and scratch at his heart, like a mouse under the floor-boards, and he suffered bitterly from secret pangs. During the memorable day when he found Malek Adel, Chertopkhanov had been conscious only of a blissful happiness. But the following morning when, beneath the low lean-to roof outside the inn, he started saddling up his discovery, after having spent the whole night by its side—for the first time he felt a certain pricking . . . He merely shook his head—but the seed had been sown. During his journey home (which lasted a week) he had but few doubts; they grew stronger and clearer as soon as he returned to his own Bessonovo, as soon as he found himself on the spot where the earlier, indubitable Malek Adel had lived . . . On the journey he had walked his horse for most of the way, swaying, looking from side to side, smoking his chibouk and without a thought in the world except occasionally to say to himself with a grin: "The Chertopkhanovs always get their way! None of your nonsense for them!" But with his arrival home, another chapter began. He kept the whole thing to himself, of course; his pride alone would never have allowed him to speak of his inner anxiety. He would have "torn in half" anybody who had even remotely hinted that the new Malek Adel was perhaps not the old one. He received congratulations on his "happy find" from the few persons he happened to meet; but he didn't solicit these congratulations: more than ever he avoided people—a bad sign! He put Malek Adel, if I may so express myself, through an almost continuous examination; he would ride off with him far away over the fields and set him a test; or else he would creep into the stable, lock the door behind him, and, standing right in front of the horse's head, would look him in the eyes and ask him in a whisper: "Are you Malek Adel? Are you? Are you? . . ." Or else he would gaze at him in silence, with a fixed stare, for whole hours at a time, now joyfully murmuring, "Yes! Yes! of course he is!" now perplexed and, indeed, troubled in his heart.

What troubled Chertopkhanov was not so much the physical dissimilarities between *this* Malek Adel and the *other* . . . of which, incidentally, there were a few: the *other's* tail and mane seemed to have been thinner, his ears sharper, his pasterns shorter and his eyes brighter—but this may have only seemed to be so; Chertopkhanov was troubled by what might be termed the moral dissimilarities. The *other's* habits were different, his bearing was not the same. For instance: the *other* Malek Adel used to look round and whinny gently every time, the moment Chertopkhanov entered the stable; but *this* one went on munching hay unconcernedly—or else drowsing with lowered head. Neither of them moved when their master was dismounting, but the *other* came at once when called—while *this* one went on standing like a stump. The *other* galloped at the same speed as this one, but jumped higher and farther; *this* one had a freer motion in walking, but a jerkier trot—and was sometimes "loose" with his hooves—that's to say, he knocked a back hoof on a fore one; the *other* had never shown such a fault—God forbid! *This* one, it seemed to Chertopkhanov, was always pricking his ears, in a stupid sort of way—quite the contrary to the *other*, who would cock one back and keep it there—watching his master! The *other* had only to see dirt around him and he would kick the walls of his box with his rear hoof; but *this* one never cared, you could have poured dung right up to his stomach. You had only to put the *other* one head to wind for him to be breathing at once with all his lungs and wide awake; but *this* one would simply whinny. The *other* was made uneasy by a rainy dampness in the air; *this* one didn't mind it at all. This one was coarser, coarser by far! And he had none of the other's charm and a mouth as hard as—but why go on! The other horse was a dear—but as for this one . . .

These were the thoughts that sometimes passed through Chertopkhanov's mind, and they had a bitter taste. But at other times he would let his horse out at full gallop over a newly-ploughed field, or make him jump down into the bottom of a hollow ravine and out again the steepest way. His heart would faint within him from delight, a loud whoop would burst from his lips and he would know, know for sure, that the horse under him was the real, the indubitable Malek Adel, for what other horse could have done the same?

Even so, however, there were frequent moments of pain and grief. Chertopkhanov's prolonged search for Malek Adel had cost him a lot of money; he no longer even thought of Kostroma hounds, and he rode about the neighborhood quite alone as before. Well, one morning, five versts away from Bessonovo, Chertopkhanov ran into the same princely hunting party, before which he had cut such a brilliant dash a year and a half before. It was fated to happen that way; as then, so again to-day—a hare jumping up from beneath a boundary fence under the hounds' noses and scuttling away across the slopes. After him, after him! The whole field went off at full tilt, and so did Chertopkhanov—only not with them, but two hundred yards to the side—exactly like the time before. An enormous ravine ran diagonally downhill and, getting deeper and narrower as it went, cut across Chertopkhanov's path. At the point where he would have to jump it, and where he had in fact jumped it a year and a half before, it was still eight yards across and fourteen feet deep. In anticipation of a triumph, so miraculously repeated, Chertopkhanov gave a victorious chuckle, shook his whip—the huntsmen were galloping too, but without taking their eyes off the daring rider—his horse was flying like an arrow, here was the ravine right under his nose—over it, like the time before! . . .

But Malek Adel jibbed suddenly, wheeled to the left, and galloped off *along* the brink, try as Chertopkhanov might to pull his head sideways towards the ravine . . .

He had refused, or, in other words, he had not been sure of himself!

Then Chertopkhanov, blazing with shame and anger, practically in tears, let out the reins and drove his horse straight ahead and uphill, away, away from the huntsmen, anywhere so as not to hear them mocking him, anywhere so as to escape as soon as possible from their accursed gaze!

With lacerated flanks, and all bathed in soapy foam, Malek Adel galloped home, and Chertopkhanov at once locked himself up in his room.

"No, he's not the same, he's not my friend! The other one would have broken his neck, but he would never have betrayed me!"

XI

What finished Chertopkhanov off for good was the following incident.

One day, mounted on Malek Adel, he was picking his way through the priest's back-yard, adjoining the church of the parish in which Bessonovo lay. With his fur hat rammed down over his eyes, slouching, with both hands dropped on the pommel of his saddle, he was moving slowly ahead; there was gloom and confusion in his heart. Suddenly someone called him.

He stopped his horse, raised his head, and saw his correspondent, the deacon. With a brown three-cornered hat on his brown, pigtailed head, dressed in a yellowish nankeen coat, girt well below the waist with a piece of blue stuff, this server at the altar had come out to inspect his plot of ground and, on catching sight of Pantelei

Eremeich, thought it his duty to pay him his respects—and incidentally to get something out of him. As is well known, the clergy
do not converse with secular people without some further purpose
of this kind.

But Chertopkhanov had no time for the deacon; he hardly acknowledged his bow, and, muttering something between his teeth,
was already waving his whip. . . .

"But what a wondrous horse you have!" the deacon hastened to
add. "It can indeed be accounted to you for honor. Verily, you are
a man of wondrous spirit; a very lion!" The father deacon prided
himself on his eloquence—and thus very much irritated the father
priest, in whom the gift of words was not inborn and whose tongue
even vodka failed to unloose. "Having lost one beast, through the
evil designs of the wicked," continued the deacon, "and no whit cast
down by this, but trusting all the more in Divine Providence, you
have taken unto yourself another, no whit worse than the former
one, and perchance even better. . . . Therefore . . ."

"What nonsense is this?" interrupted Chertopkhanov darkly.
"What other horse? This is the same one, this is Malek Adel . . . I
found him. Rambling talk like that . . ."

"Eh! eh! eh! eh!" said the deacon deliberately, as if wishing to
draw the words out, his fingers playing in his beard and his bright,
eager eyes watching Chertopkhanov. "How so, my good sir? Your
horse, if God grants me to remember aright, was stolen last year,
two weeks after the feast of the Intercession, and it is now the end
of November."

"Well, what of it?"

The deacon went on playing with his fingers in his beard. "It
means that more than a year has passed since then, and yet your
horse is now exactly as he was then, a gray roan; indeed he seems
even darker in color. How could that be? Gray horses turn much
whiter in the course of a year."

Chertopkhanov started . . . it was as if a spear had been thrust
into his heart. The deacon was right; of course a gray coat changes
color! How was it that such a simple fact had not occurred to him
until then?

"You bundle of blasphemy! Leave me alone!" he barked out, his eyes flashing with fury—and vanished in a twinkling out of the astonished deacon's sight.

So it was all finished!

Really finished, broken right up, the last card trumped! Everything had collapsed at once with the single word "whiter"!

Gray horses turn whiter.

Gallop, gallop, curse you!—but you will never be able to gallop away from that word!

Chertopkhanov rushed home and again locked himself up.

XII

That this wretched nag was not Malek Adel, that between him and Malek Adel there was not the slightest resemblance, that everyone with the slightest sense was bound to see as much at first glance, that he, Pantelei Chertopkhanov, had been most grossly taken in, no!—that he had deliberately, and with premeditation, deceived himself, wrapped himself in this fog—of all that there could not be the slightest doubt! Chertopkhanov paced up and down his room, turning on his heels in the same way every time he came to the wall, like a beast in a cage. His pride suffered unbearably; but it was not only the pain of wounded pride that rent him: despair ruled him, hatred stifled him, the thirst for revenge blazed in him. But on whom? On whom was he to revenge himself? The Jew, Yaff, Masha, the deacon, the Cossack-thief, all the neighbors, the whole world, or, finally, himself? His mind grew confused. His last card had been trumped! (He liked this figure of speech.) And he was again the most insignificant and despised of men, the most generally ridiculous, a tomfool, a blithering idiot, an object for the deacon's mirth! He imagined, he pictured clearly to himself, how that bundle of filth would tell the story of the gray horse and the stupid master. Oh, curse it all! . . . In vain Chertopkhanov strove to calm his raging bile, in vain he sought to assure himself that this . . . horse, even if not Malek Adel, was nevertheless . . . a good one, and could serve him for many years; simultaneously he would thrust this thought furiously from him, as if it contained a new cause of offense against the *other* Malek Adel, towards whom he already considered himself quite guilty enough . . . Yes, indeed! This jade, this nag, *he* had compared to Malek Adel, stone-blind oaf that he was! And as for the service which this nag could still give him . . . why, would he ever condescend to mount him? Not for anything in the world! Never. . . . Sell him to a Tartar, as food for dogs—that was all he deserved . . . Yes! That would be best of all!

For more than two hours Chertopkhanov wandered up and down his room.

"Perfishka!" he ordered suddenly. "Go at once to the pot-house, fetch a gallon of vodka! D'you hear? A gallon, and be quick about it! I want the vodka standing here on my table this very second."

The vodka was standing on Pantelei's table without delay, and he began to drink.

XIII

Anyone who had then observed Chertopkhanov, who could have witnessed the sullen fury with which he emptied glass after glass, would certainly have been horror-struck in spite of himself. Night had fallen; a greasy candle burned faintly on the table. Chertopkhanov had stopped pacing from corner to corner; he sat, all flushed, with glazed eyes which he would now lower to the floor, now turn fixedly towards the window; he would get up, pour out some vodka, drink it down, sit again, again fix his gaze on one spot, and remain stock-still—except that his breath came ever faster and his face grew ever more flushed. It seemed that within him some decision was ripening which troubled him, but to which he was gradually growing accustomed; the same thought came inexorably and incessantly nearer, the same image outlined itself more clearly before him, and in his heart, under the burning pressure of strong liquor, the irritation of wrath had already given way to a mood of brutal cruelty, and a sinister smile had appeared on his lips.

"Well, anyway, it's time to act!" he said, in a business-like, almost bored tone of voice. "Enough of this dallying!"

He drank down a final glass of vodka, brought out his pistol from under the bed—the same pistol with which he had fired at Masha—loaded it, put a few caps into his pocket "against emergencies"—and set off for the stable.

The watchman came running up to him as he began to open the door, but he shouted at him: "It's me, can't you see? Be off with you!" The watchman withdrew a little way. "Be off to bed!" Chertopkhanov shouted at him again. "There's nothing for you to guard here! This wonder horse, this treasure!" He went into the stable . . . Malek Adel, the false Malek Adel, was lying among the litter. Chertopkhanov kicked him and said: "Get up, you crow!" Then he undid the halter from the manger, took off the blanket and threw it on the ground, and, roughly turning the obedient horse round in the stall, led him out into the yard and from the yard into the fields, to the utter amazement of the watchman, who was quite unable to understand where the master could be off to in the middle of the night leading an unbridled horse. He was naturally too much afraid to ask, but simply followed him with his eyes until he vanished round a turning of the track leading to the nearby forest.

XIV

Chertopkhanov walked with long strides, never halting and never looking back; Malek Adel—for so we will call him until the end—walked submissively after him. The night was fairly light; Chertopkhanov could distinguish the jagged outline of the forest, forming a solid black mass ahead of him. At the touch of the cool night air he would certainly have got drunk from the vodka, if . . . if it had not been for another, stronger intoxication which mastered his whole being. His head grew heavy, the blood drummed in his throat and ears; but he stepped out firmly and knew where he was going.

He had resolved to kill Malek Adel. He had thought of nothing else the whole day . . . Now he was resolved!

He went about his business, not exactly calmly, but confidently, without turning back, like a man obeying a sense of duty. It

seemed to him a very simple affair: by doing away with the impostor, he would get even with "them all," punish himself for his folly,
put himself right with his real friend, and show the whole world
(Chertopkhanov thought a great deal about "the whole world")
that he was not a man to be trifled with . . . But the main thing
was that he would do away with himself along with the impostor,
for what was there left to live for? How all this fell into place inside
his head, and why it seemed to him so simple, would be difficult
to explain, though not altogether impossible. Injured, lonely, without a human soul for friend, without a brass farthing, and also
with his blood on fire from drink, he was in a condition bordering
on madness; and there is no doubt that the most absurd actions of
the insane have, in their own eyes, a special kind of logic and
rightness. Anyhow Chertopkhanov was fully convinced of his own
rightness; he never faltered, he was in a hurry to carry out his sentence on the guilty one, without, however, clearly explaining to
himself exactly whom he meant by this term . . . The truth was that
he had not thought out what it was that he intended to do. "I must
get it over, I must," he assured himself dully and grimly: "I must get
it over!"

Meanwhile the innocent culprit jogged and ambled submissively
behind his back . . . In Chertopkhanov's heart, however, there was
no pity.

XV

Not far from the edge of the forest to which he had led his horse,
ran a small ravine, half overgrown with oak bushes. Chertopkhanov
went down into it . . . Malek Adel stumbled and nearly fell on top
of him.

"Do you want to crush me, curse you?" shouted Chertopkhanov—
and, as if in self-defense, he snatched the pistol from his pocket. He
no longer felt any bitterness, but only the special feeling of wood-
enness that is supposed to come over a man who is about to commit
some terrible crime. His own voice frightened him—so wild was its
ring under the dark canopy of the branches, in the damp, rotten-

smelling fustiness of the ravine in the forest! And then, in answer to his exclamation, some great bird suddenly began flapping about on the tree-top above his head. Chertopkhanov started. It was as if he had woken up a witness to his deed—even in this dead place, where he should not have come upon a single living thing . . .

"Be off, you devil—away with you, to all the points of the compass!" he said between his teeth—and, letting go of Malek Adel's halter, struck him a swinging blow on the shoulder with the butt of his pistol. Malek Adel immediately turned back, scrambled out of the ravine . . . and fled. The sound of his hooves soon died away. A wind had arisen, which choked and hid every sound.

In his turn Chertopkhanov slowly made his way out of the ravine, reached the edge of the forest and trudged off on the road home. He was dissatisfied with himself; the heaviness which he had felt in his head and heart spread through all his limbs; he walked on, angry, morose, discontented, hungry, as if someone had injured him, robbed him of a prize, or of bread itself . . .

His feelings were those of a suicide who has been prevented from carrying out his design.

Suddenly something touched him behind, between the shoulder blades. He looked round . . . Malek Adel was standing in the middle of the road. He had followed his master, had touched him with his muzzle . . . had reported his presence.

"Ah!" cried Chertopkhanov, "you've come of your own accord, to meet your death! Very well, then!"

In the twinkling of an eye he had snatched out his pistol, cocked it, put the muzzle against Malek Adel's forehead, and fired.

The poor horse shied to one side, reared up, jumped back about ten paces and suddenly crashed heavily down, wheezed, and rolled convulsively on the ground.

Chertopkhanov stopped his ears with his hands and ran off. His knees faltered beneath him. Drunkenness, anger, grim self-confidence—all had vanished in a flash. He was left with nothing but a feeling of shame and ugliness—and the consciousness, sure beyond a doubt, that this time he had made away with himself as well.

XVI

Six weeks later, the boy Perfishka thought it his duty to stop the inspector of police as he drove past Bessonovo.

"What's the matter?" asked the guardian of the law.

"Please, your honor, come in," answered the boy with a low bow; "Pantelei Eremeich seems in a fair way to die; that's what I fear."

"What? Die?" the inspector repeated after him.

"Just so, sir. First of all he'd be taking vodka every day, and now he's gone to bed and got very, very thin. I think that now he doesn't understand anything any more. He's quite lost his tongue."

The inspector got out of his cart. "Well, I suppose that at any rate you have been and fetched the priest? Has your master confessed? Has he taken communion?"

"No, sir."

The inspector frowned. "But how is that, my friend? Is it possible—eh? Don't you know that for this . . . there's a heavy responsibility—eh?"

"But I asked the master the day before yesterday, and yesterday as well," protested the intimidated boy, "wouldn't he like me to go for a priest? 'Silence, you fool,' he says, 'mind your own business.' But to-day when I reported to him—he just looked at me and twitched his moustache."

"Did he drink a lot of vodka?" asked the inspector.

"A terrific lot! But please, your honor, come and see him in his room."

"Well, lead the way!" grunted the inspector and followed Perfishka.

A strange spectacle awaited him.

In the back room, which was dank and dark, on a miserable bed which was covered with a horse blanket, with a shaggy felt cloak for pillow, lay Chertopkhanov, no longer pale, but yellowish green, the color of a corpse, his eyes sunk under eyelids with a sheen on them, his nose grown sharper, but still red, above his dishevelled moustache. He lay dressed in his perpetual tunic with the cartridge-pleats round the chest and his blue Circassian trousers. The fur cap with the raspberry-colored crown covered his forehead right down to the eyebrows. In one hand Chertopkhanov held a hunting whip, in the other an embroidered red tobacco-pouch—Masha's last present to him. On the table beside the bed stood an empty decanter; over the head of the bed, fastened to the wall with pins, hung two water-colors: one, so far as it could be made out, represented a fat man with a guitar in his hands, probably Nedopyuskin; the other depicted a galloping horseman . . . The horse was like those galloping animals which children draw on walls and fences; but its carefully shaded roan markings, and the cartridges round the horseman's chest, the sharp points of his boots and his enormous moustache, left no room for doubt: the picture was meant to represent Pantelei Eremeich mounted on Malek Adel.

The puzzled inspector didn't know what to do next. Deathly silence reigned in the room. He must be dead already, he thought and, raising his voice, said: "Pantelei Eremeich! I say, Pantelei Eremeich!"

Then something extraordinary happened. Chertopkhanov's eyes slowly opened, his dim pupils moved first from right to left, then from left to right, stopped at the visitor, saw him . . . something kindled in their dim whiteness, a semblance of vision appeared in them . . . the blue lips gradually parted, and from them came a husky voice, already the voice of the grave:

"Pantelei Chertopkhanov, nobleman of ancient lineage, is dying; who can prevent him?—He owes nothing, he wants nothing . . . Leave him alone! Go!"

The hand with the whip tried to raise itself . . . in vain! The lips stuck together again, the eyes closed!—and Chertopkhanov lay as before on his hard bed, stretched out flat as a layer of bricks, the soles of his feet pressed close together.

"Let me know when he dies," whispered the inspector to Perfishka as he left the room; "and I think you could still go for the priest. Things must be done properly, he must have the last rites."

The same day Perfishka went for the priest, and the next morning it was his duty to report to the inspector that Pantelei Eremeich had died during the night.

When they buried him, his coffin was followed by two people: the boy Perfishka and Moshel Leiba. The news of Chertopkhanov's death had somehow or other reached the Jew—and he did not fail to pay the last tribute to his benefactor.

The Live Relic

Motherland of long-suffering—
Land of the Russian people!

F. TYUTCHEV

THE FRENCH PROVERB HAS IT THAT A DRY FISHERMAN AND A
wet hunter make a sorry sight. Never having been addicted to fishing, I am no judge of a fisherman's feelings in fine clear weather
and of the extent to which, in a downpour, the satisfaction afforded
him by a good catch offsets the unpleasantness of getting wet. But,
for the hunter, rain is a real disaster. A disaster of this kind befell
Ermolai and myself on one of our excursions after blackcock in the
district of Belevo. From daybreak the rain had not stopped. We had
done everything possible to escape it. We had put rubber capes practically over our heads, we had stood under trees to avoid the drops.
Our waterproof capes, besides hindering us from shooting, had let
the water through in the most shameless manner; and, as for the
trees—true, at first there seemed to be no drops, but then the water accumulated in the leaves suddenly burst through; every branch
poured down on us like a rain-pipe, a cold stream found its way under the cravat and ran down the spinal column . . . That was the last
straw, as Ermolai put it. "No, Pyotr Petrovich," he exclaimed at last,
"we can't go on like this! . . . We can't shoot to-day. The dogs' noses
are washed-out, the guns are misfiring . . . Phew! It's too much!"

"What shall we do?" I asked.

"I'll tell you what. We'll go to Alexeyevka. You may not know it—it's a little farm, belonging to your mother; eight versts from here. We'll spend the night there, and to-morrow . . ."

"We'll come back here?"

"No, not here . . . I know some places beyond Alexeyevka much better than here for blackcock."

I did not think fit to inquire of my trusty companion why he had not conducted me straight to these places, and the same day we reached my mother's farm, the existence of which I confess I had not suspected until then. Beside the farm we found a little pavilion, very decrepit, but uninhabited and therefore clean; in it I passed a fairly peaceful night.

The next day I woke up very early. The sun had just risen; there was not a cloud in the sky; the whole scene sparkled brightly with a double brilliance: the brilliance of the early morning rays, and of the previous day's downpour.

While my dog-cart was being harnessed, I went for a stroll in a small garden, once an orchard, now run wild, which surrounded the pavilion on all sides with its lush, scented growth. Oh, how good it was in the open air, under the clear sky, in which larks were trilling, and from which their sweet voices fell in silver beads! They had certainly carried off dewdrops on their wings, and their songs seemed drenched in dew. I took off my cap and joyously breathed in with all my lungs . . . On the slope of a shallow ravine, beside a fence, I saw a bee-garden; a narrow path led towards it, winding like a snake between unbroken walls of weed and nettle, above which towered, planted heaven knows how, the pointed stalks of dark-green hemp.

I went along the path, and came to the bee-garden. Beside it stood a little wattle shed, the place where the hives were put in winter. I looked in through the half-open door: it was dark, quite dry; there was a smell of mint and balm. In a corner there was an arrangement of trestles and on them, covered in a blanket, a sort of small figure . . . I was going away . . .

"Master, I say, master! Pyotr Petrovich!" came a voice, weak, slow and husky, like the rustling of sedge in a marsh.

I stopped.

"Pyotr Petrovich! Come closer, please!" repeated the voice. It issued from the corner where I had noticed the trestles.

I came closer—and stood stock-still from amazement. Before me lay a live human being, but what on earth . . . ?

A head completely dried up, all one color, the color of bronze, nothing more nor less than an ancient icon; a nose as thin as the blade of a knife; lips almost invisible—only the pale glimmer of teeth and eyes, and, winding out from under a handkerchief on the brow, a few thin strands of yellow hair. Beside the chin, on the fold of the blanket, slowly twisting their twig-like fingers, moved two tiny hands of the same bronze color. I looked closer: the face was far from ugly, it was beautiful even—but strange and frightening. And all the more frightening because on it, on its metallic cheeks, I could see—forcing . . . forcing its way, but unable to spread across—a smile.

"Don't you know me, master?" whispered the voice again; it seemed an exhalation from the hardly moving lips. "But how could you know me!—I'm Lukerya . . . D'you remember, I used to lead the country dances, at your mother's, at Spasskoye . . . d'you remember, I used to lead the singing, too?"

"Lukerya!" I exclaimed. "Is it you? Is it possible?"

"Yes, master, it is. I'm Lukerya."

I didn't know what to say, and gazed as if dumbfounded at that dark, motionless face, with its bright, deathlike eyes fixed upon me! Was it possible? This mummy—Lukerya, the greatest beauty of all our household—tall, plump, pink, and white—full of laughter and dancing and song! Lukerya, clever Lukerya, who was courted by all our young swains, for whom I too had sighed in secret, I—a lad of sixteen years!

"For goodness' sake, Lukerya," I said at last, "what's happened to you?"

"Oh, I've had terrible trouble! But you mustn't be put off, master, you mustn't look down on me for my bad luck—sit down over there on the cask—nearer, or you won't be able to hear me . . . you see what a fine voice I've got! . . . Well, I *am* glad to see you! How did you come to turn up at Alexeyevka like this?"

Lukerya spoke very quietly and faintly, but without faltering.

"Ermolai, the hunter, brought me here. But tell me . . ."

"Tell you about my trouble?—Very well, master. It happened some time ago now, six or seven years back. I had just been betrothed to Vasily Polyakov—d'you remember him, a fine-looking chap, with curly hair—he was serving as butler at your mother's? You had left the country by then and gone to Moscow to study. Vasily and I loved each other very much; he was never out of my thoughts. It was in the spring. Well, one night . . . It was not long before dawn . . . and I couldn't sleep: a nightingale in the garden was singing so wonderfully sweet! . . . I couldn't stay still, I got up and went out to the porch to listen to him. He went flowing, flowing on . . . and suddenly it seemed to me that someone with Vasily's voice was calling me, quietly-like: 'Lusha!' I looked round, half-asleep, you know—slipped, fell right off the floor of the porch, and went flying down, thump, on the ground! And it didn't seem as though I'd hurt myself badly, because I got up at once and went back to my room. Only it felt as if inside me—in my belly—something had torn . . . Let me get my breath . . . just a minute, master."

Lukerya paused and I looked at her in bewilderment. What bewildered me particularly was that she told her story almost gaily, without groans or sighs, never complaining or asking for sympathy.

"From then on," continued Lukerya, "I started fading and withering away; a blackness came over me, it got hard for me to walk, and then—I couldn't even use my legs; neither stand nor sit: I'd just lie the whole time. And I didn't want to eat or drink; I got thinner and thinner. From the kindness of her heart your mother showed me to the doctors and sent me to hospital. But I got no relief from it. Not a single doctor could even say what my illness was. They did everything they could think of to me: they burned my back with red-hot iron, they sat me down in broken ice—all no good. At length I grew all stiff, like a board . . . So the mistress decided that there was nothing more to be done to cure me, and as it isn't possible to keep a cripple in the manor house . . . well, they sent me over here—because here I have relations. And here I live, as you see."

Lukerya paused again and again, made an effort to smile.

"But it's a terrible plight to be in!" I exclaimed . . . and, not knowing what to add, I asked: "And what about Vasily Polyakov?"

It was a very stupid question.

Lukerya turned her eyes away.

"What about Polyakov? He moped and moped, and married someone else—a girl from Glinnoye. D'you know Glinnoye? Not far from us. Her name was Agrafena. He loved me very much . . . but he was young, you see . . . there was no reason why he should stay a bachelor. And what sort of a sweetheart could I be to him now? He found himself a good wife . . . they've got children. He lives on a neighboring estate, in the agent's office; your mother let him go with a passport, and, praise be to God, he's very happy."

"And so you just lie and lie?" I asked again.

"Yes, master, I have lain like this for more than six years. In summer I lie here in this wattle hut, but when it gets cold they'll move me inside the bath-house. And there I lie."

"But who looks after you? Who keeps an eye on you?"

"Oh, there are good folk here, too. They don't leave me to myself. And I don't take much looking after. As for food, I don't eat anything, and as for water—here it is in the mug: there's a supply of clear spring water always standing there. I can reach the mug myself: one of my hands still works. There's a girl here, an orphan; now and again she looks in on me, bless her. She was here just now . . . didn't you meet her? Pretty, she is, and fair-skinned. She brings me flowers; I'm very fond of them, of flowers. There are no garden flowers here . . . there were, but they've died out. But wild flowers are good, too, they smell even better than garden ones. Take the lily of the valley . . . What could be sweeter?"

"Aren't you bored, aren't you restless, my poor Lukerya?"

"What can I do? I don't want to lie to you—it was very sad at first; but then I got used to it, I grew patient—I came not to mind; there are some people who are even worse off."

"In what way?"

"Some people haven't even anywhere to go! And some are blind or deaf! But I, praise be to God, I can see beautifully and I can hear everything, everything. If a mole burrows underground—even so,

I hear him. And I can smell every smell, even the faintest there are! If buckwheat blossoms in the field, or lime in the garden—you needn't tell me: I'm always the first to know. So long as only a breath of wind comes from there. No, why anger God?—there are many worse off than I. For example, someone who's well can sin very easily; but even sin itself has left me. The other day Father Alexei, the priest, came to give me communion, and said: 'I need not confess you: how can you sin in your condition?' And I answered him: 'But what about sin in thought, Father?' 'Well,' he says and laughs, 'that's not a big sin.' And even in this sin of thought I couldn't be much of a sinner," continued Lukerya, "because I've taught myself not to think and, more important still, not to remember. Time passes quicker like that."

I was, I confess, surprised. "You're quite alone all the time, Lukerya; then how can you prevent thoughts coming into your head? Or do you sleep all the time?"

"Oh, no, master! I can't always sleep. Although I have no big pains, it nags me here, inside me, and in my bones, too; it doesn't let me sleep as I ought to. No . . . I just lie by myself, I lie and lie—and I don't think; I feel that I'm alive and breathing—and that all of me is here. I look and I listen. The bees in the garden will buzz and bumble away; the pigeon will sit on the roof and start cooing; the mother-hen will look in with her chickens to pick up the crumbs; or else a sparrow will fly in, or a butterfly—I enjoy it so much. The year before last some swallows even built a nest over there in the corner and hatched a family. How funny it was! One of them would fly in, drop into the nest, feed the chicks—and away. You'd look again, and the other would already be there inside. Sometimes they wouldn't fly in, but just swoop past the open door. And at once the chicks—how they'd squeak and open their beaks! . . . I thought they'd come the next year, too, but they say that some sportsman hereabouts shot them with his gun. What good can it have done him? A whole swallow is no bigger than a beetle. How cruel you are, you sporting gentlemen!"

"I don't shoot swallows," I hastened to observe.

"Then, once," began Lukerya again, "I had a great joke! A hare ran in, really he did! The hounds were after him, but he came lolloping straight in at the door! . . . He sat right close to me—sat for quite a while—kept moving his nose and twitching his whiskers—a regular officer! And how he looked at me. He must have understood that he'd nothing to fear from me. At last he got up, hop-hop to the door, looked round from the threshold—what a one he was! Such a funny one!"

Lukerya looked up at me . . . as if to say, isn't it amusing? To please her, I laughed. She bit her dried-up lips.

"Well, in winter, of course, I'm worse off, because it's dark; it would be a pity to light a candle, and what for? Although I know my letters and was always fond of reading, what is there to read? There are no books here at all, and, even if there were, how am I going to hold one? Father Alexei brought me a calendar to occupy my mind; then he saw that it was no good, and he went and took it away again. But even when it's dark, there's always something to hear; a cricket chirrups, or somewhere a mouse starts scratching. Then, too, the best plan is not to think!

"Or else I say prayers," continued Lukerya after a short rest. "Only I don't know many of them, these prayers. And why should I go and bother the Lord God? What can I ask Him for? He knows better than I do what I need. He has sent me a cross—it means He must love me. That's how we are told to understand it. I say 'Our Father' and 'Mother of God' and the prayer for all that suffer—and then I just go on lying again without a thought in my head. And I don't mind!"

Two minutes passed. I didn't break the silence and didn't stir on the narrow little cask which served me for a seat. The cruel, stony immobility of the unfortunate living creature lying before me communicated itself to me, too: I, too, was as if benumbed.

"Listen, Lukerya," I began at length. "Listen, I'm going to suggest something to you. Would you like me to arrange for them to take you to hospital, a good hospital in town? Who knows, perhaps they could still cure you? In any case you won't be alone . . ."

Lukerya just moved her eyebrows. "Oh, no, master," she said in a worried whisper, "don't move me to hospital, don't touch me.

I'll only get more suffering out of it. What's the use of treating me now! . . . Why, once a doctor came here: he wanted to look at me. I said to him: 'Don't bother me, for the Lord Christ's sake.' What was the good of asking him! He started turning me over, moved my arms and legs, bent them about; he said: 'I'm doing this for science's sake; you see, I'm in the service of science! and you,' he said, 'can't resist me, because for my troubles I've had an Order given me, and I try my best for fools like you.' He pulled me about, and pulled me about, he told me the name of my illness—a learned sort of name— and with that he went away. And for a whole week afterwards all my bones ached. You say I'm alone, always alone. No, not always. I get visitors. I'm quiet—not in anyone's way. Peasant-girls will come to me and gossip: a pilgrim-woman will look in and start telling of Jerusalem and Kiev and the holy cities. And it's not as if I was frightened to be alone. I'm even better off, I promise you . . . Master, don't touch me, don't take me to hospital . . . Thank you, you're kind, but don't touch me, my dear."

"Well, as you like, Lukerya. I just thought that, for your own good . . ."

"I know, master, that it was for my own good, but, master, dear master, who can help anyone else? Who can get inside someone else's soul? Let everyone help himself! You won't believe me—but sometimes I lie alone like this . . . and it's as if there was no one in the whole world but me. I'm the only one alive! And it seems to me, it sort of dawns on me . . . ideas come to me—and such strange ones!"

"What are they about, Lukerya, these ideas of yours?"

"That, master, I can't tell you either: you'd never make it out. And I forget them afterwards. It will come, like a little cloud, it will burst, it will be all fresh and good, but what it was—you'll never understand! Only it seems to me that if there were people near me, none of this would happen, and I'd feel nothing except my own unhappiness."

Lukerya sighed painfully. Her chest was doing its work no better than the rest of her body.

"I can see by looking at you, master," she began again, "that you feel very sorry for me. But don't feel too sorry, don't indeed! Listen, I'll tell you something: even now, sometimes, I . . . well, you remember how gay I used to be in my time? Such a lively one! . . . Well, do you know what? Even now I sing songs."

"Songs? . . . You?"

"Yes, songs, old songs, round songs, carols, songs of all sorts! You see, I used to know many of them and I've not forgotten. Only I don't sing dance songs. As I am now, there wouldn't be any point."

"So you sing them . . . to yourself?"

"To myself, and aloud. I can't sing loudly, but loud enough to understand. I told you about the girl who comes to see me. An orphan, so she's an understanding sort. Well, I've taught her; she's already caught four songs from me. Don't you believe it? Wait, now I'm going to . . ."

Lukerya collected her strength . . . The thought that this half-dead creature was getting ready to sing horrified me in spite of myself. But, before I could say a word, there trembled in my ears a drawn-out, scarcely audible, but pure and true note . . . and after it followed another, then another. Lukerya was singing *"In the meadows."* She sang with no play of expression on her petrified face; even her eyes were fixed. But so touchingly did her poor, forced little voice sound, wavering like a wisp of smoke; so hard did she strive to pour out her whole soul . . . It was no longer horror that I felt: an indescribable pity gripped my heart.

"Oh, I can't!" she said suddenly. "I haven't the strength . . . I've been so pleased to see you."

She closed her eyes.

I put my hand on her tiny, cold fingers . . . She looked up at me—and her dark eyelids, trimmed with golden lashes, like those of an ancient statue, closed again. After a moment they glittered in the twilight . . . A tear had moistened them.

I sat there motionless as before.

"Just look at me!" said Lukerya suddenly, with unexpected force and, opening her eyes wide, tried to wipe the tears from them. "Oughtn't I to be ashamed? What do I want? This hasn't happened to me for a long time . . . not since the day when Vasily Polyakov was here last spring. As long as he was sitting talking to me—I didn't mind—but when he went away—I fairly cried away to myself! Where did it all come from? . . . But tears cost nothing to girls like us. Master," added Lukerya, "I expect you've got a handkerchief . . . Don't be put off, wipe my eyes."

I hastened to carry out her wish, and left her the handkerchief. At first she refused it . . . "What do I want with such a present?" she said. The handkerchief was very plain, but clean and white. Then she seized it in her weak fingers and did not loosen them again. I had grown used to the darkness in which we both were, and could make out her features clearly, could even discern a faint ruddiness, showing through the bronze of her face, could descry in that face, or so at least I thought, the traces of her former beauty.

"You asked me, master," began Lukerya again, "if I sleep. I certainly don't sleep much, but every time, I dream—good dreams! I never dream about myself as ill: I'm always well and young, in my dreams . . . The only pity is that I wake up—and I want to have a good stretch—but it's as if I was all in chains. Once I had such a marvellous dream! Would you like me to tell you? Well, listen. I was standing in a field and all round was rye, so tall, and ripe like gold! . . . And with me there was a red dog, fierce, very fierce—trying all the time to bite me. And in my hands I had a sickle, not just an ordinary sickle, but absolutely like the moon, when it's like a sickle. And with this moon I had to cut down the rye, every stalk of it. Only I was very tired from the heat, and the moon dazzled me, and laziness came over me; and around me cornflowers were growing, such big ones! and they all had their heads turned towards me, and I thought: I'll pick these cornflowers, Vasya promised to come—so I'll make a garland for myself first . . . I've still got time for reaping. I began to pick the cornflowers, but they melted between my fingers, and melted, and there was nothing I could do! So I couldn't make my garland. But then I heard someone coming towards me, quite near, and calling: 'Lusha! . . . Lusha! . . .' Oh, I thought, what a shame—I haven't finished! Never mind, I'll put this moon on my head instead of the cornflowers. I put on the moon, just like a head-dress, and at once I seemed to be all aglow.

I lit up the whole field around. I looked, and over the very tops of the ears of rye comes sweeping quickly towards me, not Vasya, but Christ himself! And how I knew that it was Christ, I can't say—He was not as He is in pictures—yet it was Him! Beardless, tall, young and in white, but with a golden belt—and He stretches out His hand to me. 'Never fear,' He says, 'my well-adorned bride, but follow Me; you will lead the dances in My Heavenly Kingdom and play the music of Paradise.' And how I clung to His hand!—my dog at once went for my legs . . . But away we whirled! He was ahead . . . His wings spread out over all the sky, long, like a seagull's—and I went after Him! And the dog had to stay behind. It was only then that I understood that this dog was my illness, and that there would be no place for it in the Kingdom of Heaven."

Lukerya was silent for a minute.

"And then I had another dream," she began again—"or perhaps this one was a vision . . . I don't know. It seemed to me that I was alone in this cabin and that my dead parents came to me—my father and mother—and bowed low to me, but said nothing. And I asked them: 'Why are you bowing to me, father and mother?' 'Why,' they said, 'because you're suffering so much in this world that you've not only lightened your own soul's burden, but you've taken a heavy weight off us as well, and it's got much easier for us in the other world. You've already finished with your own sins; now you're overcoming ours.' And, so saying, my parents bowed to me again—and I could see them no longer: the walls were all I could see. I wondered very much afterwards what it was that had come over me. I even told the priest in confession. But he thinks that it couldn't have been a vision, because visions come only to those of the priestly calling.

"Then I had another dream," Lukerya went on. "I was sitting by a high-road, under a willow tree, holding a peeled stick, with a bundle on my shoulder and my head wrapped in a kerchief—a regular pilgrim-woman! And I had to go somewhere far, far away, on a pilgrimage. And pilgrims kept on going past me; quietly they'd go, as if against their will, always the same way: they had sad faces, all very much like one another. And I saw, winding her way amongst them, a woman a head taller than the others, wearing a strange dress, not like ours in Russia. And her face was strange, too, a stern, fasting sort of face, and all the others seemed to keep away from her; and suddenly she turned—and came straight for me. She stopped and looked at me; her eyes were like a falcon's, yellow, big, and oh, so bright. And I asked her: 'Who are you?' and she said to me: 'I am your death.' I ought to have been afraid, but on the contrary I was glad, so glad, I crossed myself! And this woman, my death, said to me: 'I'm sorry for you, Lukerya, but I can't take you with me.— Good-bye!' Lord! how sad I was then! . . . 'Take me,' I said, 'mother, dearest one, take me!' And my death turned around me, began to talk to me . . . I understood that she was telling me my hour, but darkly, as if in riddles . . . 'After St. Peter's,' she said . . . With that I woke up . . . That's the sort of strange dreams I have!"

Lukerya looked up . . . reflected . . .

"Only my trouble is this: it happens that a whole week goes by and I don't go to sleep once. Last year a lady drove by, saw me, and gave me a bottle with some medicine against sleeplessness; she told me to take ten drops at a time. It helped me a great deal and I slept. Only now the bottle has been finished long ago . . . D'you know what medicine that was, and how to get it?"

The passing lady had clearly given Lukerya opium. I promised to get her just such a bottle, and again could not refrain from admiring her patience aloud.

"Eh, master!" she rejoined. "What are you saying? What is this patience of mine? Simeon on the Pillar really did have great patience: he stood on his pillar for thirty years! And another martyr ordered himself to be buried in the ground up to his chest and the ants ate his face. And once, someone who had read many books told me that there was a certain country, and this country had been conquered by the heathen, and they tortured or put to death all the people in it; and try as the people of the country might, they couldn't free themselves. And then there appeared among those people a saintly virgin: she took a great sword, she put on herself clothes weighing seventy pounds, went out against the heathen, and drove them all out beyond the sea. And only after she had driven them out, she said to them: 'Now burn me, because such was my promise, to die by fire for my people.' And the heathen took her and burned her, and her people have been free ever since! There was a great deed for you! and what have I done?"

I marvelled to myself at this far-flung version of the Joan of Arc legend, and, after a pause, I asked Lukerya how old she was.

"Twenty-eight . . . or twenty-nine . . . less than thirty. But why count them, the years? I'll tell you something more . . ."

Lukerya suddenly coughed dully and groaned.

"You're talking a great deal," I remarked to her. "It can do you harm."

"True," she whispered, in a hardly audible voice, "it's the end of our talk, but no matter. Now, when you go away, I shall have all the silence I want. At least, I have got a lot off my mind . . ."

I started saying good-bye to her, repeated my promise to send her the medicine, and asked her to think carefully once more and tell me whether there was nothing she needed.

"I need nothing; I'm absolutely content, praise be to God," she pronounced, with extreme effort, but also with emotion. "May God grant health to everyone! And you, master, please speak to your mother—the peasants here are poor—if she would only bring down their rent, just a little! They haven't enough land, they make nothing out of it! . . . They would pray to God for you . . . but I need nothing, I'm absolutely content."

I gave Lukerya my word to carry out her request, and was already making for the door when she called me back.

"D'you remember, master," she said, with a wonderful brightening of her eyes and lips, "what hair I had? D'you remember—right down to my knees! For a long time I couldn't make up my mind . . . Such hair it was! . . . But how could I comb it! In my condition! So I cut it off . . . yes . . . Well, good-bye, master! I can't say more . . ."

The same day, before setting out to shoot, I had a talk about Lukerya with the local constable. I learned from him that in the village she was called "the Live Relic," also that she caused no trouble; there was not a grumble to be heard from her, not a complaint. "She asks nothing for herself, on the contrary she's grateful for everything; she's as quiet as quiet can be, that I must say. She's been smitten by God," so the constable concluded, "for her sins, no doubt; but we don't go into that. As for condemning her, for example, no, we certainly don't condemn her. Let her be!"

A FEW WEEKS LATER I heard that Lukerya was dead. Death had come for her after all . . . and "after St. Peter's." The story went that on the day of her death she kept hearing the sound of bells, although it is more than five versts from Alexeyevka to the church, and it was on a weekday. Besides, Lukerya said that the sound came, not from church, but "from above." Probably she did not venture to say—from Heaven.

The Knocking

"I'VE GOT SOMETHING TO TELL YOU," SAID ERMOLAI, COMING into the cabin where I was. I had just had dinner and lain down on a camp-bed to rest myself after a fairly successful and exhausting day shooting blackcock. It was in the middle of July and the heat was terrible. "I've got something to tell you: all our shot's finished."

I jumped up from the bed.

"Our shot finished! How on earth? Why, we must have taken thirty pounds from home! A whole bagful."

"Certainly; and a big bag, too: it ought to have been enough for two weeks. But who knows? Perhaps there was a slit in it; anyhow there isn't any shot . . . just about enough for ten charges."

"Whatever are we going to do? The best places are ahead of us. They promised us six coveys for to-morrow."

"Send me into Tula. It's no distance—only forty-five versts. I'll fly like the wind and bring back the shot—forty pounds of it, if you like."

"But when will you go?"

"I'll go at once. Why waste time? Only there's one thing about it: we shall have to hire horses."

"Hire horses! What are our own for?"

"We can't use our own. The shaft-horse is lame, dead lame."

"Since when?"

"Since just lately—when the coachman took him to be shod. Well, they shod him. The smith must have been no good. Now he can't even walk on the hoof—the fore-hoof . . . So he carries it . . . like a dog."

"Well, at least he's been unshod?"

"No, he hasn't, but he'll have to be unshod at once. The nail must have gone right into the flesh."

I sent for the coachman. It appeared that Ermolai had spoken the truth: the shaft-horse was indeed lame in one hoof. I at once gave orders for him to be unshod and stood on wet clay.

"Well? Shall I hire horses and go to Tula?" insisted Ermolai again.

"But can you so much as find horses in this miserable hole?" I exclaimed, annoyed in spite of myself. . . .

The village in which we found ourselves was solitary and out of the way; all its inhabitants seemed to be desperately poor; with difficulty we had found a single cabin that had no chimney, certainly, but was quite roomy.

"Yes," answered Ermolai, imperturbable as ever. "You're right about this village, but even here there lived a peasant—very clever . . . and rich! He had nine horses. He's dead now, and his eldest son manages it all. He's the stupidest man that ever lived, but he hasn't yet managed to run through his father's fortune. We'll get horses from him. If you wish it, I'll fetch him. He's got brothers—bright lads, so I've heard . . . but all the same he's the head of the family."

"How is that?"

"Because he is the eldest! That means, the younger ones have got to knuckle under."—Here Ermolai expressed himself forcibly and unprintably about younger brothers in general.—"I'll fetch him. He's a simple chap. It won't be difficult to come to terms with him."

While Ermolai went to fetch the "simple chap," it occurred to me that it might be better for me to drive into Tula myself. In the first place, taught by experience, I knew I couldn't rely on Ermolai. I had once sent him into a town to make some purchases; he had promised to carry out all my commissions during a single day—and vanished for a whole week, spent all the money on drink, and returned on foot—having set out in a racing drozhky. Secondly, I had an acquaintance in Tula who was a horse-dealer; I could buy a horse from him to replace my lame shaft-horse.

That's decided, I thought. I'll drive in myself; I can sleep on the way, too—luckily my carriage is well-sprung.

"I've brought him!" exclaimed Ermolai a quarter of an hour later, bursting into the cabin. Behind him entered a sturdy peasant, in a white shirt, blue trousers, and shoes, fair-haired, short-sighted, with a little pointed red beard, a long, swollen nose, and a wide-open mouth.

He certainly looked a "simple chap."

"Here, sir," said Ermolai, "he has got horses and it's all settled."

"That is, that's to say, I . . ." began the peasant in a husky, stammering voice, shaking his sparse hair and fingering the band of the cap which he held in his hands. "I, that's to say . . ."

"What's your name?" I asked.

The peasant looked down and seemed to reflect. "What is my name?"

"Yes; what do they call you?"

"They call me Filofei."

"Well, listen, Filofei, my friend; you have got horses, I hear. Bring three of them here; we'll harness them to my carriage—it's quite a light one—and then you drive me into Tula. There's a moon to-night, it's light, and it will be cool driving. What sort of road have you got here?"

"Road? the road's all right! It's twenty versts at most—to the highway. There's one place . . . a bit awkward, but all right."

"What's the place that's awkward?"

"You have to cross a river by a ford."

"So you're going into Tula yourself?" inquired Ermolai.

"Yes, I am."

"Well!" said my faithful attendant, and shook his head. "We-ell!" he repeated, spat, and went out.

The drive to Tula evidently held no more attraction for him; in his eyes it had become an empty and uninteresting business.

"D'you know the way all right?" I said to Filofei.

"Of course I know the way! Only, I mean, of course, you're the master, but I can't . . . all of a sudden, like this."

It turned out that Ermolai, in engaging Filofei, had declared that he need have no doubt of being paid, fool that he was . . . and that was that! Fool though he was, according to Ermolai, Filofei was not satisfied merely with this declaration. He asked me for fifty rubles in notes—an enormous price. I offered him ten rubles—a low price. We started bargaining. Filofei at first was obstinate, then began to yield ground, though stubbornly. Coming in for a moment, Ermolai began to assure me "that this fool" ("he must like the word!" observed Filofei under his breath;) "this fool has no idea of the value of money"—which incidentally reminded me how, twenty years before, a tavern which my mother had established at a busy spot at the crossing of two high roads had failed completely because the old servingman, who had been installed there as host, really didn't know the value of money, but paid out by quantity; that is to say, he would change a silver twenty-five copeck piece for six brass pieces of five copecks each, swearing heartily the whole time.

"Oh, you, Filofei, you're a regular Filofei!" exclaimed Ermolai at length, and he went out and slammed the door with feeling.

Filofei answered nothing, as if recognizing that to be called Filofei was indeed not altogether felicitous and that such a name could even be used as a term of reproach, although the whole guilt for it lay with the priest, who had not been suitably remunerated before the christening.

Finally he and I agreed on twenty rubles. He went off for his horses and within an hour brought five of them for me to choose from. They turned out to be decent horses, although their manes and tails were tousled and their bellies were large and taut as drums. With Filofei came two of his brothers, who in no way resembled him. Small, black-eyed, sharp-nosed, they certainly made the impression of "bright lads"—talked fast and much, "bubbled," as Ermolai expressed it, but obeyed their elder.

They rolled the carriage out from the shelter, and busied themselves with it and with the horses for an hour and a half; one moment they would be slackening off the string traces, the next, they would be making them fast as hard as they knew how. The two brothers wanted badly to harness the roan horse, because "he knew how to go downhill," but Filofei decided on the bay, so the bay it was that was harnessed to the shaft.

They piled the carriage up with hay and pushed under the seat the collar belonging to my lame shaft-horse—in case we had occasion to fit it on to a newly-bought horse in Tula. Filofei, who had found time to run home and return in a long white overall inherited from his father, a cone-shaped cake of a hat, and well-greased boots, solemnly mounted on to the box. I took my seat, and looked at the time: it was a quarter past ten. Ermolai didn't even say goodbye to me, he was busy beating his dog Valetka. Filofei twitched the reins, called out in a very faint voice: "Hey, my tiny ones!" His brothers jumped back on both sides, gave the side-horses a flick under the stomach, the carriage moved off, turned through the gate into the road—the bay tried to dart home to his yard, but Filofei brought him to his senses with a few blows of the whip— and there we were driving out of the village and rolling on over a fairly good road between dense, unbroken hazel-thickets.

It was a glorious, still night, perfect for driving. Now the wind would be rustling in the bushes, swaying the branches, now it would die right away; here and there in the sky you could see motionless, silvery clouds; the moon stood high and lit up the countryside distinctly. I stretched out on the hay and was already dozing off . . . when I remembered the "awkward place" and started up.

"Hey! Filofei, how far is it to the ford?"

"To the ford? Eight versts or so."

Eight versts, I thought. We shan't be there in less than an hour. I can sleep until then.

"You know the way well, Filofei?" I asked again.

"Of course, I know the way. It isn't the first time . . ."

He said something more, but I didn't hear the rest . . . I was asleep.

I was awakened, not by my own intention to wake after exactly an hour, as is often the case, but by a strange though faint squelching and gurgling right under my ear. I raised my head . . .

What in the world was this? I was lying in my carriage as before, but around the carriage—and a foot away, no more, from its edge— was a watery expanse, moonlit, quivering, and breaking into tiny, precise ripples. I looked forward: on the box, head down, back bent, Filofei was sitting like a statue, and, farther forward still, above the bubbling water, was the curving line of the shaft-bow and the heads and backs of the horses. And everything so motionless, so sound- less, as if in an enchanted kingdom, in a dream, a fairy dream . . . What in the world? I looked back over the hood of the carriage . . . Why, we were right in the middle of the river, thirty yards from the bank!

"Filofei!" I exclaimed.

"What?" he rejoined.

"What d'you mean, 'what'? For goodness' sake, where *are* we?"

"In the river."

"I can see we're in the river. And likely to drown at any moment. Is this the way to ford it? Eh? You're asleep, Filofei! Answer me!"

"I made a little bit of a mistake," said my guide. "You see, I took the wrong way, too much to one side, and now we've got to wait."

"What d'you mean, we've got to wait? Wait for what?"

"Why, just to let the shaft-horse take a look around. The way he turns will be the way for us to go."

I raised myself slightly in the hay. The head of the shaft-horse emerged motionless from the water. But it was possible to see, in the bright moonlight, that one of his ears was just moving—first forward, then back.

"But he's asleep, too, your shaft-horse!"

"No," answered Filofei, "he's now sniffing the water."

And again all was still, except, as before, for the faint gurgling of the water. I, too, sat still, as if petrified.

The moonlight, the night, the river, and we in it . . .

"What's that hissing noise?" I asked Filofei.

"That? Ducks in the rushes . . . or else snakes."

Suddenly the shaft-horse's head began to turn from side to side, his ears pricked, he whinnied and fidgeted. "Ho-ho-ho-ho-o!" came a sudden full-throated roar from Filofei, and he sat up and waved his whip. The carriage at once began to move, it lurched forward, across-stream, and moved on, jolting and swaying. At first I thought that we were sinking, going to the bottom, but, after two or three jolts and dives, the level of the water seemed suddenly to drop . . . it dropped farther and farther, the carriage emerged from it, the wheels and the horses' tails were already visible—and then, throwing up great, heavy splashes, which burst into sheaves of diamonds—no— not diamonds—sapphires, in the even brilliance of the moonlight, and pulling cheerfully together, the horses dragged us out on to the sandy bank and struck off along a track which led uphill, stepping out, as if to race each other, with their glittering wet hooves.

What'll Filofei say now, I wondered: "You see, I was right!" or something like that? But he said nothing. So I on my side didn't think it necessary to reproach him for his carelessness and, lying down on the hay, tried to go to sleep again.

But I could not go to sleep; not that I wasn't tired from shooting—and not that the anxiety which I had felt had driven away my sleep—but we were passing through a landscape of great beauty. There were vast, spreading, grassy water-meadows, with countless smaller meadows, lakelets, brooks, creeks with banks overgrown with sallow and osier, real Russian country, such as the Russian people love, the sort of country into which the heroes of our ancient folk-lore rode out to shoot white swans and gray duck. The rough track wound in a yellowish ribbon, the horses went easily, and I couldn't close my eyes—I was lost in admiration! And the whole scene floated past so softly and smoothly under the friendly moon. Even Filofei was affected.

"We call these St. Egor's meadows," he told me. "And after them come the Grand Duke's meadows; such meadows as you won't find in the whole of Russia . . . They're really beautiful!" The shaft-horse snorted and shook himself . . . "God bless you!" said Filofei sedately, under his breath. "Really beautiful!" he repeated, and sighed, and then gave a prolonged grunt. "It'll soon be mowing-time, and the amount of hay they'll get here—whew! And there are plenty of fish in the creeks. Wonderful bream!" he added in a sing-song voice. "You just don't want to die, and that's the truth."

Suddenly he raised his arm.

"Oh—look, just look! Above that lake, is that a heron standing? Can he really be fishing, at night-time, too? Oh, no! it's a stake—not a heron. I was wrong! The moon's always playing tricks!"

So we drove on and on . . . But at last even the meadows came to an end, and woods and ploughed fields appeared. Away to one side was a hamlet with two or three winking lights . . . we were not more than five versts from the high road. I went to sleep.

Again something woke me. This time it was Filofei's voice.

"Master . . . hey, Master!"

I sat up. The carriage was standing on a smooth patch right in the middle of the high road; looking at me from the box with wide-open eyes (in fact I was amazed, I had no idea that his eyes were so big) Filofei was whispering significantly and mysteriously.

"The knocking! . . . The knocking!"

"What d'you say? . . ."

"I say: the knocking! Just bend down and listen. D'you hear it?"

I put my head out of the carriage and held my breath. Indeed, from somewhere far, far away behind us, I heard a faint, staccato knocking, as if from rolling wheels.

"D'you hear it?" repeated Filofei.

"Well, yes," I answered. "There's some sort of carriage coming."

"But don't you hear it . . . eh? *There* . . . bells, and whistling, too . . . d'you hear it? Take off your cap . . . you'll be able to hear better."

I didn't take off my cap, but strained my ears. "Well, perhaps . . . But what of it?"

Filofei turned to face the horses.

"It's a cart coming . . . travelling light, wrought-iron wheels," he said, and picked up the reins. "It's bad men coming, master; just here, by Tula, they're up to all sorts of tricks."

"What nonsense! Why d'you suppose that it must be bad men?"

"I'm sure of it. With bells . . . and in an empty cart . . . Who else could it be?"

"By the way—are we far from Tula?"

"About fifteen versts still, and there is not so much as a house hereabouts."

"Well, go faster then, there's no point in hanging about like this."

Filofei waved his whip and the carriage moved on again.

Although I didn't believe Filofei, nevertheless I could no longer go to sleep. Supposing what he said were true! An unpleasant feeling stirred within me. I sat up in the carriage—until then I had been lying down—and began to look out. While I had been asleep, a fine mist had gathered—not on the ground, but in the sky. It stood high up, and inside it the moon hung in a yellowish patch, as if seen through smoke. The whole scene had grown dim and confused, although it was clearer near the ground. Around us lay a flat and cheerless landscape. Fields, more fields, small bushes, ravines— and still more fields, most of them fallow, under a sparse growth of weeds. Deserted . . . dead! Not so much as the cry of a quail.

We drove on for about half an hour. Now and again Filofei waved his whip and clucked with his lips, but neither of us spoke a word. We came out on to a small hill . . . Filofei halted the horses, and said at once:

"The knocking . . . The *knocking*, master!"

I leant out of the carriage again; but I could have remained under the shelter of the hood, so clearly, though still far off, could I hear the knocking of iron wheels, the sound of people whistling, the jingling of bells and even the clopping of horses' hooves; even, I thought, the sound of singing and laughter. True, the wind was blowing from that quarter, but there could be no doubt that the unknown travellers had gained on us by a whole verst—perhaps even by two.

Filofei and I exchanged glances. He merely moved his hat from the back of his head on to his forehead, and at once bent over the reins and began whipping up the horses. They set off at a gallop, but could not keep it up for long and fell into a trot. Filofei kept whipping them up. We had to get away!

I could not explain to myself why, when I'd not shared Filofei's suspicions to start with, I had now suddenly become convinced that they were indeed bad men who were on our tracks. I had heard nothing new: the same bells, the same knocking of a cart travelling light, the same whistling, the same vague hubbub. But I no longer had any doubt. Filofei could not be mistaken!

So another twenty minutes went by. During the last of these twenty minutes, above the rattling and rumbling of our own carriage, we could already hear another rattling and rumbling . . .

"Stop, Filofei," I said. "It doesn't matter—it'll all be the same in the end!"

Filofei clucked apprehensively. The horses stopped, as if delighted at the chance of a rest.

Good heavens! The bells were simply thundering right behind us, the cart was rumbling and jolting, men were whistling and singing, horses were snorting and beating the ground with their hooves . . .

They had caught us!

"Oh *dear*," said Filofei deliberately under his breath, and he clucked irresolutely and began to urge the horses on. But, simultaneously, something suddenly tore up out of the darkness, there was a roaring and a rushing—and an enormous ramshackle cart, harnessed to three lean horses, whirled past us obliquely, galloped ahead, and at once fell into a walk, blocking the way.

"A regular cut-throat's trick," whispered Filofei.

I confess that my heart contracted . . . I stared ahead intently—into the dim mist-veiled moonlight. Sitting or lying in the cart in front of us were half a dozen men in blouses and unbuttoned coats; two of them were capless; their long-booted legs swung and dangled over the edge, their arms rose and fell aimlessly . . . their bodies jolted . . . it was as clear as daylight: they were all drunk. Some were roaring out anything that came into their heads; one was whistling very piercingly and accurately; another was swearing; a giant in a sheepskin jacket was sitting driving on the box. They drove at a walk, as if taking no notice of us.

What could we do? We drove after them, also at a walk . . . willy-nilly.

We went on in this way for about a quarter of a verst. Agonizing apprehension! Salvation, self-defence . . . what a hope! There were six of them and I had not so much as a stick! Turn around the other way? They would catch us at once. I remembered Zhukovsky's line from the passage where he tells of the murder of Field-Marshal Kamensky:

The assassin's axe abhorred . . .

Or, if not that—strangling with a muddy cord . . . and into the ditch . . . croak there, and struggle like a hare in a trap. . . .

Oh, it was a black look-out indeed!

The others kept on at a walk and took no notice of us.

"Filofei," I whispered, "just try pulling out to the right, as if to go past them."

Filofei tried and pulled out to the right . . . but they at once pulled out to the right, too . . . it was impossible to get past.

Filofei tried again: he pulled out to the left . . . but they wouldn't let him pass the cart on that side either. What was more, they began to laugh . . . It was clear that they were not going to let us pass.

"Regular cut-throats," Filofei whispered to me over his shoulder.

"But what are they waiting for?" I asked, also in a whisper.

"Ahead of us—in a hollow—over a stream, there's a bridge . . . That's where they'll get us! That's always their way . . . at bridges. Our business is settled, master," he added with a sigh. "They aren't likely to let us go alive; so the great thing for them is that no one shall be any the wiser. There's one thing I'm sorry about, master: my three little horses will go—and my brothers won't get them."

I might have been surprised that at such a moment Filofei should still be able to worry about his horses, but I confess I had no time for such thoughts myself . . . Will they really kill us? I repeated to myself. What for? Why, I'll give them everything I've got.

But meanwhile the bridge drew nearer and nearer and we could see it more and more clearly.

Suddenly there came a shrill whoop and the horses ahead of us seemed to whirl into the air, dashed away, and, galloping up to the bridge, halted all of a sudden, as if nailed to the spot, a little to one side of the road. My heart fairly sank within me.

"Oh, Filofei, my friend," I said, "we're going to our death. Forgive me for having brought this on you."

"But it isn't your fault, master! There's no escaping your own fate! Well, shaft-horse, my faithful one," said Filofei, "go on, boy! Do me your last service! It's all the same thing in the end . . . God bless us all!"

And he put his horses into a trot.

We began to approach the bridge and the cart, which stood there motionless and threatening . . . In it, all was still, as if from set purpose. Not a sound! It was the silence of the pike, of the hawk, of every creature of prey, when its victim approaches. So we drew level with the cart. Suddenly the giant in the sheep-skin jacket jumped down from it and came straight at us.

He said nothing to Filofei, but Filofei of his own accord at once pulled on the reins and the carriage halted. The giant put both his hands on the doors and, bowing his shaggy head forward and grinning, pronounced, in a quiet even voice, with a mechanic's accent, the following words:

"Honored sir, we are coming from a party, everything fair and above board, a wedding; we've married off our boy; we've put him to bed, good and proper; our lads are all young and hot-headed—they've had plenty to drink and they've nothing to sober down with; so would you be good enough to give us just a very little money, so that we could get a pint to toast our brother? We'd drink your health, we'd call upon your honor's name; won't you be so good? . . . and please don't be angry with me!"

What could this be? . . . I thought . . . A game? . . . A practical joke?

The giant stood there with his head bowed. That moment the moon came out of the mist and lit up his face. It was grinning, this face—grinning with its eyes and with its lips. There was no threat to be seen in it, but it was full of a certain alertness . . . and such white teeth, and such big ones, too . . .

"With pleasure . . . take this," I said hurriedly, and getting my purse out of my pocket I pulled out two silver rubles from it—it was the time when silver coins were still current in Russia. "Here, if this is enough."

"Most grateful!" barked the giant, military-fashion, and his thick fingers snatched from me in a flash, not my whole purse, but just the two rubles. "Most grateful!" He shook his locks and ran back to the cart.

"Lads!" he cried. "The gentleman-traveller has given us two rubles!" They all burst out laughing together. . . . The giant tumbled up on to the box. . . .

"Good-bye and good luck!"

And that was all we saw of them! The horses darted off, the cart rumbled up the hill, it showed for a flash against the dark line dividing earth from heaven, sank beyond, and disappeared.

And soon we couldn't even hear the knocking, the shouting, the bells . . .

Dead silence fell.

IT WAS SOME WHILE before Filofei and I recovered ourselves.

"You joker, you!" he said at length—took off his hat, and began crossing himself. "A proper joker," he added, and turned to me with a happy face. "He must be a good man—he must. Go on, my little ones! Get a move on! Your skins are saved! All our skins are saved! D'you remember how he wouldn't let us pass? He was the one that was driving. A regular joker, that lad! Go on! and God bless you!"

I said nothing, but I felt good inside. Our skins are saved, I repeated to myself, and lay down on the hay. We had got off cheap!

I was even slightly ashamed of having remembered that line of Zhukovsky's.

Suddenly a thought occurred to me:

"Filofei!"

"What?"

"Are you married?"

"Yes."

"With children?"

"Yes."

"Why didn't you think about them? You were sorry about the horses—but what about your wife and your children?"

"But why be sorry about them? They would not have fallen into the hands of thieves. But I had them in mind the whole time . . . and so I have now . . . and that's the truth." Filofei paused. "Perhaps . . . it was on their account that the Lord God spared you and me."

"But supposing they weren't cut-throats?"

"How can you tell? Can you get inside someone else's soul? Other people's souls—it's a well-known thing—are just so much darkness. But it's always better, with God's help . . . No . . . as for my family, I always . . . Go on, my little ones, God bless you!"

It was almost light when we started to enter Tula. I was lying, half asleep and oblivious. . . .

"Master," Filofei said to me suddenly, "just look; there, standing in front of the pot-house, that's their cart."

I raised my head . . . so it was; their cart and their horses. On the threshold of the drinking establishment there suddenly appeared my friend the giant in the sheepskin jacket.

"Master," he exclaimed, waving his cap, "we're having a drink at your expense! Well, coachman," he added, with a wave of the head at Filofei, "you *were* scared, weren't you?"

"A very funny fellow," observed Filofei, when we had driven fifty yards past the pot-house.

And so at last we were in Tula; I bought some shot and incidentally some tea and vodka—and I also got a horse from a dealer. At noon we set off on the return journey. As we passed the spot where we had for the first time heard the cart knocking along behind us, Filofei, who had had a drop in Tula, and turned out a very talkative fellow—he had even been telling me stories—suddenly burst out laughing.

"D'you remember, master, how I kept on saying to you: 'The knocking . . . the knocking,' I said, 'the knocking!'"

He moved his arm several times in a back-handed gesture. By now this expression struck him as very amusing.

The same evening we returned to his home village.

I informed Ermolai of the incident that had befallen us. Being sober, he expressed no sympathy—simply sniffed, approvingly or censoriously—I dare say he didn't himself know which. But two days later he informed me with pleasure that, the very same night on which Filofei and I had driven into Tula, and on the very same road, a merchant had been robbed and murdered. At first I refused to believe this story: but afterwards I had to believe it; its truth was confirmed to me by a police-inspector who arrived post-haste to investigate. Was this not the "wedding" from which our hot-heads were returning, and was this not the "lad" whom they, to quote the giant-joker, had put to bed? I stayed five days more in Filofei's village. Whenever I met him I would say to him: "The knocking? Eh?"

"A funny fellow," he would answer every time, and burst out laughing.

Forest and Steppe

THE READER IS PERHAPS ALREADY WEARY OF MY NOTES. I HAS-
ten to reassure him with the promise that I will limit myself to the
fragments already printed; but, in taking my leave of him, I cannot
refrain from saying a word about the pleasures of shooting.

Shooting with gun and dog is a joy in its own right, "*für sich*," as
our fathers used to say . . . but let's suppose that you are not a born
hunter; all the same, you're a lover of nature and freedom; and you
cannot therefore help envying the rest of us. Listen to me . . .

Do you know, for example, the delight of starting out in spring,
before dawn? You walk out on to the porch . . . Away in the dark-
blue sky the stars are twinkling; from time to time a moist breeze
blows gently past: you can hear the discreet, confused murmuring
of the night; a faint rustle comes from trees deep in the shadow.
Your men are already spreading out the rug in the cart; under your
seat they put the case which holds the samovar. The horses shiver,
snort, and take small prancing steps; a couple of white geese that
have just woken up pass silently and slowly across the road. Behind the fence, in the garden, the nightwatchman is snoring peacefully; every sound seems to stand in the cool stillness of the air—to
stand, and go no farther. You take your place; the horses set off
together, and the cart rattles behind noisily . . . Away you go—
past the church, down the hill to the right, across the dam . . . The
mist is just beginning to rise from the pond, you feel the chill, you
hide your face in the collar of your coat; you begin to nod. The
horses splash their way noisily through the puddles; the coachman

whistles softly. By now you have covered about four versts . . . Near the horizon the sky is growing scarlet; in the birches, jackdaws are waking up and flapping about awkwardly; sparrows are chirruping round the dark ricks. The air grows lighter, the road begins to glimmer and the sky to clear; the clouds are tinged with white, the fields with green. In the cottages there is a red blaze of firewood, and sleepy voices come from inside the gates. By now the dawn has begun to blaze; the sky is striped with bands of gold; mists curl in the valleys; larks sing noisily, the dawn breeze blows—and the blood-red sun swims quietly up. Light fairly streams forth; the heart starts up inside you like a bird. Freshness, laughter, beauty! The eye ranges for far around. Away there behind the trees is a village; there in the distance is another, with a white church; over there is a birch-wood on a hill; behind it is the marsh for which you are bound . . . Step out, horses, step out! Forward at a fast trot! . . . Only three versts more. The sun is rising quickly into a clear sky . . . It will be a glorious day. A herd of cattle comes winding out of the village towards you. You have reached the top of the hill . . . What a view! The river winds for about ten versts, dimly blue through the mist; behind it, water-green meadows; behind the meadows, sloping hills; in the distance, lap-wings are wheeling and calling over the marsh; through the brilliance of the moisture transfusing the air, the distance stands out sharply . . . how different from the summer! How freely you breathe, how briskly you move, what strength courses through all your being, lapped in the fresh breath of spring! . . .

Or take a summer morning—a morning in July. Who but a sportsman knows the joy of wandering through the brakes at sunrise? Your footprints make a green trail across the dew-whitened grass. You part the dripping bushes, and are all but drenched with the concentrated warmth and fragrance of the night; the air is heady with the sharp freshness of wormwood, the honey-sweetness of buckwheat and clover. In the distance an oak-wood stands up like a wall and flashes and blushes in the sun; it is still cool, but you can already feel the sultriness to come. Your head is dizzy and languid, surfeited with scents. The brushwood stretches endlessly

away . . . Here and there in the distance is the yellow glow of rye
that is almost ready for the harvest; here and there, narrow strips
of reddening buckwheat. Then you hear the creaking of a cart;
the peasant driver is threading his way forward at a walk; then he
stops, and leaves his horse in the shade, before the heat becomes
too great; you exchange greetings and pass by. From behind you
comes the ringing chime of a scythe. The sun mounts higher and
higher. The grass dries quickly. By now it is already hot. An hour
passes, then a second one . . . The sky grows darker about the horizon; the motionless air exhales a tingling sultriness. "Where can
I get a drink hereabouts, my friend?" you ask a mower. "There's a
well down there in the valley." Through dense hazel bushes, tangled
with clinging grass, you drop down to the bed of the valley. Sure
enough, at the very foot of the slope, there's a hidden spring; an
oak-thicket has thirstily spread its splay-fingered boughs above the
water; big, silvery bubbles rise, swaying, from the bottom, which is
covered with a fine velvety moss. You throw yourself to the ground,
you drink your fill, but now you feel too lazy to move. You are in the
shade, breathing an air redolent with dampness; you have a sense
of perfect well-being—but opposite you the bushes in the sunlight
begin to glow an incandescent yellow. What is happening? All of
a sudden a wind gets up and blows past you; the air shivers round
about; can it be thunder? You come out of the valley . . . What is
that leaden streak on the skyline? Is the heat growing thicker?
Are the clouds piling up? . . . Lightning flickers faintly . . . Yes,
here is the storm! All around, the sun is still shining brightly: it is
still possible to shoot. But the cloud is growing. Its forward edge
spreads out like a sleeve and forms into a vault above us. Grass,
bushes—everything around suddenly darkens . . . Hurry! Over
there you spy a hay-shed . . . hurry! You run to it and take shelter . . . what a downpour! What lightning! From somewhere in the
straw roof water begins to drip through on to the sweet-smelling
hay . . . But here once more is the play of sunlight. The storm has
passed; you go out again. Heavens above! How gaily it sparkles all
around, how fresh and liquid the air, how strong the scent of strawberry and mushroom! . . .

But now evening is coming on. The glow of sunset blazes up and suffuses half the sky. The sun is sinking. Near at hand, the air has a special transparent quality, as if made of glass, and the distance is mantled in soft, warm-looking mist. With the falling dew, a crimson splendor drops on forest glades which, a moment before, were drenched in floods of liquid gold; from trees, from bushes and tall haystacks, long shadows run out . . . The sun has set. A star lights up and trembles in the fiery sea of sunset . . . Now the fiery sea turns pale; the sky takes on a deeper blue; separate shadows are extinguished and the air is saturated with mist. It is time to go home, to the village, to the cabin where you are spending the night. Throwing your gun over your shoulder, you step out briskly, weary though you are . . . Meanwhile night comes on; you cannot see twenty paces in front of you; the dogs are white shapes, hardly visible in the darkness. Over there, above those black bushes, there is a dim radiance on the skyline . . . What is it? A fire? . . . no, it is the moon rising. But down on the right the village lights are already twinkling . . . Here, at last, is your cabin. Through the window you see a table spread with a white cloth, a candle burning, and supper laid . . .

Or else you have the racing drozhky harnessed and drive away to the forest after hazel-hen. It is exhilarating to thread your way along the narrow track, between two walls of tall rye. The rye-ears beat softly in your face, cornflowers cling to your ankles, quails call on all sides, the horse trots lazily on. Here is the forest. Shadow and silence. Stately poplars whisper high above your head; the long, hanging birch-branches hardly stir; the powerful oak stands warrior-like beside the graceful lime. You drive along a green track, checkered with shadow; big yellow flies hover motionless in the golden air and suddenly dart away; a swarm of midges forms a pillar, light in the shadow, dark in the sun; birds sing quietly. The small golden voice of the robin rings out in its innocent, prattling joy: it matches the scent of the lilies of the valley. Farther, farther, ever deeper into the forest . . . The forest runs wild . . . An ineffable stillness descends on you; everything around is so drowsy and so still. But soon a breeze passes, and the tree-tops sigh, with the sound of breaking waves. Through the brown mold of last year's leaves, tall grasses grow here and there; mushrooms stand aloof under their little hats. Suddenly a white hare starts up, and with a loud bark the dog dashes after it . . .

And how delicious the same forest is in late autumn, when woodcock are on the wing! They do not lurk in the innermost recesses: you must seek them along the forest skirts. There is no wind, no sun, no light or shade, no movement, no sound; the soft air is drenched with the smell of autumn, redolent as the smell of wine; a fine mist hangs in the distance over the yellow fields. Through the bare brown limbs of the trees you see the mild featureless pallor of the sky; here and there the last golden leaves are still hanging on the lime trees. The damp earth is springy underfoot; the tall withered blades of grass never stir; long threads glitter on the faded turf. You breathe in peace with every breath, yet a strange unrest comes upon the spirit. You walk along the forest edge, you watch your dog, but all the time images and faces of the beloved, dead or alive, keep coming to mind; impressions that have slumbered for years suddenly spring to life; the imagination hovers and darts hither and thither like a bird, and all the memories it evokes move and stand so vividly before your eyes. At times the heart trembles, beats loudly, and yearns forward passionately; at times it plunges into a world of memory beyond recall. All your life unwinds as smoothly and swiftly as a scroll; all your past, all your emotions, all your faculties, all your soul, are yours to command. There is nothing around to disturb you—no sun, no wind, no sound . . .

Or take the autumn day that is clear and chilly, after a frosty morning, when the birch, all golden like a tree in a fairy-story, stands out delicately against the pale-blue sky; when the low sun has no more warmth in it, but shines out clearer than in summer; when the small poplar-wood sparkles from end to end, as if the trees found relief and exhilaration in standing naked; when there is still the whiteness of hoar-frost in the bottom of the valleys and a cool breeze is stirring faintly and blowing the fallen crumpled leaves; when on the river the blue waves rush joyfully past, gently rocking the geese and duck that float dreamily on them. From the distance comes the hammer of a watermill, half-hidden among the willows, and above it pigeons wheel swiftly, their colors shifting and changing in the brilliant air . . .

Delicious too, although not loved by sportsmen, are the misty days of summer. On such days shooting is impossible: the bird that flies up from underfoot vanishes at once in the whitish cloud of stationary mist. But how still, how inexpressibly still a world it is! Everything is awake and silent. You pass a tree—it does not stir: it is just standing at its ease. Through the fine vapor, which is evenly diffused in the air, a long dark stripe looms up before you. You take it for a nearby wood; you approach—and the wood turns into a high ridge of wormwood on a boundary fence. Above you and all around—everywhere there is mist . . . But now a breeze stirs lightly—a patch of pale-blue sky shows up faintly through the thinning vapor, which seems turned into smoke. Suddenly a golden-yellow ray breaks through, floods down in a long beam, strikes on fields, fixes on a wood—and then the whole scene clouds over again. For a long time this struggle continues; but how unspeakably bright and magnificent is the day, when the light finally triumphs, and the last waves of sun-warmed mist roll down and spread out, flat as linen, or else coil up and vanish in the blue and tender radiance of the heaven . . .

Or perhaps you have decided to visit an outlying field in the steppes. For about ten versts you have threaded your way along by-roads—and here, at last, is the highway. Past unending processions of country carts, past little inns, each with its wide-open gates and its well and its samovar hissing under the lean-to roof—from one village to another, over limitless fields, past lines of green hemp-bushes, far, far away you drive. Magpies flutter from one willow to the next. Peasant-women with long rakes in their hands plod towards the fields; a man in a threadbare nankeen coat, with a satchel of birch-bark slung over his shoulder, trudges wearily by; a land-owner's heavy travelling coach, drawn by six stalwart, well-broken horses, rolls towards you. Out of the window sticks the corner of a pillow, and behind, holding on by a cord to his perch athwart the foot-board, on a mat-bag, sits a footman in a great-coat, spattered to the eyebrows with mud. Here is the local market-town, with its crooked little houses, its endless fences, its stone mansions untenanted by their merchant owners, its ancient bridge spanning the deep river-bed. On, on! . . . The steppe-country is approaching. You look round from the hill-top—and what a view meets your eyes! Round, low hills, ploughed and sown to the summit, roll away in sweeping waves; valleys choked with bushes wind between them. Oblong islands of woodland are scattered here and there. Narrow tracks run from village to village; churches gleam whitely; a stream sparkles among willow bushes, its course broken in four places by dams; a file of bustard stands out far away in the fields; a little old manor house, surrounded by its outbuildings, its orchard and threshing-floor, nestles beside a small pond. Farther and ever farther you drive. The hills grow smaller and smaller—there is hardly a tree in sight. And here, at last, is the interminable, frontierless steppe!

Or on a winter's day, to go out hare-shooting through the deep snow-drifts, to inhale the sharp, frosty air, to screw your eyes unwittingly against the fine, dazzling glare from the soft snow, to revel in the green tinge of the sky above the reddish branches of the forest! . . .

Or the first days of spring, the glittering, melting time, when through the dense steam that rises from the thawing snow there begins to steal the smell of warm soil; when, on the thawed patches of earth, under the slanting rays of the sun, the larks sing confidently, and with a cheerful, bustling roar the flood-waters roll from gully to gully . . .

But now it is time to stop. It is fitting that I should have been speaking of spring; in spring, partings are easy—in spring, even the happy feel drawn far away . . . Reader, farewell! I wish you eternal good-fortune.